Chasing Ghosts

ISBN: 1-4515-1924-9
ISBN-13: 9781451519242

Chasing Ghosts

Philip J Reilly

Forbidden Drive Press
2011

Dedication

I would like to thank everyone who helped along the way. Fran Merlie, your editorial advice and input was invaluable. Brian Gould, Seth Krufka and Emily Paffet, thanks for lending your eyes to the manuscript. And a special thanks to my family and lovely wife Rachael for your undying support.

chapter 1

JOEY MCNEAL GLANCED down at the speedometer to confirm what he already knew. His 1995 Chevy Cavalier was inexplicably reducing speed at an alarming rate. He quickly switched lanes to exit I-95; luckily mere minutes from home. McNeal needed to meet his roommate, Ryan Cooper, to go to their weekly flag football game in Manayunk. Just as McNeal steered his car to the off ramp, the engine shut down. McNeal maneuvered the vehicle onto the shoulder and placed the car in park. He turned the car off, then attempted to restart it, but to no avail. He slammed his hands against the steering wheel. "Crap! Now is not the time to break down." McNeal pulled out his cell phone and called Cooper. "Coop, where you at?"

"Sitting here waiting for you. Where are you?"

"Sitting on the off ramp of I-95. My car just died. I probably need a new battery or something. Can you come give me a jump?"

Cooper stood up. "Yeah, I'll be right there."

Unsure of the problem, McNeal dialed AAA while waiting. Within minutes Cooper's 2002 Toyota Camry was facing McNeal's Cavalier on the shoulder. McNeal checked to make sure he was safe from traffic, and exited the car. "Impressive u-turn. On I-95, nevertheless."

"Thanks. You know how to do this without blowing each other up?"

"Dude, you do realize how many cars have died on me? I might know next to nothing about cars, but I know how to operate jumper cables."

Five minutes later, McNeal sat in his Cavalier, attempting in vain to coerce the vehicle to start. "Come on baby, come on." The engine revved, turned over a few times, and sputtered to a halt. "Maybe I ran out of gas," McNeal said. "The gauge was close to E and with these old cars, you never know how accurate they are."

"Get in. I'll take you to the gas station."

McNeal hopped into the passenger seat and Cooper drove the half-mile to the Sunoco. McNeal entered the Sunoco, purchased a plastic gasoline container, returned to the pump, and filled it up. Cooper then dropped McNeal off at the top of the exit ramp. "I'll go pour this in the tank, then meet you over in the diner's parking lot."

Cooper nodded. "Sounds good."

McNeal jumped out of Cooper's Camry and began sprinting down the I-95 exit ramp. Curious onlookers shot McNeal all sorts of looks. *It feels good to actually sprint,* he thought.

McNeal arrived to find a AAA tow truck parked next to his car. The driver stood on the road, wide eyed watching McNeal gallop down the ramp. "Sorry for leaving the scene. I thought maybe I just ran out of gas."

The driver smiled. McNeal checked his watch. It read 6:30. The game was scheduled to start at 7:20. Luckily, they rarely began on time. He attached the container to his gas tank, flipped it upside down, and funneled the gas into the tank. "Hurry up, hurry up," he implored it. Once the entire gallon emptied into his car, McNeal again attempted to start his car. This time the battery showed no signs of life. He slumped back in his seat and threw his hands up in the air.

The driver stood outside the car, chewing on a toothpick. "I can take it to the shop where we'll look at it in the morning."

McNeal stepped out of the Cavalier. "Ok. Do I gotta go with you?"

"Well, normally you ride with your car. In case anything were to happen. Why?"

"Well, I've got a football game and was hoping I could leave it and call you in the morning."

The driver ran his hand through his thinning black hair as he mulled over McNeal's question. "Sure, no problem."

McNeal immediately began running up the ramp. "Thanks, thanks a lot."

"Hey, don't you want my card? You're going to need it in the morning."

McNeal hurried back, grabbed the driver's worn out business card, and dashed up the ramp and down the road to the diner. It was now 7:00. They would assuredly be late for the game. By the time they arrived at the field, Team Bonzai trailed 14-0. McNeal quarterbacked them on a 20-0 run, but their opponents, "The Whiskey Warriors" scored a last second touchdown and successfully converted the extra point to secure a 21-20 victory.

McNeal sat on the grass and unlaced his cleats. Lonnie Mc-Bride patted him on the back. "You guys going out?" Traditionally, the team gathered post game for wings and drinks.

"Not today. I think I've had my share of excitement. I'll hang out after the playoffs."

Today's loss was the third straight in which Team Bonzai fell on a last minute score. While merely a recreational game, McNeal took losing of all sorts hard. "We should have beat those guys," he told Cooper, as they drove home. "They weren't even any good."

"Relax, Joe, we'll get them in the playoffs."

The next morning Joey McNeal awoke to more bad news. The engine on his Cavalier had blown a gasket, and needed to be replaced. McNeal could not afford the nearly $2000 needed to fix a car worth at the most $1000.

"Well, I do have an old junker here. It's a 1989 Dodge Aries, station wagon model. Don't look like much, but it runs strong. You want to come check it out?"

McNeal agreed to go see the Aries. There was just one problem. He had no means of transportation. *Good thing I'm a runner,* thought McNeal as he stepped out the door of his apartment. Thirty minutes and four miles later, a sweat soaked McNeal arrived at Al's. He walked out back where he found the Aries amid an assortment of junked cars. Off white, with a rust spot on the driver's door, a dinged bumper and a faded blue interior, the Aries would win no beauty contests. But with school scheduled to start in a week, McNeal needed something to get to his job at Second Chances Alternative School.

"She's not much to look at, but she'll get you where you need to go," said a man McNeal assumed to be Al.

"How much are you looking for?"

"Seven hundred."

McNeal put his hand to his chin and stroked his short stubble. "How about five?"

Al extended McNeal his hand. "I hope you like your new car."

~∞~

Several weeks later, the members of team "Bonzai" gathered around the table of the Main Street bar basking in the glory of another unexpected coed flag football championship. A rough regular season had transformed into playoff success. Memories of the season were rehashed, perhaps with a side serving of embellishment. Imbibing in beverages of the alcoholic variety tends to do that. Most people's attention was on the Phillies-Mets rivalry playing out on a flat screen TV hanging on the wall. Quite a few football fanatics focused on the Eagles-Ravens game, despite the fact that it was the fourth quarter of an exhibition game, prime time for the has-beens and never-weres battling it out for the final roster sports. Joey McNeal's eyes, however, remained glued to a smaller television set in the corner of the bar playing ESPN Classic. It showed highlights from the 1996 Atlanta Olympics. Michael Johnson's 200 meter dash to sports immortality currently played on the set. McNeal averted his eyes from the set and spoke up, taking a break from his diet Coke since he, as a general rule, avoided alcohol. "I think I'm gonna start running again."

"Dude, what you talkin' about? What do you think we do on Tuesdays at Allentown Athletics?" asked his roommate Ryan Cooper, a wiry fellow whose primary job on the football field consisted of preventing opposing players from getting behind him on defense.

Cooper stood 5'10, with short, dark colored hair. He often talked of growing his hair long in true distance runner fashion, but never displayed the patience to see it through. While lacking the distance runner's coif popularized by the late Steve Prefontaine, Cooper possessed a classic distance runner's physique. He weighed 125 pounds on a fat day. McNeal joked that if Cooper turned to the side, he'd be invisible. It wasn't that Cooper really watched what he ate, or ran a high amount of mileage, but somehow his internal furnace burned it all off. His incredibly fast metabolism allowed him to eat like a garbage disposal and somehow never gain weight. Numerous ex-girlfriends learned to hate Cooper as, despite their fad diet of the month, they still outweighed him.

McNeal thought for a moment about Cooper's question. "I call that eating pizza, listening to boring stories and jogging four miles with a fast finish. Let's continue this conversation while I whip your butt in table tennis." McNeal pointed to the now vacant ping pong table in the corner of the bar.

"No way, Mac. Today's the day I take you down. Anyway, it's not like we don't compete at Broad St. every year and run some other local races." The Broad Street Run was an annual ten-miler that McNeal despised, mostly because it was ten miles, about seven miles more than he was comfortable racing and nine and a half longer than he preferred.

"No, I mean I want to really get after it. See what happens after a year of real training." He tossed Cooper the ball. "Go ahead and serve, don't worry about volleying. I wanna eat right, train right, go all in and just take a shot." McNeal slammed Cooper's first serve back over the net. He then grabbed his eleventh wing of the night while Cooper retrieved the ball. At the bar, a group of his football teammates followed McNeal's plea to take a shot by downing a shot of their own.

Cooper returned to the table and served again. This time McNeal sliced the ball down the side of the table but Cooper managed to volley it back. McNeal then fired a laser return which ricocheted off the back right corner. "Lucky point. So, you got a plan here, or this a moment of sudden inspiration? Hey, guys, Joey Mac is planning on getting back into running."

Len O'Donnell and Mitch Maloney had now entered the room. Both played alongside Cooper and McNeal on the football field and each man was also a serious runner. At least at one point.

The nearly six-foot tall O'Donnell raised his eyebrows. "Seriously? It's not like you've been sitting on your ass getting fat these past couple of years. " O'Donnell and McNeal had forged a friendship over a summer's worth of battles on the local track circuit. O'Donnell had once chased McNeal at an all-comer's meet all the way to the line as McNeal ran a 1:53 half-mile, bettering his college best. The problem with all-comers meets, however, is that often no one came.

"Dude, you know I would never let that happen. Even if I never could be as rail thin as Coop here." The 5'7 McNeal currently topped the scales at 140 pounds, slightly more than in his racing days, significantly less than the average American, but he felt the difference a few pounds made. He sent a vicious backhand across the table, leaving Cooper flailing at air. "That's nine to one. Your serve."

McNeal's younger cousin Mitch Maloney sipped his beer. "That's great and all, cuz, but we're missing the sounds of the incomparable Willy's Wonka while you annihilate Cooper up here."

Cooper badly missed a McNeal serve, flailing desperately at air as it whizzed past his paddle. "I hate Willy's Wonka. I hated the movie, I hate his Chocolate Factory, and I especially hate the damn second rate, Bon Jovi playing cover band."

"Thirteen-two. Nice play. My serve. They ain't that bad, Coop. Who doesn't love a little Bon Jovi? That's classic stuff, man. You're just frustrated 'cause you're losing to an Olympic caliber table tennis player." McNeal insisted on referring to the game as table tennis. Ping pong, he claimed was played in the basement at family parties with younger cousins and drunk uncles.

"Well, the ladies like them so they're ok by me," remarked Maloney, as he touched bottles of Miller Lite with O'Donnell. "Will you put poor Cooper out of his misery so we can continue this conversation down by the band?"

"I ain't miserable," said Cooper as he made a failed attempt at a slam, sending the ball well past the end of the table.

"That's game point. I seriously need to find out how to qualify for the Olympics in this. When are you gonna stop trying to slam so much? I told you to be patient."

"I'm addicted to slamming, Mac. And just so you know, there's a whole continent of Asians who can kick your ass in ping pong. And there's probably a thousand Asian-Americans who can also crush your Olympic dreams. "

"Fine, I'm the world's greatest Caucasian." McNeal aced a serve by Cooper, flipped his paddle into the air, then blew on it like a pistol. "That's game. I'll meet you guys down by the band. I gotta go pee off these four diet Cokes."

McNeal walked across the bar to the restroom and his mind drifted. He had run for almost his entire life. To Joey McNeal, running was not merely a hobby. He had hobbies, like reading the sports section of the newspaper, playing flag football and listening to old school rap music. McNeal recognized the benefits of daily exercise but running to him represented something more significant than a way to keep in shape. No, for McNeal running symbolized something deeper. It was his passion, but more than that, running defined Joey McNeal. Talk to most anyone about him and they'd surely mention four things. They'd mention his trademark, wildly curly hair. They'd talk about his fierce competitive instinct. It showed its face in everything he did, whether a championship race, a flag football game, or arcade basketball with his kid sister. If Joey McNeal was involved, he wanted to win. They would probably mention how McNeal was a 'Philly kid' through and through. McNeal had called the city home for his entire existence and, like many Philadelphians, lived and died with the local sports teams. Sadly, in Philadelphia sports, dying happens a lot more often. Finally, or more likely first, they'd talk about McNeal's passion for running. McNeal felt blessed to be able to pass on his love of running to find a career as a high school track coach. It amazed him to get paid for something he'd gladly do for free.

After tipping the bathroom attendant a dollar, McNeal left the restroom and met his three friends at a table by the band. They sat amongst the tens of adoring fans as Willy's Wonka now belted out classic Journey songs. "What's going on, guys?"

Cooper looked up. "Not much. So this comeback of yours, how serious are you about it?"

"I'm for real, Coop. Like I said before, I need to take one last shot at it. Eat right, sleep right. Hell, I'll even lift and stretch. I'm talking doubling as much as possible, just testing my limits."

It's easy to forget how much actual work goes into being—or trying to be—an elite runner. The little things add up to big things and the truly great understand this. While missing one day of an "abs of death" workout might not seem like a big deal, the accumulation of small missed events add up.

"Don't even tell me each of you hasn't at least thought what it'd be like to get after it one final time. That you haven't looked back on your career and said 'If only this' or 'I could have done that'." McNeal paused for a moment. "Well, quite frankly, I don't want to be that guy anymore. I want to know I gave every ounce of sweat, every drop of blood, everything I had to this unforgiving sport. Then I'll know where I stand. I'll be able to look in the mirror and know Joey Mac was the best runner he could possibly be—no matter what that is."

"He's right," answered Maloney. "Every day I wake up, notice I'm twenty-five pounds overweight, remember being All-A-freakin-merican as a junior in high school and ask myself 'what the hell happened?'"

The now standing McNeal gestured towards O'Donnell and Cooper. "Well, what about you two? Do you want to go for it? Bust your balls for a year to find what you're made of? Or do you want the questions to remain? Do you want to always be haunted by the ghosts?" McNeal did not need the loosening up effects of alcohol. When on top of his game, he possessed the energy and animation of an ADHD kid with a Red Bull in one hand and a Tastykake in the other.

"Aight, Knute Rockne, I'm in. You're an SOB for pulling me back in, but I'm in." Cooper finished his beer. "I was all ready to start eating more pancakes, drinking more beer and getting fat. But I guess that can wait."

"Well, I can't let you guys get all the girls that come with running fast," said O'Donnell. "So I guess I'm in too. But I hope you remember how much dedication it takes here. This crap ain't gonna happen overnight. Now all we need is a plan."

At this, the four suddenly inspired runners got up and walked out the door and down the street to where Cooper had parked after the game.

Instead of finding Cooper's blue Camry, they were greeted by an empty patch of asphalt. "I don't believe it. I think those clowns towed my car again," said Cooper, referring to the notorious Philadelphia Parking Authority.

McNeal stopped where the car once was. "Whoa, I know there wasn't a no parking sign."

O'Donnell waved his hand, as if to correct McNeal. "You know it don't matter. Those Nazis tow whatever they want!"

Maloney echoed O'Donnell's sentiments. "That's why I hate them. Power tripping, always trying to get some money off someone. They got your nuts in a damn vice grip, I tell ya. If you wanna fight the ticket, you gotta miss work, drive downtown and sit in court for five hours and find another place to park. Probably get a ticket for that too. That or pay an arm and a leg to park in a lot."

Cooper paced back and forth, cell phone to his ear, being transferred from one clueless person to the next at the Parking Authority as Maloney and O'Donnell continued to rant about the evils of the PPA.

McNeal tapped Cooper on his shoulder. "Yo, man, I don't think your car was towed, Coop."

Cooper pulled the phone away from his ear as he waited once again on hold. "What do you mean?"

McNeal pointed to the curb. "See this pile of glass? It wasn't here when you parked the car."

O'Donnell bent down to look at the glass. "And? What's your point?"

"My point is someone broke the window of Coop's car, hot-wired it, and drove away. Coop's car wasn't towed. It was stolen."

Cooper hung up the phone as McNeal's surmise was proven correct. "They got no records of my car. Detective McNeal's right. It's stolen. Damn!"

O'Donnell stood and put his arm around Cooper. "You got insurance, right, man? It'll be covered, you'll be alright."

"What? Yeah, I got insurance. Doesn't change the fact I don't have a car and we're stuck here."

"This mean we gotta take a cab home?" asked Maloney. "Cause I hate cabs. A bunch of maniacs—probably foreign—who can't drive or speak English, trying to rip you off 'cause they think either you're drunk or you don't know where you're going. Well, I ain't the one."

Cooper folded up his phone and put in his pocket. "Thanks for the sympathy, Mitch. My car gets stolen and you're pissed about taking a cab."

Maloney frowned. "Sorry, Coop. Sometimes I get a little carried away."

As Maloney, O'Donnell and Cooper discussed their options, McNeal began to think. "I got an idea." His three friends turned to look at him. "Let's run back."

They could tell by the tone of his voice he was serious. McNeal possessed a reputation as being an "idea guy." While they may not always be the most normal or mainstream of ideas, many of them turned out brilliant. For example, one summer down the Jersey shore, after an hour of trying to ignite the grill to cook a few hot dogs in three short minutes, McNeal threw the donuts from the morning's breakfast on the grill. While Cooper and the other inhabitants of the shore house were at first skeptical, within minutes the Legend of the Grilled Cinnamon Donut had been born. Cooper, who graduated Hickory State College with a business management degree and owned a far keener sense of finance than McNeal, currently ran The Grilled Donut Café. McNeal and Cooper had taken out a small business loan to open the shop. McNeal hoped one day business would be booming and he could leave his teaching days behind, focusing on the Café and coaching.

O'Donnell rolled his eyes. "You've gotta be kidding."

"Why?" asked McNeal. "It's only 10:30, and we've all got running shoes on. It's what, five miles home? And do you have the fifty bucks a taxi's liable to cost?"

At this, the others immediately checked their footwear, then looked around, hoping to see someone with sandals or dress shoes on. Nope, McNeal spoke the truth. Running shoes every one. "You never know when a 4x8 might break out," McNeal once said. For this reason he always wore sneakers, plus kept a baton, and spikes in the trunk of his car. Not to mention a basketball, football, baseball glove, wiffle ball and bat. McNeal may not have been a boy scout, but he was always prepared for a sport of some sort to break out.

Maloney, aware that arguing with his older cousin usually proved pointless, was the first to commence trotting down the street. "Might as well start losing those twenty pounds now."

At this, they all began to follow.

chapter 2

THE PIERCING SOUNDS of barking dogs jolted McNeal from his sleep. He checked his clock. It read 6:50. He had set his alarm for 7:30, but like so many other days, the loud barking woke him early. "Darn dogs, don't you know I don't need to be up for another forty minutes," he mumbled as he trudged to the bathroom. Cooper and McNeal shared a two bedroom apartment in a working class Northeast Philadelphia neighborhood. They resided on the second floor of a triplex, one of several on their side of the block while across the street sat neatly arranged row homes, each with a red brick exterior and a small front porch. The front of the building housed a dog groomer. The soothing melody of a chorus of howling dogs could be heard at any hour of the day or night. Every night a couple of dogs slept there, probably as protection against thieves. The back of the first floor's residents changed with the seasons. Ever since sports talk call-in legend 'Northeast Billy' died, the landlord had rented out the space to all sorts of unsavory characters. There was the guy who didn't really live there, but used it as a place to get away from his wife, normally with a female friend. He followed the one-legged Vietnam Vet who routinely spent his days and nights drunk, high or both. Before him, the dealer who provided the means for getting high lived there. The list of shady characters was longer than a five-year-old's Christmas wish list. Presently, McNeal had no idea who occupied the apartment.

Philip J Reilly

Already awake, McNeal decided to go for a short run. Today marked his fifth day in a row, his longest streak in two years. Cooper had also been running regularly. Usually, the two ran together after work. This was fine during the fall and winter base building periods, but once spring rolled around, it would be time for more event specific work. McNeal descended the steps, the refreshing aroma of dogs drifting over from the neighboring groomer. He headed out the door and in the direction of the neighborhood rec center fields. As McNeal ran down the street he conducted a quick personal inventory. Breathing felt relaxed, legs had some soreness in the calves and hamstrings, but nothing out of the ordinary. All in all, McNeal felt surprisingly good.

McNeal was embarking on his second return to competitive running. The first began a year after graduating college. After five years of school, McNeal left with a degree in education, a conference title in the 500 meter dash his senior year, and a pulled hamstring that left him writhing in agony on the track after his final collegiate race. It wasn't supposed to be his last race; the plan had been to run the 4x100 and the 800. The hamstring stopped McNeal's dream in its tracks. He had hoped to win the half, thus qualifying for the NCAA Regional meet and serve as a springboard for reaching the NCAA National Championships. Like so many well-laid plans, McNeal's never came to fruition.

It had been two years since McNeal's first foray into post-collegiate racing ended. He thought back to the day he injured his left ankle during a winter run on the trails of Pennypack Park, misstepping on a leaf-covered rock. Unable to run back, he hopped, hobbled and limped the remaining three miles to his car. After getting reassurance that no break existed, McNeal resumed running in three days. While able to run, his ankle flared up periodically throughout the year, causing him to miss days here and there and making pedestrian paces feel overwhelming. Finally, after crossing the line a well-beaten third at a local summer meet in the unimpressive time of 2:01, McNeal decided enough was enough. He shut it down and by the fall was enjoying

14

himself playing football and running just for the heck of it. Which, to be honest, occurred not nearly often enough.

Alone with his thoughts, McNeal soon arrived at the rec center. The soft grass felt good underneath his feet and he decided to run a few striders. Striders allowed McNeal to run at a faster pace, not quite a sprint, but much faster than his daily distance runs. McNeal decided to run them barefoot. He sat down in the grass, slipped off his socks and shoes and ran across the grass. McNeal loved the sensation of the cool, dewy grass underfoot. After six, McNeal put his shoes back on and ran home, pushing the pace, happy with his first week back, but well aware of the long road ahead. He soon became winded and his legs began complaining about their fifth day of running. *Relax*, he reminded himself. He slowly walked up the steps of his apartment, dripping sweat and out of breath, exhausted and sore all over. *This is gonna be harder than I thought.*

࿇

Fresh out of the shower, McNeal drove the twenty minutes to work. Today was the first day of the school year at Second Chances Alternative School, a school for emotionally troubled students in the seventh through twelfth grades. The school catered to inner city students, but was located on a scenic parcel of land just outside Philadelphia. Many of the children placed there suffered from a violent and damaged past and were liable to erupt at any time. McNeal's assignment for this year was to teach middle school math. Sadly, last year he spent as much time, if not more, breaking up fights as he did actually teaching. Today would be no different. Just after lunch, a loud disagreement between two male students broke out in the back of the class. McNeal rushed over to try and deescalate the situation, but arrived too late.

"I warned you 'bout talking to my girl?" screamed Frank, a large Italian boy. As McNeal intervened, punches began to fly. McNeal grabbed Frank and pushed him back, attempting to calm him as he escorted him away. "It's not worth it, Frank, it's not worth it."

Just as things appeared to have calmed and an NTA had corralled the student, McNeal turned to discover Michael, a much smaller African American student, standing with the classroom computer in his hands, apparently about to throw it.

"Michael, put it down. Do NOT…. oh crap!"

The monitor and keyboard simultaneously came flying at him. The thought *Move or catch it?* quickly flashed through his brain. Instinctively, he reached out and grabbed the monitor, preventing it from crashing into the wall, while the keyboard dropped harmlessly to the floor. McNeal took Michael into the hallway before sending him to the discipline office. "Michael, what are you thinking throwing a computer?"

The eighth grader looked down at the floor. "I dunno. I'm tire of him pushing me around. He think cause he bigger than me he can do whatever he wants."

"Nobody likes to be bullied." McNeal emphasized with the smaller student. He tried to dig deeper into the issue. "Is there something you guys are fighting about?"

"Frank thinks he owns Amanda. But I was friends with her before he ever knew her. Not like I'm tryin' to be with her or anything."

"So he's mad at you for talking to her?"

"Guess so."

"Does he know you two have been friends for awhile? Sometimes guys get jealous of their girlfriend's friends. Maybe later we can sit down and you can tell him your side. For now, though, you need to go downstairs to the in school suspension room. There's no excuse for throwing a computer, Michael. You know better."

"I'm sorry, Mr. Mac. I won't do it again." McNeal shook the student's hand before the NTA escorted Michael downstairs.

McNeal spent the remainder of the afternoon filling out the necessary paperwork that must accompany every behavior incident. With the amount of incidents at Second Chances, the paperwork often became tedious. McNeal enjoyed the day-to-day rapport with the students, attempting to spark an interest in learning something, anything. He liked the concept of striving to better the lives of youths, many of whom lacked positive influences outside of school. But the constant police work, coupled with the voluminous paperwork often left McNeal drained and yearning for a different job. His desire to coach kept McNeal teaching. Very few jobs offered the flexibility of teaching. He was free to leave before three and pursue his coaching passion. The summers off certainly didn't hurt either.

McNeal reminded himself this as he left school thinking *Just another day in paradise.* He hopped in his 1989 K car and drove the fifteen minutes to Bishop O'Connell High School where McNeal served as the girls' cross country and track coach for the Wildcats. He had taken the job fresh out of college and originally coached the boys' and girls' teams. He successfully helped build both teams into perennial contenders for league, county and state supremacy. Last year, however, he handed over the reins of the boys' program to his assistant, Pat Myers. Myers graduated from O'Connell and possessed a passion to further the success of the team. Leaving the guys was a gut wrenching decision, but he knew in his heart it was the right thing to do. Myers, for one, aspired to be a head coach, and despite his loyalty to McNeal and the O'Connell program, may have left if offered a position elsewhere. McNeal continued helping with the guys, and Myers lent a hand with the girls, but it allowed each to narrow their focus. Separating the teams opened up room in the budget for each team to have their own assistant, allowing them to cover the field events in greater depth. This knowledge, and the ability to consult with Myers, lessened the sting of not coaching the guys.

McNeal approached Myers before the start of practice. "So, Pat, how's the team looking?"

"Good, Joe. Our junior class, the ones you had as ninth graders, has a ton of talent. I don't know if it'll be this year or next, but when they put it together, they'll be something special. How about the girls?"

"We should be in the mix. Hopefully we'll contend for the regional and state championships. You never know, though."

As usual, they would face steep competition from nearby rivals Springtown Academy. Today's practice consisted simply of a distance run between five and eight miles, depending on the girl. Afterward, each athlete completed their daily regimen of speed drills, icing and core workouts. The season opened on Saturday at fabled Belmont Plateau and the girls' squad was accepted into the championship section of the Briarwood Invitational. McNeal didn't place much focus on early season meets, but he was anxious to see how they stacked up against some of the other top-notch area programs.

A buzzing in his pocket interrupted McNeal's commute home. He pulled out his cell phone. It was Mitch Maloney. "Hey, Joe, how's that renewed commitment to running going?"

"It's a work in progress. With another year of breaking up fights at Second Chances...let's just say you don't exactly feel like pounding the pavement for an hour after breaking up three fights in the course of the day."

Maloney laughed. "You think taking night classes and working construction with my pop are conducive to the runner's lifestyle?"

McNeal felt a ping of regret for complaining about his situation. Maloney lived in a tiny row home in the Badlands of Kensington with his parents. His older sister and her two kids also shared the place. Making matters worse was the fact both his mother and sister smoked like chimneys. "Nah, man, not at all," he answered. "That's why I'm always telling you to get out of there."

"Where am I gonna go?"

"Move in with me and Coop."

"I'll think about it. Alright, I gotta go. I'll call you later this week to set up a run."

"Later, Mitch."

Ten minutes later, McNeal walked in the door of his apartment, saw Cooper on the couch and yelled the traditional "Bonzai!" Neither remembered quite how it started, but in honor of the Karate Kid, Mr. Myagi and their flag football team, "Bonzai" long ago replaced hello as the customary greeting. "What's for dinner, Coop?"

"I dunno. Check the fridge."

McNeal opened the refrigerator. "Do you want...Coors Lite, unopened milk two weeks past the expiration date or a box of pizza?"

"What's on the pizza?"

"Umm, let me see...Half pepperoni and half...mold. No make that all mold, half pepperoni,"

Cooper now stood in the kitchen doorway. "I guess we're calling Francisco's again."

"Well, that or we get risky and go food shopping." McNeal tossed Cooper a menu. "Start dialing."

Thirty minutes later they were chowing down on an upside down pizza, Francisco's specialty. Pizza washed down with good old Philly tap water. McNeal bit into a slice, the grease soaking his paper plate. "Now this is living the dream."

chapter 3

SATURDAY MORNING, MCNEAL woke early with anticipation. The first big invite of the cross country season always excited McNeal. The smell of fresh cut grass, the endless rows of colorful tents, and the hope that springs eternal at the start of every season all added to the buzz. McNeal grabbed a banana and a water and drove to Bishop O'Connell.

Before the Wildcats loaded up the bus, McNeal reminded everyone to use the bathroom one last time and to continue drinking water. The bus ride to Belmont was a boisterous one. The girls shared the bus with the guys for most meets, sitting in the front of the bus while the noisier guys sat in the back. McNeal had learned early in his coaching career not to allow mixed seating. The girls, in contrast to their male counterparts, were much more mellow, listening to their MP3 players, and quietly talking amongst themselves.

McNeal stood up and faced the girls. "Listen up, ladies. JV girls run first. Varsity girls are in the Championship section. We're the only unranked team in there according to the preseason coaches' poll. Let's show the pollsters what a top-notch cross country team really looks like." The girls yelled and clapped loudly. "Remember to stay under control the first mile, push the woods and take no prisoners the last mile, ladies. Be positive and confident and good things will happen. Let's go have some fun."

The team was senior-dominated with the exception of one freshman, Kelsey Sullivan, who joined the team with outstanding credentials. She recorded a victory in the USATF national championships 800 meter run as a seventh grader. While Sullivan specialized in the 800, she was no slouch on the cross country course. Today marked the freshman phenom's high school debut, and she appeared extra jittery. McNeal made a mental note to talk with her before the race. The rest of the varsity seven consisted of five seniors and one junior. The seniors had grown together as a team since their freshmen year. Four of them ran cross country as freshmen, while the fifth signed up for winter track expecting to be a sprinter. By the spring, she was racing 800s and that fall, she was running 5Ks as a member of the cross country team. Another successful conversion.

McNeal initially worried about how his seniors would handle having a new top dog on the team, but his fears soon dissipated at the summer workouts, barbeques and team picnics. Sullivan blended in with the upperclassmen like peanut butter mixes with jelly. It was as if she had known them her whole life and the upperclassmen realized she enhanced their shot at a state title.

McNeal waved Sullivan over to talk to him. "Hey, Kelsey. Come here for a minute."

The pig-tailed, blonde haired freshman walked over to McNeal. "What's up, Coach?"

"How you feeling? You seem a little jittery, not your normal jovial stuff. You ok?"

Sullivan looked at McNeal with confusion in her eyes. "Jovial?"

"Uh, happy, talkative. Anyway, you feeling alright?"

"Yeah, just a little nervous, Coach."

"Relax. Take a deep breath. You've run in way bigger races than this. Just stay relaxed the first mile, work the woods, and then let your speed and instincts take over the last mile."

Sullivan still looked nervous. "It's just…well I've never run a 5K before Coach."

"We've run way farther in practice, Kels. The distance won't be a problem."

"Yeah, but that's different. This is a race. What if I die?"

McNeal took a deep breath. "Kelsey when you worry about dying, what are you thinking about?"

Sullivan stood silent for a moment, searching for the right answer. "Dying?"

"Exactly. Which means you're allowing the possibility that you might not succeed to enter your head. It's ok to be nervous; it means you care. But even when you're nervous you need to control your thoughts. Be nervous, but be excited to try and run your best, not worried about messing up or dying. Kels, do what you know how to do and have some fun. That's what it's all about right?"

The freshman laughed. "Fun, yeah. Thanks, Coach." She ran to join her teammates in their final pre-race drills.

At 2:00 the girls' race began and the Wildcats entered the woods a mile into the race in good position. Sullivan led the way with a pack of five girls tucked behind her. McNeal joined the other coaches and spectators at the mouth of the woods where he could do nothing but wait. Cross Country was not always spectator friendly and this was one of those times. The leaders would remain in the woods for ten minutes. Ten minutes that felt like hours. Tensions built as rival coaches stood side-by-side, each eagerly awaiting the appearance of the lead runners. When the harriers began emerging from the woods, McNeal knew his Wildcats had a shot at the title. It appeared to be a three-way battle between Bishop O'Connell, nearby rival Springtown Academy, and visiting national power Chaminade, who made the trip from New York. Five minutes later, however, it was clear the Wildcats, while game, were third best today. If the race had been 2.9 miles they might have won, but their excited charge up the final hill left too little in the tank for the stretch run. Final scores read Springtown 73 Chaminade 77, Bishop O'Connell 86. Losing to a nationally ranked team like Chaminade was expected, and to be honest, Springtown had gotten the best of the Wildcats more often than not, but to see

Springtown upset the ninth ranked team in the nation added salt to the wounds. McNeal gathered his girls for a quick post-race pep talk before instructing them to cool down. "Today was a good start, ladies. It showed everyone that you ladies mean business and come the end of the year we'll be right in the mix. Stay positive, stay confident, and get a good cool down in. Upperclassmen go long tomorrow. Sullivan: nice debut—take tomorrow off. Again, good race, ladies."

At this, McNeal darted across the plateau to wish the guys luck. "Go get 'em, Wildcats." He ran by the starting line and nodded at Myers who pumped his fist. McNeal missed the intensity near the line immediately before a guys' race. When he first began coaching McNeal learned the hard way that coaching girls took a different tact than coaching guys. While McNeal thoroughly enjoyed coaching the girls' team, moments before a big race left him wishing he remained the head boys' coach.

chapter 4

SATURDAY NIGHT MCNEAL had plans to go out to dinner and a movie with his girlfriend, Kelly. McNeal met Kelly at a Halloween party the previous fall. Kelly found his Flash costume to be cute. It wasn't often that grown men ran around in red tights.

She had been seductively dressed as Princess Leia from the Return of the Jedi scene where Jaba the Hut held her hostage. "So, Mr. Flash, what made you decide to be, uh, the Flash? Do you often run around in tight pants?" she asked him that night.

"Well, Princess Leia, just as you did not choose to be born a princess, I did not choose to be a superhero. I was born with the gift of speed, and I guess the rest is history."

Kelly held in a chuckle. "I meant, why did—what's your name?"

"Joe. Joey McNeal."

"Ok, so why did Joey McNeal decide to dress up as the Flash for Halloween?"

"Well, he's fast. And I'm fast. Plus, I look good in tights."

Kelly rolled her eyes. "Are you?"

"I said I was."

"Well, just so you know, I'm not that kind of girl. I like to take it slow."

"What? No, not fast like that," McNeal stammered. "Running fast."

"Oh, I see. How fast?"

"Umm, how am I supposed to answer that? Like in miles per hour, like a car?"

Kelly giggled and gently touched McNeal's arm. "No, I mean are you Olympian fast, or just regular fast?"

"While I wish I could tell you I was Olympian fast, I guess I'm somewhere in between the two. Probably the fastest person you know, though."

Kelly put her hands on her hips and tilted her head to the side. "How do you know? Maybe I know someone who's Olympian fast?"

"Maybe, but doubtful. They don't exactly grow on trees. So, why are you dressed up as Princess Leia?"

"Well, my parents always told me I was a princess. Plus, I read somewhere that most guys fantasized about Princess Leia. Halloween's the one day I get to dress a lil on the slutty side and not be judged."

McNeal raised his eyebrows. "What's your name, again?"

"Again? That's the first time you had the courtesy of asking me my name."

McNeal frowned. "Sorry."

Kelly slapped him gently on the arm. "Just messing with you. It's Kelly. Kelly Polaski. It's a pleasure to meet you, Mr. Flash."

"And also with you."

McNeal enjoyed the challenge she provided. She didn't immediately agree to go on a date. Only after he insisted it wasn't a date, but rather, an outing, did she relent. After several weeks of outings, Kelly admitted they were in fact dating. A few weeks later, the two were officially a couple. McNeal's friends chided him the first Friday night he wasn't able to hang out because he was attending an Art Gallery open house. While never one to forget his friends, McNeal had learned sometimes you just have to swallow your pride when it came to the fairer sex. It was not a lesson he had learned easily, but he, nevertheless, learned it.

For dinner, McNeal and Kelly decided to eat at Caeser's, a local Italian restaurant.

Kelly swallowed a bite of her chicken parmesan. "So, Joe, what does this 'Going back to training' mean?"

McNeal smiled. "Well, for one, it means you'll get to eventually see me race."

"Well, that'd be cool, I guess. I've always wondered what it'd be like to see the great Joey Mac in action." Kelly lacked interest in sports. She worked out and even ran—or more precisely jogged—but was strictly fitness and health motivated. Kelly was the going-to-the-gym-to-get-in-shape-for-the-beach kind of girl. She couldn't understand why McNeal still needed to play games like flag football. She thought it was time for him to grow up and wasn't shy about telling him. "Does this mean there's no more football? You said the main reason you played football was because you didn't race."

"Most likely," McNeal answered. "Although, we do move up to the top tier and I'd love to see how this arm holds up with the big boys."

"Of course. 'Cause the Greater Philly Flag Football 'A' Division is without a doubt the 'big boys.' So it's not going to affect us though?"

It was a legitimate question. McNeal already had his hands full with coaching, teaching, family, Kelly and once a week football games. Kelly understandably didn't want to lose some of the precious little time they spent alone.

McNeal saw the concern in Kelly's eyes. "No, Kell, it won't." He hoped to God he was telling the truth.

chapter 5

McNEAL LEFT PRACTICE on Monday after the last of his runners had driven off or been picked up by their parents. The girls had just completed one of McNeal's favorite workouts. It consisted of a mile-and-a-half warm-up and cool-down with five sets of three minutes at race pace with three minutes relaxed in between. They ran it around a small, hilly loop at a park down the street from the school. The leaders looped back during the recovery phases to pick up anyone who fell off the pace. This enabled a girl not quite ready to run with the top group to take a chance if she felt particularly strong at the end of the workout. It also taught the girls to run by feel rather than by being slaves to their watch or to the track. McNeal believed this helped hone their instincts as a runner. This was a bread and butter workout for McNeal and he used variations of it throughout the season. The plan was to build up to four minutes on four minutes off, then cut the rest to three minutes and as they approached peak season, they'd reverse the process until it was three minutes on, four minutes off. McNeal left practice upbeat about the remainder of the season.

Philadelphia may not possess the reputation of Eugene, Oregon, Denver, Colorado or Flagstaff, Arizona but it does own a thriving running culture of its own. Numerous running specialty stores serve the community, many of them hosting weekly runs and serving as meeting places for local running clubs. The city plays host to the Penn

Relays, the oldest and largest track meet in the country. High School harriers compete regularly at Belmont Plateau, one of the more fabled cross country courses on the East Coast. Fairmount Park and Pennypack Park, two of the largest urban parks in the nation, sit within the city limits each equipped with a wide assortment of trails to run on. In addition to the park system, Kelly and West River Drives provide a scenic, flat eight and a half mile loop for runners to enjoy. Today, McNeal was meeting his cousin Mitch for a run at Kelly Drive.

McNeal arrived at the designated start by Boathouse Row at 6:00. Maloney sat on a small patch of grass, reaching for his toes. "Bout time you got here, Joe."

McNeal bent down to ties his shoes. "Nice to see you too. You know how tough it is to make good time on the Schuylkill at this hour? It's insane."

"Whoa, dude, just messing wit ya. Of course I remember. For four years I sat shot gun with you on that ride."

"The best four years of your life, I'm sure. So how you want to go tonight?"

"That ain't sayin' much. How about five miles?"

"Sounds good."

After a few more minutes of stretching, the two runners began. McNeal ran this route along the river countless times as a high school athlete. The path ran parallel to the Schuylkill River and was the preferred route of numerous runners, bikers, and in-line skaters. On a nice, warm day, the Drive, as it was commonly called, could be home to what McNeal liked to refer to as "the scenery." Today was one of those days. Endurance athletes of all sorts showed off their well-toned physiques along the path.

The scenery was just one benefit of running at Kelly Drive. The Drive marked every quarter mile, allowing a runner to lock into a pace. With neither runner too far along the comeback trail, the pace wasn't anything to write home about, just a tad under seven minutes per mile. After reaching the half way mark and making the turn for home, Maloney began to push it.

McNeal matched Maloney's cadence. "Feeling good today, Mitch?"

"Sometimes it's nice to just run, you know. If you feel good, run faster."

In his high school days Maloney had been known for wild inconsistencies. On his good days, few runners could challenge Mitch. That was the Mitch Maloney who had won numerous age group championships in his younger days. But the days Mitch didn't quite have it were another story completely. McNeal theorized that Mitch's bad days were somehow related to the amount of second-hand smoke he inhaled at home. When Maloney spent the night before a meet at McNeal's, he generally performed at a high level. When sleeping at home, anything could happen. It appeared Mitch felt good today. By the time they were a mile from the finish line, the pace dropped down to six flat. McNeal was impressed with Maloney, considering four years had passed since his competing days. Mitch never ran in college, so high school, up to now, represented the apex of his running life.

Maloney was now breathing heavily. "What do you say we do something different, Joe?"

"Well, I guess that depends on what it is."

"Let's run up the Art Museum steps, you know, like Rocky."

McNeal looked quizzically at Maloney. "What?"

"Do the steps. It'll be fun."

McNeal shrugged his shoulders. "Sure, why not."

Despite being a life long Philadelphian, a huge Rocky fan, and an avid runner, McNeal couldn't remember actually ever running up those steps. He had never ventured inside until one Sunday morning in college when he and a roommate double dated with a pair of coeds named Jess. Sundays were free of charge, enabling them the rare opportunity to look sophisticated and classy without breaking the bank.

McNeal and Maloney passed their starting point and continued towards the steps, a quarter mile away. Upon reaching them, they began bounding up the steps, leaping two at a time, flying by the beaming tourists and joggers who normally frequented the steps. McNeal marveled at the joy the simple act of running up the steps seemed to bring people. At the top, they did the traditional celebratory dance, pumping their fists while bouncing up and down, raising their arms up into the air. Maloney grabbed McNeal in a bear hug. "I'm ready to do this, man. I'm ready."

"Good to have you back, Mitch."

They descended the steps and walked back to their respective vehicles, Maloney still beaming about the run and his new found love for the sport. "That felt good, Joe, real good."

"Great run today, Mitch. Give me a call and we'll get together later on in the week. But don't make that your next run."

"Of course, Joe. Gimme some credit. I'll call you this weekend."

McNeal stopped at the local deli on the way home to pick up a Gatorade. He grabbed a bunch of bananas as he approached the counter, handed the cashier a five-dollar bill and returned to his car. Minutes later, McNeal walked in the door to find Cooper sitting on the couch watching Sportscenter, eating a Tastykake chocolate junior.

Cooper chewed on his Tastykake. "I thought you were running with OD tonight?"

"What? I thought you and OD were getting together for a run. I just ran with Mitch. We did a little over five at Kelly Drive and then, in a moment of divine inspiration, Mitch decided we should run the Art Museum steps. He was all fired up, saying he's ready to run again. You got any more Tastykakes?"

"No, sorry. The steps, eh? Nice. I ran at lunch today thinking I was eating dinner at my parents' house, but then I realized that's tomorrow, not today."

Knock! Knock! The door at the bottom of the steps swung open and in walked Len O'Donnell. "Bonzai!"

"Bonzai!"

"Wow, I didn't think both you guys would be here. What a freakin' treat. You both ready for a run?"

Cooper swallowed his last bite of chocolate junior. "Oh, yeah. Definitely, OD. Right, McNeal?"

McNeal figured if Cooper could double today, than so could he, lack of recovery be damned. "Yeah. Yeah, I'm in."

The three runners followed a five-mile loop of the neighborhood. It wasn't a particularly hilly loop, but it finished with a grueling twelve hundred meter climb. The lack of a true shoulder on the road, combined with the darkness of night running, forced the runners to head up the hill single file. OD claimed the spot at the front of the line, and twelve hundred meters of pain ensued as OD, oblivious to the fact that McNeal and Cooper both already ran, pushed the pace up the hill. McNeal thought his legs were going to give up and collapse as he struggled to match OD's rhythm. Each step he took felt more difficult than the previous. He peered over his shoulder to find Cooper dealing with struggles of his own, wobbling up the hill, barely keeping contact, apparently hurting from his previous run and the Tastykake dinner. "You ok, Coop?"

"Just trying to survive. Literally."

Upon cresting the summit of the hill, only a few blocks remained. McNeal and Cooper managed to hang on, each finishing with OD.

O'Donnell peeled his shirt off his head. "Nice run, guys."

McNeal laughed. "Especially since I just got done running with Maloney. And Coop here ran at lunch. We had some miscommunication."

"What? Why didn't you say something? I thought you both looked like you were struggling."

Cooper patted O'Donnell on the back. "We didn't want you to suffer 'cause of our stupidity. And Mac walked in the door about thirty seconds before you."

"Well, thanks."

The three ate some leftover hamburger helper McNeal had brought home from his parents. O'Donnell left soon after dinner and within minutes Cooper and McNeal retreated to their respective bedrooms. McNeal slept soundly, exhausted from his unplanned double.

❧ ❧

Thursday morning, McNeal visited the Café on his way to work. The Grilled Donut Café sat in a busy shopping center in Northeast Philadelphia. They catered mostly to on the go workers looking for a quick bite on their way to the office while providing a social setting for cyber commuters. Cooper ran the day-to-day operations and kept the books while McNeal stopped by whenever possible, usually about once a week. McNeal and Cooper tried to make the Café a pleasant community, without morphing into a Starbucks clone. Regular customers who dined in kept mugs at the shop, helping to reduce waste. Today he found a group of regulars sitting on the thrift-store-purchased couches drinking their teas and coffees and eating their respective breakfasts. McNeal approached the table. "How's everyone doing today?"

"Good," answered an older gentleman, eating a bowl of oatmeal.

As the name implied, their specialty was grilled donuts, grilled as only Cooper and McNeal could. They also grilled other "pastry of the day" items. As relatively health conscious individuals, they did not use trans fats in their foods and strived to keep the food, if not healthy, at least not too bad for you. All pastries served at the Café contained 100% whole grain ingredients; they sold fresh, locally grown fruit, and blended fruit drinks and shakes. Cooper also cooked a mean turkey chili usually available for the lunchtime rush. McNeal saw a large container containing the sauce on the second shelf of the Café's refrigerator. "That'd make a good lunch." He reached in and grabbed the container. "Yo, Coop. Get over here and smell this sauce. Let me know if it's any good."

"Smell it? What do you think I am? The health department?"

McNeal held the glass bowl in the air. "Come on, Coop. You got a nose like a bloodhound. That's why they call you Hot Sauce."

Cooper stared quizzically at McNeal. "Who calls me Hot Sauce?"

"Everyone, darn it. Now sniff it and tell me if it's any good."

Cooper grabbed the bowl. "Well, first of all, this sauce is a minimum of three weeks old. I don't need to smell it; I know for a fact it's no longer anywhere near edible. And next, I have not once ever heard someone call me Hot Sauce."

McNeal took the sauce from Cooper and disposed of it in the sink. He then concocted a new batch of sauce and threw it into one of his trademark recipes, an unusual mixture of instant mashed potatoes, honey barbeque sauce, melted cheese, and diced tomatoes. McNeal considered cooking an art and he rarely followed a recipe or a plan when he cooked. Rather, he cooked by pure inspiration and feel, choosing ingredients on the fly. Surprisingly, the results were often delicious. Customers eagerly asked if there were any "Joey Mac Specials." Cooper originally doubted his methods, but the first meal McNeal served changed his tune. If McNeal claimed "Thanksgiving Stew" was a winner, most likely it was a winner. "There you go, Coop, today's lunch time special."

"Special? Yeah, looks real special," said Cooper as McNeal walked out the door.

chapter 6

THE FOLLOWING MONDAY McNeal, Cooper, O'Donnell and Maloney gathered at Cooper and McNeal's apartment to watch Monday Night Football, eat pizza and discuss long-term training plans. They agreed to spend the fall building a base and improving general fitness. McNeal also wanted to get back into the habits of lifting and doing speed drills. He followed the "Use it or Lose it" philosophy regarding speed, believing some form of speed work necessary throughout a training cycle. They then planned on racing a little indoors to test their fitness. They hoped to really be flying by the late spring and into the summer.

Maloney leaned forward in his plastic fold up chair. "Are we gonna try and hook up with a training group, or just do our own thing?"

Cooper walked in from the kitchen. "Well, we could see what Allentown is able to offer us."

McNeal rolled his eyes. "Well, I reckon we could, but my guess is it'll be the same as always—next to nothing. Not that I'd offer four guys with dreams of being fast anything either."

Cooper took his seat on the couch. "You reckon? Who are you? Wyatt Earp?"

"Actually, I've always been preferential to Doc Holliday." Tombstone ranked up there with the Rocky saga as one of McNeal's favorite movies. He was a sucker for sappy sports movies with underdog themes. It probably had something to do with the fact he considered himself the quintessential underdog.

O'Donnell sipped on a Coors Lite. "What about coaching? Are we going to coach ourselves or should we come up with a group plan?"

McNeal shook his head. "Well, I don't think we should coach ourselves. I think if we want to go somewhere with this, we need an outside voice, someone who can evaluate our workouts in an objective manner. What about Seamus O'Toole?"

O'Donnell placed his Coors Lite can on a wooden end table. "Didn't he get banned from coaching?"

"From high school coaching. Last time I checked, we're not in high school."

Cooper stood up to get a third slice of pizza. "Not that you couldn't pass for seventeen."

While nearly thirty years of age, McNeal had a boyish face to match his short stature.

Cooper bit into a slice of pepperoni pizza. "Seriously though, do we want to associate with a cheater?"

Maloney stood up. "This chair is so freakin' uncomfortable. Anyway, what'd he get in trouble for? I think that's important."

"It wasn't anything really." McNeal slid over on the couch and gestured for Maloney to take a seat next to him. "He was accused of recruiting runners from another school's territory. When he heard another coach was talking behind his back, he confronted him and it escalated. End of story."

O'Donnell looked towards McNeal for further explanation. "Escalated? Meaning...?

"They got into a fight, O'Toole won, so he faced the brunt of the punishment."

Cooper remained skeptical. "I don't know, man. I know he coached you back in high school, but I don't know if he's the guy."

Maloney sipped on his glass of water. "Can the guy coach? That's all I need to know. If he knows his stuff, then I'm willing to forgive him. If I got banned from track for every ass whooping I dealt, let's just say I wouldn't be here. It's not like he's a drug cheat."

O'Donnell agreed. "Why don't you give him a call, Mac, and see what he thinks about consulting us? The more information we have available, the better. Maybe he can give us an outline or something."

"Alright, I'll call him later this week."

With that decided, they turned their focus to switching between the football game between the Eagles and the Giants and Monday Night Raw. As the Eagles game turned into a rout—the Birds lost 38-17—they narrowed their attention to their favorite trash TV. Upon first moving in with McNeal, Cooper showed reluctance at watching wrestling. He quickly became hooked, however. One Monday, McNeal walked in the door after a night out with Kelly to find Cooper glued to the male soap opera that was professional wrestling. Each subsequent Monday, they tuned in to watch the latest plot twists. An hour into the show, one of them would inevitably question why they were wasting valuable time—time that could be spent sleeping or performing any of a long list of chores—on watching grown men in tights hit each other with chairs. But return each Monday they did. Before Maloney and O'Donnell left, the four men agreed to meet on Wednesday to run hills, as well as on Sunday morning for the obligatory weekly long run.

chapter 7

McNEAL WOKE EARLY on Wednesday morning, ready for what promised to be a busy day. He arrived at work at 7:30, an hour earlier than normal to sit through the mind numbing bi-weekly faculty meeting. As usual, McNeal and the rest of the faculty sat in the conference room for half an hour while waiting for someone from administration to arrive. "So, Steve, what time do you think we get this started?"

Steve was McNeal's only real friend on the staff. "I would say any minute now since I hear them talking in the hall."

Moments later John Lyons entered the room. McNeal struggled to stay awake as various members of the faculty moaned about their students. McNeal knew teaching at Second Chances was difficult at best, but the constant complaints certainly didn't raise his spirit. To make matters worse, Lyons reminded the staff about the upcoming standardized tests and told them they were expected to spend the next week preparing their classes for the test.

McNeal walked with Steve down the hall to his class. "It's not that I have a problem with standardized tests themselves. But to spend a week getting ready so we can falsely inflate our scores? I hate that."

Steve nodded in agreement. "Don't let it get to you, Mac. It'll be over soon enough."

"Impossible. Then it'd already be over. Have a good day, Steve."

"You too, Joe."

McNeal spent the school day attempting to explain to his students why they needed to take, in the words of Michael, one of McNeal's more talented students, "a stupid freakin' test that we don't even get a grade for." Michael, like many of the students at Second Chances, had a less-than-stellar home life. Currently, he lived at Second Chances. Michael excelled in his math classes and enjoyed playing basketball. McNeal often reminded Michael that his grades had to come first.

At the end of the school day, McNeal hustled down to Belmont Plateau for the Bishop O'Connell's weekly league meet. He gathered his girls around to review strategy for the race. "Alright, ladies, remember, today we work on pack running. No offense to the other teams, but we should be able to hold back a little and still win the meet. Stay with your assigned group and help each other out."

The Wildcat harriers followed McNeal's instructions and recorded a league victory. Their only league loss up to this point had been to Springtown Academy. They hoped to avenge their defeat at the end of the season in the Regional and State Championship meets. "Good race today, ladies. You girls are looking stronger and stronger each week."

McNeal left the plateau and drove to Lorimer Park to hit some hills. Hills provided a break from the daily grind of distance runs for McNeal. They allowed him to work on his strength and speed. Hills have often been referred to as speed work in disguise. They granted him an opportunity to really test his fitness. Ever since Monday night, McNeal had been looking forward to this workout. The plan called for 8x300 meters up Gypsy Hill with a jog down recovery. To boost their mileage, they would also warm-up and cooldown two miles. McNeal dreaded long cooldowns; he wanted to be done when he was done. Cooper and O'Donnell often ran the cooldowns faster than McNeal preferred. His cool downs on the track often resembled the "sprinter shuffle". To further complicate matters, he had a date with Kelly at 9:00. The two of them planned on seeing a movie, a favorite mid-week date of theirs.

At 6:00, the four runners began warming-up on some of the flatter areas of the park and by 6:30 they were sprinting up the first hill. Cooper immediately charged to the front of the pack. McNeal sat on his shoulder with O'Donnell and Maloney tucked in behind. Exactly a minute later they reached the summit. Cooper fist bumped McNeal and turned around to begin the descent down. "One down guys."

Maloney clapped his hands. "Seven to go."

They jogged down to the bottom and without missing a beat, turned right back around to run back up. This time Maloney led the foursome to the top with the others just a step back. Fifty seven seconds.

McNeal took a deep breath before turning around. "Two down."

"Six to go," again responded Maloney.

At the bottom, O'Donnell decided to take his turn and lead this repeat. McNeal responded and ran right on his shoulder as Cooper and Maloney both fell into line. Fifty-six seconds up the hill. O'Donnell put his hands above his head. "Three down."

Maloney sucked in a deep breath before turning around. "Five to go."

At the bottom, McNeal decided he'd serve as the pace setter and took off up the hill. Determined to continue the pattern of dropping time each one, he set a blistering pace. "Strong and relaxed," he reminded himself. He focused on keeping his arms at his sides, pumping back and forth and exaggerating his knee lift slightly. Fifty-three seconds read the clock at the top. McNeal crossed the line first and pumped his fist. "Half way there, fellows."

"Four to go," was Maloney's robotic answer.

Cooper clapped his hands. "Let's make the second half better than the first." Again they jogged back down. Each time down the hill, the pace slowed just a little as they all struggled to suck in one extra breath. As they began to return up the hill, Cooper darted to the front and pushed the pace. Again, McNeal responded. He could feel the burn setting into his quads. Hills had a way of inflicting pain upon a runner that few other workouts matched.

I can't believe I was looking forward to this, thought McNeal.

Just as his mind wandered, O'Donnell passed him on his left, causing him to snap out of his moment of self pity and go with him. Again the four runners finished within a yard of each other. This marked the first time they didn't drop time; the clock again read fifty-three seconds.

O'Donnell rested his hands on his knees. "Five down."

"Three to go."

McNeal was the first to begin jogging. "Next two are the toughest everybody."

Maloney glared at McNeal. "Don't remind me."

The last repeat was always easiest on a runner's psyche. Being so close to done you could practically taste the post workout Gatorade. It was the final few leading up to the end that inflicted the most suffering.

This time, Maloney decided to lead. It was not meant to be, however, as 100 yards from the apex his form began to break down. He appeared to struggle more with each passing step. McNeal sensed this and passed him, encouraging his younger cousin as he did so. "Let's go, Mitch, you got this." It was in vain as Mitch could not sustain pace. McNeal, Cooper and O'Donnell crossed the top in fifty-one seconds, with Maloney two seconds back.

McNeal patted Maloney on the back. "Six down."

"Two to go. At least I hope I got two to go."

Cooper slapped Maloney on the butt as he jogged by him. "Stay strong there, man. You got this."

The next to last one was a struggle. O'Donnell dutifully took his turn at the helm and McNeal fell in, a step behind. He felt the lactic acid mounting in his legs as they begged him to stop. They reached the summit in fifty-three seconds, the first repeat they had run slower than previously.

McNeal paused for a moment at the top, his sweat-soaked shirt sticking to his chest. "Damn."

One small word summed up each of their thoughts.

Maloney didn't wait for anyone to announce "Seven down." "One to go."

At the bottom, they nodded at each other. The last one was always every man for himself. As they took off, McNeal dashed to the front, pumping his arms furiously, legs churning up the hill. He gapped everyone but Cooper by ten yards before they reached the halfway mark of the hill. He accelerated as they neared the 200 meter mark.

"Pump and lift, pump and lift," he repeated to himself, straining to keep his form the final half of the hill. Cooper matched him stride for stride as they charged up, finishing side by side in forty-eight seconds.

An exhausted Cooper beamed a happy but tired smile. "Way to go, man."

"You too. Let's go, guys, finish strong!"

O'Donnell and Maloney crossed in fifty-one seconds, matching their best efforts of the day. O'Donnell collapsed to the ground and laid on his back. "Eight down!"

Maloney slumped to one knee. "Zero to freakin' go."

At the bottom, the four runners gathered their breaths, gulped some water and began their cooldown. McNeal checked his watch. "I need to cut this short, guys. I'm supposed to pick up Kelly for a nine o'clock movie. I'll cool down a mile instead of two. Good workout everyone."

McNeal hopped into his car and left the parking lot. *No rest for the weary,* he thought as he drove off. He made a quick pit stop at the apartment to freshen up before heading off to Kelly's. Lucky for McNeal, Kelly had offered to cook him dinner and a plate of chicken, mashed potatoes and broccoli awaited him. "Dinner looks delicious, Kell. Thanks a lot."

She reached around the now seated McNeal and hugged him. "No problem. I knew you had a hard work out. How'd it go anyway?"

"Good, real good. Real hard, but real good. We did eight 300 meter hills." He bit into a piece of chicken. "Wow, this is really good, babe. Anyway, me and Coop were able to hit forty-eight for our last one."

"That's good. " She pretended to know hitting forty-eight seconds for an uphill 300 was good. In reality, McNeal could have been speaking Greek when he talked times with her. She tried to be interested and he helped her learn the lingo but it was at best a work in progress. After dinner, the couple went to see the latest Adam Sandler movie. Unlike running, Adam Sandler comedies were a passion they shared. They had looked forward to this installment of comic genius since the first preview several months ago. As usual, Sandler did not disappoint.

McNeal grasped Kelly's hand as they left the theater. "What'd you think?"

"Hilarious. I especially loved the part where he fell down, sang a silly song and fell in love. Amazingly funny. You?"

McNeal opened the passenger side door of his Aries. "Agreed. Well worth the price of admission." He dropped Kelly off at her place and kissed her goodnight. McNeal drove home, struggling the whole way to keep his eyes awake. He walked in the door at 12:37, the first time he had stepped foot home since 7:15 that morning. McNeal brushed his teeth, washed his face and was fast asleep by 12:41.

chapter 8

THE PIERCING SOUND of his alarm clock jolted McNeal from his sleep. Six thirty comes real quick. McNeal rolled out of bed, wiped the sleep out of his eyes. "Why am I up? I don't leave for work until 7:45? Oh, yeah, I'm supposed to double today. Geesh."

He drank a glass of water, ate half an apple, and headed out the door. McNeal planned on only running a nice loosening up three miler. With every step he took, he felt yesterday's hill workout. Hopefully, the morning run would serve as a nice shake out and he would feel better later in the day. After the run, McNeal showered, grabbed a bagel and a glass of orange juice and drove to work.

School had been strangely peaceful the past week. Today would end that. Just prior to lunch two girls were involved in a loud shouting match that apparently stemmed from an incident the previous night at the residential hall. Outside occurrences often spilled over into the school day and caused disruptions.

Sonya, a large seventh grade African American girl with her hair in braids stood in front of another student's desk, pointing her finger. "I told you not to touch my stuff!"

Monet, a slight, light skinned African American eighth grader, got out of her chair and stood toe to toe with Sonya. "I didn't touch any of your nasty stuff. Not like I want to get a disease or something from your poor self."

Before the situation escalated, McNeal stepped in and managed to settle things down. Soon after, the lunchtime aides escorted the class to the cafeteria. McNeal took a minute to relax, then walked out to his car to grab the peanut butter, honey and banana sandwich he left on the passenger seat. As he took his first bite, McNeal noticed Sonya had left the cafeteria undetected and was presently walking alone toward the edge of campus. McNeal waited a second, hoping to see someone pursuing her. No one appeared. Leaving his sandwich, he began to jog towards her. "Hey, Sonya, where you going?"

"I'm leaving this stupid place. Tired of people callin' me poor. I'm gonna go back and live with my Mom," she answered without stopping.

"That's a pretty far walk there, Sonya."

The girl continued walking away from the school. "So. I don't care. I can walk far if I wanna."

McNeal gently placed his hand on her shoulder. "Well...Why don't we head back to the class and give you some time to calm down before you start walking home."

Sonya pushed McNeal's hand away. "Get your hands off me! I wish you and everyone else would just leave me the hell alone."

McNeal sensed this would not be easy. He used his cell phone to call the office for back up; hopefully they would send someone in a car to get Sonya. As McNeal waited for the office to answer, Sonya darted into the street, stopping smack in the middle of the busy road. Cars flew by in each direction. She stood on the yellow divider lines, screaming obscenities and waving wildly at passing cars. McNeal hung up his phone and did his best frogger impression, carefully dodging traffic. He firmly grasped Sonya's wrist, attempting to lead her back across the street. Sonya smacked his hand away and began yelling for help. A few drivers stopped to ask McNeal what was going on. McNeal tried to explain the situation, calm Sonya down and again call the office all at once. Frustrated at getting the system's voice mail, and unsure of how to resolve the situation on his own, he called 911. Sonya posed threat to her own safety as well as those around her.

Five minutes later, an emergency response team arrived. Seconds later, back up finally appeared from Second Chances. Mrs. White, the school counselor, tried to take Sonya back with her, but the ERT insisted she go with them for further observation. McNeal felt the icy glare of the counselor as Sonya was taken in. He now wondered if calling 911 was the appropriate move.

"Mr. McNeal, you do realize we are all supposed to be equipped to handle these type of situations, don't you?"

"What was I supposed to do? Sonya was endangering herself as well as others. I called the office and after twenty minutes, there had been nothing. What would you have done?"

The bespectacled Mrs. White stood inches from McNeal's face. "Students under my watch never would have been in that situation."

"She wasn't on my watch. Sonya left during lunch. As I was beginning my lunch break, I saw her wandering off unattended. So I called the office to report it and missed my lunch to follow her."

"Well, Mr. McNeal, there will be a meeting about this situation. I'd tell you to be there, but we both know that once the bell rings, you vanish in a puff of smoke, Mr. Olympian."

McNeal hated other employees referring to his leaving of work early. The director of the school granted him explicit permission to leave at the bell on the day he was hired. He bit his tongue, not wanting to get into a verbal sparring match with the counselor. "Well, if it's before school or during lunch I'll be available. Otherwise, I'll write up a report like I always do. Now, if you'll excuse me, I've got a class to attend to."

"For now you do, for now you do."

McNeal walked off in disbelief. How could he be blamed for this? What right did Mrs. White, the school counselor, have to admonish him? He shook his head and returned to his class room.

By the time McNeal left for practice, his head was pounding. As he did countless other times, McNeal tried to use the drive time to calm down and relax, listening to Bob Marley. He didn't like to carry over a bad day teaching into practice. Nevertheless, a few times in the past his runners—usually some goofball guys back when he led both programs—felt the brunt of an already fed-up McNeal.

"Alright, girls let's bring it in," McNeal called out as he walked into the track office. "Today's a recovery distance day. You know the routine by now, ladies, forty-five minutes for the rooks, and sixty for the vets. Run with your groups, stay on soft surfaces and have some fun. After the run we'll reconvene for the post run routine—speed drills, foot drills, core and flexibility work. See everyone on the flip side."

After practice ended, McNeal left for home, the day's earlier events still fresh on his mind. He remained in shock that Mrs. White actually threatened his job. While teaching at Second Chances Alternative School was far from his dream job, it paid the bills. He had no idea what he would do if fired. Thoughts swirled throughout his head. Part of him wanted nothing more than to go home, lay on the couch and turn on the TV. The other part of him wanted nothing more than to run the day's problems off. Pound the pavement into submission until they disappeared. He picked up the phone and called Cooper to see if he wanted to get some mileage in. "Yo, Coop, you want to run tonight?"

"Um, yeah, of course. What'd you want to do?"

"I don't know. I ran an easy three this morning so I was thinking about an hour nice and smooth."

"Ok, sounds good. See you in a few."

McNeal arrived home in a little more than thirty minutes and quickly changed into his running gear. At 7:15, they left the apartment, McNeal ranting to Cooper about the incident with Mrs. White.

"That's messed up, man. You need to get outta there."

"Ha, I also need to pay the bills. Maybe next year though."

Running at night in the city provided some interesting challenges. Busy roads should be avoided when possible. At the same time, dark deserted back roads presented their own dangers. Generally the neighborhood toughs did nothing more than yell a few well thought out insults or comments their way. "Run Forrest, RUN!" rang out from a crowd as the two runners passed.

Cooper shook his head. "If I hear that one more time..."

"You know, when it first came out, I had no problem with Forrest Gump. In fact, I think Tom Hanks was terrific in it. It truly was a great movie."

"Let's be careful about how we throw the word great around here."

"Seriously, man, it won a freakin' Oscar. I think."

Cooper remained unimpressed. "Whatever."

McNeal's legs were beginning to loosen up, slowly getting into a rhythm. "But it's been thirteen years and I think people need to find a new way to heckle runners—I mean is it too much to ask for a little bit of creativity when a car drives by or I run past a group of the neighborhood's finest?"

"I would think not. Creativity's always nice when being heckled. Personally, I like a good old fashioned mama joke." Cooper checked his watch, saw it had just passed thirty minutes and stopped to turn around. "How you feeling, Joey Mac?"

McNeal turned around to begin the trek home. "Decent, a little sore from the hills but nothing serious. Yourself?"

"About the same."

As the conversation lagged, the pace quickened. Within minutes they were dropping off miles at a sub-six minute clip. McNeal had begun thinking about the day's frustrations and the more he thought, the more frustrated he grew and the faster he ran. Cooper responded by running stride-for-stride alongside McNeal. The two runners covered the distance home in less than twenty-seven minutes.

Cooper stopped to stretch before heading back inside. "Nice run. You were really in the zone at the end, Mac."

McNeal smiled. "I guess I was trying to pound the day away. Sorry about the sudden pace change."

"Not a problem. I can handle it."

"I've got no doubt about that."

chapter 9

Seamus O'Toole stood in lane four of the West Oak Lane track, working with some local age group wonders and weekend warriors when Joey McNeal and Mitch Maloney stopped by for a visit. "Joey Mac! How the heck are you? It's been a long time, lad."

McNeal and O'Toole embraced. O'Toole spoke with a mixture of an Irish brogue and a small hint of a Jamaican accent. It was quite the interesting mix. His mother, born to a Jamaican mother and a visiting white father, was a champion sprinter who met his father, an Irish miler, while competing for Villanova. O'Toole himself was a world-class half miler in the late 1970's. He qualified for the 1980 Olympics running for his parents' adopted country of the United States but never was able to compete due to the American boycott of the Soviet Union-hosted Olympiad. The Irish team was already set, thus, for all intents and purposes, dashing his Olympic dreams. By 1984, O'Toole was past his prime and finished well off the pace in the first round of the Olympic Trials. He then turned his focus and energy to coaching.

McNeal tried to engage O'Toole in small talk before breaching the topic of coaching. "Coach O, you look great! How you been?"

"Ha, look great. I'm losing hair and gaining weight, Joseph. Other than that I'm 'bout as fine as can be. What brings you here?"

"Well, I heard you were coaching again. Looks like you've got some good guys." McNeal nodded in the direction of the track.

O'Toole glanced at the collection of joggers and shook his head. Never one to waste time, O'Toole cut right to the chase. "What can I do for you, Joseph?"

"I was wondering if you were interested in helping me and some of my buddies out."

O'Toole looked suspicious. "Depends on what the help is. I learned many moons ago not to answer questions if I don't know what the question is asking."

"Well, you see, me, my cousin Mitch here, and a couple other guys are looking for a coach. We're hoping to get after it, but wanted some guidance. You interested?"

"Hmmmm. Coach ya? I don't know. Ever since...You know, I haven't really done much coaching." O'Toole's voice quieted as he finished the thought.

Maloney looked at the track and challenged O'Toole's assertion that he wasn't coaching. "Aren't you coaching right now? All these guys out here, aren't they running for you?"

"This—ha—this ain't really coaching. I'm just helping some regular Joes get into shape to run some fund raising races- you know Race for the Cure and the like. That's a lot different than trying to coach a few wannabe elites. That's like comparing camping at a campground in a hooked up thirty-foot RV to roughing it on the Appalachian Trail. The same in name only, but in reality, two different worlds."

Maloney again challenged O'Toole. "I thought you almost made the Olympics? I thought you knew what it took to be great? I guess Joey Mac was wrong about you."

O'Toole walked away. "Another lifetime my boy, another lifetime." O'Toole looked towards the heavens and sighed. "Seamus has to leave. I got work to do here." After a few steps, he turned and faced the pair of runners. "Do you guys even realize what it takes just to smell that level? I doubt it. Nice to see you again, Joseph."

McNeal turned around and walked off the track. "That went surprisingly well. I guess we can get out of here."

Maloney shook his head. "Yeah, wasn't a waste of time at all. That guy's a wack job."

McNeal remained hopeful. "Maybe he'll change his mind."

"Yeah, and maybe if we're lucky he won't. I know he's your boy and he used to be a stud, but Joey, that guy's nuttier than Jiff."

"There's a thin line between madness and genius. You know that."

"Whatever, man, whatever," Maloney relented. "Let's go run."

After running, the pair returned to McNeal's apartment to find Cooper angrily talking on the phone to an insurance representative. "But I've had the same coverage for six long years. You mean to tell me I miss one stinking payment and you just cancel me. Are you really that cold?"

"I'm sorry, sir. We're just doing our job," replied the voice on the other line.

"Your job my ass. Your job cost me my car. Thanks a whole helluva lot."

"Sir, do not talk to me like that. How were we to know you didn't cancel your coverage? Is there any other way I can help you today?"

"Another way to help? No, there's not another way to help me 'cause that would require you to have actually helped me already. How about you help me in the first place? How about you replace my stolen car? How about you pay for the car I've been renting the past month while you guys 'investigated the incident' only to tell me I'm out of luck? How about that?" Cooper angrily hung up the phone. "Let's go."

McNeal sat down on the couch and kicked off his shoes. "Where?"

"Running, where do you think?"

Maloney opened the refrigerator, searching for a cold drink. "Uh, Coop, me and Joe just ran five miles after talking to that lunatic O'Toole."

"Well, that's fine and dandy but I just lost my car and I'm going for a run and I think you two—especially you McNeal after the other night—should join me. And fill me in on how meeting with O'Toole went."

McNeal and Maloney looked at each other. They hadn't run all that hard earlier but neither was in the mood for another.

Cooper glared at the two of them. "What? Neither of you ever doubled before?"

McNeal began to put his shoes back on. "Well, normally it's morning followed by evening. Not evening followed by later evening. But I guess we'll go for another, but no more than, uh, five."

Unable to find anything in the fridge, Maloney sipped from a glass of tap water. "We? Why you speaking for me?"

Running shoes now on, McNeal stood up. "Mitch, you know you're in if I'm in."

"Fine, fine I'll do it. But if you clowns try to hammer this I'm kicking the crap out of you when we get back. You might be able to outrun me right now, but I'll still beat both your asses. Let's go run."

So they did. Cooper and McNeal both heeded Maloney's warning, keeping the run at a conversational pace.

After pounding the streets of Northeast Philly, the three runners returned to the apartment. O'Toole's refusal to coach the runners further fueled Cooper's fire. "Man, I wasn't 100 percent in favor of this guy coaching us. But I hate coaching myself. It just don't work for me. But what gets my goose is he had the audacity to say no and question our commitment. Not that we're a bunch of world-beaters, or anything, but I mean he's working with a bunch of has-beens and never-weres who want to complete some charity runs. But he can't coach us? That's ridiculous. Call OD. We're going out tonight."

Maloney's eyes lit up. "Now that's what I'm talking about. At least I didn't run ten miles for nothing. I got first shower."

McNeal shook his head. "I'm in, but I need to pick up Kelly. She wanted to go out tonight, so I'll need to get that first shower, Mitch, before I pick her up."

"Can't break the old ball and chain for a night, eh, Joe?" chided Maloney.

"Man, it ain't even like that. We'd been planning on hanging out tonight. You guys are lucky I can go out at all. She finds your antics amusing."

"It's true. We are lucky to have the great Joey Mac out with us for a night." Cooper wrapped his arm around McNeal. "I mean he may be a future Olympian. So we should be thankful for the opportunity to be graced by his presence."

Maloney bowed. "Truly grateful."

Two hours later McNeal was driving his 1989 Dodge Aries down I-95 South with Kelly sitting shotgun and Maloney, Cooper and O'Donnell tightly piled into the back. Upon arriving, McNeal and Kelly headed for the basement where they listened to a lonely performer sing Irish folk songs while Cooper and the gang caused mischief upstairs. The quiet, relaxed atmosphere downstairs provided quite the contrast from the noisy rock band and swaying, sweaty crowds of the top two floors. Above them, newly minted couples danced close together, brought together by the combination of alcohol, the rhythmic beats and suggestive lyrics sung by "Willy's Wonka," and the yearnings of lonely hearts. The action in the basement moved decidedly slower. A few happy members of a bachelorette party danced a jig in the middle of the small dance floor. Men sat at the bar, their eyes watching an assortment of sporting events as they sipped on their Guinness. It was here McNeal and Kelly preferred to hang out, sitting at a table and talking about their respective days. After Kelly finished her second fruity drink of the night, the couple went upstairs to join Maloney, Cooper and O'Donnell. They found the three of them in front of the stage. Maloney was break dancing on the floor as Cooper and O'Donnell desperately tried to negotiate with the band's bodyguard to allow them to sing a song causing McNeal to shake his head and laugh.

Kelly looked concerned. "Should you go get them?"

"Nah, they'll be fine. They're great singers."

Before Kelly could voice her objections to them being great singers, the crowd parted like the red sea, revealing several bouncers dragging Cooper and O'Donnell out the door. A bewildered Maloney was following them, trying to find out what was wrong.

A large, bald man with a black scorpion tattoo on his left bicep opened the door and pushed the pair out. "We told you guys to stay away from the stage. Get out of here and stay out!"

Maloney followed them outside. "Man, you guys ruined it for me. I was feeling it in there. Didn't you see me breaking it down?"

Before either could answer, McNeal and Kelly joined them on the sidewalk out front of the bar. "So I guess you guys found out the hard way it wasn't karaoke night?"

Cooper and O'Donnell were about to defend themselves when they caught an icy glare from Kelly and decided against it.

O'Donnell ventured across the street. "Uh, what do you guys want to do now?"

Cooper quickly answered. "Go get some steaks."

McNeal squelched that idea. "Not tonight, gentlemen. I'm ready to go home. Let's go."

They had parked about four blocks away. As they walked, O'Donnell stopped twice to vomit.

McNeal shook his head and put his arm around Kelly. "Another reminder as to why I don't drink."

Kelly pulled away from McNeal. "You don't have to be an idiot when you drink. You've never seen me puke or try and steal the microphone from the band, now have you?"

"No, I haven't. You know there are other reasons I don't drink." In college McNeal felt he needed every advantage possible, so while other members of the team spent their weekends drinking, McNeal played the role of designated driver. Coupled with alcoholism running in the family, the decision was easy for McNeal.

"I know, Joe. I just don't like to be grouped with them."

McNeal and Kelly took their places in the front seat of his car, waiting for the others to hop into the back.

Maloney knocked on McNeal's window. Unable to roll it down, McNeal cracked open his door to listen to Maloney. "Dude, we can't leave yet. O'Donnell's still outside. He said he wants to make sure he's done puking before getting in."

McNeal got out of the car to find O'Donnell sitting on the ledge of a wall on the outskirts of a small urban park. His head bobbed back and forth as he struggled to stay awake hoping to coerce the last vomit out of his system. Cooper had fallen asleep in a small ivy patch a few feet from O'Donnell. As McNeal attempted to hurry them, a homeless man awakened from a bench nearby and angrily approached McNeal, stopping inches from his face. "What are you doing?!"

McNeal backed away with his hands in front of him and tried to explain the situation to the enraged man, but to no avail. Kelly watched on in open-mouthed horror from the safety of the passenger seat. The man turned his attention to O'Donnell for a split second before realizing O'Donnell was in no shape to process what he was saying. Cooper had just awoken from a short nap to find the homeless man facing him.

"Do you want to know what I'm about?!" The man's arms flailed in all directions and his head bobbed back and forth.

Cooper sat there, dazed and confused, completely speechless.

The angry man raised his voice even louder. "Well, do you?"

The bewildered Cooper rose to his feet. "No, I don't."

"You're damn right you don't! Cause you can't handle what I'm about."

Maloney just now realized what was going on and approached the situation.

McNeal stepped in front of him and tried to take control. "Okay guys time to go! Get up and get in the car. Let's go—NOW!"

"You boys better be getting out of my house!"

O'Donnell opened the back door and slid across the seat. "His house? We're on the street out front of a park."

"But he lives here, man. The fact that he's homeless is irrelevant. Yeah, it's a city bench he's sleeping on, but it's after one o'clock in the morning. I'm not defending his actions, I'm just saying that's why he's so mad. That's like you waking up one night to see three dudes sitting on your couch watching TV. You'd be a fired up mug." With everyone safely inside, McNeal started the car and began to drive away. He could only imagine what tomorrow's long run would be like.

McNeal woke at eight the next morning. He needed to run early because he was going to a wedding that afternoon with Kelly. Kelly, too tired to drive home, had crashed at McNeal's. McNeal rolled over to get out of bed and run, but Kelly wrapped her arm around him. "Joe, can't you just stay here this one morning? We never get to sleep in together."

Kelly's offer tempted McNeal. She rarely slept over, and the simple act of laying down next to her, feeling her soft skin, caused McNeal to pause. He thought of the consequences of sleeping in. He needed a long run. If he didn't run now, he never would. But his bed was so comfortable, and the sweet look in Kelly's tired eyes made the choice difficult. "How about I lay here for fifteen minutes, then I go run?"

Kelly looked up at McNeal and smiled. "Ok. I guess that'll do."

McNeal smiled, laid back down and cuddled next to Kelly. It felt good to lie next to her, her blonde hair falling into his face, his arm wrapped around her waist. Fifteen minutes passed quickly, and just before falling back to sleep, McNeal reluctantly got out of bed. "Ok, Kell, I gotta go now. I'll see you at your place, ok?"

"Ok, Joe. Have a good run. See you soon."

McNeal bent over to kiss Kelly, then left the room. As he descended the steps he found Cooper, O'Donnell and Maloney all still fast asleep. He didn't bother waking them. McNeal drove the ten minutes to Pennypack Park where he hoped to run his first ten-miler of the year. Pennypack Park contained a nearly eight-mile asphalt path, marked every quarter-mile. On either side of the Pennypack Creek, an assortment of rolling dirt trails. The fall foliage on the trees colored the park a wonderful assortment of bright reds and golden yellows.

McNeal chose the dirt trails for today's ten-miler. While the 800 lasted less than two minutes, McNeal believed a strong base built in the fall and winter was necessary to complete the speed workouts of the spring and summer. The trails at Pennypack were soft, but challenging. It was these very trails where he injured his ankle two years ago, an injury that eventually prompted him to temporarily retire. When he first returned to the park, he avoided the trails, instead running on the asphalt bike path. He knew, however, the intense climbs and descents on the hard surfaces could be brutal on the joints and he eventually became comfortable enough to return to the trails. He simply exhibited a little more caution, his eyes glued to the path, looking for any roots and rocks that could threaten his legs. Every now and then, however, he caught himself flying down a descent, the wind blowing through his curls, his legs turning over faster and faster as he effortlessly sped towards the bottom. He missed that feeling of free falling speed. It reminded him of primal man, running through the forest in search of prey, on the hunt for dinner to support his family.

McNeal soon realized he was getting careless and eased up slightly. Ten miles was a long time to be alone with your thoughts, and McNeal's mind wandered. Two weeks from now, Bishop O'Connell had their regional championships. Would they have enough to win? He wondered if he could rely on Cooper, Maloney and O'Donnell as training partners. All three were talented runners, and three of McNeal's best friends, but to train at the top level required a huge commitment of time and dedication. Could they sacrifice some of their social life when the time came to get serious? If this morning was an indicator, the answer was no. Could he successfully coach himself? He knew how to coach the 800, he had coached countless half-milers at Bishop O'Connell, but self-coaching was different. Was he wasting his time out there? What was he hoping to achieve? His thoughts traveled to his job at Second Chances. He ran faster as he thought of how much he had started to dread going to work there. Every day held the potential for disaster, not a pleasant thought to wake to. He tried to refocus his thoughts. He thought of Kelly. Would his running allow him to give her the attention she needed and deserved? Again his pace quickened as he tried to avoid the answer that deep in his heart he knew. Kelly was a sweet girl, but she struggled to understand his issues when it came to running. She thought it was a great hobby, good for your heart and a great sport for kids, but for a grown man to dedicate himself to dreaming? She could not comprehend that. A little more than an hour later, McNeal finished his run. He stretched, downed a bottle of water and hopped back into his car to drive home. The wedding was two hours away in upstate New Jersey and he had to be at Kelly's by 11:15. He knew he'd be cutting it close. Hurriedly, he showered at the apartment, trying to avoid any conversations with the guys. He knew every moment was vital. "Alright, fellows, I got to get out of here. See you guys later. Make sure you get some running in."

Maloney lifted his head from his pillow. "Nice white suit."

McNeal descended the steps. "You know how I roll." He arrived at Kelly's house at 11:22. *Darn, almost made it*, he thought as he knocked on her door. "You ready?" Secretly, he hoped she needed more time to get ready to clear him of his tardiness.

Instead, she walked out the door. "Of course, why wouldn't I be?"

"I don't know, I know how long it can take for girls to get ready for these things."

"Precisely why I got an early start."

"Well, it worked. You look great." McNeal kissed Kelly on the cheek. "Got the directions?"

"Yeah, babe."

McNeal and Kelly sat amongst the crowd at the ceremony, held in a beautiful old Catholic Church. The church had large Cathedral-like ceilings with paintings of angels that looked as if Michaelangelo himself could have painted them. The windows were ornately decorated stained glass with vivid Bible images on them.

McNeal looked around the church in awe. "This place is beautiful, Kell. Almost as beautiful as you."

Kelly blushed. "I'd love to get married at a church like this one day."

The talk of marriage unnerved McNeal and his eyes roamed the church again. The groomsmen stood in front of the altar, looking like five penguins, wearing black and white tuxedos with red cumberbuns and matching red vests. The organist soon began to play and the bride processed down the aisle, marking the beginning of the ceremony.

At the reception two hours later, Kelly convinced McNeal to join her on the dance floor where he gave his best efforts to the Electric Slide and the Twist. Kelly sipped on her mojito and moved in close to McNeal. "You don't look like you're having fun?"

"What? I'm fine, babe. You know I love dancing with you. I'm just a little sore from this morning's ten-miler."

"Oh, ok. Why so far? Ten miles seems kinda far. Isn't your race only half a mile long?"

"Yeah, but I need to get strong before I can get fast." McNeal stood still. "Can I rest a minute?"

Kelly frowned. "Sure go ahead and sit down. I'll dance with my girls."

"No, that's ok. I still got some life in these legs."

Kelly pushed him away. "No, really. Sit down and rest for a few songs then come on back up. Wouldn't want your little running legs to get too tired."

Exasperated, McNeal walked to the bar, ordered a diet Coke and sat down. Later that night, as they were driving home, McNeal asked if she had a good time.

"It was nice to see everyone again," she answered. "Would've been more fun if you could've moved a little on the dance floor, however."

"Sorry. I'll oil up these old joints and do better next time."

chapter 10

THE FOLLOWING MONDAY McNeal arrived at work an hour early to finish up his report cards. They were due by the end of the day and with McNeal unable to stay after school, he needed to complete them before school. McNeal walked into his classroom, garnished with assorted fall and Thanksgiving decorations. McNeal logged onto his computer, took out his student folders, and waited for the report card application to appear on the screen. The computer network at Second Chances was frustratingly slow. While waiting, McNeal walked around his room, adjusting some orange and brown leaves and pumpkins that fell from the walls over the weekend.

When the computer finally retrieved his report cards, McNeal sat back down, opened the files for his fifth period Algebra class and began to input the data. He had input the grades for his first four classes into the system before the weekend and was now expecting to just add his final two classes. But his online report cards showed none of his previous work. *Oh, you've got to be kidding me,* McNeal thought.

It would be virtually impossible to redo four full periods of transcripts in the little more than half an hour he had until students began filing into class. McNeal quickly took out his grade book and turned to the section dedicated to his first period students. In ten minutes, he had reentered all of their information. McNeal then moved onto his second period class and within ten minutes was halfway through his third period class. McNeal stopped to check his watch. It read 8:50. Class began at 9:00. At some schools McNeal might be able to get away with giving the class an assignment, and finishing up his grades while they worked independently. McNeal contemplated doing this for a minute, but quickly decided otherwise, realizing it would be a recipe for disaster. McNeal was able to finish the report cards for his first three periods before the school day began and logged off the computer as his students entered the room. He hoped to find some time at lunch to work on his final three periods. When lunch arrived, however, it became apparent this would not be possible. The classroom lunch aide had called in sick, the tenth time this year. With no floater available to take her spot, McNeal would be required to help out in the lunch room. McNeal saw Maria Richards in the cafeteria, a first year school nurse who also taught a few girls' health classes at Second Chances, and asked her opinion

She ran her fingers through her curly brown hair. "Well, from what I've heard, they never get the report cards out in time. Why don't you come in early again tomorrow and get the final few done? I doubt anyone will even notice if your grades are incomplete. Besides, I can't imagine you'll be the only one."

"You're probably right. I'll go to practice like normal and just get here nice and early tomorrow. Thanks for the help, Maria."

McNeal followed her advice and headed out the door a shade before three. He was confident in his ability to perform under pressure, and had no doubt he could finish his grades early tomorrow morning. His only concern was that an administrator might check to see if all of the grades were completed. Even if someone did, he figured, there would be several other teachers whose grades were incomplete. McNeal drove to practice, his mind wandering between his report card grades and the taper he planned for his runners to do this week. It is common practice in distance running to "taper" before an important race. McNeal considered the taper to be the hardest aspect of coaching to master. Much had been written about the importance of tapering and of how to properly execute it, but it seemed the more McNeal read, the more conflicting theories he found. The most common belief is that a reduction in mileage while maintaining the same percentage of faster running resulted in the best peak. Research has shown anywhere from a half percent to a three percent increase in performances after a properly executed taper. This may seem like chump change, but a three percent drop from a twenty minute 5K would be would be thirty-six seconds, a pretty significant PR and quite a few points in a championship race.

McNeal walked in to the track room to find his girls already in a circle, doing their dynamic stretches before they went out for a light warm-up run. Today's run would be a four-miler, followed by drills, striders and a visualization session. The top seven returned from their four-miler in about thirty minutes. They took off their shoes and did their striders in the grass behind the soccer field barefoot. McNeal thought barefoot striders strengthened the tendons in their feet, hopefully preventing injuries and adding a little pep to their step. They combined this with a regimen of foot drills, also done barefoot. Since McNeal had implemented these small practice additions encompassing a mere fifteen minutes, he noticed a significant decrease in the number of shin splints and lower leg injuries his girls suffered.

Kelsey Sullivan took off her shoes, felt the cool wet grass beneath her feet and wrinkled her nose. "Coach, do we gotta do these today? I just got a pedicure."

"I'm sure a little mud won't kill you, Kels. Besides, don't they use mud at some fancy spas? It's probably good for your feet. Now get moving."

The freshman pouted before beginning her first strider. "Smooth and fast, smooth and fast!" McNeal reminded Sullivan and the others as they passed a third time. "Smooth and fast" was a catch phrase McNeal often used in workouts and races to keep his runners focused on their form. They all knew what was expected of "smooth and fast" so upon hearing it, most would attempt to make the necessary adjustments.

McNeal believed training the brain was just as vital as training the body. After seven years at O'Connell, he had his team buying into the concept. Post-striders, they gathered in the room, turned on some relaxation music, and began "making the movie" as University of Colorado head coach Mark Wetmore called it. McNeal began the exercise by going step-by-step through the race itself, discussing different tactics and parts of the course. They focused on the strategy for the given race and tried to picture the proper execution. McNeal told his team that their bodies didn't know the difference between the real and the imagined. The whole process lasted about twenty minutes. After it ended, the team emptied their ice bags, gathered their things and were free to leave.

"OK ladies, good practice today. Go home, ice down again, eat a good dinner, keep drinking your water, visualize one more time, and get a good night sleep. Remember, little things make big things. This weekend's the regional champs. Let's make it special. See everyone tomorrow."

The rest of the week passed uneventfully. McNeal awoke, went to work, followed by practice, followed by a run. Every day it grew dark just a bit earlier, the temperature dropped a few more degrees and less and less leaves remained on the trees. Cross country training began in early July, in the midst of long hot days, the trees full of life and ended in the cold, shorter days of November, with the leftover leaves holding on for dear life, much like a distance runner in the latter parts of a race.

On Saturday, McNeal woke at seven, well before his alarm was set to sound. He almost always rose early on the day of a big meet. He had woken up periodically throughout the night, and checked the clock, fearful of oversleeping. With a noon departure, that was unlikely.

McNeal arrived at Bishop O'Connell just before noon. As each runner arrived, McNeal made sure to greet them, telling everyone "What a great day for cross country!" Indeed it was. The sky was clear, the air brisk, simply perfect cross country weather. McNeal hoped his runners would respond to such a great day with equally great performances. The girls were scheduled to run in the first race of the day. It was expected to be a three-team battle between Bishop O'Connell, Springtown Academy, and Northfield West. McNeal spoke to the girls just before they left the bus. "Alright Wildcats, this is the day we've been waiting for. You girls have been working for this day since July. Think of all the hot weather runs, the hills, the tempo, the core, the workouts. All season long we've been baking a cake. We've already mixed the ingredients, we've put it to the fire, and today we ice it. If everyone does what they're capable of, good things will happen. Remember, run smart, run tough, run with passion. Every spot's a point so in that last loop, just let it all loose. Go get 'em and have some fun." McNeal clapped his hands at the conclusion of his speech and the girls followed suit. He preferred to give the "psych up speech" on the bus, rather than right before the race. He had learned his lesson as a rookie coach, seeing all of his kids start aggressively and be upfront a mile into the race, but falling further and further back throughout the last two. Cross country was not football; it required controlled passion, not unbridled aggression.

At three o'clock the gun sounded and the O'Connell girls started aggressively. At the mile, his top five were all under six minutes and in the lead pack. McNeal hoped this wouldn't prove to be too fast. Time would soon tell. McNeal, the other coaches, and the spectators now played the waiting game while the runners ran the woods. The Greater Philadelphia Area Championship was held at Belmont Plateau, a course the O'Connell harriers knew well. The middle mile, actually closer to a mile and a quarter, was a grueling stretch of gravel, dirt, and cinder that included the infamous Parachute Hill. Adding to the drama was the fact that coaches and spectators were not permitted inside the woods during the race. McNeal nervously paced back and forth as he waited for the runners to emerge. At 14:05, the first girl appeared. It was Springtown Academy's number one, Maureen Harrison. She was the two-time defending champion. McNeal grew more anxious as he waited to see who would be next. Another Springtown runner soon followed. *Oh, crap,* McNeal thought. *Come on ladies, come on.*

A loud roar erupted from the Wildcat cheering section as the next four runners all wore the purple and gold of Bishop O'Connell. The top four girls today were seniors who had run cross together since ninth grade. They came into the season determined to bring home a title.

"Awesome running, ladies, awesome. How do you feel?" In unison, the four seniors shouted back, "I feel great!"

McNeal saved this tactic for the very big races to keep his runners in a positive frame of mind during the last part of the race. He knew how tough the mental battle could be at the end of a distance race and played around with different mind games to help his girls break through the pain barrier.

The next five runners represented different schools before three more Springtown Academy runners emerged. Ten seconds behind their fifth was Kelsey Sullivan. She began the year as their number one runner but recently battled a severe stomach bug.

"You look great, Kelsey. How ya feeling today?"

"Feeling great, Coach," she lied.

McNeal raced across the plateau to meet the girls at the half mile to go mark. Coaching was not a standstill, passive activity for McNeal. He wasn't sure how to log the running he did at a meet, but he knew his legs couldn't tell the difference between that and loggable mileage. McNeal arrived there seconds before the leaders; the Springtown runners remained one-two. The Wildcat pack had separated as the next three passed by close together, but the fourth had dropped back. The third Springtown runner had moved up to eighth. Springtown's fourth ran several strides behind McNeal's fourth, who was badly laboring. McNeal shouted several words of encouragement, hoping to spur her on for one last kick. She looked back, saw the hard charging Springtown runner and dug deep, barely finding the energy to hold her off. Through four runners the Wildcats of O'Connell were tied with Springtown Academy. Springtown's fifth runner currently ran five seconds ahead of Sullivan.

"Just an 800, Kelsey, just like the track. Catch one more spot and we're golden," McNeal urged her on.

At this, Sullivan began shifting gears. She had been slowly making up ground the entire last mile, but now it seemed as if she was inching closer with every stride she took. With two hundred meters to go, she remained several strides back. As they made the final turn for home, both runners were in a full out sprint. The Springtown runner was game, but no match for the pure speed the frosh from Bishop O'Connell possessed. Kelsey Sullivan crossed the finish line in fourteenth place, one step ahead of Springtown Academy's fifth girl. McNeal anxiously ran towards the finish line where several of the JV girls were scoring the meet. They had just finished adding it up as he arrived. "Did you get it ladies? Did you get the scores?"

Freshman Molly Haywood waved the paper in the air. "We win Coach! We win!"

McNeal couldn't believe his ears. "Really?! What's the score?"

"Forty to Forty-One."

"You added it up and checked it twice?" He wanted to be certain of the score before telling the varsity seven and before believing it himself. For all the O'Connell harriers had accomplished—from county records to All-American relays—a team area title had eluded them. This would end that drought.

The excited freshman beamed from ear to ear. "Yeah, me and Michelle both added it twice. I'm positive."

"Awesome! That's amazing. Go tell the girls!"

McNeal watched as the two runners ran over to tell their teammates the results. Within seconds, the O'Connell girls were yelling and screaming as they jumped for joy. The five seniors ran over to the O'Connell tent and grabbed the Gatorade cooler. They carried it over their heads and soaked McNeal as he stood next to Myers, wishing him luck in the boys' race. He tried to fake anger, but the smile on his face gave him away. Cold and sticky never felt so good.

chapter 11

McNEAL ROSE EARLY on Thanksgiving morning to get ready for the local Turkey Trot 5K. It represented his first venture into competitive running in a little more than two years. Cooper and O'Donnell were also competing. Maloney had opted against running the race. He was going down to watch and support the guys, however.

McNeal banged on Cooper's door. "Yo, Coop, you awake in there? We've got to go meet OD and Maloney at the Turkey Trot."

Cooper pulled the covers over his head. "I'm up, I'm up."

"Coop, it's 6:30. We need to be at Kelly Drive in an hour. The K-Train leaves in twenty." McNeal walked into the bathroom.

"Train? What train?" Cooper sat up in his bed. "I thought you were driving."

McNeal squeezed the last drop of toothpaste onto his toothbrush. "You know, the Dodge Aries K Train. It leaves in twenty and I'm the conductor."

Cooper hurriedly dressed and stuffed his gear into his track bag. "How are you so damn wide awake at 6:30 Thanksgiving morning?"

McNeal spit into the sink. "Dude, we're racing. How can I not be juiced for this?"

"You do realize it's a 5K road race, not an 800 on the track?"

"Yeah, yeah, whatever. It's a race, man. We've been busting it hard for about three months and now we get to go out there and see what we got. I don't know about you, but I'm fired up, man. Fired up." McNeal left the bathroom. "Fifteen minutes and the K train departs."

McNeal walked into the living room and double-checked his bag to make sure he had everything. Inside he saw his singlet, road flats, MP3 player, spare socks, dry t-shirt, extra pants and sweatshirt, and his trusty tube of Icy-Hot. Applying Icy Hot was a ritual for McNeal. Before any race or important work out, he faithfully applied large amounts of the muscle warming goo to his hamstrings, quads, calves and anywhere else in need of some "instant warm-up."

Cooper walked out of the bathroom, toothbrush in hand. "Dude, you used the last of the toothpaste. What am I supposed to brush my teeth with?"

McNeal looked up from his seat on the couch. "I did not. There's always a little left."

Cooper denied McNeal's claim. "No way, man. It's bone dry."

McNeal stood up, walked into the kitchen and grabbed a knife. "I'll prove it to you." McNeal grabbed the rolled up tube of Crest and flattened it out on the sink.

Cooper looked skeptical. "Who do you think you are, Mc-Gyver?"

"Watch and learn, my friend, watch and learn." McNeal sliced the tube down the middle, exposing enough toothpaste for Cooper to brush with. "Enjoy, Hot Sauce."

A couple minutes later, McNeal was driving towards Kelly Drive. The course on The Drive was flat and fast. O'Donnell and Maloney waited for them in the parking lot near the start. Maloney planned to run the warm-up with them, then take some pictures and keep an eye on their stuff while they raced. Maloney had never tried his hand at road racing and wasn't about to start.

They warmed up by jogging easily for ten minutes together. Cooper added on another ten minutes. Maloney went with Cooper while McNeal and O'Donnell waited in the expanding line for the Port-A-Potties. Without fail, McNeal needed to use the restroom before every race. Often more than once. When Cooper returned, each runner went through his own stretching routine. Occasionally, Maloney would assist in stretching someone out in partner-assisted stretches. McNeal switched the music in his MP3 player to some of his favorite songs from the Rocky soundtracks. He walked away from his teammates to do some drills in a small patch of grass a few feet away. Twenty minutes remained before race time. McNeal kept reminding himself to slow his breathing down and relax. The 5000 was a race that required discipline at the start. An over-excited runner tended to get out too fast and suffer the consequences in the middle of the race. It was the rare 5K won during the first two to three minutes, but countless had been lost by an over zealous runner expending too much energy too soon. McNeal fell victim to this numerous times in the past and tried to relax. He took a deep breath, and counted down from ten, talking himself through the beginning phases of the race.

Cooper tapped McNeal on the shoulder. "Yo, Mac, let's go. Time to go to the line."

McNeal removed his headphones. "Alright, let's do it."

Maloney high-fived each runner as they headed to the line. "Go get 'em, fellows."

As they stood on the line, McNeal's mind filled with doubt. Was he ready to race a 5K? He had been seriously running for three months, enough time to get into decent shape, but not enough to be really race ready. He took a deep breath, smacked himself in the head and refocused. "Oh well, I guess I'm about to find out how the Joey Mac comeback trail is going."

The starter went over the normal pre-race commands. Before he knew it, a siren sounded and McNeal, Cooper and O'Donnell shot out to the front, joined by four runners from Philadelphia Running Club. *Stay relaxed,* McNeal thought to himself. Four hundred meters into the race, he found himself in the uncomfortable position of leading. McNeal didn't want to be the sacrificial lamb, but once in front, he figured he might as well stay there. He heard the pit-pat sounds of several runners, telling him he wasn't alone. McNeal held his position through the first mile, hitting it in 4:48. *I hope that's not too quick,* he thought. At the turnaround, McNeal remained in the lead. As they rounded the orange cone marking the halfway mark, Cooper made a break. Immediately, two runners from Philadelphia Running responded.

McNeal surged to keep contact. *React, react.* Despite his best efforts, McNeal found himself struggling to stay with the newly formed lead pack. The race had transformed into two distinct races; one for the lead between Cooper and the first two Philadelphia Runners, and a second featuring the chase pack of McNeal, O'Donnell, and the two remaining Philadelphia Runners.

O'Donnell pulled up alongside McNeal. "Let's go, Mac, let's get back in it."

McNeal sucked in a deep breath. "Alright, OD, let's go."

The pair tried in vain to close the gap. However, with each step, the leaders appeared to pull further away. The gap grew and with half a mile to go, McNeal trailed by over twenty seconds. A quarter mile from the finish, the front two PR runners dashed into the lead. Cooper tried to match their move, but his legs did not cooperate. Cooper crossed the line in third place with a time of 15:24. McNeal was next in 15:45, followed by O'Donnell in 15:50.

McNeal bent over at the line, his hands on his knees. "How'd you feel, Coop? Sweet move at the halfway mark."

"Not enough to shake those PR guys."

O'Donnell shook Cooper's hand. "You sure shook me and Mac."

McNeal exited the finish chute. "Shook us like a salt shaker."

Maloney joined the trio for their cool down. "Nice race, guys."

O'Donnell exchanged fist bumps with Maloney. "Yeah, not a bad starting point."

Cooper led the foursome on their cool down. "Let's make sure that's all it is, a starting point."

McNeal pulled up the rear. "Amen, brother, Amen."

෨෴

McNeal loved Thanksgiving; it was one of his favorite holidays. Although corporate America had moved the start of the holiday season to sometime before Halloween, Thanksgiving officially kicked off the holidays for McNeal. He relished the opportunity to spend time with family, relax, and eat a home-cooked meal. While Cooper and McNeal ran the Grilled Donut Café, home cooking was not their specialty. Dinners often consisted of Café leftovers, take-out, and quickly made mixtures of instant potatoes and whatever else was in the kitchen cabinets. McNeal and Kelly were eating dinner with her family and going to McNeal's parents for dessert. Today marked their first holiday spent with each other's families. McNeal picked Kelly up at noon to drive to her parents' house. "Happy Thanksgiving, Kell."

Kelly reached across the front seat and kissed McNeal on the cheek. "Thanks, you too, Joe. How'd the race go?"

"Not bad. Coop ran pretty well. OD and myself were decent, maybe a lil' better. I guess it was a good first race back."

"Cool, so were you satisfied?"

"Happy, I guess, but not satisfied. When you're satisfied you stop being hungry. Can't be satisfied, even if number one."

"Got it. Can't get no satisfaction."

McNeal laughed. "Just like the Stones say. Only different."

Kelly's parents lived in a large single home in a suburb west of Philadelphia. They resided in the same house Kelly grew up in. They would be joined at dinner by Kelly's older brothers, Ted and Ron. McNeal met them several times previously and wasn't looking forward to seeing them again. They both worked as highway patrol officers and didn't think of special education as a manly profession. Regardless, he planned on being on his best behavior. Kelly's mother greeted them at the door. "Kelly!! How's my little girl doing?"

"Mom, I'm fine, and I'm not exactly your little girl, anymore. I am twenty-five, ya know."

Kelly's father descended an elaborate wooden staircase into the living room. "Aw, Kelly, you know you'll always be your Mom's and my little girl. Come here and give me a hug." Mr. Polaski stood about 6'3, slightly taller than Kelly's two brothers who each measured 6'1.

McNeal was keenly aware of his height when he visited Kelly's family; even her mother stood 5'8.

Mr. Polaski hugged Kelly then turned to face McNeal, extending his hand to shake. "So, Joe, Kelly tells us you've gotten back into running seriously. How's it going?"

"Great, it's going great." McNeal shook Kelly's father's hand. "I just had my first race back this morning."

"Really? On Thanksgiving morning? How'd it go?"

"It was a start. It was just nice to shake off some of the rust and let loose a little bit, ya know?"

"Not really. But that sounds great." Mr. Polaski took a seat in the family room in front of the television. "So what are you trying to get into shape for anyway? You're a little young for a mid-life crisis now aren't ya?"

McNeal was uncomfortable talking about why he was getting into shape especially with people who didn't understand running. He wasn't totally sure himself; it was just something he needed to do. In his mind, he didn't even have a choice. He had to take one last shot in order to get a full definition of himself as a runner, to know what he was capable of. If he didn't make one final attempt, he was certain he'd go crazy. Before he could attempt to answer Kelly's father, she came to his rescue.

"Dad, of course he's too young for a mid-life crisis. Is there something wrong with getting into good shape? More people should run in this country, maybe we'd have less health problems. It looks like you could use a little running." Kelly pointed to her father's ample waist.

Everyone laughed and McNeal breathed a sigh of relief, thankful his girlfriend had taken him off the hook. He joined Kelly's brothers in the living room to watch the Dallas Cowboys traditional Thanksgiving football game. This year's opponent was the Houston Texans, an inner-state rival in name only.

Ted, the elder brother, turned to greet McNeal. "Hey, Joey Mac, how are you?"

While both brothers stood 6'1, Ted was the broader of the two. He weighed about 235 pounds, while his younger brother was closer to an even 200. Both brothers had dirty blond hair and kept it cut close, almost a military buzz cut. Ted sported a goatee while Ron was clean-shaven.

"Pretty good. How about you guys?"

"As long as Romo leads the 'Boys to a win, and Mom don't burn the bird, then I think we'll be just fine." Ted turned and high-fived his brother Ron.

"Sounds about right to me."

McNeal shook his head. A rule for most Philadelphians was you don't root for the Dallas Cowboys in football. It ranked up there with staying loyal to your favorite cheese steak shop. McNeal never understood how someone could grow up in the Philadelphia area and adopt the most hated rival of the local team. "Do you guys have family from Dallas?"

"No, why?" Ron sipped from his bottle of beer.

"Just trying to figure out why you'd root for the Cowboys."

Ted reached into a bowl of chips. "Just always have. Don't you like a winner?"

"I guess I'm just a homer. My favorite teams have always been the local ones."

"Well, that's great if you can't think for yourself. Just root for who all your neighbors root for," teased Ron.

McNeal walked towards the kitchen. "Cause rooting for the Cowboys is the choice of a true individual thinker. Hey, Kell, what are you doing?"

He was trying to avoid any more conversation with her two brothers. It seemed to never go well and Thanksgiving was not a good day to argue about your choice of teams to cheer for.

"Helping out my Mom with some of the food. We're having candied yams." She held up a can of sweet potatoes for McNeal to see, aware they held a special place in his heart.

"Oh, sweet. That sounds good."

"You watching the game with my brothers?"

"Um, yeah. I guess I am." McNeal took a seat on a red fold up plastic chair.

"Have fun," Kelly responded, apparently oblivious to the fact that fun was not an option for McNeal right now.

"Definitely."

For the next thirty minutes McNeal, Ron and Ted made small talk about fantasy football and who they thought would reach the Super Bowl. McNeal was surprised at how well it actually went.

Mrs. Polaski poked her head out from the kitchen. "Dinner's ready, boys."

The three of them joined Kelly, her parents and Ted and Ron's wives in the dining area. The meal was truly a feast. There was the traditional array of foods available including some of McNeal's personal favorites: turkey, sweet potatoes, stuffing, homemade mashed potatoes and biscuits with butter. Each dish was passed around the table and McNeal, not wanting to insult Kelly's mother, sampled everything. "Wow, this is really good, Mrs. P. Everything's delicious."

"Thanks, Joe. Make sure you have seconds."

McNeal reached for another biscuit. "I'm pretty stuffed but maybe I'll have a little more sweet potatoes and another biscuit."

Mrs. Polaski looked up from her plate. "You can't be stuffed. We need to put some meat on you, Joseph."

"Actually, I need to drop a few pounds." McNeal buttered his biscuit. "For racing."

Mrs. Polaski shook her head at the thought. "If you lose any weight you'll wither away."

Kelly's father cut off another slice of turkey. "How are you supposed to lose weight and be able to protect my little girl?"

"I think I'll manage. I'm not dieting or anything. I just know what weight I race best at, and I'm a few pounds over that."

Ted took a break from scarfing down his meal. "Maybe you just need to add some more muscle to your scrawny body."

"Yeah, cause carrying 200 pounds around the track would be real efficient."

Ted stopped his stuffing-covered fork just sort of his mouth. "You calling me fat?"

"No, I'm just saying bulking up won't help me." McNeal sipped from a glass of water and tried to change the topic of conversation. "Anyway, how's the business going Mr. P?"

Kelly's dad ran an insurance office in the King of Prussia area. "Going great. Hopefully I'll be able to retire soon."

"Me too," joked McNeal. "Tons of special-ed teachers and track coaches have been striking it rich and retiring before thirty."

Everyone shared a laugh and the meal continued in peace. After eating, McNeal and Kelly left to visit McNeal's family for dessert. "Thanks for everything Mr. and Mrs. P. The food was outstanding," McNeal said as he walked out the door. "Happy Thanksgiving!"

Kelly bid her family farewell and met McNeal in the car. McNeal drove the forty-five minutes to his parents' home in Northeast Philadelphia. McNeal's family lived in one of the nicest neighborhoods in Philadelphia. They resided on a tree-lined street full of twin stone houses. McNeal came from a whole family of runners. His father was the patriarch of the running McNeals, a lifelong runner who had done some coaching but was unable to do so on a long term basis due to job pressures. McNeal's mother was a fitness runner, the kind found at the track mixing running with walking. But unlike many fitness runners, Mama McNeal knew better than to jog in lane one. Walking and jogging in lane one ranked as one of McNeal's top pet peeves and there may have been a time or two when he, or one of the other guys, had traded terse words with an uncooperative walker or two. McNeal's sister Teresa was a twenty-three year old nurse. Teresa dabbled in a variety sports in her youth and was currently a member of McNeal's Team Bonsai flag football team. The final member of the McNeal clan was his youngest sister, Kimberly. Kim was an 8th grader who recently picked up running, but had been playing soccer since age five. Despite his parents' complaints, McNeal preferred to simply be young Kimberly's older brother and only offered sports advice when prompted. It wasn't that McNeal wasn't interested in her exploits, he merely figured his parents gave her more than enough attention and advice when it came to the athletic arena.

McNeal fiddled with the radio dial as he drove. "So, you looking forward to some dessert?"

"Eh, I'm pretty stuffed but there's always room for pumpkin pie."

"You know it." McNeal pulled into his parents' driveway and parked the car. The two walked into McNeal's parents' home to find the family gathering around the table.

Mrs. McNeal stood at the kitchen sink, rinsing dishes with Teresa. "Hey, Kelly. Hi, Joe. How was dinner?"

"It was good. How about you guys? How was dinner?"

Teresa embraced Kelly and kissed her on the cheek. "Delicious. Mom outdid herself again."

McNeal's mother opened the refrigerator. "Who's ready for some pie? We've got pumpkin and pecan. What do you want, Joe? How about you, Kelly?"

McNeal joined his family at the table. "Can I get one of each, Ma? You know I can't turn down either."

Kelly elbowed McNeal in the ribs. "So much for trying to lose a few pounds. I'll take a piece of pumpkin. Pecan's a little too sweet for me."

"Kelly, you know I've got a sweet tooth. One day of having two pieces of pie won't kill me. Make 'em small though, Ma."

Sweets were McNeal's kryptonite. He easily avoided the grease-covered foods of the fast food enterprises. But offer McNeal cookies, cake or anything chocolate, and his guard melted like a cup of ice in the hot summer sun. McNeal sat down and bit into a slice of pumpkin pie. It did not disappoint. "Can I get some milk?"

McNeal's sister Teresa was not shy about speaking her mind. "You got legs, why don't you get your own milk? Mom wants to eat too, you know. And while you're at it, get everyone else a glass."

"Alright, alright, I got it. Who wants milk?" McNeal stood up and opened the fridge. "One, two, three, four, five, six, alright six glasses of milk coming right up."

McNeal promptly poured six glasses of milk and did his best waiter impersonation, nearly spilling them as he set them on the dining room table. He sat down and enjoyed the opportunity to spend time with his family.

Mrs. McNeal sipped her glass of milk. "Are you guys going to be at Uncle Neal's fiftieth birthday bash?"

McNeal swallowed a bite of pecan pie. "When is it again, Ma?"

"December 9th. We're hosting it here. He doesn't know about it yet. He thinks he's coming over here for something small, but the whole family's gonna be here."

"I need to check my schedule. I think my girls have a meet in the morning, but that night I was planning to race in New York at the Armory. It was going to be my first race back on the track."

Over the past several years, McNeal's coaching had taken quite a toll on his ability to see his extended family. Birthday parties and holiday gatherings often fell on the weekend, and it was a rare Saturday that McNeal did not have some sort of track obligation to attend. He still made time for his parents and sisters, but visits with aunts, uncles and cousins were few and far between. After so many misses, sometimes he wasn't invited at all. McNeal hated the look of sadness his mother gave him when he had to tell her that once again he would be missing family for track. He often wondered if the price he paid was worth it, a question he could not answer. One day he hoped to have a family of his own and realized changes would need to be made. Until then, he just juggled everything the best he could.

Mrs. McNeal sighed. "It's ok, Joe. Just make sure you let us know for sure."

"For sure, Mom. I'll let you know. So Kim, how's soccer going?"

Kim didn't look up from her cell phone. "It's ok."

McNeal's father spoke up. "She's got a tournament this weekend in Harrisburg."

McNeal patted his younger sister on the back. "Good luck, sis. Have fun!"

She put her phone in her pocket. "Thanks, 'bro. How's coaching?"

"Indoor starts Monday, so I'll have a better idea of how the team's going to be in a week or so. But based on cross country, it should be a good one. Maybe next year we'll have one Kimmy Mac running for the Wildcats."

Mr. McNeal carried his plate to the sink. "Maybe. We'll see if we can work that out."

Kimberly rolled her eyes, before breaking into a smile. "And if I want to go there."

After eating more than his fair share of pumpkin and pecan pies, McNeal bid his family farewell. "Thanks for having us, guys. I'll let you know about the party. Love ya'll."

McNeal drove Kelly home, humming to the Christmas music now playing on the radio. "You have a good time?"

"Yes, I did. It was nice to see both of our families, don't you think?"

"Of course. It's always nice to see the fam during the holidays."

Kelly turned the radio down. She was not a fan of Christmas music more than a week a before Christmas. "And on birthdays too, you know, Joe. Running isn't everything. It'd be nice if we could go to your uncle's surprise party. I bet he'd appreciate it."

McNeal sighed. He felt like he was stuck in the middle of a game of tug of war. "I know, Kelly. We'll see what happens."

"I'm sure we will." Kelly undid her seatbelt as they arrived at her apartment. "Anyway, thanks for today. It was fun. Good night."

"Good night, Kelly." McNeal gently kissed her goodnight. He watched Kelly walk up her steps and into her apartment. McNeal sat there a minute, inhaled a deep breath and slowly drove home. He went straight to bed for what proved to be a restless night as he lay awake in bed, staring at the ceiling. He wondered if he would ever find the proper balance in his life. The conflicts never ended between running and family, or coaching and teaching, or Kelly and running. McNeal felt as if he was running uphill in the mud. Slipping and sliding, slipping and sliding.

Something has to give, McNeal thought as he fell asleep. Soon enough, something would.

chapter 12

McNeal struggled to climb out of bed on Monday morning. A long holiday weekend only served to make the return to work more difficult for McNeal. He walked to the bathroom where he tried to visualize his lessons for the day. Much like race strategies, plans at Second Chances often fell apart and McNeal had to wing it. He had been winging it in his life for so long now he had it down to an art form.

McNeal did not eagerly anticipate getting back into the swing of things at Second Chances. The students at Second Chances typically behaved poorly after a long weekend. Those lucky enough to visit home for the holiday frequently reverted to the same habits that led them to Second Chances. Those who had nowhere, or no one, to go home to were usually in a justifiably unhappy mood. The combination often proved combustible. Monday was no different. McNeal broke up three fights before noon. The afternoon went slightly better and McNeal left work hoping Tuesday might actually approach peaceful.

Monday marked the opening of indoor track. McNeal referred to the first day as "organized chaos." Unlike cross country, where every girl was united in purpose and task, track season divided the team into several smaller groups, such as distance runners, sprinters, throwers, hurdlers and jumpers. Some gifted athletes crossed boundaries between groups, making the design of their practice schedule truly challenging. The championship run of the fall created a buzz in the school and new sign-ups abounded. Past history told McNeal a large portion of the newcomers wouldn't last past the first week. Still the sight of fifty-seven girls excited him. Numbers most years averaged in the twenties or thirties, so if they maintained a number in the forties, McNeal thought it could translate to greater success. After all, the more mud you throw at a wall, the more that sticks.

McNeal's phone buzzed at 7:30 on Friday night. He and Cooper had just finished a seven-mile fartlek run and were set to begin a core workout. They had worked up to thirty-minute core workouts consisting of thirty-second intervals of different exercises with ten push-ups in between. They began in September with an eight-minute routine, which left the two of them laying motionless on the floor with abs so sore it hurt to laugh for days. McNeal checked the caller ID but didn't recognize the number. "Probably another bill collector."

"Calling your cell? That sucks, man."

"Tell me about it. Can't outrun them." His phone again buzzed loudly, signifying a message had been left. "That's weird, they don't normally leave a message."

Cooper sat at the computer desk in the living room corner, sipping on a water bottle. "Listen to it, then we'll knock this core workout out. I'll pull up some tunes."

McNeal dialed in the digits to check his voicemail. It wasn't a bill collector; it was Seamus O'Toole. He had called to discuss the possibility of coaching McNeal, Cooper, O'Donnell, and Maloney. McNeal put his phone down. "O'Toole wants to meet with us. He's interested in coaching us."

Cooper stood up from his seat and raised his eyebrows. "Really? I thought he wanted nothing to do with us."

"Must have seen those rolling Turkey Trot 5ks from last week."

Cooper lay down to begin the core workout. "Yeah, that's the ticket. Alright, let's get this crap out of the way."

They started with thirty seconds of straight crunches followed by ten push-ups. The next exercise was twists, where they sat with their feet a couple inches above the ground and twisted from side to side. They had progressed to doing it with a ten-pound weight. Push-ups again followed. The sounds of Linkin Park blared from Cooper's computer. Another set of crunches, this time in slow motion. After the push-ups, they moved to bicycle kicks. Each exercise more difficult than the previous. Half way through the regimen, the strain was apparent on both of their faces. Another fifteen minutes later, after three hundred push-ups, and thirty gut busting exercises that worked their abs, back, and hip flexors, McNeal and Cooper sat on the floor drenched in sweat, sore all over.

McNeal slumped to the ground and stared at the ceiling. "Yo, man, nice workout."

Cooper stood up and walked towards the kitchen. "Thanks. I hate you." McNeal had instituted the core routine in September and Cooper had not yet forgiven him.

McNeal drug himself off the ground and grabbed his phone. "I'm going to call O'Toole back. Can you grab me some water?"

"No problem. I still hate you."

"Figured as much." McNeal dialed O'Toole. "Hello, Seamus. This is Joey McNeal returning your call."

"Joseph? How the hell are you today? Well, I've been thinking. I might take you up on your offer. One condition, however." O'Toole spoke quickly as if in a hurry to move on to the next thing on a long to do list. He wasn't trying to be rude; he simply talked fast, the same way he ran back in the prime of his career.

"OK. What's the condition?"

"Well, first of all, no questions about the 1980 Olympic boycott. I've moved on in my life and so should you. Second, if you're going to do this, then you've got to do the bloody thing the right way. No short cuts. No excuses. Got it?"

O'Toole gave McNeal no time to respond as he continued his list of one. "You need to keep a daily log and I'm going to check it each week. I understand there will be days when you guys need to fit your run into that God forsaken mess you bastards call a life. Whatever. Write them down for me to see. Got it?"

Again McNeal attempted to answer, but the words never made it out of his mouth. Cooper watched this unfold with a grin on his face as McNeal listened to O'Toole, unable to get a word in. "You need to make sure you take care of yourselves. That means eat right, stay hydrated, no late nights drinking fire water and chasing dames. The body needs to recover."

McNeal hesitated before speaking. "Is that all?" If this was one condition, McNeal dreaded doing a workout of twenty quarters.

"Is that all? Maybe I was right and you guys aren't ready for good ol' Seamus O'Toole. Yes, damn it, that's all. Before we start, I insist on meeting with anyone I'll be coaching. How about Monday, your place at 7:00? I'll see you guys there." O'Toole hung up the phone before McNeal could respond.

McNeal stood in the center of the living room, still holding his phone to his ear. "I think we're meeting with O'Toole here on Monday at seven. We need to tell OD and Mitch."

Cooper looked confused. "You think? What's that mean?"

"I never confirmed it. In fact, I never really said much of anything."

"I know. I was listening. Or rather watching since there was nothing to listen to. Monday ought to be interesting."

McNeal nodded. "Indeed. Indeed."

The weekend passed uneventfully and O'Donnell and Maloney arrived at the apartment around 6:30 on Monday. McNeal and Cooper had just completed a seven mile run. Maloney brought with him two pizzas—one sausage and one pepperoni. O'Donnell carried a case of beer, and a two liter diet Coke for McNeal. Forty-five minutes later, the four friends sat on McNeal's couch, their bellies full, but with no sign of Seamus O'Toole.

O'Donnell stood up to go to the bathroom "You think he's coming?"

"Yeah, he's coming," McNeal assured him. At 8:00, McNeal wasn't so sure. By 8:50, he had little doubt Seamus O'Toole would not be showing up.

"Dude, I told you he's crazy. First, he won't coach us. Now all of a sudden he's calling you to tell you he changed his mind." Cooper stood up and pointed to his chest. "I mean I'd want a piece of this too if I was an out of work coach. Why the hell not?"

McNeal defended O'Toole. "Coop, you and I both know there's a thin line between genius and madness. I mean how many people thought we were crazy when we opened the Grilled Donut Café. Now look at us."

O'Donnell exited the bathroom and rejoined the conversation. "Yeah, look at you guys, living above a dog groomer and God knows what else. I wouldn't call the Grilled Donut Café a huge hit just yet. I mean I it has potential and all, but I'm just saying…"

Maloney looked around the apartment. "OD's right. This ain't exactly a penthouse suite here, Joe."

McNeal looked out the window, checking for a sign of O'Toole. "Both you guys who are criticizing le chateau still live at home if I do say so myself. Not that there's anything wrong with saving a few bucks."

O'Donnell returned to his seat. "Yo, man, you know me and Leslie are getting a place together. And we all aren't as old as you, Mac. Living at home at twenty-four aint' what it would be if your old ass was living at home at—what are you now—thirty?"

"Watch it there big guy. Twenty-nine. Won't be thirty til May."

"Stop bickering like a couple of grade school girls. RAW's about to begin." Cooper opened the refrigerator. "Who wants another beer?"

BANG! BANG! BANG! "Joey Mac, get the hell down here and let me in!"

Maloney shook his head in disbelief. "You got to be kidding me."

McNeal ran down the steps to let Seamus O'Toole in. "About time you got here, Seamus. Thanks for the call."

O'Toole walked through the door. "Shut your bloody trap. Seamus O'Toole doesn't own a cellular telephone. I've made it this far without one, and I sure don't plan on changing now. And SEPTA is run by a bunch of donkeys." O'Toole wrinkled the nose on his well-traveled face and sniffed. "What the hell's that smell?"

McNeal pointed to the wall. "Dogs, we're standing next to a dog groomer."

O'Toole marched up the steps. "Well, it reeks! How do you live with that stench?"

McNeal followed O'Toole up the stairs. "It ain't that bad. You get used to it. It don't really make it upstairs, anyway."

"Maybe a couple clowns like you can get used to it. Not Seamus O'Toole." O'Toole climbed the top step to find Cooper, Maloney, and O'Donnell sitting on the couch watching Monday Night Raw, drinking beer, and eating pepperoni and sausage pizza. Apparently unhappy with what he saw, he exploded into a tirade. "What in the blue hell is this? This looks like a house of disrepitude, not a place where men run. Drinking beer, eating crappy pizza and watching a bunch of half-naked steroided-up buffoons beat on each other. You think this gets you ready to run with the big boys, do you? Not with Seamus O'Toole in town. Oh, bloody no." O'Toole waved his arms above his head furiously as he spoke.

Cooper, O'Donnell and Maloney sat on the couch dumbfounded. No one dared open their mouth. Besides, who knew what to say to the raving lunatic who had just entered Cooper and McNeal's home—two hours late.

McNeal attempted to reason with O'Toole. "Seamus, calm down. We already ran tonight and no one's racing anytime soon. We're just having some fun, eating dinner, watching TV, while waiting to talk to you about coaching us."

But it was to no avail. "And that's exactly what I'm about to do now!" O'Toole pointed at the couch. "Manny, Moe, and Jack, state your names and events. And turn off that brain-numbing nonsense you're watching on the television."

The three men looked at each other, no one wanting to talk first. O'Donnell bravely decided to give it a shot. "Uh, I'm Len O'Donnell.

I run the 800 and mile on the track, as well as the 5000 on the roads. I might be moving up though."

Cooper went next. "Ryan Cooper. Distance."

O'Toole scratched what little red hair remained on his head. "Of course you're a gosh danged distance runner. I certainly wasn't going to confuse your scrawny skin and bones with a sprinter. Now, Mr. Cooper, do you run the mile or the marathon?"

"Neither, mostly the 5000. I love Broad Street. That's a ten miler and I've run some miles and halves on the track."

"Thank you Mr. Cooper. I am aware of the distance of Broad Street. I didn't think that you merely had some odd affection for the street itself."

Maloney was last to answer. "My name is Mitch Maloney. I run the 400 and the 800 and I was wondering, no disrespect intended, why the hell are you so damn mad?"

If looks could kill, Mitch Maloney would be dead. Luckily for all involved, they do not.

"Why am I so mad? Is that what you want to know? Well, let's get one thing straight here, McGillicutty. Seamus O'Toole is not mad. You want to see mad? I've been mad just twice before and trust me, young man, it is not a pretty sight. You don't want to be around the third time Seamus O'Toole is angry." O'Toole walked into the kitchen. "Who actually lives in this God-forsaken shack?"

Cooper followed O'Toole to the kitchen. "Uh, myself and Joe. And Mitch might be moving in."

"Why the hell would he want to do that?" O'Toole wondered. "Where do you live, Maloney? The depths of hell? That's about the only place worse than this. Dogs downstairs, crap all over the place, bunch of flippin' thugs hanging on the corner."

"Close," answered Maloney. "Kensington."

O'Toole opened the refrigerator and found the usual suspects that resided in McNeal and Cooper's fridge. "You blokes do realize food is fuel. What you eat is what you are. How do you expect to achieve anything in the great sport of track and field if you eat and drink like a bunch of common American slobs?"

He reached into the refrigerator grabbed a bottle of beer and dumped it down the sink. Cooper opened his mouth to protest, caught a glimpse of the crazed look in O'Toole's eyes and thought better of it. O'Toole proceeded to do this ten more times as the four runners simply watched, mouths agape. "You want to run for me? You'll do as I say," O'Toole told them. "No alcohol. It's only useful purpose is getting ugly guys chicks. Well, maybe you gents might need some booze for that reason. But not when you're running for me. Save it for when you're retired." O'Toole then grabbed the diet Coke. It too was soon dumped down the drain. "Soda? Not in my house."

No one ventured to remind O'Toole that he was, in fact, not in his house. Next, O'Toole opened the cabinets and found a box of Tastykakes. "Ah, peanut butter candy cakes, a wee piece o' heaven on earth. Seamus O'Toole's favorite. Good taste. Great taste, even. Bad fuel. I'll be taking these with me. By the end of this week I want some real food in here if you know what's good for you."

McNeal and company knew not what O'Toole considered real food. Based on his bizarre behavior, he may have a totally different idea of what good fuel was.

O'Toole now stood at the top of the steps. "Get your spikes. We're going to the track."

Cooper, his face red with anger, protested. "We're going where? Seamus I don't know what you do, but we all work tomorrow and it's almost ten o'clock at night. There's no way in hell we're going to the track."

O'Toole turned to face Cooper. "If you want to run for Seamus O'Toole, you'll get your bloody spikes and meet me downstairs. If you want to spend the rest of your life watching wrastlin', getting fat before your time, and never amounting to anything worthwhile, stay here, I insist. For anyone who wants to learn how to be a runner, I'll be outside. I need to smoke a cigarette."

As O'Toole descended the steps, the four runners stood there, open-mouthed, yet speechless. No one could believe what they just witnessed. McNeal warned them of O'Toole's eccentricities but none of them expected this.

Maloney broke the silence. "Joe, what the hell just happened?"

McNeal shrugged his shoulders. "I really don't know."

Cooper sighed. "Does he really think we're going to the track now?"

O'Donnell couldn't help but smile. "Do you think this guy jokes around? I don't think he even knows what a joke is."

McNeal agreed. "He's serious, man. He's definitely serious."

The door at the bottom of the steps opened and in popped O'Toole. "What are you ladies doing? Putting on your make-up or something? Jiminy Crickets, we're going to the track, not the gosh-darned prom!"

They all looked at each other, waiting for someone to take the lead or say something to O'Toole. Maloney walked to the corner of the den, grabbed his bag with his running clothes and spikes and slowly walked down the steps.

O'Donnell looked at Cooper. "I guess we're actually gonna do this?"

Cooper shook his head. "Looks like it. Let's go."

They descended the steps and piled into O'Donnell's 2003 Ford Taurus. McNeal opened the door to get in the front seat next to O'Donnell before Seamus grabbed his arm. "Seamus O'Toole doesn't do the back seat."

Joey Mac bowed his head and reluctantly squeezed into the back seat with Maloney and Cooper. O'Donnell drove the ten minutes to a local high school track and parked his car in the dark, vacant lot. McNeal walked towards the gate. "It's probably going to be locked up. It always is at night."

"Don't matter, we'll just hop the fence," said Maloney, as he stepped out of the car. "Never stopped us before."

For the first time all night O'Toole smiled. "That's the first thing I heard all night that I liked. Now that we're on a roll jog a mile to warm-up. I don't have all day."

McNeal and the others hopped over the chain link fence onto the track. The well worn track was black in color, adding to the darkness of the night. Tall trees surrounded the track, the last of their leaves brown and holding on for dear life. The four runners circled the empty track in silence, trying to comprehend the events of the night. McNeal had worked out in the dark before, but never quite so late on a track quite so dark. On their fourth lap, Cooper said what each man was thinking. "What do you think he'll have us do?"

McNeal stopped to start stretching. "I don't even want to guess."

He wouldn't need to guess as O'Toole's voice soon filled the cool, crisp air. "Alright, gentlemen. This is what we're doing tonight. It's an old favorite of mine. I think it's fitting for the occasion. We used to call it 'Chase the ghost.' Here's how it works. You guys each run a 400, one at a time, relay style. Our ghost friend ran a four minute mile. You guys have to run a four minute mile. Each of you. So that means four quarters in sixty seconds or better. Your rest is your teammates run. If anyone doesn't break four, we do it again. Any questions?"

No one spoke. "Ok, then see me at the line in five minutes."

McNeal did some speed drills followed by four hard striders down the backstretch. Cooper jumped up and down several times. "You know—and I'm going to regret saying this in about ten minutes—but it actually feels good to be out on the track."

Maloney looked up from tying his spikes. "Yeah, tell me how good it feels after the first two quarters."

"Hey, I said I was going to regret it."

O'Toole clapped his hands. "OK, gentlemen. Let's get this baby started. Seamus O'Toole would like to go to bed tonight, if that's alright with you. Maloney, OD, Cooper, McNeal—that's the order."

Seconds later, Maloney ran off into the night. He had always possessed the habit of going out too fast and tonight appeared no different. Maloney flew off the first turn and powered down the backstretch, driving his knees high into the air with each stride, resembling Michael Johnson's trademark upright running style. He passed the 200 meter mark in twenty-six seconds before disappearing into the deep darkness of the far curve. The strain of the early pace began to show as Maloney emerged from the shadows and entered the homestretch.

McNeal watched from the infield. "Let's go, Mitch."

Maloney held form as he ran the final hundred meters. O'Donnell pulled Maloney out and grabbed the baton as the clock hit fifty-six seconds. O'Toole scribbled Maloney's time into a small spiral notebook. "Fifty-six? Not too shabby, Maloney. You might pay later on though."

O'Donnell ran more conservatively than Maloney, hitting the 200 just under thirty seconds before he disappeared into the abyss for a hundred meters. O'Donnell reappeared then accelerated down the stretch, handing Cooper the baton in 59.5 seconds.

McNeal stepped on the track to wait his turn. "Nice job, OD."

O'Toole continued watching from the infield. "Let's go Cooper! Move those chicken legs, this ain't bloody Broad Street!"

Despite O'Toole's yelling about Cooper's lack of speed, the wiry runner reached the 200 in twenty-eight seconds, well under pace. McNeal peered into the darkness to try and watch Cooper sprint around the turn, but it did him no good. Cooper emerged at the three hundred meter mark. He seemed to run out of gas as he neared the exchange, his stride growing more rigid with each step.

O'Toole counted the seconds as they ticked off his watch. "57-58-59-60.60.5. Five tenths to make up."

McNeal took the stick from Cooper and flew through the first turn. Like Maloney, he'd blown many a race by setting too furious of an early pace. Despite this, he stubbornly remained a frontrunner. He felt more comfortable in the lead, out of traffic. McNeal passed the first 200 in twenty-seven flat. Surprisingly, he felt good. He knew that would soon change. The track was nearly pitch black on the far curve and McNeal struggled to see as he sped through the turn, hoping not to step on anything. He ran the final straight smoothly, hitting the quarter in 55.5 seconds. Maloney received the baton and began his second repeat more relaxed. His 200 meter split read 29.5 but he looked to be laboring. When Maloney tired, he had the tendency of leaning back, looking like a marching toy soldier at times. He appeared on the verge of losing form as he entered the third hundred meters and disappeared from sight.

Cooper clapped his hands as Maloney entered the final hundred. "Keep it together, Mitch. Get forward."

Maloney regrouped, and finished his 400 with a flurry, sprinting the final fifty meters and handing off the baton in 59.5 seconds before collapsing into the grass. "I'm out, man. Ain't no way I got two more sub-sixtys."

McNeal attempted to encourage his cousin. "You don't need two sub 60's. You got some time in the bank."

Maloney peered up at McNeal from his knees. "Do I got an hour in the bank? 'Cause that's probably what I need."

McNeal watched as O'Donnell methodically went about his business again. He hit the 200 in 29 flat, vanished into the shadows and sped through the final hundred and handed Cooper the stick, again in a time of 59.5.

McNeal slapped O'Donnell on the back as he stepped onto the track. "Nice job, OD. You look good."

"Thanks. Wish I felt good instead of the bag of rotting monkey feces I feel like."

"Thanks. Nice visual." McNeal turned towards Maloney. "I better see you standing here when I'm finishing, Mitch."

"I'll be there. I'll be there." Maloney sounded like he was trying to convince himself.

McNeal hopped up and down as he waited for Cooper. "Let's go, Coop."

Cooper hit the 200 in 28.5 seconds before disappearing. He looked strong as he appeared off the turn and headed for home. He handed McNeal the baton in 59.8 seconds, dipping under, but still needing to make up three-tenths of a second.

McNeal again moved with ease down the backstretch. "I can't believe how good I feel," he thought as he sped through the 200 in 26.5 seconds. "Those hills must be working."

O'Toole, silent for much of the workout, looked up from his notebook. "Let's go, Joseph. Show Seamus O'Toole why he should coach you!"

McNeal entered the final straightaway and powerfully ran towards the finish line before handing off in a time of fifty-five seconds flat. He walked off the track, clapped his hands and shouted words of encouragement to Maloney, who was already laboring as he rounded the first turn. While he had shed ten pounds since returning to running in September, he still carried an extra fifteen. Maloney hit the 200 in 31.5, and things looked bleak. O'Donnell stood on the line waiting for Maloney to emerge from the shadows. "Come on, Mitch, you got this." Maloney pumped his arms and fought against the fatigue but by the 350 mark, there was little fight left and Mitch struggled across the line in sixty-seven seconds.

O'Toole continued taking notes. "First one a bit saucy for ya, Mr. Maloney?" Maloney glared at O'Toole from the infield, hands and knees on the grass, but said nothing.

O'Donnell took the baton and again went about the business of running a sub-sixty second quarter mile. O'Donnell worked in finance, and he approached each 400 with the same business like mindset he approached a day at the office. He hit the 200 in a shade under twenty-nine seconds, maintained his form throughout and again handed off the stick in 59.5 seconds.

O'Toole looked up from his notes. "Pretty consistent."

Cooper grabbed the baton from OD, and took off much quicker and more aggressively than in his first two efforts. He hit the half way mark at 27.8 this time, churned his legs though the turn, and began opening up his stride as he approached McNeal. Cooper handed off the baton in 57.1, more than making up the necessary three tenths.

O'Toole said nothing and continued writing in his notebook. Cooper stepped off the track and stared at the silent O'Toole. "Go get 'em, Mac!"

McNeal hit the backstretch and began pouring it on as he motored down the track. O'Toole looked at his watch as McNeal approached the 200 meter mark. It read twenty-six seconds flat. O'Toole nodded his head in approval as McNeal came off the turn and showed signs of fatigue for the first time. McNeal's head drifted back and his stride shortened. Despite this, he managed to cross the line in 54.8 seconds, recording the fastest split of the day. Maloney grabbed the baton and gamely went out hard, hoping to muster something for his final 400. By the time he hit 150 meters however, it was clearly not to be. O'Toole scratched his head, apparently in thought. A drop of rain hit O'Toole in the head and he looked up at the sky, ready to burst at any moment. "Seamus O'Toole is old, tired and cold. And apparently about to be wet. So this is what I'm gonna do. If the four of you break four minutes for this last set, then you're done. By the looks of Mr. Maloney, it looks like you three gentlemen might have to do some real running tonight."

Maloney hit the 200 in thirty-three seconds. A consistent pattern of rain now fell to the track. Cooper and O'Donnell looked at each other with raised eyebrows. Neither seemed confident about their hopes of breaking four. Maloney would be lucky to break seventy and ten seconds was an awful lot to make up.

Cooper paced nervously back and forth on the infield. "Come on, Mitch, suck it up. Stay strong!"

Maloney labored badly as he entered the final hundred. McNeal and Cooper stood in the infield, urging him on. Maloney turned towards them, lowered his head and lifted his knees as he approached O'Donnell, crossed the line and collapsed. McNeal and Cooper grabbed Maloney under his shoulders and helped him to the infield.

O'Toole grinned. "Sixty-nine! You guys are gonna have to average under fifty-seven to get out of here."

O'Donnell's consistency, such a good thing only minutes earlier, no longer looked so great. O'Donnell began slightly faster this time, but his legs had already settled into the rhythm of running 59.5. The icy rain now falling didn't help matters. O'Donnell disappeared into the dimly lit turn for the final time. Fifteen seconds later he sprinted off the final turn, fighting for every inch. He pumped his arms furiously as his legs turned stone like, crossing the line in 59.2 seconds. The rain was now a full blown downpour.

O'Toole reached into his leather satchel and pulled out a small black umbrella. "Well, well, Mr. Cooper. Was that fifty-seven a mirage or do you have something else to show old Seamus O'Toole? What are those chicken legs made of?"

Cooper snatched the baton and took off like a bat out of hell, running as if he had something to prove. He hit the 200 in twenty-seven and flew into the darkness. He was running all out now, bobbing his head as he sucked in each breath.

McNeal toed the line and waited his turn. He jumped up and down, trying to stay warm on the cold, wet night. "Let's go, Coop, you got this!" Cooper burst upon the final turn with all he was worth, legs churning, arms vigorously thrusting back and forth, his t-shirt stuck to his chest. Maloney took a break from heaving up pizza and beer to watch Cooper pass the baton to McNeal. Cooper had run 56.8 seconds, not only his best effort of the night, but his fastest quarter mile in years. Despite this, McNeal still needed to run a fifty-four second quarter mile.

Maloney gingerly rose to his feet. "Come on, Joe."

McNeal aggressively ran the first turn, knowing if he relaxed his legs would settle into too slow of a rhythm. Taxed and spent, he needed this to be his best effort of the night. He accelerated out of the first turn and hit the halfway mark in just under twenty-five seconds. The rain fell sideways as he entered the turn. McNeal's curls were now glued to his forehead, rain dripping down his face.

"I hope that's not too fast for Joey," worried O'Donnell.

Maloney placed his hand on O'Donnell's shoulder. "He'll be ok."

McNeal fought to keep his form on the far turn, pain written all over his face. The shadowy turn seemed to last forever. *Lift and pump, lift and pump*, he thought as he finally entered the final straight.

Cooper, Maloney, and O'Donnell lined the track cheering McNeal on. O'Toole stood there silently, staring at the clock, watching each second tick off. Each step grew increasingly difficult for McNeal. His eyes struggled to maintain focus and he strained to see. He felt like he was pulling a sled through soft sand. His form deteriorated with each stride. A few meters shy of the finish, McNeal's spikes caught the track, causing him stumble. His arms awkwardly flailed over his head as he fought to stay upright. McNeal did all he could to lift his knees and pick his feet off the ground. At last, he crossed the line, completely devoid of energy, and crumbled to the wet track. O'Toole looked down at his watch. Maloney ran over to check the time, making sure the old man didn't try to cheat McNeal. He glanced over O'Toole's shoulder to read 52.8. McNeal had done it, running the time needed for them to break four with a second to spare. Maloney gripped McNeal in a bear hug. "Fifty-Two freaking eight!"

McNeal wobbled over to the grass, sat down and removed his spikes from his throbbing feet, each home to friction marks on the instep. "How was that, Seamus?"

"Not bad. Now put your pants and shoes on and cool down."

Cold and wet, McNeal and the others cut their cool down to a half mile, gathered their things and walked to the car.

O'Donnell led the way. "Where's O'Toole?"

"I bet that S.O.B. is already in the car getting warm while we shiver out here," grumbled Cooper. "Mac, I wanna trust you about this guy, and I realize I don't know him very well, but I hate that overgrown Jamaican Leprechaun."

They arrived at the car, expecting to find O'Toole in the passenger seat. Instead they found a note taped to the front window.

"Good workout. I'll be in touch. Seamus O'Toole."

O'Donnell unlocked the doors and started the car. "How do you think he was getting home?"

O'Donnell handed McNeal a towel to lay on the front seat. McNeal took the seat next to O'Donnell. "I guess the bus."

"It's pouring rain and nearly midnight."

McNeal shrugged his shoulders. Ten minutes later, O'Donnell dropped McNeal, Cooper and Maloney off at the apartment. The rain had now stopped. With it already midnight, Maloney decided to spend the night on their couch.

"Good job tonight, guys," said O'Donnell.

McNeal shut the passenger side door. "Later, Len."

The three tired runners trudged up the steps to the apartment. Cooper slumped onto the first chair he saw. "I have no idea what just happened. All I know is I'm beat and I do not want to wake up at six to manage the Café."

Maloney laughed. "I can't wait to move furniture for eight hours. I am so stoked for that, man, so stoked."

McNeal handed Maloney some dry clothes, a towel, pillow and blanket. "Well, I guess I won't complain. But you know how much I love teaching at Second Chances."

McNeal and Cooper each went to their respective bedrooms while Maloney attempted the impossible, a good night's sleep on their fifty-dollar thrift store couch.

chapter 13

McNeal awoke early on Wednesday December 14th to run with Maloney. Maloney now slept on their couch with increasing frequency, providing McNeal another regular training partner. A small but growing pile of his clothes lay in a corner of the living room. The difference in his running after a couple of days of breathing smoke-free air was usually obvious. O'Donnell often guessed where Maloney had slept based on how he fared in a workout. Today McNeal and Maloney planned on doing a sixty-minute run with some light fartlek in the middle. They stepped out of the apartment at 6:40 to find a fresh carpet of snow on the ground.

Maloney walked back inside to fetch a pair of gloves. "What a beautiful day for an hour with pick-ups. Don't you agree, Joe?"

"Indeed. Ain't it always? Hopefully, Whitaker Ave will be plowed so we can pick up the pace without worrying about slipping all over the place. The last thing we want to do before racing is strain a groin or something."

They spent the first fifteen minutes dodging traffic, periodically ducking behind a parked car for cover before they reached Whitaker, a wide road that wasn't heavily traveled. Already plowed, it provided a safe spot to run fast when getting to a track wasn't possible. For the next thirty minutes the two runners alternated hard segments of thirty and sixty seconds with corresponding easy parts. They focused on remaining relaxed and fast, not an easy task in sub-freezing temperatures with mounting snowfalls. The wind gusts made half their repeats feel like they were being pushed faster and faster by an invisible force, while conversely, running on the other side of road felt like trudging uphill.

McNeal paused at a red light. "How you feeling, Mitch?"

"How you think I feel? My toes are numb, I got snot frozen to my face and my lungs are searing. I'm freezing my balls off, man, that's how I feel."

The light turned green and McNeal started running. "Glad to know you're OK."

"Yeah, whatever. How many more do we got?"

"One more. Let's let it rip a bit."

"Let's do it."

Within ten seconds, they were stride for stride, cutting through the wind like a warm knife through butter. Two blocks later, they eased up, pounded fists, and began the easy fifteen-minute run home.

"Nice workout, Mitch."

"You too, Joe. I can't wait for Saturday. I know I'm not there yet, but it feels good to be in the same ballpark again. To remember what it feels like to be fit and fast."

"Well, I don't know about fit. But you sure looked fast today," McNeal kidded Maloney.

Maloney had dropped most of his excess weight and almost looked runnerish. McNeal enjoyed seeing the transformation of his younger cousin back into a competitive runner. It gave Mitch something to shoot for, an alternative to the everyday doom and gloom so many faced in Kensington. "Man, look at me. I might not be stickman thin like Coop, but I'm as light as I've been since high school. Now I know I'm a young buck compared to you, cuz, but it's been a few years still."

"Gotta make an old joke, don't you?"

"Hey, man, you started with the fat jokes."

The two laughed as they headed home. "How do you think we're gonna do?" Maloney turned suddenly serious. "I haven't raced in three years. I'm nervous, even if it's no big deal."

"You'll be alright. Just like riding a bike. Put yourself in it, and let instinct take over."

"Joe, I haven't ridden a bike since my Huffy was stolen the day after my twelfth birthday. But I know what you mean, instinct. Yeah, instinct."

The remainder of the run was completed in silence as each man wondered what would happen upon their return to the track. They would find out soon enough.

Saturday afternoon McNeal returned from Lehigh University, where his girls' competed in an indoor meet. They finished second in the 4x800, behind rival Springtown Academy, who ran a state-leading time of 9:37. He paced around the apartment as he waited for Seamus O'Toole to arrive. O'Toole was driving the foursome up to race at the MAC Holiday Classic in a rented mini-van. Kelly was also riding up to watch. She had never seen McNeal run a serious race and was looking forward to finally getting a firsthand view of what made him tick. McNeal and Maloney were both running the mile, while Cooper and O'Donnell were competing in the 3000. Maloney had only run the mile once in high school. His senior year, he opened outdoors with a 4:51 on a cold, blustery day. With such a limited track record, Maloney had no choice but to improve. "You ready to rock that mile, Mitch?"

"Define 'rock.' I guess I'm as ready as I'm gonna be." Maloney sipped on his water bottle. "How about you?"

McNeal smiled. "I'll tell you after the race."

"Haha, yeah, me too."

The loud honking of a horn signified O'Toole's arrival.

"Coop, OD, let's go. O'Toole's here."

The four runners grabbed their track bags, double-checking to make sure they had everything they needed—spikes, uniform, racing socks. For McNeal, it also included a Powerbar and a tube of Icy Hot. They piled into O'Toole's silver van. Maloney grabbed shotgun, with

OD and Cooper in the front row. McNeal headed to the back. "Seamus, we got to make a quick stop and pick up Kelly. She's on the way to I-95, though, so it's not a big deal."

O'Toole was not fond of McNeal's girlfriend going to the Armory with them. He liked the idea of picking her up even less. "In the name of St. Patrick himself, Joseph, why isn't the lass here?"

"She had to finish getting ready."

"Finish? What time did she bloody start? It's two o'clock in the blessed afternoon. She's had the whole damn morning to get ready. It's a track meet, not a fashion show. Damn you, McNeal, you better run fast. You know how I feel about women and racing!"

O'Toole was of the "women weaken legs" school of thought and believed they posed a distraction.

"Don't worry about it, Seamus. It's all under control."

Ten minutes later, Kelly joined McNeal in the backseat and they were heading north on I-95. "Nice to meet you, Mr. O'Toole." She turned to McNeal to see if she said the right thing. She had heard stories about his ranting and raving and did not want to set him off on a tirade.

O'Toole resumed driving, never turning his head. "Pleasure is mine."

Kelly took the open seat next to McNeal. "Hey, guys, how's it going?"

Cooper turned in his seat. "Good."

McNeal kissed his girlfriend on the cheek. "How you doing, babe?"

"Good. You ready to run?"

"I think so. Ask me again when I'm done."

The remainder of the nearly two hour trip evoked memories of high school track trips for McNeal. The guys spent the time joking about various topics, occasionally having to apologize to Kelly for an off-color remark. It felt good to be traveling to a meet and have that old feeling of being a part of a team. It prompted them to decide to formally form a track club. They had not yet come up with a name but some ideas floated around, including Upstarts Track Club, Philadelphia Freedom Runners, and McNeal's personal favorite, Bonzai Athletics.

O'Toole remained true to himself, mumbling a barely audible "How about Team Misfit?"

As the van approached the George Washington Bridge, traffic slowed to a crawl. O'Toole slumped over the steering wheel as they came to a total stop. "Where the bloody hell is everyone going on a Saturday afternoon?"

"Just the greatest city in the world," responded O'Donnell.

"Last time I checked, the George Washington Bridge led to New York stinkin' City, not Dublin."

Luckily, the traffic soon picked up and before long, they were over the bridge and driving down Ft. Washington Ave. The surrounding neighborhood caught Kelly off guard. Ft. Washington Avenue was the home of various high-rise apartment complexes and retail shops, featuring such stores as 'Barbara Guatemala's Wine Shop,' and 'La Avenue Check Cashing.' "You guys traveled all the way up here to run around this?"

McNeal put his arm around Kelly's shoulders. "We won't be running around the neighborhood, Kell. The track's inside, and I told you, it's one of the best in the nation. There's nothing like it in or near Philly. Besides, it's not that bad around here. Just don't go wandering the streets by yourself."

"Trust me, Joe, you don't have to worry about that."

"Wait 'til you see inside the place, anyway, it's like a track museum. Downstairs is the indoor hall of fame, and the history of the sport just oozes from the walls," said O'Donnell.

Cooper nodded his head in agreement. "It's like the mecca of indoor track."

"I got it, I got it. It's a pretty special place for you runners."

O'Toole stopped the van at 168th and Ft. Washington, right in front of the Armory. "Eh, it's a little overrated in my opinion. Frankly, the whole racket of indoor track is overrated. Winter should be used for gettin' ready for outdoor track. In fact, outdoor track is redundant, since all track ought to be run outdoors."

McNeal unbuckled his seat belt. "Then why are we here again?"

"Ah, shut the hell up."

McNeal, Kelly and the rest of the gang exited the van in front of the red brick building before O'Toole set off on the unenviable task of finding a parking spot large enough for a mini-van in the heart of New York City. As they entered, remnants of the afternoon's high school meet were leaving the premises. The Armory directors had organized the day to allow high school athletes the opportunity to stick around and watch some of the elite and sub-elite runners. The hot races of the night were scheduled to be the Men's 400 and mile events.

O'Donnell and Cooper led the way up the stairs to the third floor track. Blue plaques with white writing lined the stairwell walls commemorating every National and World Record set at the Armory.

"Nineteen thirty-one? You see that, Kelly? That's over seventy years ago!"

Kelly feigned interest. "Yeah, that's really old, Joe."

O'Donnell and Cooper checked in at the registration table while McNeal, Maloney and Kelly staked out a place to set up camp for the night. Radiators surrounded the stands above the track, often pushing the temperature close to eighty degrees. For this reason, Mc-Neal picked a spot track level, deciding that cooler temps were more important than actual seats.

"Joe, you didn't tell me I'd have to sit on the floor. I'd have brought a chair if I'd known."

"Sorry, babe. I wasn't thinking."

One of the charms of the Armory was the fact that track was a big deal in the old arena. A full-size scoreboard displayed up to the minute results while a large video screen showed replays of the races and highlights from the field. Inspirational music blared from the speakers. The track itself was banked on the turns, raising them five-feet up in the air. This made the Armory track much faster than a normal indoor track. McNeal brought his girls up to the Armory at least once a season to experience what track could be like.

Cooper returned from the registration table. "Joe, it looks like me and OD are running at 6:50 and you and Mitch will probably go off around eight. At least that's what the time schedule says. But you know the way these meets go."

Indoor track, and the Armory in particular, had the bad habit of falling incredibly far behind a time schedule.

"Aight, me and OD are about to go outside for a nice two mile warm-up."

O'Toole had just entered the track area. After circling the block for twenty minutes, he decided to pay the thirty dollars and park in the hospital garage across the street. "Thieves, I tell you. A den of thieves. Thirty dollars to park a van! You guys get the time schedule?"

"Yeah, Seamus. Len and Coop are out warming-up and Mitch and I should be racing around eight. We're set up off the first turn if you want to go sit down for a while."

"I'm gonna walk around a bit first, talk to some people. Did you make sure you were in the seeded heat? I called earlier this week but best to double check."

"I assumed I was, but Coop did the registering, so I'm not positive."

"You know what they say about assuming, Joey Mac? Well, I don't know about you, but Seamus O'Toole isn't an ass for anyone. I'll check on that now."

"Uh, thanks. I'm gonna go start getting ready."

McNeal walked over to the blanket where Kelly sat. "What do you think of the place, Kell?"

"It's interesting. There's a lot going on. How you feeling?"

"A little nervous, but that's normal. I'll be alright. Can't ever really tell until it starts. Thanks for coming again, babe."

"No problem. I figured I needed to see what it is that keeps calling you back. This addiction of yours."

McNeal laughed and pulled his MP3 player, a Powerbar and a bottle of water out of his bag. "Time to get in the zone. Mitch, you want to warm-up in half an hour?"

"Sounds good. Joe, I've got more butterflies than a butterfly-a-toreum."

"A what?"

"You heard me. A butterfly-a-toreum."

"Dude, what the heck is that? You made that word up."

"You know, one of those parks where all the butterflies live."

"I think that's a conservatorium, or maybe just a 'butterfly park'. But, whatever, man. Relax, we're just trying to see where we're at."

"That's what I'm afraid to find out. I might not like the answer."

McNeal shrugged his shoulders and smiled. He too was worried about what questions might be answered today. He put on his headphones, walked over to a corner and laid down, visualizing his race. McNeal tried to visualize for most races. When in good shape, he could see the whole race play out without losing focus. It seemed when he wasn't quite there yet, remaining focused on the race proved difficult. It was as if he knew he'd be unable to maintain the whole race and couldn't convince himself otherwise. Just as he was getting into the thick of his mental rehearsal, O'Toole interrupted him.

"You're in the seeded heat. There's a $500 dollar first prize, so there's some pretty steep competition in there. A few guys from West Chester Track Club, and a couple Boston Athletics and Central Park fellows are also in there. Let them pull you through the first half, and then see what you got left in the tank. Should be fun."

McNeal wasn't sure if he agreed with O'Toole's assessment of fun. His first track race back, with cash on the line, running the mile wasn't exactly a Night at the Roxy. McNeal walked over to where Cooper and O'Donnell were stretching and wished them luck. Minutes later, Cooper and O'Donnell were circling the track, rhythmically hitting thirty-five second 200s. Their plan was to run the first mile in 4:40, see where that placed them in the pack, and then race the last mile with whatever remained in the tank. They passed the mile five

112

seconds under pace, trailing the leaders by about thirty meters. With a half mile to go, Cooper had closed to within twenty meters, with O'Donnell slightly behind. Cooper hit the quarter mile to go mark in 7:20, a mere stride off the leader. He continued his pursuit, inching closer with every step and as he hit the bell, Cooper flew by the leader, a college kid from NYU, and hammered the last lap, finishing in 8:25. O'Donnell crossed the line in third place in a time of 8:33. For both runners, it marked a more-than-solid start. Their performances gave McNeal a shot of confidence, knowing they had basically followed the same plan.

Maloney and McNeal left the building to run their warm-up. The crisp December air served as a welcome relief from the dry, warm air inside the Armory. The Armory shared its building with a recovery home for homeless drug addicts. It provided a real-life reminder that there were some problems bigger than track. Upon returning indoors, McNeal went through his routine of stretches and drills. Ten minutes prior to the start, the announcer called for all fifteen hundred meter runners to report. McNeal walked over to Kelly, kissed her for good luck, earning a sigh and a roll of the eyes from O'Toole in the process, and jogged to the check in area. Cooper and O'Donnell passed McNeal as they left the paddock. "Good luck, Mac."

McNeal nodded his head and gave his name to the clerk at the table. The seeded heat would run first, followed by Maloney's race. The two exchanged fist bumps as McNeal stepped onto the track to run a couple striders in his spikes. It felt good to let loose. McNeal could feel his legs preparing to get tested in a matter of moments. The starter called for all competitors in the Invitational Mile to make their way to the line. When McNeal heard Ian Brooks' British accent over the loudspeaker, his stomach tightened just a bit more as he knew if the Armory's "A" announcer was doing the race, there had to be a reason. Brooks, clad in purple velvet pants, announced the participants, providing a brief bio on each. While none of the runners were Olympians, they possessed solid credentials. No one in the field was expected to make a run at the mythical four minute mile, but there were a handful of sub 4:10 guys. McNeal wondered what would be said about himself as Brooks announced the other runners.

"From Philadelphia, running unattached, Joey McNeal."

Short and to the point, McNeal thought. He stepped to the starting line to await the starter's instructions.

"On your marks!"

The gun loudly followed the starter's voice and McNeal instinctively darted straight for the lead. Remembering it was a mile and not his preferred 800, he settled down as he entered the homestretch of the first lap. He had not wanted to lead the race, but the lead is exactly where he found himself.

O'Toole glanced at his watch as McNeal passed. "Thirty-one."

Stay relaxed. Stay relaxed, McNeal reminded himself. He focused on staying smooth as he led a pack of five. The lead bunch included a pair of native Kenyans who currently competed for the West Chester Track Club. While they were considered "B" Kenyans, they were still more-than-capable runners. Also amongst the front was Bruce Millington, a runner from Greater Boston who had run collegiately for Harvard, and Sean Stevens, from NYAC, a local runner who had prepped at St. John's back in the '80s. Stevens was the lone athlete with a sub four minute mile under his belt, but at the age of forty, was well past his prime. He was still capable of popping out a quality performance, however, and was rumored to be training to take a shot at the master's American record in the mile.

O'Toole fidgeted nervously alongside the track. "Sixty-three."

It was in the middle half mile that the race got difficult. The opening quarter of a top-notch mile race would pass by nearly effortlessly. It was the middle two quarters, four laps on an indoor oval, that tested the toughness of a runner. Only the runner himself would know if he had truly run to his limits or if had fallen victim to the pain, or worse, the fear of the pain.

Sam Kiplegat, one of the West Chester Kenyans assumed the lead at the four hundred meter mark. He was joined at the side by his compatriot and fellow West Chester runner Joe Magui. McNeal reacted to their move and kept the third position, five meters off the leaders. The split at the half mile was 2:07. It had turned into a four-man race as McNeal, the two Kenyans and Stevens had distanced themselves from the field. The pair of East African runners made the 135 pound McNeal look large in comparison to their slight frames. Kiplegat, the taller of the two, stood 5'10 but weighed no more then 115 pounds soaking wet, while Magui was a diminutive 5'3 and topped the scales at 105 pounds. Stevens dwarfed all three as he stood over 6' and weighed close to 160.

The pace quickened in the third quarter, as they passed the 1200 meter mark in 3:09, a 61.7 split. O'Toole slapped his hands on the elevated track imploring McNeal to make a move, but McNeal continued patiently biding his time. Brooks was furiously searching for information on McNeal as they sped down the track on the seventh and penultimate lap.

"And it looks like it's gonna be a battle here folks, as the unknown Joey McNeal, here from Philadelphia PA, battles the pair from West Chester Track Club and Sean Stevens, the local favorite. Can Stevens go to the well one more time? Can the upstart from Philadelphia do it? Who's got a kick? Who's got a kick!?"

McNeal wondered the same thing as he struggled to keep contact.

Cooper cupped his hands and yelled at McNeal from the sideline. "Relax your face and drop your hands!" He had seen many a McNeal race where his form fell apart rendering him helpless and unable to use his lethal closing kick. McNeal reacted to Cooper's advice, dropping his hands as he fought to maintain contact down the backstretch.

Just stay here for one more lap, damn it, McNeal implored himself as he struggled to stay smooth. Magui had shot into the lead and Kiplegat appeared to be fading. McNeal passed Kiplegat and was closing on Magui as they entered the final lap. Brooks was screaming into the microphone as Eye of the Tiger blared from the speakers.

"Uh-oh, OD, they're playing Rocky music. Mac's about to lay the smack down," an excited Cooper told O'Donnell.

"I hope so, man, but that old son of a bitch Stevens is flying. Look at him."

McNeal shot off the turn onto the backstretch and into the lead as he passed Magui.

"LIFT! LIFT!" shouted O'Toole.

McNeal struggled to maintain his form as he entered the final turn. Each lift of the legs grew increasingly more difficult. As he entered the homestretch, McNeal still held the lead, but Stevens was closing fast.

I've got this, just fifty more yards and it's mine.

But it was not to be today. Thirty yards from the line, Stevens showed that yes, he did have some pop left in his legs as he passed McNeal and crossed the finish line in 4:10.42. McNeal, arms flailing as he tried to fight off Stevens, held on for second in 4:11.09. It represented an indoor best for McNeal and eventually he would be pleased with it. Right now, however, he was upset about being out-kicked, and barely able to stand, let alone walk. His world was spinning. He felt as if everything he ever ate was desperately trying to escape. McNeal tried to recover as he watched Maloney's race, leaning against the rail on the outside of the track. Maloney also ran a PR, as he won the unseeded section in 4:31. He had sat off the pace for 1200 meters, then unleashed a blistering kick over the last quarter mile, covering the distance in an impressive fifty-nine seconds flat.

All told, it was a successful trip for the four runners. It confirmed that the steady diet of mileage, hills and tempo runs O'Toole fed them was working. McNeal felt aerobically stronger than ever. He knew he needed to get into the weight room and be more consistent with his post run speed drills and striders.The drills and striders would put some pop back in his legs and ease the transition to the speed work they would be doing come spring.

"If you get serious with that strength work and those drills I gave you, you'll drop that guy Stevens likkity-split," O'Toole told him.

116

They stopped at a rest stop on the New Jersey Turnpike on the way home, grabbed some burgers and waters and continued home. The only downside of the trip was the four cases of "indoor track cough" they had acquired. Racing indoors often had the unusual side effect of leaving a runner with an annoying, dry, hacking cough.

"Between barely being able to stand, and hacking like a sixty-year-old life-long smoker, Joe, I can see why this indoor track stuff is so much fun," joked Kelly.

"Haha, you have no idea."

Joey McNeal soon rested his head on Kelly's shoulders and drifted off with visions of much more than sugarplums dancing in his head. He was right about Kelly, however. Tired from the long trip, she truly did not understand what it was all about.

chapter 14

JOEY MCNEAL ROSE on the morning of Monday December 17th in justifiably good spirits. For the first time in his life, he felt like everything was coming together. He had a beautiful girlfriend in Kelly. She may not understand his need to run, but he definitely thought he out kicked his coverage with her. He was part owner of a somewhat successful business. He had just ran faster than he had in his life. The Bishop O'Connell track team was primed for a big season, and while Second Chances wasn't his dream job, he at least had a job. He ran a quick three miles, showered, dressed and hopped into his car. He turned on Soft Hits 103, the station that began playing Christmas carols on Thanksgiving. Anything to boost the mood on the way to work. But when McNeal walked into his classroom, he sensed something amiss. He couldn't quite put his finger on it, but something didn't feel right. After ten minutes, it hit him. The students' desks were empty. No books, pens, pencils, nothing. Puzzled, McNeal walked down the hall to talk to John Lyons, the principal of Second Chances. McNeal knocked on the door and waited. He soon heard his name called from down the hall.

"Joe! I was about to come talk to you. I see, however, you've beat me to the punch." Lyons was walking towards him. He opened his door, entered the office and gestured for McNeal to follow.

"Mr. Lyons, why are the desks in my classroom empty? What's going on?"

Lyons took a seat behind a large mahogany desk. He motioned for McNeal to sit. "Joe, are you happy here?"

McNeal remained standing. "Excuse me? Am I happy here?"

"That's what I said. Are you happy at Second Chances? I don't think you are. I mean you have an awful lot on your plate. Coaching, running, teaching. To be perfectly honest, it seems to me teaching here is your third priority. Quite frankly, that's not fair to our students. Their needs require one hundred percent dedication and commitment. Are you capable of that?"

"I think the job I've done for the past four years speaks for itself. When I was hired, it was with the understanding that I coached and had to leave by 3:00. What does what I do when I leave have to do with my ability to teach?"

"Well, if I remember correctly your report card grades were handed in a day late. True?"

"Yes, but the system crashed over the weekend and erased everything I had done. I wanted to work on it during my lunch hour, but my aide was absent—again."

"I believe most of your colleagues completed theirs in the afternoon after school. So it seems, your coaching does in fact hinder your job here."

"So what are you trying to say?" McNeal braced himself for the answer.

"Well, the bottom line is that myself and the rest of the administrative staff have decided your services are no longer needed here, Joe. We need someone we can depend on to be here on a full-time basis. There's a lot to be done after three o'clock." Lyons stood up and opened the door to his office. "Clean out your desk before the students arrive. Then go see HR about a severance package. I was generous enough to include one for you."

"What about my students? What will happen to them?"

"They'll be divided amongst other classrooms. I think it will be best for them."

McNeal walked out of Lyons' office, stopped to say something, took a deep breath, shut the door and left. He strode down the hall with his head down, completely in shock.

Maria Richards looked up from hanging a fruits and vegetables poster in the hall. "Joe, what's wrong?"

"Lyons just fired me. I need to clean out my stuff and go to HR."

"Oh my God, I'm so sorry. Did he say why?"

"Some crap about me not being able to fully commit to the school and the students."

"That's not right. These kids here love you and you do a great job teaching them."

"Thanks, Maria. Not sure how true it is, but thanks for the effort."

Maria stepped closer as if to hug McNeal but stopped short. "No, Joe, it's true. You're a good teacher. You've seen them fire other people, it's not like it's you. Anyway, what are you going to do now?"

"I just told you. I'm going to clean out my stuff, and go to HR. Hopefully before any of my students see me so I can avoid the embarrassment."

"No, that's not what I meant. I meant work wise, do you have any options?"

"Oh, my bad. I don't know. I mean I was just fired seconds ago. I could probably sub somewhere. Maybe I'll join Coop at the Café. I'll figure something out."

"The Café? What Café?"

Maria and McNeal didn't talk outside of work. She had no idea what the Grilled Donut Café was.

"The Grilled Donut Café. My roommate and I own it. It's a little shop, been open about a year. Maybe I could work there for a while." McNeal shook his head. "I really don't know what I'm going to do. I'm just shell shocked. I got to go. I'll talk to you later."

121

"You own a place called the Grilled Donut Café?"

"Yeah, there's a long story behind it. I'll fill you in some other time. I want to get out of here before the students start filing in. That would just be way too awkward and embarrassing. Thanks for, uh, being here to listen and all." McNeal opened the door and entered his former classroom for the final time.

"Bye, Joe. Good luck and I'm sorry. The school's going to miss you." Maria sighed deeply and watched with sad eyes as McNeal hastily emptied his desk and gathered his belongings. He walked them out to the car, trying to avoid any spots where he might encounter a student. McNeal then walked to the HR office to find out what type of payment he would receive as a final farewell for three plus years of service.

A grey-haired middle-aged woman stood behind a Plexiglas window. "Joseph McNeal, come to the counter, sign your name and we'll have your package in a minute. Have a seat while you wait."

McNeal signed his name then took a seat near the wall, laid his head back and closed his eyes. He had never been fired before. Not even as a teenager working summer jobs. It hurt; it hurt a lot, even coming from a job he didn't exactly love. McNeal's stomach felt queasy and his head began to throb as he thought about the events of the morning. A voice from the counter jolted him back to reality. "Joseph McNeal. We have your package ready."

McNeal walked to the service desk, grabbed a manila envelope that contained his immediate financial future, and opened the door.

"Have a happy holiday, Mr. McNeal."

Did I just pick up my severance package and get wished a happy holidays all in the same breath? That's amazing. Oh well. Good-bye, Second Chances.

Merry Christmas, Joey McNeal.

≈∽

The first thing McNeal did when he got home was what he knew best; he laced up his trainers and ran. McNeal didn't know how far or where he would go, he just needed to go. In the past when things unraveled, he found the best way to figure them out was to go out for a run, and just think through it.

McNeal settled into a rhythm as he ran down the asphalt. Three miles later he found himself at Pennypack Park. He decided to do four in the park and then return home. That would give him an even ten for the day and a good hour to think. The first thing he would do is talk to Cooper about the financial feasibility of working at the Café. He refused to take someone else's job so if there wasn't room for another salary, he would find something else. Like he told Maria, he could substitute teach if needed. It paid about a hundred dollars a day. One problem with subbing was that either the timing or location might not be compatible with coaching. "I can't imagine walking into a different classroom every day," he thought. McNeal enjoyed establishing a rapport with his students and subbing made that difficult.

Tired of pounding the pavement, he turned off the paved path and onto a dirt trail. While soft on the legs, the path posed its own dangers. Fallen leaves hid the rocks and roots scattered throughout the trail, making it an ankle-breaker waiting to happen. Re-injuring his ankle, however, was the last thing on his mind, and McNeal began picking up the pace. He hammered up the hills and sped the downhills, running faster and faster as he grew more angry at Lyons. Soon enough, he exited the park and began the return run home.

While running back he wondered how he would tell Kelly he lost his job. He feared having to tell his parents. Telling someone you love you have just been fired—in essence been told you weren't good enough—was hard. McNeal felt embarrassed and ashamed. He felt as if he had failed. The more he thought about it, the larger the knots in his stomach grew. McNeal reminded himself that he at least had some options. With the economy suffering, many people didn't.

An hour after he set foot out the door, McNeal returned home. Unsure if he accomplished anything besides a ten mile run and an hour of putting off reality, McNeal wearily walked up to the second floor apartment, entered his bedroom, lay down and tried to sleep the day away. Maybe when he woke up, he'd realize it had all just been a horrible dream.

Sixty minutes later, McNeal woke from a restless nap and pinched himself to see if it had in fact just been a dream. But the manila envelope staring at him from his bedside desk reminded him that his firing was very real. He quickly showered and headed to the Café. "Yo, Coop," he said as he walked in the door. "I need to talk to you."

McNeal's arrival caught Cooper by surprise. "Alright, man. What's up?"

The two walked into Cooper's closet sized office behind the counter. "I just got fired."

"What? Why?"

"I don't even know to tell you the truth. Something about teaching being my third priority and the students deserving better."

"Ouch. That sucks, Joe. I'm really sorry. What are you gonna do?"

"I'm not sure. I could do some subbing."

"What about at Bishop O'Connell? Would they hire you?"

"I thought about that, but it ain't that easy. First of all, they don't do their own hiring. Downtown handles all that. Plus, my degree is in special education and they don't have any special-ed classes."

"Oh. I didn't realize that."

"What about here? How are we doing? Can we afford to add another salary?"

"Well, we did just lose someone from the morning shift. We could use a floor manager so I could focus more on the books and less on the day to day stuff. That might just work. You got practice today?"

"Yeah, I'm going there after I leave."

"Good. I'll let you know how it looks when you get home." Cooper paused for a moment. "Joe, you are half-owner, so if you want a job, it's yours."

"Coop, I don't want to push off my problems on somebody else. That just ain't right. I also don't want to overburden the shop. We're barely getting by here as it is. Alright, man, I gotta get to practice. I'll see you tonight."

"Later, Joey."

Practice at O'Connell was uneventful. The distance runners ran, the hurdlers hurdled, the jumpers worked on their steps and technique, while the throwers split time between the weight room and the circle.

After practice McNeal sat in the parking lot known as I-76 during rush hour. McNeal wondered why it was called "rush hour;" currently McNeal's Aries was rushing along at ten mph. Each day of winter seemed to prolong the commute home. The colder and darker the day, the slower traffic moved. And if rain or snow were involved, then McNeal might be better off running the twenty miles between school and home. McNeal figured this would be as fine a time as any to call Kelly. "Hey, Kell, it's Joe. How you doin'?"

"I know it's you, Joe, because when my cell phone rings it says Joe. You don't have to introduce yourself like we're talking on rotary phones. Anyway, I'm good. You?"

McNeal inhaled. "Well, that's what I wanted to talk to you about. Today wasn't exactly a great day."

"Awww, I'm sorry. Tough day at work again?"

"You could say that."

"Why what happened? You didn't have another computer thrown at you did you?"

"Haha, no not this time. A bit worse actually."

"Really? Oh my god! What happened?"

"They fired me, Kelly."

"They did what? Why?"

"They told me they think teaching is my third priority and the students need better. I don't think the new principal likes the fact I leave at three, even though when I was hired that was part of the deal. He wasn't around then."

"So they fired you?"

"Yeah. Told me my running and coaching take up valuable time and energy that could be spent on teaching."

Kelly was silent for a moment. "Wow. I'm sorry, Joe. What are you going to do?"

"I'm not sure yet. Maybe sub somewhere. Maybe work at the Café. I'll figure something out."

"Yeah, I'm sure you will. Do you want to get together and talk over dinner?"

"Yeah, I'd like that. How about eight? I'll meet you at the Pilgrim Diner?"

"See you there."

Traffic had picked up and McNeal soon arrived home. He walked in to find Cooper furiously shuffling through a stack of papers. "It looks good. I think we can fit you in. Here's the big question though: How long will your benefits from Second Chances carry over? If we don't need to add you to the company benefit package, we'll be able to pay you a little more. Diane had two kids and herself on her plan. So if you're still covered, that's money in the bank."

McNeal and Cooper believed all their full time workers deserved health insurance. It was costly, but they felt it helped them attract better workers, and more importantly, it was the right thing to do. The bank loan officer told them they were crazy when they discussed this but it was non-negotiable. Cooper and McNeal wanted to sleep at night and if their pockets grew fat while their employees couldn't afford to take their kid for a physical, they'd be a couple of insomniac runners.

"I should be covered for three months. We always redid our plans in March. Plus they gave me six weeks pay. So I'll put that in the bank, and after three months I should be able to get a basic **HMO** for the rest of the year."

"Then I'd like to congratulate you as the newest member of the Grilled Donut Café. Be there tomorrow by 6:30."

"Aw, man, I forgot about that. That's going to make doubling real difficult."

126

"Tell me about it. Usually I bike to work, then squeeze in a thirty minute run at lunch. Luckily, there's a shower in the bathroom so I don't stink up the place and scare away all the customers."

"Well, I guess I'll have to get used to it. Alright, I need to get ready. I'm meeting Kelly at eight."

"You tell her yet?"

"Yeah."

"How'd that go?"

"Oh, just wonderful. 'Hey, babe, your boyfriend's now an unemployed bum. Do you still want to be with me?' Hah, I guess it went ok, though. I'll tell you after tonight, I guess."

"Well, the good news is you're no longer an unemployed bum. You're just employed someplace new. You might still be a bum, however."

"True, I'll see how she handles that take."

"Alright, man, good luck."

"Thanks, Hot Sauce".

Thirty minutes later, McNeal was sitting at the Pilgrim Diner, eating a plate of pancakes while Kelly ate a chicken Caesar salad.

"I don't know what you like about this place, Joe. My salad is at best average."

"You're at a diner. Everyone knows the best things on the menu are the breakfast foods. And the worst things on the menu are the seafood—never, ever eat diner seafood—and then the salads."

"I guess everyone but me. So tell me about your plans?"

"Well, Coop told me that Diane, the former manager, just left. So I'm gonna run the floor while he handles the behind the scenes stuff. Second Chances gave me six weeks severance and my benefits will be good for another three months."

"Joe, you're going to actually manage the Grilled Donut Café? Wasn't your degree in education?"

"Yeah, it was, but that's not all I can do. I'm not just a one trick pony, you know?"

"I know that, Joe, I was just saying. I'm sure there's a lot about running cafés you need to learn. That's all."

"It's not like I'm a total stranger to the business. I am part owner. Besides it might be fun to see how the place really runs."

"Fun? Is that all you worry about? Joe, life's not all fun and games. Do you really think that's a good career choice? What about benefits? Retirement plan, health insurance? I don't want to be a naysayer, but what if the Café fails? Then what?"

"I told you, I'll be able to keep my benefits for three months from Second Chances. They also gave my six weeks severance pay. I'll put that aside for when my insurance expires. Give me some credit, I've thought this out."

"Well, that's good. But three months will go by before you know it. Joe, you're just about thirty years old. Don't you think it's about time you started thinking long term? Maybe you need to start taking your career as seriously as you take your track comeback? You're dedicating all this time for what? To see if you can run faster than you did in college? Who really gives a damn? It doesn't matter. You were and still are a great runner but you spend more time and energy running and coaching than you do on your future, hell, than you do on me? Your boss was right, your top priorities are running and coaching. Where does that leave me, Joe? Third string? We've been dating for over a year and I feel like I'm still second fiddle to these childish games of yours. Every weekend you have a meet to go to, sometimes two. Then after that's over, you're out running a workout of your own. By the end of the day, you're so god damn tired that we don't do anything but sit on the couch and watch TV. Is that what I have to look forward to? Is it?"

McNeal sat there shell shocked at Kelly's reaction. "When did this turn into a conversation about our relationship? I thought we were talking about what I was going to do for a job? I never said I was gonna manage the shop for the rest of my freakin' life, Kell. I said I could do it for now. Maybe it will go under, who knows, but maybe it won't. Maybe it'll be a big hit and Cooper and I can earn a living off it? I can always go back to teaching; it ain't goin' nowhere." He took a sip of water. "And you want to know why I'm running hard? Because

I still can. It's what I do, heck, it's what I am. If I'm not training hard for something, then I feel like something's missing. Ever since I was twelve years old, I've run. I tried to replace it the last couple years with football and stuff, and I had a lot of fun playing with the guys, but it wasn't the same. I just need to know. I need to know how good I can be before it's too late. I know I'll be thirty this spring, you don't gotta remind me. Every time I wake up in the morning with aches in muscles I didn't even know I had, I realize I ain't twenty years old anymore. But I sure ain't dead either. I know I don't have that many more fast years left. I hope I still have one, but I'm not even certain of that. But if I do have one, I want to run to the best of my abilities and try to be great. Didn't you ever want to be the best at something?" McNeal paused for a second, waiting for Kelly to respond, but no response came. "And how can you think you're my third priority? Kelly, you know I love you. I don't know what else you want though. I can't stop being who I am. I'm sorry if what I am isn't good enough but I'm never gonna be a shirt-and-tie-wearing kind of guy who follows the norm. It's not me and I thought that was what you loved about me. I'd do anything for you and for us, but one thing I can't do is change who I am."

"Joe, I'm not asking you to change who you are. And yes, I do like how you're spontaneous and funny and all, but there needs to be a balance and there needs to be some focus on your future, on our future. Right now, I think you have too much stuff going on in your life to treat me the way I want—the way I deserve—to be treated."

Kelly was sobbing as she spoke. Her hands trembled and her voice grew shakier by the word. McNeal sat there, still in shock. He hated to see her cry, but felt helpless to do anything. His eyes began to well up with tears as he sat there, searching for the words to say. "You really don't think I treat you right? Why didn't you say something before?" He reached across the table to hold her hands, but she pulled them away. "I'm sorry. I want you to feel special because you are. I know I can take care of you and run the way I want to run. Trust me, I can. Just give me the chance to show you."

Kelly wiped the tears from her face. "I'm sorry, Joe, but I can't. And you can't. Not now, not anymore. You're not Superman and you can't do everything. I just can't do this anymore. Good-bye, Joe." Kelly stood up, kissed McNeal on the forehead and left, leaving him alone with his thoughts, with his emotions, dumbfounded over what had just happened. This morning, he felt on top of the world. Now, he sat there not knowing where his life was headed. He had just lost his job and girlfriend in the space of a day. Joey McNeal had just come face to face with the Mac truck known as the rest of his life.

❧❦

BANG BANG BANG!!!

McNeal woke up to the loud banging on his bedroom door. He rolled over and glanced at his alarm clock. It read 5:30. He didn't normally wake up for another hour and a half.

Cooper continued pounding on McNeal's bedroom door. "Joe! Wake up! If we're gonna double before work we need to go now—like immediately, man!"

McNeal had forgotten all about yesterday. He forgot he was fired, that Kelly broke up with him. He had hoped he could sleep it all away but Cooper's loud knocking jolted him back to reality. He contemplated just rolling over and telling Cooper he would start working tomorrow and was taking today off from running.

"Mac, if I got to come in there..."

McNeal sat up. "Alright, alright, stop banging on the door. I'll be out in a minute." He got out of bed, dressed in sweat pants and a hoodie, grabbed his hat and gloves, slipped on his running shoes, and walked out his door. They descended the apartment stairs and stepped out into the cold December air. Some left over snow remained on the ground from the last storm. What was once a beautiful covering of white fluff, now was a dark mixture of dirt, exhaust and ice. "So much for a white Christmas. More like a black Christmas."

"Dude, it ain't Christmas yet," said Cooper. "Anyway we've only got time for three miles."

"Fine, that's fine with me," mumbled McNeal as he wiped the sleep from his eyes.

"Do the fields loop?"

"Whatever, man."

"So how'd last night's dinner with Kelly go?"

McNeal didn't know how to answer. He didn't really want to discuss his dumping at 5:30 in the morning. "You don't want to know."

"Yes I do. Or I wouldn't have asked."

"Alright, here's the short version. She broke up with me. Told me I need to get my priorities straight, start thinking about the future and quit playing games. Told me she couldn't deal with being what she thought was my third priority. Now, I don't mean to be rude, but can we just run?"

"Damn, that sucks, dude. I'm sorry. You had an ass getting kicked kind of day. Damn, and like a week before Christmas?"

"Yeah, you could say that again. I'm still kind of in shock from the whole thing. You know?"

"Yeah, that's a lot of crap for one day."

They ran the remainder of their run in relative silence, except for the sounds of their breathing and the gentle pit-pats of their footsteps. Less than twenty minutes later, they were back at the apartment.

"Alright, hurry up and get a shower. We've got to be out of here by 6:10," Cooper told McNeal. "Don't be too long 'cause I need to get a quick one too."

"No problem." McNeal entered the bathroom, pulled open the shower curtain and twisted the handle all the way to the right, turning the hot water on full throttle causing the tiny bathroom to fill with steam. Minutes later, he was showered, dressed, and driving himself and Cooper to the Café.

"You think you can handle manning the front today? We'll have Tom here to help out, but he usually mans the grill. I'll be in the back going over orders, talking to vendors, etc. etc. You can run the register and make sure everything goes smoothly, ok?"

McNeal nodded his head. "This can't be that difficult."

By seven thirty, a lengthy line had formed and McNeal was beginning to wonder what he had gotten himself into. An angry male customer walked to the front of the line, fruit shake in hand. "I asked for a banana blueberry blend, this is clearly a blueberry banana blend."

McNeal stared at the man for a moment.

"Well, are you going to give me the right shake or just stand there?"

Cooper heard the disturbance and walked to the counter. "Hey, Jack, what can I do for you?"

"Ryan, I ordered my usual grilled cinnamon donut and banana blueberry blend, but I got a blueberry banana blend."

"Oh, I see. Sorry about that, let me fix it for you. Hey ,Tom, can you man the register for a second while I show Joe the difference?"

Tom, a nineteen-year-old college freshman nodded and took his spot at the register.

McNeal followed Cooper to the juice blender. "Dude, what's the difference between the two?"

"Percentages. The first fruit listed is 75% of the blend, the second 25%, unless the customer asks for an even mix. If there's three or more fruits listed, then it's even Steven for all of 'em. I should have told you."

"Nah, that's my fault. I should have remembered. I did help design the menu. My head's just a mess today."

"I'm sure. You want to go home for the day?"

"No, that's alright. I don't want to wallow in self-pity. That certainly won't do me any good." McNeal brought the customer his new drink. "Sorry for the mix-up. Have a nice day!"

The breakfast rush slowed by 9:00 and McNeal took the time to reacquaint himself with the menu. The downtime also allowed McNeal to dwell on yesterday's events. He still couldn't believe he had been fired. He had even more trouble comprehending the fact that Kelly dumped him. It still seemed surreal. By eleven, business had picked back up and McNeal no longer could afford to be lost in his thoughts. "Hey, Coop," he yelled back. "We need quarters."

"I'm going to the bank at one."

"Don't we have any rolls in the back?"

"No, not today. I didn't get to go to the bank yesterday. If you remember, I had other stuff to work on."

"Oh, yeah." McNeal counted out seven dimes and a nickel to give his current customer her 75 cents change. "Sorry about the dimes."

The elderly grey haired woman smiled. "Eh, they all spend the same."

At two o'clock, McNeal walked to the door and switched the sign from open to closed. "Thank goodness, that's over."

Cooper walked out from his office. "So what'd you think about actually being behind the scenes?"

"Pretty overwhelming, I'm not gonna lie. I'm exhausted. If I never grill another donut or count another dime, I'll be happy."

"Well, Mac, I got bad news for you, unless you plan on quitting, you'll be doing the same thing tomorrow."

McNeal drove Cooper home on his way to practice. "Yo, Joe, what are you going to do with Kelly's gifts? That's probably the last thing on your mind, but it's a legitimate question."

"Well, Coop, I guess it's a good thing today's December 18th and I don't normally start shopping til December 23rd. So, I don't have any Christmas gifts to return."

"There you go then. Things are already starting to look up."

"Indeed." Somehow he didn't feel things were looking up quite yet.

❧❧

Wednesday night, McNeal and the guys met Seamus O'Toole at the track to run mile repeats. It was his first run since Tuesday morning. Cooper had tried to convince McNeal to run after practice on Tuesday, but McNeal declined the offer, instead opting to indulge in a bowl of rocky road ice cream while watching Seinfeld reruns. Today's session called for five by a mile repeat in five minutes with a one minute break between. Maloney, not yet as fit or strong as the others, would run the first twelve hundred of each.

O'Toole stood in lane five, twirling his yellow stop watch. "You fellows ready to get this going? I've still got some shopping to do. McNeal did you get that dame of yours some nice jewelry? She's a diamond diva, now isn't she?"

"Actually, Seamus, I didn't get her anything. She dumped me the other day. Same day I got fired." McNeal had told Seamus about his firing, but not about Kelly dumping him.

"Wow. That's a nutcracker. Ok, gentlemen, step to the line. Seventy-five seconds a lap."

As usual, they would rotate shifts at the lead. McNeal took the opening stint at the front. "Remember, Mac, we got five of these. Don't go trying to run away your troubles on the first lap," warned O'Donnell.

McNeal heeded O'Donnell's advice for the first lap, hitting the quarter in seventy-five seconds. "Well done, that's the pace," yelled O'Toole from the sideline. By the second lap, however, McNeal's head was racing and he began picking up the pace, covering it in seventy-two seconds.

"Easy there, Joseph."

McNeal paid O'Toole no mind, continuing to pick up the pace, running the third quarter in seventy-one seconds. Maloney stepped off the track after passing the 1200 and shook his head. "I'm glad that's all I got."

Cooper and O'Donnell weren't so lucky. They continued to follow McNeal for one more loop around the track, this one in seventy seconds flat, for a total time of 4:48. "Yo, Mac, don't go messing up our workout cause you're pissed off," said Cooper.

"Sorry guys, but I didn't make you stay with me."

"Joe, the deal was we take turns leading at the predetermined pace. It was your turn," said O'Donnell.

Maloney tried to break the tension. "So this means, we only need to run 5:12 pace for the next one. Joe was just trying to put some time in the bank."

"Alright, quit your bickering lassies, and step to the line,. This repeat is yours Mr. O'Donnell, so you can ensure the pace is correct."

O'Donnell did just that, hitting each four hundred between seventy-four and seventy-five seconds, running the mile in 4:59. McNeal and Cooper finished right with O'Donnell, while Maloney ran step for step with them for 1200 meters. A minute later, and Cooper was setting the pace, running slightly faster than five minute pace. O'Donnell ran on Cooper's shoulder with Maloney and McNeal a stride behind. Maloney again finished a lap early and McNeal was left on his own for the last lap. Cooper turned up the intensity a notch on the final lap, closing in seventy flat, totaling 4:54 for the mile. McNeal never responded to Cooper's move and crossed the line five seconds back.

"Come on, Mac, you shouldn't be getting dropped," Cooper told him.

McNeal didn't respond, just mumbled to himself, "I thought we didn't want to go too fast."

On the fourth repeat, Maloney assumed the lead. Mitch ran the opening quarter in seventy-three seconds, before settling into the seventy-five second a lap rhythm. McNeal trailed the pace from the outset. Maloney paced the 1200 in 3:43 and instead of stepping off the track, dropped back to McNeal, who passed the mark at 3:50. "Let's go cuz, you're better than this. Sulking in the workout damn sure ain't gonna do you no good. It won't get your job back, it certainly won't get Kelly back, but it might make her right cause you are just out here wastin' your freakin' time." Maloney shadowed McNeal for the remainder of the lap, and they both finished in 5:10, eleven seconds behind O'Donnell and Cooper.

O'Toole called McNeal over before the fifth and final repeat. "Joseph, get over here." McNeal walked over to O'Toole his head down. "Look at me damnit, Joseph. When I agreed to coach you, you assured me you were serious and ready to do whatever it takes. A damn dame breaks your heart and you go out there and run like absolute garbage. Do you think your former lady is somewhere pouting?"

"Seamus, it's not just that."

"Oh, it most definitely is. Work is work. It's called work 'cause it sure ain't play. You're working at a damn café, not wiping the crap from elderly blokes' arses, and there are folks who do that, you know. But I assure you, Joseph, not only is she over you, she's under some one else. Now quit your pity party, and go run your last repeat."

By this point, O'Donnell, Cooper and Maloney were one hundred yards into their last mile. McNeal, now fuming at O'Toole for insinuating his former girlfriend was currently with another man, took off determined to catch them. This would be no easy task as they opened in seventy-three seconds. McNeal was faster, however, hitting it in seventy-one. *Close the gap,* he told himself, converting his whirlwind of emotions into fuel. By the half mile, McNeal was ten seconds back, having run his opening half in 2:22.

"What are you waiting for, Joseph? Turn it up and run your bloody arse off."

McNeal responded to O'Toole's words with a hard surge. By the time he reached the backstretch, he was flying. He ran his third quarter in sixty-five seconds. He now sat six seconds back, as the guys had also dropped their pace. Maloney decided to run the entire distance for the last repeat and he, Cooper and O'Donnell were covering ground quickly. McNeal had set his sights on them, however, and was determined to do whatever necessary to catch them. McNeal hit the proverbial bell lap and again intensified his effort. His stride lengthened and his turnover increased as he steadily wheeled in his friends. With two hundred meters to go, McNeal lay three seconds back, and began kicking as if in a race. He flew by O'Donnell and Cooper as they exited the curve, but Maloney responded and the two ran side by side the final one hundred meters. McNeal ran the last quarter in fifty-nine seconds, giving him a total time of a 4:26. Maloney finished his mile in 4:45, while O'Donnell and Cooper ran 4:48. McNeal collapsed to the track immediately upon crossing the line. O'Toole walked over to the exhausted runner and placed his hand on his shoulder. "4:26, impressive. I heard the new fellow ran 4:25."

chapter 16

CHRISTMAS MORNING, MCNEAL rose at seven to run before meeting his family at the ten o'clock Mass. McNeal ran thirty minutes, showered, ate breakfast and drove to St. Genevieve, his parents' church. After Mass, McNeal and his family drove to his Aunt Emily's home in South Jersey. Expecting to see Kelly, various family members hit McNeal with a barrage of questions and comments.

"Oh, but she was such a nice girl."

"You guys were so cute together."

Even his mother got in on the act. "Joe, why don't you just give her a call?"

"And talk about what, Mom?"

"Well, you could tell her you'll change."

"So you want me to lie to her?"

"What? No, I don't want you to lie to her. I'm sure you could make some changes. Everyone has to change sometimes."

"Mom, I don't want to change. I like me. Even if I wanted to, Mom, I couldn't. Not now."

"Why not now?"

"I've run my whole life. Just now I'm starting to get somewhere. And I'm supposed to suddenly give it up?"

"Joe, I don't think anyone wants you to give up running. I just think maybe you need to get your priorities straight. Think about it, ok."

Exasperated, McNeal agreed to "think about his priorities" but told his mother he wasn't going to be able to make the changes necessary to get Kelly back.

Christmas night McNeal returned home to find Cooper in a state of panic.

"Did you forget we're hosting a New Year's Eve Party?"

"No. Did you forget today's Christmas Day, not New Year's Eve?"

"Six days, man, six days. We don't know who's coming. We don't know what we're doing for food. We don't have a theme. We don't have nothing, man, nothing. If we're not careful, this party's gonna be a bust. Do you want that on your soul?"

"What?" With everything else going on in his life, McNeal hadn't thought much about the annual New Year's Eve Party.

"I said do you want that on your soul, Joey Mac? Do you want to be known as the guy who ruined New Year's Eve? What kind of way is that to start 2008?"

"I guess it'd be a bad one, but not like my life can get much worse. Correct me if I'm wrong, but I thought we already picked a theme. 'Christmas in Hawaii.' What's wrong with that? We've got a finely decorated light up palm tree and a bunch of other decorations throughout the apartment. Get some cocoanuts and pineapples, pour some sand in the kitchen. You know, really do it up."

"Did you just say 'pour some sand in the kitchen'?"

"Yeah, why?"

"Well, 'cause if we pour sand in the kitchen, it's going to be tracked all over the flippin' apartment. I don't think we want that."

"Alright, then this is what we're gonna do. We'll get a kiddie pool, and put the sand there. Throw a bucket and a little yellow shovel in there, and it'll be like lil' Wildwood."

"I thought the theme was Christmas in Hawaii?"

"Fine, lil' Hawaii."

"Does the shovel have to be yellow?"

"No, but I think yellow goes well with the sand."

"Alright, that works, but Joe, where on God's green earth are we gonna get a kiddie pool? You do realize it's December in Philadelphia? Not exactly prime time for the kiddie pool market."

"Coop, last year when you said we needed a palm tree for the beach bash, did I get us a palm tree?"

"Yes, you did."

"You're damn right I did. Joey Mac the Party Starter will secure a kiddie pool full of sand or my name isn't Joey Mac the Party Starter."

"Since when is your name…"

"Silence. Let's finish this conversation over a run."

"At 10:30 on Christmas night?"

"It's called a holiday not a day off."

"Indeed. Spoken like a true champion."

"Shut up and let's go run."

Sixty minutes and nine miles of pavement pounding later, Cooper was feeling much better about the party prospects.

"So, we'll call OD tomorrow, to see if he's making those ridiculous wings?"

"Yeah, Mac, I'll do that tomorrow afternoon. See if he wants to run, too. You in for some tempo and hills after work at the Café?"

"Yeah, I should be. Alright, Coop, I'm spent. I'm gonna go catch some zs. You have no idea how exhausting it is explaining to your whole family why you were dumped."

"I can only imagine. What about your, uh, career change? Was that a big topic of family discussion?"

"Surprisingly, not so much. You've seen the tabloids. Sex trumps everything. Later, Coop."

"True. Well, that's good, I guess. Good night, Mac. Merry Christmas."

"Merry Christmas, Hot Sauce."

๛

McNeal, Cooper and OD returned to the apartment after a track session on the afternoon of December 31st. They had just completed a 10x1000 meter workout with Maloney, who returned home to prep for the party. McNeal's legs ached with every step and his lungs seared from breathing in the cold air. "I'm spent, man. I think I need a nap."

"Joe, in all the time I've known you, I've never known you to take a nap. Now, like I said before, do you want to be forever known as that guy who ruined New Year's Eve?"

"No, Coop, I do not want that blemish on my soul for all of eternity."

"Alright, then let's get down to business. Len, how are your wings looking?"

"Like pure deliciousness. Pure deliciousness." OD had marinated the wings the previous night and soaked them in his secret sauce overnight. He claimed it allowed the full wing to seep with flavor, rather than just the outer layer, which is what you get with most wings.

"So how many do you have again, OD?"

"One hundred and ninety-one."

"Good Lord. One hundred and ninety-one wings? We don't even know enough people to eat that many wings. Not to mention the majority of people we do know, won't be here."

Cooper glared at McNeal. "There you go again, Mac, trying to ruin New Year's."

"Huh?"

"Most people we know won't be here?"

"No, most won't. Like my cousins, aunts and uncles—they won't be here. Except for Mitch, of course. I don't think their not showing up is going to ruin anyone's New Year. I mean, this apartment is not that big."

"Negative Nancy. If they come, we will fit them."

"Thanks, James Earl Jones. Just let me remind you who's the man who thought of getting the kiddie pool of sand? Oh, yeah, that's me, Joey Mac the Party Starter. Pardon me if I actually want room for people to mingle and not be stuffed in here like sardines in a can."

OD peeked his head out of the kitchen at the mention of sand. "Did I hear you say sand? As in bringing sand to the apartment?"

140

"Yeah, why?"

"Well, just the small problem of where are you going to find sand? And if you do manage to acquire sand, do you really want that tracked all over the apartment?"

"Lenny, my boy. Don't you think this has been thought of? I'm not some noob, you know. That's what the kiddie pool's for."

"Oh, the kiddie pool. Good luck finding a kiddie pool, Joe. I'm gonna get back to cooking these bad boys."

"Coop, let's go. We've got work to do. We need sand, a pool, more grub, and drinks."

"We don't have much time," said Cooper. "It looks like a cyclone hit this place. It's gonna take a good two hours of cleaning. It's already three o'clock."

"Then let's rock, Hot Sauce. OD, good luck with the wings."

"Yo, Joe, I've been thinking. If I make the wings, why does Cooper get to be Hot Sauce?"

"'Cause that's the way the cookie crumbles. Get to work on those wings, Mr. Winginator."

"Winginator, eh? I guess that works."

Seventy-five minutes later, Cooper and McNeal returned in a moment of glory. Cooper carried a bag full of the party necessities of chips, dip, and various other snacks and drinks. In his arms, McNeal clutched several rolls of left over Christmas wrapping paper, four pineapples, and a couple of cocoanuts.

"No sand I see?"

"Always noticing the negative, OD. How about Cooper's bag of goodies? Or how about all this tropical fruit? By the way, the wings smell insanely good."

"Thanks. Um, nice work with the motley assortment of crap you have, but where's the sand and pool?"

"Cooper, I don't think OD believes there's going to be sand in little Hawaii tonight. Should we tell him there's a fifty pound bag of sand out in my trunk?"

"Go ahead, Mac. Tell him there's a fifty-pound bag of sand in your trunk."

"OD, guess what?"

"There's a fifty pound bag of sand in your trunk?"

"You better believe there's a fifty-pound bag of sand in my trunk!"

"Now does the fact I haven't seen or heard a mention of a pool mean you guys plan on covering the kitchen floor with sand?"

"Of course not. What do we look like? Amateur hour at the Apollo? This ain't our first day. Mac, tell him about the pool."

"Well, we checked several stores—Lowes, Toys-R-Us, Home Depot, etc.—to no avail. So I called a guy."

"You have a guy who can acquire a kiddie pool in December?"

"None other than Mitch Maloney. He said the five and dime on Kensington Ave had one left over from the summer. They practically gave it to him."

"Well done, guys. I apologize for ever doubting you."

Cooper put a hand on O'Donnell's shoulder. "If those wings are as good as they smell, there'll be no hard feelings at all."

"Don't worry, Hot Sauce, they will be."

With that, a blizzard of cleaning began. Vacuums buzzed, floors were swept and mopped. The dishwasher rumbled. Tables were scrubbed. Even the bathroom sink was shining like the moon on a cool, clear night. As the cleaning of the apartment ended, the decorating began. Pineapples were strategically placed throughout. Cocoanuts hung from the ceiling. The electric palm tree was adorned with garland and tiny red Christmas balls.

"May I ask what the wrapping paper's for?" O'Donnell wondered.

McNeal held the roll in his hand. "Well, all Christmas items were half off at the dollar store. So how could I turn down fifty cent wrapping paper?"

"True, but what purpose does it serve?"

"See that chair by the wall? Well, we're going to wrap the wall behind it. Make it look like a gift. Then we're gonna put a bow on it, a name tag and BAM—there you have it."

"There you have what?"

"A gift wrapped wall, that's what."

Cooper hopped up onto the tan lounge chair, one of the few pieces of furniture not purchased at a thrift shop. "Yo, Joe, toss me the stapler, so we can staple this wrapping paper up on the wall."

McNeal grabbed the stapler from the bookshelf on the other side of the room and tossed it to Cooper who proceeded to staple the shiny gold wrapping paper onto the wall. "How's that look, guys?"

OD peeked his head in from the kitchen and shook it back and forth. "Classy."

"What?"

"It looks awesome, Coop. OD, you worry about your two tons of wings. We'll worry about gift wrapping the wall."

"No problem, Mac. No problem at all."

McNeal handed Cooper a red sheet of wrapping paper that was used to make a vertical stripe on the "gift." McNeal then stuck on two tiny white bows while Cooper used his long dormant art skills to create a name tag to tape onto the middle of their present. It read "To Apt 357, Love, Santa Claus."

O'Donnell reentered the room from the kitchen. "I have to admit it, guys. The gift wrapped wall looks surprisingly good."

"Thanks, OD. It's good to know you're on board. Mac, what time did you say Mitch is coming over?"

"He said sometime around seven. What time is it now?"

"6:40. You want first or second shower?"

"I'll take first."

"Yo, Coop, what about me? Don't I get an option?"

"No, Len, you don't. You don't live here, so you get what's left, which is third shower. Hopefully, there'll be some hot water left for you."

"Some thanks I get for slaving all day over these wings."

"Sorry, man. That's just the law of the jungle."

Maloney arrived just before eight. No one else had yet arrived. He had with him his new girlfriend, Holly, as well as a 10-foot by 8 ½-foot plastic kiddie pool. It was even decorated with tropical flowers to add to the theme of the night.

Cooper beamed with happiness. "Well done, Mitch. Well done, indeed."

"My cousin Joey knows I wouldn't ever let him down. He's the reason I'm here today."

"Yeah, Mitch that's cause I invited you. Did you drive here, Holly?"

"Yeah, how'd you know?"

"Cause Mitch always likes to tell me how I saved his life after he's had a few drinks. You pre-gaming tonight, Mitch?"

"Maybe a little." Maloney's lips turned up into a slight smirk. "It's New Year's Eve, cuz. Don't worry, I won't be drinking during training. I've been good."

"I'm not judging, just asking, man."

Maloney placed the pool in the kitchen and McNeal poured the fifty-pound bag of sand into it. They then drug it to the small walkway between the living room and kitchen. Not big enough to be a true dining room, it served as a cross between computer station and hallway.

Maloney stood in front of the gold-wrapped wall. "I like the gift wrapped wall. Great idea. We should take pictures in front of it. When a guest arrives, they get a lei and a picture with Doc."

Doc was the plastic elf McNeal acquired five years earlier when a neighbor gave him a box of old, unwanted Christmas decorations. McNeal kept him out all year, calling him a guard for the apartment. Since then Doc had found a few friends and now led what Cooper and McNeal referred to as the welcome committee. There was a tall wooden Santa, a golden statue of Mickey Mouse with one ear, a stuffed green eagle, a Bob's Big Boy bank, and a pair of bean bag balls with faces. A more motley crew may never have been assembled. Female visitors generally disliked Doc. He creeped them out, they claimed.

The stickers that he had for eyes made him appear to be watching them, wherever they moved.

"That's brilliant, Maloney. Pure brilliance. McNeal must have taught you well when you were growing up," said Cooper.

By nine o'clock, the party started to heat up. Cooper's sisters had arrived. OD's girlfriend Liz had come with two of her friends, Katie and Karen. Everyone had their picture taken with Doc upon arrival. Cooper used his digital camera, and then printed them out as party favors.

A few minutes after ten, McNeal's friend Steve from Second Chances arrived at the party. McNeal had not spoken to anyone from the school since his firing, so he was slightly shocked at Steve's arrival. Steve carried a bottle of champagne and was accompanied by Maria, the school nurse.

McNeal gripped Steve in a bear hug. "Steve! I didn't expect to see you, buddy. Thanks for coming by."

"Did you think because those jerks at work let you go we wouldn't be friends still? Once I got the email, I was in."

"I just felt kind of embarrassed, man, you know."

McNeal turned his attention to Maria, whose arrival truly shocked him. "Wow, Maria, I really didn't expect to see you here. Happy New Year, Merry Christmas, and anything else you celebrate."

"Uh, that's it, Joe. It's nice to see you. How you been holding up?"

"Joey Mac has never been finer! Ryan Cooper, at your service. You are?" Cooper extended his hand for Maria to shake.

"Maria, Maria Richards."

"Pleased to meet you, Maria."

"Like wise." She turned her attention back to McNeal. "So, Joe, what's new? The place looks, uh, interesting." Interesting summed up the apartment nicely.

"I've been ok. Trying to stay busy with coaching and running. Also been working with Cooper over at the Café. I'm getting used to it. It's kind of early though. I never realized how lucky we were to not start until nine."

"I'd be careful about how you throw around the word lucky. But yeah, it's nice to not begin until nine o'clock. How's coaching going? You coach track and cross country, right?"

"Yeah. The girls are doing well. It's getting tough though with coaching and running. I sometimes come home just physically and emotionally exhausted and still need to get a run in. There also might be some conflicts with my races and the team's races."

"Ouch. That sucks. What are you going to do?"

Maria stood a shade above 5'2 and weighed a tad under 115 pounds. McNeal never noticed the curves on Maria's body that her tight black dress now showcased. Maybe it was because she always dressed more conservatively at work. Maybe it was because he tended not to notice those things while dating Kelly. It wasn't that he hadn't realized Maria was an attractive girl previously. That was tough not to notice with her bright smile and long curly brown hair.

"I wish I knew. I wish I knew."

"Yo, Joe," yelled Steve from across the room. "Where's Kelly tonight?"

"Um, not here. Would you believe she dumped me the same day I got fired?"

"What? No way! I'm sorry, man, I didn't know."

"How could you? It's not like it was broadcast on the news or anything."

"So you got fired and dumped in the same day? The nerve of her," said Maria. "I didn't even know you had a girlfriend."

"I did. Not anymore."

"Well, yeah, obviously. That's a kick in the teeth. That might be one of the worst days ever."

"In modern mankind, I believe it ranks pretty high up there. I think how high depends on whether you include days with deaths on the list or if they are a category unto themselves."

"Definitely their own category."

"Anyway, Maria, that's enough about my sad and pathetic life. You need to get your picture taken with Doc."

"With who?"

"Doc, the elf who guards the apartment."

"Oh, yeah, that Doc. You have an elf guarding your apartment? You really are quite the character, Joey Mac. Where do I go for my photo shoot?"

"Right in front of the gift-wrapped wall. You want a solo shot or do you want it with Steve, since you guys came together?"

"Um, solo. I don't want Doc to get jealous or anything."

"Doc? Jealous? Never. He doesn't have a jealous bone in his body. In fact, he doesn't have any bones in his body. He's made of plastic."

Cooper took Maria's picture and printed her out a copy as a keepsake. "Mac, I've got a great idea."

"Let me have it, Coop."

"Introductions."

"Haven't we already introduced everyone to each other?"

"That's not what I meant. NBA style intros, rock music and all. They come up the steps as I play music from the computer and you announce them Michael Buffer style."

McNeal ran his hands across the stubble on his chin. "That's good stuff. Real good stuff. Let's do it at 11:30 to lead into Dick Clark and Times Square. Plus it'll allow people some time to prep for their moment of fame."

"Prep? You mean get a lil' drunker?"

"Whatever they need to walk the catwalk."

At 11:30, McNeal grabbed a hairbrush from a bookshelf and used it as an impromptu microphone. "Ladies and gentlemen, the moment you have all been waiting for has arrived."

"It won't be New Year's for another thirty minutes!" yelled someone from the crowd. McNeal thought it was one of Cooper's sisters.

"Not that moment. The OTHER moment you have all been waiting for. It is time for the introductions. Hot Sauce, hit the music."

As the music blared from the speakers, McNeal introduced each guest at the party. For some he included information such as birthplace, age, or height. For others he used make believe facts and statistics. He referred to Mitch's girlfriend, Holly as hailing from "Parts Unknown," and having the distinctive honor of dating Maloney. When he arrived at Len O'Donnell, McNeal bestowed upon him more nicknames than were given to Apollo Creed. "Now entering the party, the Winginina-tor, Len OD- Len Dog, Len Diggity, the man with the plan to make wings taste good—Len O'Donnell."

Cooper and Maloney erupted into applause as the speakers blared "I'm too Sexy" by Right Said Fred. OD circled the apartment high fiving and hugging each and every guest. By now it was 11:55 and all eyes turned to the television, glued to the conclusion of Dick Clark's Rockin' New Year's Eve, an American tradition.

10-9-8-7-6-5-4-3-2-1!

The apartment exploded with energy as everyone screamed "Happy New Year!" In true Philly fashion, pots and pans could be heard banging outside. Cooper circled the apartment pouring shots of champagne for everyone to toast. Even McNeal had one. Cooper stood on a red fold up chair. "To 2008! May all your wishes come true. Cheers!"

Everyone raised their glasses to the sky and then sipped their champagne. McNeal turned around to see Maria waiting for him.

"Happy New Year, Joe. Hope this one begins better than the last one ended for you."

With this she kissed him on the cheek and gave him a hug. The new year was already off to a better start than the previous year ended.

chapter 17

McNeal left the Grilled Donut Café at 2:00 for practice on Thursday. It had just started lightly snowing, but none was laying. As he neared Bishop O'Connell, the snow intensified. The weather guy on the radio had said it wouldn't begin until after six, and even then it was supposed to start as rain. "Must be nice to have a job where you can totally blow it, and still get paid," McNeal mumbled. By the time McNeal arrived at practice, a thin coating of snow covered the ground. McNeal originally had scheduled a track workout for the girls, but it looked like that would have to change. One of the keys to coaching at the high school level was flexibility. Not flexibility as in the ability to touch your toes, but flexibility as in the ability to adapt your plans for the day depending on things like weather, sickness, and available time.

"OK, ladies, bring it in. We need to change our plans. Sprinters, I want you to go through all of your speed drills, followed by eight striders. Follow that with 10x30 meters coming out of the blocks. Focus on exploding out. Distance girls, we're going to use the hallway to do repeat 200s. We'll do them in sets of three with low recovery within the set. Sprinters, you can use the auditorium. It should be clear. Throwers, head to the weight room and do circuit one."

McNeal hated days like this. Conducting practice totally indoors was like running a three ring circus. The girls shared the halls with the boys team, and both squads were only granted access to a small area of the school. On the second 200, senior half-miler Mary Sherman collided head on with a freshman boy. Sherman, thirty pounds lighter, took the worst of the collision.

"You ok, Mary?"

The senior popped up off the ground. "Yeah, I think so." She tried to hop back in for the third 200, but McNeal noticed she was laboring and shut her down for the day.

"I'm fine, coach, I'm fine."

McNeal knew Mary worried about losing her spot on the 4x800 and reassured her. "Missing one workout won't kill you, Mary. Go put some ice on your knee and rest. You'll be fine, I'm sure. And nobody's bumping you from the relay cause of one day."

Sherman sighed and reluctantly headed to the trainer's room for ice. After the second set of 200s, McNeal received the first phone call of the day. It was the mother of one of the freshmen, informing McNeal that she would be there in five minutes to pick her daughter up. McNeal went outside to check the conditions. The snow was still falling at a decent rate.

"Anybody who drives, cool down five minutes and leave. Drive carefully and slowly. If you're getting picked up, call your ride and tell them practice is over."

McNeal sent his assistant home and told Myers he would wait alone today for all of the runners to get picked up. Over an hour later, McNeal was still waiting. Finally at just past six o'clock the last of his athletes left the school. McNeal hopped into his car, and began the slow trek home. What was normally a thirty minute commute was tripled and McNeal walked into the doors of the apartment at 7:50.

"Yo, Mac. Long day, huh?"

"I hate the snow, Coop."

"Ah, you don't mean that. The snow's a kind creature who's never done you harm."

"First of all, the snow is not a creature. Second of all, it did me wrong three times just today. For one, it messed up our practice. For two, I had to wait 'til after six for the last kid to get picked up. Finally, my normal thirty minute ride home took over an hour and half. And we still haven't run yet. So there's my beef with the snow."

"Interesting points, one and all. What are we going to do about running tonight?"

They had both already taken a day off that week. Cooper was a little under the weather on New Year's Day, and McNeal had planned his one day off every third week to coincide with New Year's Day. While he hadn't been drinking the night before, he figured he would be tired and could use a day of rest.

"I guess we'll head down to the avenue and hope we can find a safe spot to run. Maloney and myself ran in the snow last month and were able to get some decent running in, but that was during the day when cars could see us."

The two runners quickly dressed in their warmest gear and walked down the apartment steps to head outside. The winds were picking up and the temperature had dropped below twenty degrees. The same weatherman who earlier said it would be mostly rain, now called for over a foot of snow and advised against venturing outside.

McNeal and Cooper ran about two miles before deciding it was time to turn around. The snow was swiftly accumulating creating a dangerously slippery surface. When they were within a mile of the apartment, Cooper was hit in the back with a snowball. "What the heck was that?" Cooper spun around to find a gang of laughing teenagers.

"What you gonna do about it, running man?"

"Let it slide, Coop. No need for us to get into an all out snow war with a bunch of punks."

"Can't I throw just one snowball back?"

"And then they throw another? Next thing you know..."

"I get it, I get it. No need to fuel the fire."

The two runners continued their run in the dark cold of the winter storm. Nights like this made McNeal yearn for a winter in the warm sun of Florida. He had always enjoyed his trips to Florida, whether visiting an aunt in Palm Beach, or vacationing in Disney World. He thought of it as the one place he would be able to relocate to happily. He just could never sum up the courage to pack up and leave everything behind. Maybe if he could convince some friends or family members, he'd get up and go, but not alone. He once discussed the idea of moving south with Kelly and she had been open to considering it. That was no longer an option.

"So Mac, have you talked to what's her name since the party?"

"No, I haven't actually."

"Well, what the hell are you waiting for? You got her number, right?"

"Yeah, she gave me her phone number. I don't know, Coop. Kelly just dumped me a couple weeks ago, you know. It ain't that easy to just throw yourself back in the game."

"What are you some sort of chick? How much recovery time do you need? Like Rocky Balboa said in his last movie, "Life's not about how many times you get hit and knocked down, it's about getting back up and hitting back.""

"I'm not sure if that's exactly what Rocky said. And even if it is, I'm even less sure of how it applies here."

The two runners arrived at the corner of their block. "It means get back on the dating merry go round. Damn. You want to do a few striders?"

"In the snow? No way, man. I'm not trying to slip and get hurt. Let's go inside and do some drills and core."

"If you insist. But seriously, man, you got to call her."

The two runners moved the remainder of their workout indoors. McNeal wondered whether or not he should pursue Maria. He wasn't even sure if she was interested in him. After all, a couple glasses of champagne on New Year's Eve can tend to distort how a girl sees you. He also didn't want to get involved with Maria to find out that once again, he just couldn't make everyone happy. What if it wasn't Kelly? Maybe she was right. Maybe he really couldn't do everything.

"Mac, I'm not saying you need to start dating this broad for real or anything exclusive like that. All I'm saying is it was obvious she had a thing for you, and I know you think she's cute. Right?"

"Um, yeah. Maria's a good looking girl for sure. I just don't know if I'm ready to hop right back in the saddle."

"Look, give her a call, invite her to hang out down at Third Street Pub. Tell her to bring some friends. We'll invite O'Donnell and his old lady, Mitch too, and it'll be a good time."

Normally, McNeal found himself in the position of providing Cooper with female advice. With the tides turned, McNeal wasn't sure what to do. "Alright, if it'll get you off my back, I'll call her tomorrow."

"Tomorrow? Tomorrow's Friday. Call her tonight, see if she wants to hang out on Saturday."

"Dude, it's getting late. I'll call her tomorrow."

"Late? It's five after nine. I was allowed on the phone later than that in eighth grade. And you know how mean my Mom was."

"Yeah, she was real mean. But not nearly as mean as she was fat," replied McNeal. "I'll call her now."

"Well played with the mom joke. I'm going to shower. Let me know how it goes."

"No problem." McNeal began searching through the contacts in his cell phone. He pressed send upon finding Maria's name, and waited for it to go through. Nerves caused his stomach to churn and his palms to sweat as he waited.

Date the same girl for over a year and you forget how to talk to them, he thought. His pulse quickened as he wondered what he'd say when she picked up. He'd have no such worry, however as after four rings it went to her voice mail. Leaving a message was even worse than talking to the actual person. Your words disappeared into the air when you talk to someone. A voice mail message is saved forever, though. Or at least fourteen days.

"Hey, Kell, it's me Joey Mac, from Second Chances. I was just— oh, damn I'm not talking to Kelly's machine. What the hell do I do now?"

"Press two," Cooper yelled from down the hall. "That'll let you start over."

"Thanks, you eavesdropping son of a gun."

"You're lucky I'm an eavesdropping son of a gun or you'd be in a world of trouble."

"Whatever."

McNeal pressed two, and rerecorded his message, this time using the correct name. McNeal told Maria he hoped she had a good time at the party, apologized for not calling earlier, and told her he'd be at the Third Street Pub in Center City Saturday night with some friends if she wanted to stop by with a couple friends. McNeal then checked outside on the snow, saw it was still coming down at a rapid rate, and went to bed. Six AM comes pretty quickly he'd been learning.

❧❦

McNeal felt as if he was starting to get the hang of working at the Café. Even though he owned half, he never before was involved with the day-to-day operations. McNeal spent the majority of the time talking to customers, testing how different pastries respond to grilling and trying to create a relaxed and welcoming environment. McNeal and Cooper believed a happy customer stayed a customer. The drain of working at the Café surprised McNeal. He wasn't sure if it was the early hours, the constant time on his feet, or the utter chaos the morning rush could be. All he knew was that between working at the Café and coaching, he found himself frequently exhausted when it came time to run.

A typical day had McNeal working the grill early in the morning. McNeal knew that the surest way to lose a customer's business was to keep make them late for work. He was now familiar with some of the regulars and began prepping their orders when they came in the door. There was the construction worker who showed up each morning at 6:53 wearing ripped jeans, overalls and a yellow helmet. Without fail, he could be counted on to order an herbal spiced tea, no sugar, and a whole grain bagel with lox. There was the business man with a different three piece suit for each day of the week whose daily order consisted of an extra large coffee, heavy on the cream, heavy on the sugar, one grilled cinnamon donut, and a breakfast sandwich. McNeal's favorite regular had to be the elderly gentleman who each day arrived with that day's *Daily News* and *Inquirer*. He sat at the same table near the window where he could watch the outside world and absorb the sun's warmth. He could be counted on to order a small orange juice and one "Cinnamon De-Light." The De-Light was for the customer who wanted the flavor of a good old fashioned donut, but was more health conscious. It was made of whole wheat flour, and utilized organic cinnamon and agave nectar for flavor. It contained only six grams of fat, and just two of them were saturated. Like all of the Café's products, it was trans-fat free. It felt good to serve people tasty breakfast foods and at the same time help them follow a healthy diet. McNeal and Cooper were as concerned with their role in the big picture as they were with fattening their wallet. While it may have been helping their customers to eat better, and their employees to live better, it was, at this point in time, not allowing them to see the fruits of their labor. They were hopeful, however, that like all good things, large-scale profits would come with time. Today was a particularly slow day due to yesterday's snow storm. Only the hardiest of customers made it to the Café. School was canceled at Bishop O'Connell so there was no practice. It was against school policy to hold practice when the school had been closed due to inclement weather. With over a foot of snow on the ground, and temperatures not likely to climb out of the twenties, McNeal worried that it might not just be his team unable to run today. O'Toole had recently traveled to Ireland, but left them an outline to follow. Today they had planned on completing a workout of alternating a thousand meters run at two mile pace with three hundred meters at mile pace. As two o'clock rolled around and the last of their customers departed, McNeal's attention turned to running. "Yo, Coop, where are we going to get this workout in today?"

"I have no idea, Mac. We could call around to some local gyms, see if any have an indoor track."

"I'll get online and check it out while you close out the books."

An hour later, McNeal had made a handful of phone calls to local health clubs. McNeal and Cooper left the Café and made a trip to check out a few gyms whose sales reps said they had a track. The first stop on project "find an indoor track" was a Bally's near the Franklin Mills Mall. The two runners walked in the front door and approached the front desk. A young woman worked the front desk. "Hello, we're considering joining the gym and were wondering if we could check out the indoor track first?" asked McNeal.

The blonde haired worker looked puzzled. "The track? Do you mean the treadmills?"

"No, I mean the indoor track. The woman on the phone said there was a track circling the fitness center."

"Oh, yeah. Wow. There's a small...uh, track that encircles the free weight room. Are guys looking to run on this?"

"Well, that was the plan. Why?"

"It's just...well, why don't you go check it out for yourselves. Go straight down the hall and turn right. You'll see the free weight room on your right."

McNeal and Cooper walked down the hall, none too hopeful this would be a decent place to run. As they walked into the free weight area, McNeal immediately realized why the girl at the front desk seemed confused when they asked about an indoor track. Encircling the weights was a small, two lane oval. It couldn't have measured any longer then sixty meters. Dumb bells protruded onto the so called track in various places, creating an obstacle course. Huge muscle bound men filled the room, lifting hundreds of pounds at a time, ending each lift with a loud drop of the weights and an equally loud grunt or scream. Several heads turned to see who the newcomers were when McNeal and Cooper entered their abode.

"I don't know about you, Mac, but I don't think it'd be a very good idea for us to be running workouts here."

"What would give you that idea?"

"Well, there's that whole twenty-nine laps per mile thing. The weights that are not just inside the track, but actually on it. And the 'What the hell are you doing here?' stare we're getting, to name a few."

"Picky, picky. OK, let's go see what else we can find."

They turned and left the weightlifters in their own world. The girl at the counter was barely able to contain her laughter as they opened the doors to leave. "Did you find the track?"

"Oh yeah, we found the, uh, 'track,'" answered Cooper.

"Not what you're looking for?"

"No, sorry."

"Have a good night." McNeal heard her barely muffled giggles as they exited.

McNeal and Cooper preferred a track to treadmills. Treadmills would suffice for a basic distance run, but for anything faster they'd need to be on dry land. The next stop on the find a track whirlwind tour was the neighborhood YMCA. McNeal played basketball there before and remembered there was a track above the basketball court. He couldn't recall its dimensions or any of the particulars, however.

This time the front desk was manned by a graying middle-aged woman who appeared to need to spend more time working out at the Y, and less time behind the desk.

"Excuse me, Ma'am. I was wondering if we could see the indoor track? We were thinking about joining, but wanted to check out the track to make sure it's runnable first," Cooper asked.

"Well, of course it's runnable. What kind of question is that? It's a track isn't it?" Her attitude was no more pleasant than her appearance.

"No offense, but when we use the track we like to really run up there." Cooper tried unsuccessfully not to sound like a running snob as he spoke to the woman. "We're not your typical recreational joggers, or anything."

Just as he finished speaking, a rather rough looking gentleman appeared behind the desk. "So you guys want to join the gym just for the track?"

Apparently runners joining the gym was an unusual occurrence at the Y.

McNeal stepped to the desk. "Well, you know we'll be lifting too and maybe using the pool for some work-outs. I might even shoot some hoops, but we need the track to be right. It doesn't make sense for us to sign up first and spend money on something that isn't gonna work."

The woman behind the desk sighed heavily. "Go ahead and run but don't you go breaking anything on me."

"Excuse me?" a slightly confused Cooper asked. "Like what? The track?"

"No, well, yeah, don't break that either, but I mean don't go getting hurt on my watch."

The woman buzzed the two runners into the gymnasium. They climbed the steps to the second floor track. A yellow plastic sign hanging on the wall stated that it was twenty laps per mile. McNeal hung his coat on a hook in the corner. "That's a lot of left turns."

The track was slightly banked at the turns and the surface was similar to a hardwood basketball floor. A chain link fence ran along the inside. It made hugging the turns a dangerous proposition. McNeal and Cooper jogged the mile warm-up and stretched. The track held up ok, at least for light running. Just before beginning, an adult volleyball game began on the basketball court under the track. McNeal paid it no mind and strode powerfully down the track to loosen up. Cooper was to set the pace for the first 1000 and McNeal the 300, then they would switch roles for the second set. The goal was seventy seconds per quarter for the 1000, and forty-six for the 300. That might not be possible running on a twenty lap per mile track.

"You ready, Mac?"

"Define ready."

"Let's do it."

Cooper took off and the two runners were flying over the wooden track. THUMP! THUMP! THUMP! The volleyball line judge stared open mouthed at the two runners. Cooper checked his watch after five laps, the supposed quarter mile mark. "Eighty-one!" Definitely the most difficult eighty-one second quarter mile of either runner's life.

"This has got to be long!" McNeal mumbled between breaths.

"Effort, let's make sure we get the right effort."

They continued charging around the elevated wooden rectangle, hitting the 800 mark in 2:42. At least Cooper was locked in as they maintained pace for the last 200 meters.

"That was rough," Cooper said.

"Yeah, tell me about it."

"Good luck trying to handle a fast 300 up here."

They finished their 200 meter recovery and McNeal set off on leading them through the 300. Cooper struggled keeping the turns at the faster pace and grazed the unforgiving metal fence, ripping open a gash on his upper left calf. "Damn!"

"You alright, man?"

"I think so, just gashed myself on the steel cage we're running around."

As McNeal looked over his shoulder to check on Cooper an errant bump sent a volleyball flying onto the track directly in front of him. McNeal nimbly hurdled the ball, which bounced up and nearly nailed Cooper in the face.

"Nice dodge ball skills, Coop."

"Thanks. I've been watching Vince Vaughn."

They finished the 300 in fifty-two seconds, frustrated at the apparent lack of accuracy and the myriad of challenges.

"A little help!" A green shirt clad volleyball player called out from the court below.

Cooper scooped up the volleyball and dropped it over the railing.

"You ready for the next set, Coop?"

"As ready as I'm going to get."

This time McNeal led the 1000 meters. He consciously pushed the pace, only to check his watch in frustration at the quarter mile mark to again see the number eighty-one staring at him.

As they circled the track for the sixth time, another errant volleyball bounced onto the track, glancing off McNeal's shoulder after hitting the wall. McNeal just shook his head and tried to remain focused. Again the cry of "A little help" rang out from below. Locked into the workout, they ignored the plea this time. Annoyed at the lack of a response, a particularly agitated fellow on the red team stormed up to the track as they were finishing the second 1000.

"Thanks for the help, guys, really appreciate having to walk up these steps to get the ball. Nice shorts by the way."

Cooper was wearing a typical pair of running shorts, a bit shorter than your everyday shorts. OK for a runner, a little too short for the volleyball player's taste. "Little extra exercise might do you some good."

McNeal tried to diffuse the situation. "Sorry, buddy, we were in the midst of a workout, can't really stop to get a ball."

"Workout? I don't see any weights up here? I just see a couple of sticks jogging around the track."

Jogging was a pet peeve of McNeal's. He hated when it was used in reference to his own running. Jogging was for middle aged women wearing spandex trying to lose three dress sizes for their daughter's wedding. What McNeal and Cooper practiced was a far cry from jogging. "First of all, buddy, we ain't jogging up here. If you think we're jogging, I suggest you hop in and try to keep up. Second of all, if I get hit with one more volleyball while I'm *running* I'll give you a little help. But it won't be the help you're looking for."

"You threatening me, little man?"

The referee was now standing in the doorway to the track. "Hank, just grab the ball and come back to the game. I'll report these guys to the front office for their unsafe practices."

"Our unsafe what?" asked Cooper.

The striped referee looked at Cooper, looked back at Hank and began talking again. "The spirit of the Y, gentlemen, is one of cooperation. If you guys can't cooperate with other members of the Y, I'm going to have to ask you to leave."

The overweight volleyball player grabbed the ball and smirked at McNeal as he walked away. "You're lucky I'm hitting this ball and not your face!" He laughed menacingly as he descended the steps.

"Alright, fellows get your stuff and get out of here."

"Mr. Ref, I don't think it's very 'cooperative' of your Y members to expect us to stop on a dime and drop the ball down. When we don't get around to throwing the volleyball down, the same ball that hit me while running, he comes up here and picks a fight with us. That's real cooperative."

The referee began to say something before McNeal interrupted him. "It's alright, Coop. Don't waste any more breath on these guys."

Cooper grabbed his stuff and the two runners descended the steps into the lobby. The grey-haired woman was still sitting at the desk, scowl strewn across her face. "So did our track meet your needs?"

"Not exactly. Apparently we're supposed to stop moving every time a ball bounces up there and immediately throw it back down. Heaven knows what would happen if the Greater Northeast YMCA Adult Volleyball league had a short halt in the action," answered Cooper.

"It would also be a crying shame to ask one of those physical specimens to walk up a flight of stairs in order to retrieve their own ball. Not to mention the hassle of having to halt their match just so a couple of loons can continue looping around the track. Sacrilegious almost."

Cooper pulled open the glass door. "Have a nice night."

McNeal couldn't help but shake his head and laugh as he walked toward his car. "Well, I guess we won't be signing membership papers for the YMCA."

"Guess not. So this just leaves the Family Fitness Center."

"A project for tomorrow, I assume."

"Yeah, Mac, we'll squeeze that in before we go out. Maria call you back yet?"

"Not sure. Left my cell phone at the apartment. I'll check after I drive through this winter war zone."

By now, the main roads were mostly clear, but many of the small side streets that made up their Northeast Philadelphia neighborhood were too small for a full sized snow plow to navigate. A few roads appeared to have been cleared by smaller, privately-owned plows attached to the hood of SUVs. Quite a few streets, however, looked as if from the frozen tundra of Antarctica. McNeal carefully piloted his Dodge Aries through this polar wasteland. The most difficult aspect of driving the roads was the hump in the middle of the roads. The wheels of oversized trucks and SUVs left a track where their tires tore through the snow. Left behind was a four foot wide area where nearly two feet of snow remained. This hump made maintaining control difficult for smaller cars like McNeal's. Several times during the course of the trip home, McNeal temporarily lost control of the vehicle, only to regain it in the nick of time. Cooper's hands turned ghostly white from clinging to the passenger side door with a vice like grip. All color drained from his face, leaving it a matching shade of white. A couple miles from the apartment, McNeal's faithful Dodge became stuck as he attempted to turn left up a small street. McNeal futilely tried to gas his car through the snow only resulting in tires spinning and snow flying into the air as the engine roared and squealed.

"That's why we need an SUV or something," muttered Cooper as he opened the passenger side door to try and push the car out of the snow.

"We? Just 'cause we're roommates, doesn't mean we share everything, man. This car is mine and, well, you don't have a car."

"Thanks for rubbing salt in the wounds. By the way, I want no part of this car."

Cooper vainly tried pushing as McNeal went through a series of reverses followed again by trying to move forward, futilely cutting the wheel left and right, anything to try and get a better grip on the road. Five minutes later, they remained in the same spot. The only difference was that Cooper was now exhausted and covered in the blackened ice-dirt mix that had flown in every direction each time McNeal hit the gas. He opened the passenger side door and slumped into his seat. "What do we now?"

"I guess we do what we do best?"

"Grill donuts?"

"No, the other thing we do best."

"Watch TV? Where we gonna do that?"

"At the apartment after we run home. Dude, we're like two miles away. It's perfect cause we didn't get to finish our workout."

"Mac, no disrespect, but running two miles home in the snow—the same reason we're looking for a gym to run at—while we leave your car here is far from what I consider 'perfect.'"

"Well, maybe perfect wasn't the right choice of words."

"No, maybe it wasn't. Not to mention it wasn't you out here trying to push your two ton piece of junk out of the snow."

"Easy there, Coop, don't go hurting the Joe-Mobile's feelings."

"Screw the Joe-Mobile's feelings." Cooper slammed his door shut and began trudging down the snow-covered road.

The two runners arrived back at the apartment fifteen minutes later. McNeal picked up his cell phone to see if he had any messages. He dialed in his password and waited for the automated voice to tell him. "You have seven new messages."

The first four were from runners asking what the plan was for tomorrow since school had already been canceled. The next message was from Maria, saying she was unable to go out on Saturday, but she'd be interesting in getting together some other time. "Damn."

"What's wrong, Mac?"

"Maria's no good for Saturday."

"Then we'll just have to raise some Cain."

The next message was another runner calling to see what the plan was for tomorrow. The final voice was Seamus O'Toole's, calling from Ireland.

"It's O'Toole. What do you think he wants? He's all the way in Ireland."

"I don't know, Mac. Why don't you listen and find out?"

McNeal played O'Toole's message. "Oh my God! I don't believe it."

"What's wrong, man? Is Seamus OK?"

"Nothing's wrong. Quite the opposite, actually. O'Toole said I got invited to run the Wanamaker Mile at Millrose."

"No way, man. No freakin' way. That's phenomenal, Mac. Call the guys and tell 'em."

"I will in a minute. I need to call my team to arrange tomorrow's meeting. You mind if I leave work at noon?"

"Nah. Why?"

"Since we didn't get to practice today, I was going to take advantage of the day off to sneak into Lancaster Liberal Arts College. Their coach sometimes lets us in if we're out before 2:30, which obviously is impossible on a school day."

"Yeah, ok. Make it quick 'cause this is huge, dude. Huge."

"Alright, alright, stop fussing. It's not that big a deal. I don't even know if I'm gonna do it."

"WHAT?"

"I just realized, that's Meet of Champs for O'Connell. I can't miss that, man."

"Joe, I know how dedicated you are to coaching. It's real honorable and I admire you for it. You're a helluva coach but this is a once in a lifetime opportunity. Not to mention your girls will get to brag about their coach running at Millrose. How many other teams can say that?"

"I don't know. There's a few former studs coaching in the area."

"Exactly, former studs. You're gonna go toe to toe with Bernard Lagat and Buster Mottram. You can't turn this stuff down. If you do, you might as well hang 'em up. Isn't this why we're busting it day after day? Ain't this why you came back? Why we stopped playing football? Hell, it's what guys like me and you and Mitch and OD have been dreaming about our whole lives. The chance to run with the big dogs. Now you got that chance. You sure as hell ain't gonna pass it up. No way, man. No freakin' way."

"You're right, I know. But, it's hard to miss a championship meet. In all the years I've been coaching I've never missed a day, not one single day of practice. Not for sickness, not even when I had my wisdom teeth pulled. Now I'm supposed to miss one of the biggest meets of the year?"

"That's great, but sometimes you need to make time for you. You just called it one of the biggest meets of the year. Well, Millrose, that's the biggest race of your life. Commitment and loyalty are both great character traits, but if you don't do this now, you're never going to forgive yourself. You'll never find the answer you're searching for."

Deep down, McNeal knew Cooper was right. It was his biggest dream and his worst nightmare coming true simultaneously. He had feared if his comeback went as planned, then conflicts may arise between running and coaching. His worries had proven to be right. No time to dwell on that now, though. McNeal made the necessary phone calls to arrange for his varsity girls to work out at Lancaster Liberal Arts College. While he hated to make distinctions with who was allowed to practice, McNeal knew showing up with a large crowd of teenage girls would not sit well with the staff at the college.

The next day McNeal left work at noon to meet his top fifteen runners at the indoor track. With no race this weekend, today would be a challenging workout. The distance girls began with 2000 meters on the track at tempo pace. This would take the edge off, forcing them to run the rest of the workout with a little less in the tank. McNeal's believed this helped them maintain pace late in a race. Sullivan and the Sherman sisters led the pack for the 2000. The remainder of the workout called for six times a 400 with a 200 meter recovery jog in between. The girls were supposed to run at their mile pace for two, their 1200 pace for two, and run the last two at their 800 pace. Sullivan and the Shermans shuffled position for the first four before junior half miler Brittany A sped to the front for the final two, running each in under seventy seconds.

"Nice job, Brittany A."

The track was full with other event groups working out alongside the distance girls. It was slightly organized chaos, especially with no one else from his staff able to arrive be there. McNeal wore two stopwatches around his neck and the wristwatch that remained on his arm at all times. Back when coaching both the boys' and girls' teams it wasn't unusual for seven or eight workouts to run simultaneously so McNeal was well versed in juggling stopwatches. McNeal gathered the girls after they completed their respective workouts. "This weekend, if you've already had a day off, try to get a pair of runs in.

Philip J Reilly

Distance ladies, go long one day, about an hour, and about forty-five minutes with striders and drills the other day. Sprinters do your drills and striders each day, and try to get two to three miles in also. Good practice today girls and enjoy the weekend."

"You too, Coach Mac," said Sullivan.

McNeal dreaded telling his team he would miss the Meet of Champs. It was one of the meets they had been focusing on the whole season. It marked the kick-off of "championship season." McNeal decided to ask Pat Myers if he would accompany Coach Williams, the girls' assistant. Frank Williams knew the field events inside and out and was an asset to the team. McNeal wasn't totally confident, however, in his ability to handle head coach duties for a day. His normal meet day routine entailed heading to whichever field event he was asked to work, "set up shop" as he called it, and not be seen again until the end of the meet. McNeal dialed Myers' cell phone as he drove home. "Pat?"

"Speaking. What's up, Joe?"

"I got a problem. You think you can help me?"

"Well, that depends on what the problem is. If you're stranded in the Amazon jungle, I don't think that's a problem I can solve. One of the girls need help coming out of the blocks, I'm the guy."

"Well, I'm not stranded in the jungle. I'm running at the Millrose Games."

"Wow, that's awesome, man, congratulations. What's the problem?"

"It's the same night as Meet of Champs. As talented as I am, I haven't figured out how to be in two places at once."

"What about Coach Williams?"

"Pat, you and I both know that what Frank does, Frank does very well. But what he doesn't do, he doesn't do. I was hoping you could go in case something happens and Frank's down at the jumps, we'd have someone else there."

Myers sighed. McNeal had done a lot for him over the years, as a coach, and as an athlete. The day of Millrose, however, was his three-

166

year anniversary with his longtime girlfriend, Nicole. Not to mention the following morning was the guys' Meet of Champs. McNeal performed that dirty double many a time in the past and knew what an exhausting weekend it made.

"Alright, Joe, just for you. Nicole's gonna have my head, you know. But I know if I don't go, you'll be so distracted up in New York that you'll crap the bed. I'd hate to be responsible for that."

"Thanks, Pat. I appreciate it. Tell Nicole I'm sorry."

"No problem."

"Oh, Pat, one more thing."

"Yeah, Mac, what is it?"

"Joey McNeal doesn't crap the bed."

chapter 18

SATURDAY MORNING MCNEAL, Cooper, O'Donnell and Maloney went out for their weekly long run. They headed over to Tyler Park to hammer some good hills during the run. The plan called for a thirteen-miler, McNeal's last run over ten miles before Millrose. While O'Toole didn't want McNeal peaking for Millrose, he believed it best to have fresh legs when taking such a large step up in class. McNeal had run in his share of big races, but nothing in comparison to Millrose, and against no one on the level of Bernard Lagat, the double gold winner from the 2007 World Championships in the 1500 and 5000 and Australian Craig "Buster" Mottram. Mottram won the bronze medal in the 5000 meters at the 2005 World Championships, the first non-African to medal since 1987.

Thirteen miles over the hilly terrains of Tyler Park promised to be eighty minutes of suffering. By the three mile mark, Cooper and O'Donnell were pushing the pace. McNeal and Maloney begrudgingly fell in line.

"So, Mac, you got the limo for tonight?"

"What? No, Coop, no limo for tonight."

"Ah, I thought since we had these two going out sans their lady friends, we'd really do things right."

"Well, I thought renting a limo because OD and Mitch are allowed to have a guys' night out wouldn't be the wisest of fiscal decisions."

"Cooper, I'm a little disappointed you think we'd need a limo to have a legendary night. What are we a bunch of Hollywood honchos?" asked OD.

"I agree with OD that we don't need a limo to cause a ruckus out on the streets of Philadelphia. However, I do feel it'd make for a great night. Maybe we can celebrate Joey Mac's upcoming big win over Bernard Lagat with a limo ride around town."

"Whoa there, cuz. Just 'cause I'm in the same race as Mr. Lagat, doesn't mean I'm returning from Madison Square Garden with a win over him on my resume. Now, Mitch, let's not let your mouth cash a check I can't cover."

"Which is precisely why we should celebrate tonight you being invited to Millrose with a limo," proclaimed Cooper.

The runners were now approaching one of the more challenging climbs of the park. The animated discussion about the upcoming night out had helped them survive the middle miles of the run. Upon clearing the next hill, they'd only have five miles remaining in the run. McNeal could still vividly remember the first week struggling to finish a five miler in under thirty-five minutes. Now he was eight miles into a thirteen miler, thinking he 'only had five to go'. All this while clipping off mile after mile in sub 6:30 pace. How drastically things can change in four and a half months.

"Guys, how about we resume this conversation at the conclusion of the run?" asked Maloney. "Or at least at the top of this mountain."

The hill they were now climbing measured three quarters of a mile. Since the dirt trails were covered in snow and mud, the runners remained on the asphalt path encircling the park. This particular patch of pavement was an unforgiving climb that shot sharp pains throughout McNeal's legs. His quads burned more with each passing step. He pumped his arms, and consciously pushed onto the balls of his feet as he neared the summit. On a hill like this, the best way up was to get into the zone and roll. By the time he crested the hill, McNeal had put thirty meters on the others.

"Sorry guys. I just wanted to get to the top."

His apology was met with a combination of grunts and breathless "don't worry 'bout its." With all conversation ceased, and McNeal having already dropped the hammer, the last five miles of the run more closely resembled a race than a training run. The pace first dropped to six flat pace. A mile later, it was down to 5:50, another mile later 5:45. With three miles to go, Cooper took the helm and hammered a 5:37 mile dropping everyone but McNeal. McNeal hung tough, determined not to get dropped, fresh legs for Millrose be damned. Cooper continued pushing the pace, running the twelfth mile in 5:30 with McNeal glued to his shoulder. Cooper seemed determined to prove that while McNeal might be the top dog on the track, Cooper still ruled the roost when it came to the long stuff. McNeal was driven by a more primal motivation. He simply needed to prove to himself he could handle anything. He knew Mottram and Lagat would never allow themselves to be dropped in a training run. He harbored no illusions of beating either man at Millrose, but if he was going to lace 'em up against the best of the best, he needed to know he was ready. Four minutes and fifty-nine seconds later, he knew. There may have been times in his life when he possessed greater speed, but Joey McNeal had never been stronger in his life.

♾

Back at the apartment, Cooper resigned himself to the fact that there would be no limo. "No offense, Mac, but driving around in your Dodge Aries doesn't compare to styling and profiling in a stretch."

"We can take my car tonight," said O'Donnell. "Mac, you can drive the Matrix."

"Thanks, OD. Every time I get to rest the K-Train means one more ride down the road to glory."

The night began with a trip to Tony Luke's, the legendary sandwich place in South Philly. McNeal was a huge fan of the food there, especially the roast pork with provolone and spinach. He considered it the ultimate Philadelphia sandwich.

"You guys were really rolling those last five miles," said Maloney between bites of his chicken cheese steak.

O'Donnell nodded and finished chewing his cheese steak with fried onions. "Yeah, I tried to go with you guys, but once the pace dropped into the five's I wasn't messing with that."

McNeal didn't really like to talk about runs after dropping the other guys. He knew they would do the same thing given the opportunity, but he had been on the other side before and it was no fun. "Thanks guys. I was just riding Cooper's coattails out there."

"Yeah, sure, Mac. You were right there with me. It's freakin' frightening to think how dangerous you're going to be on the track this summer. This mileage you're doing, plus those crazy wheels you got, man, damn."

"Eh, you already drunk, Coop?"

"No way, Joe. I'm serious, you're going to be deadly on the track. That's all I'm saying."

Maloney nodded in agreement, finished his steak and stood up. "Alright, let's get out of here and head to Third Street."

McNeal drove the five minutes to Third Street Pub in the Old City section of Philadelphia. The "Pub" catered to an eclectic clientele. There was the standard t-shirt and jeans kind of guys, proponents of the classic American style, unchanged since the days of James Dean. They were joined by those who kept the jeans but replaced the t-shirt with a button down shirt or a v-neck sweater. They probably numbered the majority. Finally, there were the tough guys with their hats tilted to the side and their jeans two sizes too big. McNeal and company sported jeans, but since they had decided tonight was a "special night" they accessorized their outfit with blazers. Maloney, while he agreed to the look, was not a huge fan. "What the hell am I doing wearing a damn suit coat? I feel like a royal monkey."

"Mitch, it's a sport coat, not a suit coat. What the hell is a royal monkey anyway?" asked OD.

"I'll tell you that when you tell me the difference between a sport coat and a suit coat?"

OD opened his mouth to answer but Maloney simply shushed him.

Like the guys, the girls at "The Pub" dressed in a motley assortment of styles. They ranged the gamut from the conservative sweater wearers, to the nicely dressed skirts, and then, as in most establishments where the two sexes mingled, danced and drank, there were the ladies who weren't afraid to show some skin. McNeal referred to them as the "Dress to impress with flesh" crowd.

Although for many runners there is an unwritten rule that Sunday is for church, watching football and long runs, O'Toole's philosophy was to save Sunday as a recovery run. This allowed Sunday to be a make-up day if circumstances required a day off earlier in the week. Despite the snowstorm, all four runners completed their first six runs. This meant tomorrow would be a recovery day. With no major events coming up, it also meant Cooper, O'Donnell and Maloney would be imbibing in beverages. McNeal knew it could be a long night. He ordered a diet coke and a water, sat down at the bar and turned his attention to the 76ers game.

Cooper took a seat next to McNeal at the bar while OD and Maloney went to the men's room. The walk to the restroom also served as a mechanism for getting a feel for the night. One of the guys' favorite bar games was to meander around the establishment, high-fiving random people, usually punctuating the slap with a loud "Wooo!" McNeal could hear Maloney's voice ringing out from across the bar as he watched the game on the flat screen above the bar. "Sounds like Mitch's on top of his game."

"Yeah. The real question is will you be on top of yours at Millrose?"

"I suppose. I'm gonna need to be if I want to be competitive."

"That's a great opportunity you got there, Mac."

"I know, Coop. I'm still a little in shock about the whole thing. We'll see what happens."

"It'll be a great experience for you no matter what happens. How many guys get to say they rubbed elbows with two of the best distance runners ever to walk the planet?"

"Not many. I guess I'm one of the lucky ones now, eh?"

"Lucky? Nah, man, you're not lucky. You've earned this shot. Make the most of it. That's all I'm saying. Make the most 'cause you don't know when opportunity like this knocks again."

"I still say I'm lucky. Guys like me are a dime a dozen. How many 4:10 to 4:15 types would die to be in this position."

"I don't know, Mac. Probably quite a few. So you need to make sure when you step out onto the wooden boards of the Garden, you run every step for all of us guys who've been busting it trying to reach that level."

"I'll do my best. Let's go see what those knuckleheads are up to."

"Oh, Mac, one more thing."

"Yeah, Coop?"

"You're right. There probably is a little bit of luck involved."

"Why do you think I got us an Irish coach? Sometimes it's better to be lucky than good."

"Best to be both."

McNeal and Cooper found Mitch and OD at the bar on the opposite end of the pub, surprisingly sitting down conversing with each other. Cooper glanced at McNeal as if to say "What is this?" McNeal merely shrugged his shoulders.

"Yo, fellows, what's going on?"

"Not much, Mac. Just chatting a little about life. Your cousin has quite an outlook on some of the finer things."

"The finer things?"

Maloney wore a sheepish look on his face. O'Donnell had a penchant for philosophizing when he drank more than a few beverages, especially when they were of the mixed drink variety. Mixed drinks affected him differently than a few bottles of beer. "We were just talking about how lucky each of us are."

McNeal raised his eyebrows. "Care to elaborate?"

"Well, Mitch and myself both are in the best shapes of our lives, got a great set of friends, and have lovely ladies waiting for us at home. We don't need this meat market anymore."

Cooper shook his head in disgust. "I thought this was a guys' night out? Sounds more like a 'let's talk about how wonderful my woman is' party. I think I'm gonna puke."

"Alright, Coop, relax," said O'Donnell. "What kind of havoc were you and McNeal causing?"

McNeal grabbed an empty seat next to Maloney. "The track talk havoc."

"Whoa, now, let's not get too crazy," joked Maloney.

O'Donnell stood up from the bar. "Yo, Mac, we're gonna go walk through and find a spot closer to the stage. You coming?"

"I'll catch up. Gotta see the end of the game."

"Of course. The world depends on it."

"Just as much as it depends on me being closer to 'Jolly Molly.'"

McNeal ordered another diet Coke. The Sixers held the ball, down 97-96. They were just exiting a time-out, and with less than twenty seconds left on the game clock, it was likely the final possession of the game. Andre Miller, the 76ers veteran point guard, dribbled at the top of the key as the seconds ticked off. As the clock hit five, Miller drove hard towards the rim, pulled up and drained a seven-foot jumper as time expired. McNeal let out a loud yell as the ball dropped through the hoop. At the same time, he heard a familiar female voice scream for joy. He turned around to see Maria, standing ten feet away, watching the game with a small group of friends. His feeling of joy at the sight of his favorite hoops team's last second win was short lived. He figured if Maria was there, and had not called him back, she must not have wanted to hang out with him. Not to mention, a large, blond-haired fellow was draped over her shoulders like a cape. His hunch had been right; it probably was the alcohol talking on New Year's Eve. McNeal tried to slip past Maria as he headed towards the stage in search of his friends.

"Hey, Joe!"

McNeal contemplated pretending not to hear Maria's voice, but this proved to be a moot point as she ran over and hugged him. "Joe, I've been looking for you all night. How are you?"

"I'm good, Maria. What are you doing here?"

"My friends and I were looking for a place to take my roommate for her birthday. So we figured we'd come here, and maybe I'd get lucky and see you, too."

"Oh, so you were looking to kill two birds with one stone."

"If you want to call yourself a bird, then sure."

"So you want to kill me, eh?"

"Now you're putting words in my mouth. Where are your friends?"

"They're up by the front of the stage. So you're a Sixers fan, Maria?"

"Huge. Played basketball my whole life."

"I didn't know that."

"Joey Mac, there's a whole lot about me you don't know."

"Well, maybe we can change that."

She smiled. "Maybe."

"Alright, I'm going to look for Coop and the guys. Do you want to come with me? Or should I leave you with that guy?"

"Bret? Haha, no that's quite alright. That's my roommate Gina's brother. He's all over me every time we go out, but trust me there's nothing there."

"Does he know that?"

"Not sure, to be honest with you. He should, but not sure if he does."

"Gotcha. I have that problem all the time."

"Really? With who?"

"Nah, a guy can dream though."

McNeal and Maria fought their way through the sea of bodies to reach Cooper, Maloney, and O'Donnell near the stage. Cooper was in the midst of having his picture taken with a group of girls who appeared to be celebrating someone's birthday while Mitch and OD talked to a couple of red heads from the group.

"Hold on a second, Maria."

"Alright, what's up?"

McNeal quickly jumped in front of the camera, put his arms around a slightly overweight brunette, gave the thumbs up sign and flashed his best million-dollar smile. He then shook the hands of each girl in the group, patted Cooper on the back and resumed talking with Maria.

"What was that about?"

"I couldn't let Coop get in a picture without me. It's kind of fun to see the reaction of people when some random guy hops into their picture."

"You're a strange man, Joey McNeal."

"Normal's overrated. Not to mention boring. And I prefer unique to strange. Sounds much nicer."

"Hmmmm. How about weird?"

"Weird. No, that's just as bad as strange. Maybe worse."

"Goofy?"

"Um, sure, yeah. I like the Disney character Goofy. Goofy works."

McNeal and Maria spent the next hour sitting at the bar talking until a popular dance song played in between sets of the band. Maria excitedly hopped off her stool. "I love this song. Wanna dance?"

McNeal thought for a moment. He hadn't danced with a girl since Kelly dumped him. "I'm not sure if you're ready for this."

Maria grabbed his hand and drug him to a spot on the floor where they could actually move. Maria proved to be quite the hip shaker and McNeal gave his best effort to keep up. "You really got some moves there, Maria."

"Haha. Well, I was kind of a dork growing up. I used to practice dancing in my room, watching myself in the mirror."

"Wow, you were a dork. But I don't think too many dorks can move like that."

Maria moved closer to McNeal as the song ended and a slower one began. She put her hand on his lower back, looked up at him and smiled. Her eyes sparkled when she smiled. "You and your friends are certainly interesting."

"I thought I was weird and goofy."

"Well, at least your friends are interesting. You, however, are kind of goofy. Cute, but goofy."

McNeal blushed slightly. He was still getting used to being back in the game. A long-term relationship will definitely put some rust on your ability to flirt and interact with the opposite sex. Luckily for McNeal, he found it easier to flirt with a woman he already knew. It helped reduce the awkward conversation often faced when meeting someone new.

"So where'd you go to school? Oh, I know someone who went to IUP."

"What was your major? Archeology? Wow, I love rocks."

"So you're from New Jersey? Cool. The shore's awesome."

These were just a few of the typical conversation starters likely to be overheard at the local bar, neighborhood bookstore, or the frozen foods aisle at Whole Foods. Already knowing the person provides a certain level of comfort.

"I should probably go find my friends," said Maria. "They're probably worried about me."

"So I'll call you sometime this week?"

"I'd like that. Maybe we can grab a bite to eat."

"Sounds good. Have a good night."

"You too, Joe."

The two hugged and McNeal wondered where this was going. What had she meant by calling him cute? Was it "Awww you're so cute, like a baby or a teddy bear?" Or was it more of an "I'm attracted to you" type of cute? Time would tell.

chapter 19

McNEAL ARRIVED AT school early on Monday to speak to the athletic director, Butch Flouers. Butch also coached the football team and the other coaches in the school knew as long as they didn't interfere with football season, Flouers granted them free reign. Back when coaching the boys, McNeal had quickly grown tired of dealing with Flouers, trying to convince him of the benefit of allowing his football players to run. A cooperative football coach is almost essential in developing a top-notch boys' track and field team. The majority of your throwers and sprinters can be found on the football team. A football coach who encouraged participation in track and field knew his players would get faster and stronger, two vital needs for any serious football player. Butch Flouers, however, was a controlling man with the need to oversee everything his players did throughout the year. This made football a twelve-month commitment at Bishop O'Connell. Mostly, a twelve-month commitment to losing. With McNeal's sole focus on coaching the girls, he had one less battle to fight. The stench of his many heated debates with Flouers lingered and McNeal could barely disguise his contempt for the man. Flouers was a balding man, about fifty years of age. His hair was once a dark shade of brown, but what remained was mostly grey. Flouers had the build of an offensive lineman. He stood six feet tall and weighed upwards of three hundred pounds. Flouers didn't arrive at school until twelve o'clock and typically departed around four o'clock, later during football season.

McNeal arrived just as Flouers was returning from lunch. He was winded from walking up the flight of stairs from the teacher's lounge, his face flush, matching the slightly too small red sweater he was wearing.

"Joey Mac! My finest hire! To what do I owe the pleasure of your presence?"

McNeal resisted the urge to roll his eyes. "I wanted to tell you that I won't be at the girls' Meet of Champions this year."

"Really? That's not like you to miss a meet, especially one of such importance, Joe. Have you informed the team yet?"

"Not yet, I'm telling 'em at practice today. I just wanted to give you the heads up first."

"May I ask why you're going to miss a championship meet?"

"Well, I was invited to run in the Millrose Games at Madison Square Garden in the Wanamaker Mile. Some of the best runners in the world will be there. It's an opportunity I can't turn down."

"Congratulations. Sounds like quite the achievement. I think the team will be excited to hear. I assume you've talked to Coach Myers about filling in for the meet?"

"Yes, I have. He assured me it would be no problem."

"Very well, then. I just have one concern here, Joe."

McNeal sighed. He knew it couldn't possibly be this easy.

Flouers leaned forward in his chair, resting his elbows on the desk. "What if this type of conflict occurs again? I understand this is a great opportunity for you as a runner. But where do we draw the line? You do realize the school is paying your salary with the understanding that coaching will be your top priority."

"Butch, for the last eight years, I've put my heart and soul into this program. Heck, I've missed so many family gatherings that I've got cousins whose names I don't even know."

"Joe, I think you're misunderstanding what I'm saying. I am not questioning what you have given to the Bishop O'Connell community.

I'm questioning what you will be able to give in the future as you chase this…what is it that you're chasing?"

"Excuse me?"

"What are you chasing? There must be some sort of goal here for you. What is it? How will it impact your coaching? I think that's a fair question."

"I'm just trying to see how good I can be. As a former athlete, I think you understand that need. Especially now that I'm just about thirty, I don't know how many good years I have left."

"Oh, to be thirty again." Flouers scratched his balding head to emphasize his point. "Life doesn't end at thirty, you know, Joe."

"I'm sorry, Butch."

"No need to apologize. I am well aware of my increasing age."

"I know life doesn't end at thirty. But my event is dominated by runners in their early twenties. If you're still at your peak at twenty seven-years old, then that's something. In the last World Championships Final, there wasn't one athlete over twenty-eight years old. The majority were under twenty-five. I'm not saying I'm getting old but I really don't know how much longer I'm gonna be able to really get after it and be fast."

"Joe, again, I'm not arguing that fact. But you need to answer this question yourself. 'What am I trying to achieve?' Then ask yourself if you can coach while doing that? You owe it to the girls, Joe. They need to know they can count on you. You owe it to yourself too, Joe. I know you, and I know that when you're up in New York getting ready to run whatever it is you run, half your thoughts will be with your team. Then what's going happen when you step out there against some African destroyer? I might not know much about the sport as you have reminded me so many times but I know enough about sports to know you better be on your game."

McNeal sat there, not saying a word. He couldn't believe it, but Flouers was right. The man he had spent the past eight years jousting with over things like football players running and funding for the team, was unequivocally, one hundred percent right. McNeal got up to walk away, but Flouers gestured for him to wait a minute.

"Anyway, Joe, think about what I said. I know you and I haven't always seen eye to eye, but despite this, I do realize you have done a lot for the track and field programs here at O'Connell. I'd hate to lose you, Joe, but my number one responsibility is the kids. They need to know they have a head coach they can count on to be there on the day of the big race. So just do me a favor and make sure you're still that guy. OK?"

"Yeah, sure, Butch. Now if I decide that, for the time being, I'm not 'that guy' but by the fall, I've done what I need to do, will I be able to return to my position?"

"I guess that depends on how we handle the situation. If we hire from within and just have the current staff take over, and see if we can get a faculty member with some experience to help out a little, then yeah, I don't think that would be a problem. But if for some reason, Myers doesn't think he can take over the girls' and still be effective coaching the boys' team, and we hire from outside, then...well then it wouldn't be fair to whoever it was, to fire them after one season, especially if they were successful."

McNeal sighed. "Alright, Butch. I'll talk to you later."

McNeal rose from his chair, opened the door and walked down the hallway toward the track office. Eighth period, the last of the day, had just let out and the hallways bustled with activity as kids rushed to their lockers before catching their bus home. Athletes headed for the locker room, equipment bags in hand, ready to change into their practice gear. McNeal had discovered many an athlete simply by patrolling the halls, looking for students that had "it." What "it" meant was hard to define, but McNeal had a knack for knowing when he saw it. Sometimes, it was a tall, slender future high jumper, or maybe a brutishly large football player to throw the shot and discus. Today, though, discovering the next high jump champion was the farthest thing from his mind. While it was true that Millrose might just be the beginning of conflicts between competing and coaching, he couldn't help but think Flouers might have an ulterior motive. McNeal couldn't get over the possibility that Flouers might have just been jumping at an opportunity to rid himself of a thorn in his side. A novice coach would be less likely to have the whiskers necessary to stand up to Flouers. Regardless of Butch Flouers' intentions, McNeal needed to address the upcoming conflict with his team.

The Wildcats completed their usual warm-up routine of jogging and stretching, mixed in with the usual mix of giggles that came with large gatherings of adolescent girls. McNeal then called the ladies in to gather for the usual pre-practice meeting.

"Alright ladies, before we get started with practice I need to address something."

The girls scanned the room with worried looks on their faces, wondering if they had done something wrong.

"Don't worry girls, no one is in trouble," McNeal said to alleviate the looks of concern. "I've got good news, and I've got not so good news. I'm going to start with the good news. As most of you know, I've been seriously training the last several months. And it's been going pretty well. So good, in fact, that I was invited to run the Wanamaker Mile at next week's Millrose Games. Now for those of you who don't..."

McNeal was interrupted by the excited screams of the girls on the team who knew what a big deal Millrose was.

"Coach, we know what Millrose is. What do you think we are a bunch of noobs?" asked senior sprinter Kelly Barnaby.

"Sorry, Kell, but some of the freshmen and newcomers actually are a bunch of 'noobs'."

"Trust me, Coach, we all know that this is like, a huge deal. Won't that Kenyan guy who's now an American be running?"

"Yes, Bernard Lagat will be in the race."

"Didn't he win, like, two gold medals at the Olympics or something last year?" asked Kelsey Sullivan.

"Well, he won two gold medals last summer, but they were in the World Championships, not the Olympics, Kels. The Olympics are only every four years, and this is an Olympic year."

"How about that big Aussie? You know the one who always says crazy stuff on TV like about the...well you know the one?" asked Brittany Ansley.

"I assume you're referring to Craig Mottram, Brit? Good job editing yourself, by the way. Yes, he'll also be in the race."

McNeal's runners impressed him with their knowledge of the sport. He had tried to impart a love of track and field through exposure to big meets, bringing in newspaper and magazine clippings about different runners, and showing movies like Pre and Chariots of Fire.

"So, uh, Coach, we knew you were fast, but we didn't know you were that fast. That's pretty impressive stuff," said Barnaby.

"Thanks, I guess, Kell. I'm not quite that fast, anyway. I mean, I'll be in the race with those guys, but I don't think they'll be too worried about me beating them. They shouldn't be anyway."

Sullivan jumped all over McNeal. "Whoa, Coach! What's up with that? If one of us ever said that, you'd jump down our throat! No negative thinking."

"I'm not being negative, I'm just saying."

"Exactly! Just saying means you're thinking it too. Geesh, don't you learn anything from us?" The girls erupted into laughter as McNeal stood there, smiling and shaking his head. If he did have to resign, he was certainly going to miss them.

"So, Coach, what's this bad news?" asked Elissa Ellington, a promising 6' tall sophomore high jumper.

"Well, the Millrose Games are next Friday night in New York, the same night of Meet as Champs."

Sullivan frowned and shook her head. "So you're not running at Millrose? That sucks."

"Not exactly, Brit. I will be running Millrose. It's too good an opportunity for me to turn down. I won't be at the Meet of Champs. Coach Myers and Coach Williams will be accompanying the team."

A few of the underclassmen groaned upon hearing the 'bad news'. Some of the older girls shot a quick glance at them and they immediately quieted down.

"It's alright, Coach. We'll be ok. You don't need to worry 'bout us none," said senior distance runner Mary Sherman.

"I'm sure you ladies will be just fine. If I've done my job at all this year, you will be just fine. And trust me, Coach Myers and I will be in constant phone contact so I'll be getting updates about what's going on."

"And we'll be getting updates about you."

"Well, if it's good you will, Kell."

"It'll be good, Coach Mac, don't even sweat it."

"Thanks." McNeal wished he had the same sense of confidence.

chapter 20

THE SUNDAY BEFORE Millrose brought another major snowstorm to the Eastern seaboard. The local TV meteorologists had been hyping the "winter event" since mid-week, promising significant accumulation. Significant accumulation could range from a couple of inches to upwards of a foot. In this situation, it would eventually mean a whopping thirty inches for Philadelphia. McNeal stared out the window as the snow fell for an eleventh consecutive hour with no sign of letting up. "This is exactly how I envisioned the last week before the biggest race of my life beginning."

Cooper tried to be positive. "I guess we're finally giving the Family Fitness Center a try."

"Guess so, Coop, I guess so." McNeal continued staring out the window, watching the snow pile up, his thoughts wandering from Millrose, to his conversation with Butch Flouers, to Maria Richards. They had spoken several times in the past week, but had not yet met for dinner.

Cooper walked to his bedroom. "Alright, Mac, I'm going to bed. Get some rest and we'll get to the gym tomorrow night."

McNeal's eyes remained glued to the snow. "Goodnight, Coop."

The next night found McNeal and Cooper testing the indoor track at the Family Fitness Center. The elevated, wooden track numbered sixteen laps to the mile, creating some tough turns. It measured six-feet wide, divided into two separate lanes, a walking lane on the inside, and a jogging lane on the outside. There was no designated lane, however, for those who planned on hurling around the small oval at breakneck speeds.

McNeal had called Seamus O'Toole earlier in the day asking if he could do some real, honest to goodness speed work. He wanted something to tell him his legs were sharp and prepared to take on the likes of Lagat and Mottram. O'Toole remained steadfast in his belief that now was not the time. "Joseph, if we put the cow out to graze too soon, do you know what's going to happen?"

"I'm going to run faster than if I stay in the barn all day."

"You might, Joe. You very well might. But you know what else is going to happen. The bloody cow is going to get fat and become dinner. We need to stick to the plan, Joseph. I told you when I agreed to coach you guys that first we get strong, and then we get fast. Just because you got into the Millrose Games doesn't mean we scrap the whole damn plan. It doesn't work that way. You should know better, Joseph McNeal. Besides, between the drills, the hills, and the once a week short sprints, you'll have plenty of speed in the reserves."

McNeal hadn't expected such a powerful response from O'Toole, who was waiting in a London airport for his return flight to the states. O'Toole did relent slightly and allow him to run thousands, albeit at a pace much more pedestrian than he would encounter at Madison Square Garden. The workout called for 10x1000 at 2:20 pace for the 800 meters, with a 200 meter jog in between. After a two mile warm-up, McNeal and Cooper stepped into a yoga room that served as a makeshift warm-up area for stretching and drills.

Cooper sat on the ground and reached for his toes. "What do you think of the track, Mac?"

McNeal swung his leg back and forth as he supported himself against a wall. "It's got some bounce. I'm curious to see how well we navigate the turns once we turn up the intensity a notch."

"Especially if it gets crowded. Could get ugly."

During the warm-up, their sole company consisted of an elderly woman walking on the inside. McNeal stepped onto the track, to find a pair of chatty teenage girls walking side by side across the entire width of the track, save for a small two-foot space on the inside. To further complicate matters, both wore headphones, making communication with the two gum chompers extremely difficult. "Let's jog a lap to get started here, Coop, and ask the girls to give us some room on the outside."

Cooper nodded his head in agreement and they set off around the elevated oval.

McNeal paused as he approached the pair of walkers. "Excuse me, ladies?"

The taller of the two removed her earpiece, looked at her friend and rolled her eyes, probably mistaking McNeal for a gym prowler whose primary interest in working out at a gym is talking to women. "What?"

"My buddy and I are gonna be zipping around the track pretty quick and I was just hoping you girls could give us the outside."

"Oh." She glanced at her friend, who nodded in approval. "Sure. No problem."

McNeal smiled. "Thanks. Have a good walk."

McNeal and Cooper jogged across the track to the designated starting line. It was right near a pair of plastic potted palm trees. McNeal heard the two teenagers giggle as they ran off.

"Nice work there, McNeal. That was easier than I thought it would be."

"A little bit of niceness goes a long way, Coop."

"A little bit of niceness and your teeny-bopper appeal with that flowing mane of curls."

"Coop, before we get this workout started, I just want to let you know that you are never to refer to my hair as a 'flowing mane of curls' again. Two-twenty pace, that's thirty-five seconds a 200?"

"Yeah, or 17.5 per lap. How about luscious locks of gold?"

"Coop, my hair's brown. Now enough about my hair. Let's go."

The plan was to alternate the lead each repeat. McNeal had the odds and would therefore lead the first one. He passed the 400 meter mark in seventy seconds flat and continued on pace for the remainder of the rep. The three walkers on the track had not proven to be an obstacle. Cooper's legs slipped out a little on the far turn, as he attempted to adjust to the dimensions of the track. McNeal, with a more compact stride, was better equipped to handle the turns. Despite this, Cooper paced the next thousand perfectly, hitting each two hundred in thirty-five seconds flat. They maintained that precise rhythm for the first half of the workout.

"How you feel, Coop?"

"Pretty good, Mac. Getting used to these tight turns. Does it seem easy?"

"Kind of. I think it's the quickness of the lap change. Every hundred meters you get to check on the pace. There's no time to fall asleep."

By now it was time to go. The track had completely emptied. McNeal decided to pick up the pace a bit on the seventh to see how he felt. This time they hit the quarter mile mark in 68.7 seconds, held it through the half at 2:17 and finished in thirty-three seconds, for a total time of 2:50, five seconds faster than the previous six.

Cooper cautioned McNeal as they jogged the recovery. "Let's not get too carried away, Joe. Remember you got Millrose on Friday."

"I know, Coop. Just pushing it a little bit. Still felt relaxed right?"

"Agreed. Remember, though Millrose isn't just any race, now is it? Make sure you keep those legs fresh."

McNeal nodded. "Point taken. We'll stay under control."

Cooper kept the pace as he led the eighth repeat, again hitting 2:50. The final two repeats dipped slightly into the 2:40s with times of 2:49 and 2:48. While circling the track one last time a large weightlifter type of fellow walked through the door to the track, which opened right into lane two, the running lane. Cooper barely missed running into the mountain of a man, but McNeal was not so lucky. McNeal ran into the side of the behemoth, spun to his left, lost his footing and began falling towards the ground, reaching for the guard rail that circled the inside of the track. McNeal braced himself as he prepared to hit the floor. His thoughts switched from finishing the last repeat, to now, just hoping to be 100% at Millrose. An instant before crashing into the ground, McNeal felt a tug at his shirt and was yanked into the air. His arms and legs dangled in the air. He looked over his shoulder to see the mountain man holding him by his shirt collar with a big grin on his face.

McNeal's capturer softly placed him back on the track. "It looked like you were about to hurt yourself there, buddy. You guys ought to be careful up here."

McNeal blinked. "Yes, sir. Uh, thanks for the...save. Sorry 'bout almost running you over."

The flannel clad man laughed a hearty laugh, fitting for a man of his stature. "Running me over? Ha! No offense, fellow, but I don't think you were running anybody over. Maybe bouncing off me, but surely not running over me."

McNeal took a good look at the man. He certainly would not have run him over. He was a rugged looking fellow, with a blonde buzz cut. His face was covered by a reddish-blonde beard, thick like a lumberjack. He wore a red and black flannel shirt and thick, grey cotton sweat pants. "So why you guys zooming around here like a couple of headless chickens in the barn?"

"Well, I've got a big race this week up in New York, and with all the snow outside, there's not exactly a lot of places to run."

The mountain man's lips turned up into a large smile. "Well, sweet corn on the cob! You runnin' Millrose?"

McNeal was shocked this large man with the decidedly southern mannerisms knew what the Millrose Games were, not to mention that they were this weekend in New York. "You know about Millrose?"

"Know about? Why, I won the shot put there three times. Once for college competitors when I was matriculating at Appalachian

State, and then two more times in the open competition. Gosh, I miss those days."

Cooper had now joined the conversation. "Wow, that's awesome. Do you still throw competitively?"

"Ha, I wish. No siree, I'm afraid that train left the station a long time ago. Well, boys, I'll let you get back to your workout and go lift a lil' weight. Maybe I'll come back up here when it's safer. Don't want to get run over or anything. Good luck, big fellow." The jolly giant laughed a loud hearty laugh as he opened the door to exit the track.

"Thanks. We're just about done. Nothing left but the cool down, I'm sure we could all fit. What's your name?"

"Hank. Hank Brasington. Yours?"

"I'm Joey McNeal, this here is Ryan 'Hot Sauce' Cooper."

"Hot Sauce, eh? Well, good luck. See you fellows later."

McNeal and Cooper jogged ten minutes for a cool down, the entire time talking about the gentle giant who had held McNeal in the air by his t-shirt.

"Dude, if only we had that on tape, man, you and Hank the Tank would be YouTube legends."

"Could have won the grand prize on America's Funniest Home Videos."

"Get with the times, Mac. A YouTube legend is way bigger than America's Funniest Home Videos. Way bigger."

McNeal's thoughts soon shifted to something else that could make him a YouTube legend, and more: beating the great Bernard Lagat. Nothing wrong with a little dreaming.

∂∞∾

Seamus O'Toole called McNeal the morning of Millrose to see if McNeal was feeling up to the challenge. "I'm feeling strong, Seamus, strong as I've ever felt."

"You're damn right you're as strong as you've ever been. That's no accident."

McNeal shook his head at O'Toole's unsurprising demeanor. O'Toole was nothing if not consistent.

"So I'll pick you up in an hour, Joseph. Any of the guys going up to watch?"

"Yeah. We've got one of the assistants running the Café today, so Coop's going with us. Maloney and O'Donnell are taking the train up after work. Could they hitch a ride back with us?"

"Sure, what does Seamus O'Toole care if those blokes ride back with us. I've got two concerns. The first is your race."

"Uh, what's the second concern, Seamus?"

"Getting a piece of New York style pizza, of course."

"New York style pizza? What's wrong with Philadelphia pizza?"

"It's a bloody mess. That's what's wrong with it. The sauce is too sweet, the crust isn't thick enough. I won't even begin to discuss the cheese. Make sure you're ready when I get there."

McNeal hung up the phone and double-checked his track bag for the usual assortment of necessities. Satisfied that he had everything, he made a peanut butter and honey sandwich on whole grain bread and sat down to watch SportsCenter.

O'Toole soon arrived in a rented mini-van. The ride up to Madison Square Garden proved uneventful. They left early enough to avoid most of the rush hour traffic. Traffic in New York could never be completely avoided, no matter what the time, but it could at least be minimized. As they approached the Lincoln Tunnel, traffic slowed to a crawl. McNeal reached into his bag and pulled out his MP3 player. He found his favorite songs from the Rocky soundtrack and began picturing the perfect race in his head. Soon enough, O'Toole had the van at the corner of 42nd St. and 7th Ave. "McNeal, the Wanamaker Mile is the marquee event of the night," interrupting McNeal's visualization. "As such, it'll be the final race to go off. Go ahead in while I park. Check in with the officials, get your number and anything else you need and find a nice spot to relax."

Cooper accompanied McNeal into the historic arena. Legends like Joe Frasier and Muhammad Ali once battled in the old arena. Willis Reed limped onto the court to lead the New York Knicks in the NBA finals. Mark Messier hoisted Lord Stanley's Cup on the Garden's ice. Hulkamania began at the Garden. Elvis shook his hips on the Garden's stage. Eamon Coughlin earned the title of "Chairman of the Boards" at the Garden. Tonight Joey McNeal would step on the same hallowed grounds as those American icons.

Cooper stopped in the hallways of the Garden. "How you feelin',Mac?"

"Nervous, man, real freakin' nervous."

"Relax, man. There's no pressure on you. No one even knows who you are. Run your race and see what happens. Heck, most people who see your name are going to assume you're just out there to get your butt kicked."

"I know there's no external pressure on me, Coop. But internally, I'm all knotted up. I mean this is what, my second race of the year, and I'm in water way deeper than anything I've ever done before. It's all just a little crazy. I mean it seems like just the other day we were hanging out after football when I said I wanted to start training again. Six months later I'm running Millrose."

"Hey, I got to admit I was skeptical at first on how far we were going to see this through. How many times before did one of us lament the sad shape we were in, and vow that next year would be different, that we'd lay it on the line for a year. Next year would come and go and we'd be making the same empty promise. This time was different. The last six months me, you, OD and Maloney have really gotten after it. That's why you're running at Millrose tonight. Maybe you haven't run as many races as you'd like to have, or done as much track work, but right now, you're in the best shape of your life. Go for broke and let the chips fall where they may. Besides, like O'Toole said, this meet isn't the end of the line. It's just a stop in the middle."

McNeal knew that Cooper was right but that didn't get rid of the butterflies. Countless times he had preached to his team about the difference between good and bad nerves and now he was fighting that same battle. He walked to the registration table to check in. "Joey McNeal, mile."

A bespectacled gentleman wearing a blue USATF blazer carefully looked over the papers in front of him. "McNeal? Let me check my list here. Hmmm."

Hmmm can't be good, McNeal thought.

The man behind the table looked up. "McNeal you say? In the mile?"

"Yes sir. M-c capital"

"It's not the spelling that's messing me up, Joseph. It's not like you've got some Polish surname ending in ski or something foreign."

McNeal fought the urge to laugh. "What's the problem then, sir?"

"The problem is you're not on my start list. Let me go back and check the computers. Don't go anywhere, alright."

"Uh, sure," McNeal answered, wondering where the official expected him to go. He reached into his jacket pocket and pulled out his cell phone, looked up O'Toole's number in his contacts and pressed send. McNeal held it to his ear, listening to the repeating ring, waiting for O'Toole to answer. After the tenth ring, O'Toole's answering machine picked up. "You have reached Seamus O'Toole. At the present moment, I am unavailable. Leave me a message and I will return your call at my earliest convenience."

"Aw, what the?" McNeal had forgotten that O'Toole did not believe in a cell phone. O'Toole felt if he wasn't home, then he didn't want to be bothered. A lot of good that was doing McNeal now.

The man in the USATF blazer returned to the registration area. Other athletes entered the area, checked in, got their hip numbers and went on their way. None of them appeared to have the problems McNeal faced. "What team do you run for again?"

"Team? I don't run for a team."

The man sighed and walked away from the table again. McNeal felt himself getting red. He could feel the glare of the other athletes as he held up the line. Other clerks were checking people in, but the lines would move considerably faster if McNeal could just get his number and be gone. McNeal again pulled out his cell phone, this time dialing

Cooper's number. Cooper, unlike O'Toole, owned a cell phone. "Yo, Coop, it's Mac."

"Yo, Mac. What's up?"

"They don't have my name on the start list. Is O'Toole nearby?"

"He's down by the track talking to Marcus O'Sullivan. I'll go get him and send him over."

McNeal waited as Cooper ran down to trackside. He didn't envy Cooper interrupting O'Toole's conversation with Marcus O'Sullivan. O'Toole possessed a quick fuse as it was and he could only imagine his reaction when Cooper butted into a conversation with a former world record holder. An Irish former world record holder, at that. He paced back and forth in the registration area, trying to stay loose. Finally he looked up to see O'Toole approaching. O'Toole shuffled over to the registration tent. "What's the problem here, Donald?"

"I don't see Mr. McNeal's name on the start list."

"You don't have Joey in the Wanamaker Mile?"

Donald looked up from his charts. "Wanamaker? Really?"

"Yes, really. What mile were you checking in?"

Donald's face turned a crimson shade of red. "The high school mile. I'm terribly sorry Mr. McNeal. With your boyish face, I just assumed you were still a schoolboy."

In less than two months McNeal would turn thirty and hadn't graced the halls of his high school in over a decade. The three men shared a laugh as Donald gave McNeal his hip number, lucky number thirteen. "Again, I'm sorry for the mix-up. Good luck out there, Joe."

"Thank you, sir. Don't worry about it."

McNeal could do nothing but shake his head and laugh at the misunderstanding. To think, he simply needed to tell the clerk he would be competing in the Wanamaker Mile and he could have avoided the last thirty minutes. "I guess that's what happens when nobody knows who you are," McNeal said to no one in particular.

O'Toole overheard McNeal's self talk. "Well, Joseph, I guess we're going to have to change that. What do you say?"

McNeal smiled an uneasy smile.

"Trust me, Joseph. You're ready to step up to the big leagues. I know you're worried about the amount of speed and anaerobic development you've done, but with your natural wheels and the aerobic base we've laid down, you're an animal right now. A caged, wild animal. Once that gun goes off, let those animal instincts take over. Mottram is probably going to push the early pace, right behind the rabbit, and Lagat is going to go with him. I want you to be right in the thick of the next pack."

McNeal nodded his head at O'Toole's instructions.

O'Toole moved closer to McNeal, practically whispering in his ear. "Put yourself in the mix. Stay there until you've got a quarter mile left and then run like the bloody wind."

McNeal listened to O'Toole's plan before jogging to the bathroom. The nerves had wrecked havoc on his digestive system. Five minutes later, he opened the stall door and walked straight into Craig Mottram. "Sorry 'bout that," mumbled McNeal, unaware of who he just bumped.

"No problem, Yank."

McNeal immediately noticed the Australian accent. His first thought was to ask the charismatic Aussie for his autograph. He quickly thought better of it, realizing he'd be a competitor of Mottram's in a matter of hours. McNeal imagined it in his head, him trotting up to the line, Mottram seeing him thinking "Isn't that the bloke who asked for my signature in the pisser?" McNeal had no idea how many more races he would run at this level, but he didn't want to be known as that guy. Instead he wished Mottram luck and told him he'd see him on the line. A surprised Mottram stopped in his tracks. "Really? Who the hell are you?"

McNeal knew of Mottram's outspokenness from watching interviews on TV and reading quotes on various message boards, but was taken aback when confronted by the frankness of the Australian record holder in person. "Joey McNeal."

"No offense, McNeal, but I thought I pretty much knew my competition and I've never heard of you. You expect that with a Kenyan or an Ethiopian. Some twenty year old African bursting onto the scene to run a 3:50 mile. You damn sure ain't no African."

"Well, you're right about that, Craig. I ain't no African."

Mottram chuckled, nodded his head, and entered a stall. "Well, good luck to you, mate."

The mile was slated to start at ten o'clock, still two hours away. McNeal headed to the stands to talk to the guys and momentarily ease his mind. His parents wanted to come up for the race, but Kim had a playoff soccer game. McNeal assured his father it was okay to miss, even if it was the biggest race of his life. He had his time as the focal point; it was now Kimmy's turn. Besides, with the marvels of modern day technology they could watch it live on the internet after the game. McNeal gave Myers a phone call to check on the O'Connell runners. Myers assured him that everything was under control. In fact, the girls' had just won the 4x800 meter relay in a state leading time of 9:29.34. McNeal pumped his fist and told Myers to keep up the good work. Soon enough, nine o'clock rolled around and McNeal left the stands to warm-up. Before leaving, O'Toole reminded him of the race plan, and he exchanged the customary man hugs with Cooper, O'Donnell and Maloney. McNeal grabbed his bag and put on his headphones. Today's choice of music was "Number One" by Nelly. McNeal listened to others, like Chariots of Fire, and various songs from Rocky, but he kept coming back to Nelly, hoping to convince himself he truly was number one.

McNeal jogged for ten minutes, then entered the paddock area where he saw is old pal Donald. McNeal nodded as he walked by. The butterflies were still in full force. In fact, they felt more like small birds flying around his stomach. He couldn't ever remember being this nervous. He sat down to visualize his race hoping to take some of the edge off. McNeal took a deep breath and closed his eyes. He imagined floating over the Madison Garden Track. A thousand meters into his race, a loud voice jolted him back to reality.

"Milers, let's go. Time for final check in." The sound of the official's voice quickly returned McNeal to the present moment. He applied Icy Hot generously to his hamstrings and calves, making sure to also rub enough on his quads and hip flexors. Before a collegiate race, McNeal learned the hard way that the groin was a no-no when it came to the wonders of Icy Hot. A little bit of a slip up meant a world of unpleasantness. McNeal peeled off his pants and put on his spikes, keeping his t-shirt on. He wore a Bishop O'Connell shirt over his singlet, figuring maybe it would bring him and his team some luck. He also figured that today was not the day to wear a "Flash" t-shirt. The only miler in the field without a PR of sub four, McNeal had never felt like more of an underdog in his life. He approached the check in table where Donald, the USATF official, remained seated. Before he could say his name, Donald shooed him away, assuring McNeal that he remembered him. The mile was next on the track, the final race of the night. Back in the fifties, the Wanamaker Mile started shortly past ten o'clock so it could be broadcast on one of the more popular radio shows of the day. While the days of radio coverage were long gone, the mile retained its status as the marquee event of the meet.

McNeal took a deep breath, stepped onto the track and did a hard strider. It was his first opportunity to actually get a feel for the boards. The turns were sharp. His recent work at the Family Fitness Center might actually help him hold the tight turns.

"All milers to the starting line."

The moment of truth had arrived. The announcer introduced each runner to the crowd. He would save the crowd favorites Mottram and Lagat for last. The Garden announcer called McNeal's name third, simply stating that he was "unattached and from the cradle of liberty, Philadelphia, PA." McNeal toed the line, awaiting the starter's final instructions. McNeal wore black racing shorts, with a plain white singlet, a decidedly unassuming outfit.

The starter stood ten yards down the track, clad in a yellow jacket and kaki pants. "Gentleman, stand one step back from the line. I'm going to give two commands. Runners set, and the gun. Keep your elbows in. If you hear a second gun, come back to the start. Alright, gentleman, let's give them a good show."

Give them a good show? McNeal hadn't thought of it like that before. It was easy for the starter to say "Let's give them a good show." His job was easy. Fire the pistol into the air and avoid being run over. The job of the runners was a bit more difficult.

"Runners set!" Bang!"

The sound of the gun exploded and the runners took off, each jostling for position. A Kenyan runner, Noah Mgeny, was the designated rabbit. His job called for him to take them out in twenty eight seconds flat at the two hundred meter mark. Mottram and Lagat closely followed. The chase pack trailed, about five meters back after the opening lap. With the odd number of laps, the two hundred meter splits lay at various locations around the track. McNeal heard the timer call out "twenty-nine" as he passed the 200 meter mark firmly in the middle of the pack. McNeal felt constrained in the crowd, as if stuck on a congested subway car. He remained there through the four hundred meter mark, passing the quarter in sixty seconds flat.

"My God, he's on four flat pace," gasped Cooper.

O'Toole stood along the railing in the front row. "Be patient, Joseph, be patient."

O'Toole's words came too late as McNeal fought his way out of the pack at the 500 meter mark. He couldn't take the feeling of being trapped in the box, even if the pace easily bettered his personal best. McNeal shot into lane three and surged down the backstretch. He couldn't believe it; he was actually gaining on Lagat and Mottram. The rabbit still led the two, and they hit the 600 meter mark at 1:29. McNeal followed at 1:30, with the chase pack another second back.

Cooper, Maloney, and O'Donnell jumped up and down, frantically urging McNeal on as he passed. By the 800 meter mark, Mgeny had dropped out and McNeal joined Lagat and Mottram, passing the half in 1:59. What most observers figured would be a two-man duel was now a three-man race.

Go for it! Take the bull by the horns and go for it! McNeal told himself as he pulled even with the leaders.

O'Toole was beside himself. He didn't know whether to be angry at McNeal for not following the race strategy or to be happy since his protege was currently battling the greatest runners in the world. O'Toole's answer soon came as the crowd roared in excitement as McNeal took the lead. The buzz in the crowd was deafening as people tried to figure out who this interloper was.

"That's my cousin, Joey freakin' McNeal!" Maloney yelled to a group of fans paging through their programs trying to find the identity of the mystery man.

McNeal led the threesome through the 1200 meter mark in 2:59. The question now was, would McNeal be able to match the fearsome finishing kicks of his competitors. McNeal may have been known for his speed on the local track circuit, but this was a whole new world. As they neared 300 meters from the finish, Mottram flew by McNeal. McNeal tried to react. But his body was screaming for help, lactic acid filling his legs, causing them to feel as if they weighed a ton apiece. McNeal fought to remain smooth, but it was no use. Soon after Mottram moved, Lagat passed the now struggling McNeal. McNeal couldn't believe how quickly a gap formed. It was if the first 1200 meters of the race hadn't happened at all.

"Wake up, Joseph! Refocus and finish the race!"

McNeal heard O'Toole's voice and tried to respond. He dropped his hands so they swung close to his hips, trying desperately to stay relaxed. He was tightening up from his brow to the bottom of his legs. As Mottram and Lagat waged their war for the win, McNeal struggled in vain to hold off the rest of the field. The rigor mortis set in for good at the fourteen hundred meter mark. McNeal felt as if running through quicksand. The more he fought, the worse it became. The split on his final four hundred meters was sixty-eight seconds, making his total time a 4:07, ten seconds behind the victorious Lagat. McNeal crossed the line in seventh place, stumbled into the infield and collapsed. He gasped for air, sucking each breath into his lungs. Every muscle in his body throbbed, his head pounded and he felt his heart beating in his temples. All of Madison Square Garden spun in circles above him. McNeal soon climbed to his knees and crawled to the nearest trashcan where he deposited what seemed like a week's worth of food.

"Welcome to the big time, chap," said Mottram as he walked by, patting McNeal on the shoulder as he passed. "Good race. Hope to see you out on the circuit again sometime."

McNeal barely managed to get out the words "Thank you" before again puking into the trashcan. Welcome to the big time, indeed. He wrapped his arms around the yellow can and held on for dear life. "Dear Lord, please make it go away," he pleaded. The pain of the race was nothing compared to how McNeal felt now, his body shaking as he vomited. McNeal had thrown up after races previously, but never so violently. In the near future, McNeal would think about tonight's race with pride. He had actually led Bernard Lagat, a World Championship gold medalist, with four hundred meters to go. Granted Lagat and Mottram gapped him by ten seconds in the closing quarter, but McNeal still managed to run a personal record of 4:07. But right then and there, as he knelt on the Garden infield, McNeal harbored no thoughts or feelings of pride. More primitive thoughts like *When is this building going to stop spinning?"* and *"God, I hope I survive,"* filled his brain.

☙ ❧

Thirty minutes later, McNeal staggered up the stands to where O'Toole and the guys were seated.

"Good race, Mac."

"Thanks, guys."

O'Toole simply nodded at McNeal, but the grin on his face told McNeal that Seamus was pleased. O'Toole walked over to McNeal, placed his hand on his shoulder and began to talk. "Now in all of the days old Seamus has been watching track races—and I hate to admit, but it has been a wee bit more than a day—you, unknown, unproven, Joey McNeal running with—no—leading—Bernard Lagat and Craig Mottram might have been the gutsiest race Seamus O'Toole's eyes have ever seen. Might also have been one of the dumbest, but damn if it wasn't pure guts."

McNeal chuckled. *Even when complimenting me, Seamus has to call me stupid. Can't say I disagree.*

"So, Joseph, what do you want?"

"Excuse me? What do I want?"

"Damn it, Joseph, did I stutter? Yes, what the bloody hell do you want?"

"Seamus, I don't even want to think about eating right now. I just deposited a week's worth of food in a trashcan."

"Is that all you think about? Food and that damn dame. No, Joseph, what do you want from this comeback you and your merry men are on? What do you want to accomplish? I think we need to set some goals and I'm not talking about frying small fish here."

"Then what are you talking about?"

O'Toole's eyes lit up. "Beijing. I'm talking about the Olympics."

"Seamus, I think we're getting a little ahead of ourselves. I mean, 4:07 is a nice time, but there's a world of difference between that and an Olympic level time."

"4:07 with virtually no speed work. 4:07 on the boards of Madison Square Garden. Besides, we both know where your heart lies on the track."

McNeal allowed himself to smile. "Yeah. The 800."

"Exactly. Imagine for a second the kind of eight you'll be capable of with all of this strength you now possess."

McNeal grew silent for a minute as he imagined the prospect of running an eight hundred once he put the speed on top of the strength. It truly was a frightening thought.

"Scary, isn't it, Joseph? Seamus O'Toole thinks it be damn scary. I'm not saying to write it down in blood, or even ink, but what I'm saying is you need to start wrapping your mind around that thought. Make it part of you, breathe it, eat it, sleep it. Then maybe, just maybe, there'll be a chance."

"Ok, Seamus. I'll think about it, but wow, it just seems, like, I don't know, it seems a little crazy."

"Sometimes life's meant to be a little crazy."

With this O'Toole stood up, scooped up his bag, and descended the steps. McNeal, Cooper, Maloney, and O'Donnell followed suit and headed for the van and the two hour ride down the Jersey Turnpike back to Philadelphia. Prior to getting on the Turnpike, O'Toole got his wish as he grabbed a pair of whole New York style brick oven pizzas for the ride home. McNeal, still feeling queasy, passed on the pizza, instead electing to eat a Powerbar and drink water.

Maloney's house in Kensington would be the first stop. O'Toole exited I-95 at Allegheny Avenue and steered the van towards the infamous corner known as K and A, underneath the El tracks. Maloney lived a stone's throw from the corner. At just past one on a Friday night, Kensington Avenue was in full form. Women of the night, clad in faux fur coats and little else, walked the strip, gesturing to passing cars, hoping to lure a customer. Wobbly patrons from local bars wandered the avenue. Maloney, visibly embarrassed at the condition of the neighborhood he called home, attempted to distract everyone by asking about the following day's run. "So we going long tomorrow, right?"

McNeal noticed his cousin's embarrassment and tried to keep the conversation moving. "Sure, Mitch. Pennypack, anyone?"

Before anyone answered, O'Toole pulled the van to a halt in front of Maloney's rowhome. Across the street lay a vacant lot, strewn with garbage, needles, and other items more fitting for a trash dump than the midst of a residential block. For years, an abandoned building had stood there. It had served as an abode for squatters until the complaints of Maloney's family were finally heard. Looking at the current state of the lot, McNeal had to wonder if it was an improvement at all. Maloney's family had tried in vain to keep the lot in nice condition. Maloney, not exactly a green thumb, even planted a garden. McNeal participated with Mitch's family in a lot clean-up last year. But the task soon became overwhelming. The lot, which originally showed so much potential as a place of beauty in an otherwise ugly urban jungle, had disintegrated beyond the point where one family could cleanse its filth. Maloney's father attempted to involve several neighbors, but the lack of interest in their own block disheartened him. Eventually, Mr. Maloney called the city and had a ten foot high chain link fence erected, hoping to dissuade the dumpers and derelicts.

Vagrants had torn a gaping hole in the fence within a week of its placement. Each hole Maloney or his father patched was soon replaced by a larger one until an eight foot section of the fence had been knocked down, providing open access to the lot. Tonight, with the temperature in the low twenties, the lot was alive with action. A large metal barrel stood in the center of the yard, ablaze with flames dancing towards the sky. Several homeless men encircled the sphere, rubbing their hands together for warmth as they passed around a brown paper bag, sipping from whatever was inside. Mitch glanced over his shoulder at the group of men as he gathered his belongings to exit the van. He shook his head in a mixture of disgust, pity and embarrassment. Maloney briefly opened his mouth to say something, thought better of it, gave a nod and stepped into the cold night air. O'Toole fidgeted uncomfortably in the front seat. Maloney's unzipped backpack spilled onto the concrete sidewalk as he walked towards his steps. McNeal hopped out of the front passenger side seat of the van and helped him gather his belongings. "Yo, Mitch, don't sweat it, man. You don't need to be embarrassed. We come from the same place."

Maloney placed a book back in his bag. "At least you got out, man."

McNeal looked Maloney in his eyes. "You still can, Mitch. You know Coop and me would let you stay with us."

"Just leave my folks here in this hellhole?" Maloney shook his head from side to side. "I can't do that."

"Mitch, if I know your parents the way I think I do, they'd be happy for you. Heck, they could probably use the extra space with your sister and her kids living here now."

As McNeal and Maloney conversed, a familiar young face walked by, entered the lot and approached the group of homeless men. McNeal couldn't believe his eyes. "I know that kid."

"Who? The kid talking to Earl over there?"

"Yeah, his name's Michael. I taught him at Second Chances. What's he doing out at this hour?"

Michael was a thirteen-year-old African-American boy. He never knew his father, currently serving a prison sentence. His mother had been in and out of his life, battling a drug addiction. Michael bounced in and out of foster homes throughout his childhood, leaving him angry and with a short fuse. A short fuse that led him to Second Chances after getting into one fight too many. Despite his troubled upbringing, Michael excelled in the classroom and possessed a sincere desire to do good. He read at an eleventh grade level and was proficient in algebra. Currently, however, Michael appeared to be delivering drugs to Earl, one of the neighborhood drifters.

McNeal and Maloney walked across the street to find out what was going on. Inside the van, Seamus O'Toole wore a worried look on his face. "I don't like the looks of this."

McNeal approached the boy. "Michael, what you doing out at this hour? I thought you were living at Second Chances?"

The boy turned to see McNeal. His eyes opened wide and he began to stutter. "Mr. Mac, what you doin' here?"

"Dropping off my cousin. What about you? It's past one o'clock in the morning. This is no place for a kid to be hanging."

Michael became defensive and lashed out at McNeal. "Man, don't act like you care now. Not after you just got up and left us. You just like everyone else. You act like you care, like you wanna help, then when something else comes up, when it gets too tough, you pack up and leave. What'd you find a job teachin' those white girls you coach? We not good enough for you anymore?"

McNeal's heart sank. "Michael, it wasn't like that." He contemplated telling the youth what happened, but now was not the time. "But that's not important right now. What exactly are you doing? What'd you give to Earl?"

McNeal gestured across the lot to the vagrant who Maloney was now having an animated discussion with. "Earl, I thought you were done with crack. I thought we had an agreement. Every night I fed you with the understanding you'd keep drugs out of the lot. Now this?"

Earl stood clad in old, dirty grey sweatpants and a yellow parka, stained with what could have been alcohol, but just as likely was urine. He bowed his head as Maloney spoke to him, ashamed at being caught red handed. Earl's face and hands were leathered and his eyes hollow, the look of a man who had long since given up on life. His weathered appearance made it difficult to gauge Earl's age, but he appeared about sixty. Earl sighed and handed the drugs to Maloney.

Michael looked over his shoulder nervously. "Mr. Mac, I gotta go. I gotta bring this money to Big T. At least he don't think he too good for the hood."

"Yo, Mitch, who's Big T?"

Mitch and Earl approached McNeal and Michael as three other homeless men set up camp on the other side of the lot, oblivious to their conversation. The expression on Mitch's face told McNeal "Big T's" involvement was not a good thing.

Before Maloney could answer a black BMW whipped around the corner. The car was adorned with all of the trimmings popular in the inner city, tinted windows, spinning rims, a loud radio. Out of the car stepped "Big T", the local drug dealer, with four of his henchmen. "Big T" wore baggy blue jeans and a long fur coat with multiple gold chains dangling from his neck. "Yo, Mike?! What's the deal? You were supposed to make the drop off and then come back with my money."

The boy's eyes grew wide with fear. Stories abounded in the neighborhood of what happened if you crossed Big T. None of them had a happy ending. "I was just about to when..."

McNeal, infuriated at seeing someone so young with so much potential swallowed by the trappings of the street life, pushed Michael behind him and confronted Big T. "You know how old this kid is? He's thirteen and you got him out running deliveries at all hours of the night?"

Big T was not used to such flippancy. "Who you think you are telling me what I should and shouldn't be doing? Where you think he's gonna go? He ain't got no family, no nothing. We his family now. I suggest you fellows mind your business if you know what's good for you."

Big T pointed to the four men surrounding him, each nodding their heads. O'Donnell and Cooper continued to watch the developing situation but now stood outside the van.

Maloney stepped forward and handed Big T the bag of drugs. "Take it back. Earl don't need this no more, not around here."

Big T turned his attention to Earl. "Is that right, Earl? You don't need your crack anymore? Yeah, ok. Earl, you know you ain't nothing but a bum and a fiend. You'll be back tomorrow. Either way, I need my money. It was in your hands, it's sold. This ain't K-mart. We don't have no return policy here. Mike, did that maggot give you the money?"

Michael opened his mouth to answer but never had the chance as Earl sprinted and tackled the unsuspecting Big T. His crew stood there, momentarily shocked before dragging him off. McNeal and Maloney watched as Big T hopped up off the pavement, blood dripping from his lip. Two of his thugs held the now trembling Earl. "Oh, you're gonna get it now. Earl, I treated you real good. Didn't I? Let you get a discount. Hell, I even let you pay late a few times and this is how you repay me. You guys are about to see first hand what happens when you piss Big T off."

Big T pulled a seven-inch knife from his pocket and menacingly pointed it at Earl's throat. The blade of the knife reflected the light of the moon. He stepped closer to Earl. Just as Big T lunged at Earl, Maloney grabbed him from behind and wrestled him to the ground, knocking the dagger out of his hand and across the street. Cooper and O'Donnell rushed into the lot to aid their friends. The two men holding Earl threw him to the ground and engaged Cooper and O'Donnell. McNeal punched the closest thug in the face before he was hit in the head with a bottle. Instantly dazed, McNeal dropped to one knee. He felt the warm blood gushing from his head and knew he was badly cut. Maloney noticed McNeal in serious trouble and let go of

Big T. He dove in front of McNeal, taking a steel tipped boot intended for McNeal's head square on the shinbone. The impact made a loud, sickening thud and Mitch fell to the ground, clutching his leg in pain. Earl, free of Big T's henchmen's grip, again was on top of Big T punching him in the face. One of Big T's associates opened the passenger side door and pulled a gun from the BMW's glove compartment and walked toward the lot. Seamus O'Toole, who had frantically searched each runner's bag for a cell phone to dial 911, stood outside the van and raised a pistol into the air, firing two shots. The sound of sirens could be heard rapidly approaching. Upon hearing the combination of sirens and gunshots, Big T and his crew retreated to their car and sped away, first spraying a barrage of bullets in the direction of McNeal and his friends. Somehow, no one was hit.

O'Toole stood in the street, pointing at the van. "All of you, get in the van. Cooper and O'Donnell help Joseph and Mitch. They need to go to the hospital. Young fellow, you're coming with us."

Earl dashed at the sound of the police, not realizing getting picked up might mean a soft bed, a hot shower and a warm meal.

O'Toole started the van. "Hurry up, fellows. Who knows if those hooligans will return."

O'Donnell opened the passenger side door. "Seamus, I didn't know you had a gun."

"Len O'Donnell, I'm afraid there's a lot about Seamus O'Toole that you don't know. Now you and Cooper need to get those two in the van, pronto."

O'Donnell and Cooper propped up Maloney in the back seat where he stretched his leg across the whole row. O'Donnell then helped the staggering McNeal to the front seat. Young Michael joined them in the middle row.

With everyone safely inside, O'Toole began driving. "Joseph, do you remember where you were tonight?"

McNeal, still holding his head, looked over at Seamus. "I had a race, right? I must have a concussion 'cause I think I raced Bernard Lagat. Is that true?"

"Well, Seamus agrees you do have a concussion, but yes, my boy, you did race Bernard Lagat a matter of hours ago."

McNeal shook his head, but the intense pain caused him to stop. He felt groggy and wanted nothing more than to sleep. Cooper sat behind him in the van, trying to keep him alert, aware that falling asleep could be dangerous. O'Toole turned onto Frankford Ave and raced towards Temple University Hospital. He swerved in and out of traffic, from one side of the road to the other, ignoring all traffic laws. Cooper and O'Donnell sat in the second row, each buckled tightly into their seats and gripping the "Oh crap" straps located on the sides of the van above the sliding doors.

"Oh crap!" O'Toole whipped the van around a right hand turn onto Broad Street throwing O'Donnell into the window.

O'Toole sped through two red lights on the way before slamming on the brakes in front of the Emergency Room entrance. Cooper dashed into the waiting room, grabbed a pair of wheelchairs, and returned to the van.

O'Donnell opened McNeal's door. "I'm not sure when I was more worried. Fighting those thugs or holding onto that strap for dear life."

"Bite your tongue, Len O'Donnell. Seamus O'Toole is the best damn driver this side of the legendary Dale Earnhardt. The original, God bless his soul, not his kid. Although he's not so bad either."

"You like Nascar, Seamus?"

"Like I said, Len O'Donnell, there's a helluva lot about Seamus O'Toole you blokes don't know. Now cut the chit chat and get these two into the hospital."

O'Donnell pushed the reluctant Maloney in one wheelchair.

"I told you, Len, I can hop to the ER."

"Mitch, I know you're a tough son of a gun, but I'm not letting you hop there."

"Just wait 'til I'm back on my feet. Not only will I kick your ass on the track, I'm gonna literally kick your ass."

Cooper carted McNeal alongside Maloney. "Glad to see Mitch is still Mitch."

"Who'd you expect? Mother Theresa?"

O'Toole parked the van. "Let's go, young fellow. I'm sure they'll take a good look at you before sending you someplace safe."

Michael got out of the van. "Old man, I don't think I've got someplace safe to go."

O'Toole stood silent for a moment. "Well, hopefully that can change."

"Doubtful."

O'Toole and the youth entered the hospital. Michael walked up to McNeal's wheelchair. "Mr. Mac, I'm sorry."

McNeal looked up at his former student. "It's alright, Mike, it's alright. Just promise me you won't go back to Big T?"

"After the way you guys beat on them, I couldn't if I wanted to. Not to mention that when people find out his crew got beat up by a bunch of..." Michael's voice trailed off.

O'Donnell finished Michael's sentence. "White dudes?"

"Yeah, skinny white dudes. He's gonna be laughed at anyway. His rep's finished. But, if I were you guys, I'd watch out. He's gonna want revenge."

Cooper parked McNeal's wheelchair in the waiting room. "Mitch, do any of those guys know you or know where you live?"

Maloney stood on one foot, leaning on the back of his wheelchair. "Nah, I don't think so. Probably best if I stay with you guys awhile though, just to be safe."

O'Toole walked to the nurse's station to check them in. He made sure Michael was evaluated and taken to the pediatric ward. McNeal needed to fill out insurance forms before being treated. Maloney currently had no health insurance. Once McNeal handed the nurse his information, she soon called for him to go to the back. Cooper accompanied McNeal to explain the situation to the doctor. Maloney completed several pages of paperwork detailing his medical history as

Seamus O'Toole assured the front desk clerk he would pay for Maloney's care himself.

"That's why you bloody Americans need universal health care," complained O'Toole as a nurse finally wheeled Maloney back into a room.

A woman behind the desk looked up. "Remember that Mr. O'Toole when you cast your vote for president this year."

O'Toole cast the woman an icy glare. "Seamus O'Toole will remember what Seamus O'Toole wants to remember."

O'Donnell stood to O'Toole's right. "Do you vote, Seamus?"

"Do you vote, O'Donnell?"

"What? That's what I asked you."

"And that's how I answered you."

O'Donnell shook his head, and followed O'Toole into the emergency room area. A young Indian doctor walked out of McNeal's room. "You guys with the patient in room 101A?"

O'Donnell peeked into room 101A, saw McNeal and nodded in agreement.

"Your friend here is lucky. He lost a lot of blood, but he's going to be okay. He needed seventeen stitches. He's also got a concussion. He's going to need to stay overnight for observation. He should be able to go home tomorrow."

Mitch Maloney was not doing as well, however. The blow to his leg cracked his shin bone. The bone splintered, leaving tiny fragments of bone floating in Maloney's leg. Surgery would be performed in the morning. The breaking of the bone also pulled on Maloney's knee, causing his meniscus to slightly tear. The full extent of the damage wouldn't be known until after surgery. Mitch might need meniscus surgery at a later date, once the inflammation goes down.

After his evaluation, the doctor put Maloney on the powerful painkiller codeine and he was stationed in the bed adjacent to McNeal. With only the immediate family permitted to stay, O'Toole drove the reluctant Cooper and O'Donnell home.

McNeal propped himself up in his bed. "Yo, Mitch, how you feeling?"

Maloney grinned. "Not too bad since they gave me happy drugs."

McNeal tried to laugh but the shaking of his head caused too much pain.

"How about you, Joe? How you doin'?"

"Doc says I've got a concussion. He stitched me up. Took seventeen stitches. Worst part of it is he had to cut out a clump of my hair. What is Joey Mac without my beautiful curls?" Again McNeal began to laugh, only to stop once the pain resumed.

Maloney sat up in his bed. "A bad dude, that's what. You took on Bernard Lagat and the neighborhood drug dealers in one night. Not too shabby. You can't even notice the hair, anyway. Nice job out there by the way. I knew you could run but I didn't know you could scrap."

"Ha. Don't think I can. I was just getting' your back, cuz, like you got mine."

"Yeah, look where that got me."

The short-lived smile disappeared from McNeal's face and he looked down. "Sorry, man."

Maloney sat quiet in his bed for a minute. "What do you think'll happen to Michael, Joe?"

"They'll probably return him to Second Chances. Maybe put him back into the foster care system. At his age, it's unlikely he'll ever be adopted. Working for "Big T" notwithstanding, he really does wanna be a good kid. It's tough when you got no one to show you the way though."

"Yeah. Lucky for me I had you."

"Ha, your parents wouldn't have let you get away with too much even if I wasn't around."

"Yeah, you're right. But you showed me there's more to life than Kensington. That doing things right can take me someplace better."

"Yeah, to a hospital bed right next to me."

Maloney chuckled quietly. "Yeah, I guess the Mitch Maloney comeback story is over."

"Nah, Mitch. Temporarily paused. Just a minor setback."

"Not sure what your definition of minor is but I'm probably on the shelf for a couple of months. You know what this means?"

"That you're finally moving in with me and Coop?"

"Well, maybe. But besides that."

McNeal shook his head. "No, what?"

"You're running for both of us now. Every time you lace up your spikes I'm gonna be right there. You got to carry on the family legacy yourself now." Maloney saw McNeal grin and resumed talking. "I'm serious, Joe."

"I know you are, Mitch. I'll do my best. Thanks again for being there tonight."

"Just like you've always been there for me. Anyway, I know you'll do your best, Joe."

For Joey Mac, there was no other way.

chapter 21

SATURDAY MORNING, MCNEAL returned home. The events of the past twenty-four hours were a blur. In the span of several hours, he went from leading the number one miler in the world to standing in an abandoned lot fighting for his life. He felt somehow responsible for Maloney's misfortune. As the older cousin, he had always looked out for Mitch. Now Mitch was out of commission, no longer able to chase his dreams with McNeal, Cooper and O'Donnell. Mitch finally took McNeal up on his offer and moved in. O'Toole had placed a few phone calls and arranged for Maloney's leg to be operated on by a doctor he knew. When asked how he arranged it O'Toole said the guy "Owed him a favor." O'Donnell briefly thought of asking Seamus what the favor might be, but quickly remembered O'Toole's words. "There's a lot about Seamus O'Toole you don't know."

Late Saturday afternoon, Cooper, O'Donnell and McNeal headed to Pennypack Park to run an hour. Cooper placed his left leg on the rear bumper of O'Donell's Matrix to stretch his hamstring. "You sure you're up for this, Mac?"

"Yeah, I'm fine. Well, not fine, but I can run. How you feeling?"

"Eh, so-so. A little tight, but nothing out of the ordinary. How 'bout you OD?"

O'Donnell whistled. "Fresh and clean as a whistle."

Ten minutes into the run, McNeal dropped off the pace. Cooper turned back to check on McNeal. "Mac, you ok?"

"My head just—it's throbbing. I think I need to rest after last night."

McNeal assured the other guys he'd be fine walking back to the car and Cooper and O'Donnell continued on. Upon returning, they found McNeal sitting on a bench, head clasped in his hands. Cooper took a seat next to McNeal. "Dude, you alright?"

McNeal looked up. "Yeah, yeah, I'll be fine. My head's just killing me. It's like the whole world is spinning."

O'Donnell joined the two on the bench. "Hate to break it to you, Mac, but the whole world is spinning."

"Shut up, OD. You know what I meant. Anyway, I'll be fine. I think I just need to go home and lay down for a while. I mean, it sounds kind of crazy, but within the last day I've battled Bernard Lagat on the track, and a gang of thugs off it. I felt like I was going to die up in New York, then actually thought it was possible at one point last night."

Cooper stood up and walked towards O'Donnell's car. "When you put it that way, that's a helluva twenty-four hours. Kind of like that MASE song. If you had twenty-four hours to live what would you do....."

"Coop, classic song, but I don't think I'd spend any of my last twenty-four in an abandoned lot in Kensington."

O'Donnell opened his door. "How 'bout in a hospital getting stitched up?"

"I think I'll pass on that one too."

The runners piled into OD's car, and for the remainder of the ride home, discussed just what each would do if they had twenty-four hours to live. Opinions varied greatly, but consensus generally involved a favorite food, quality time with friends and family, and a treasured past time. For McNeal this entailed running one more half mile race, cooling down with a bunch of friends and family in Pennypack Park, a game of two on two basketball in his parents yard, and it definitely meant some of his mother's cinnamon French toast. Maybe coaching one last 4x800 meter relay somewhere in there if time permitted.

OD dropped Cooper and McNeal at their apartment. McNeal trudged up the steps, went to his bedroom and collapsed. He slept for several hours, dreaming a multitude of dreams. They rotated between dreams focusing on the events of the previous night and dreams recalling events of his youth. One centered on twelve-year old McNeal sitting in the bleachers at a basketball court waiting to get into a game but never getting picked. McNeal woke up in a cold sweat and walked into the living room to find Mitch and Coop playing playstation2. "Hey, Mitch, how you feeling?"

"Never felt better, Joe."

"Really?"

"Well, besides the broken shin bone and torn meniscus, I've never felt better. Plus, the pain pills make me feel a little giddy. So, yeah, I'm alright. Don't worry, Joe, I'll be back. I know I only ran one race at the Armory. But it woke the beast. And ain't no small setback putting the beast to sleep. Once the swelling goes down, I'll get my surgery, and before you know it I'll be back to the good old ass-kicking Mitch Maloney. Besides, old man, I just turned twenty-two. I've still got some time, unlike you. Heck, you should be out running now, 'cause that clock is tick-tick-ticking. You don't see many half milers breaking 1:50 after thirty."

McNeal took a step back. "Geez, Mitch, I guess those pain pills include a side helping of honesty. Chronologically, I may be the oldest guy in the room, but I've got a lot of life left in these legs. Not to mention, ladies love me, little kids adore me, and when old men reminisce about how good they used to be, they think of me. Anyway, I got winner. One of you dudes is going down. You think those guys in the lot were tough, wait til Joey Mac puts you in the figure four leg lock. Ric Flair himself would be jealous. Wooo!"

❧❧

Later that evening, McNeal and Maria went out to dinner at Applebee's. They originally planned on seeing a movie afterwards but

Philip J Reilly

McNeal felt worn out after dinner, and they decided to rent one instead. McNeal called Cooper's cell to make sure nobody was watching television.

"Yo, Coop? Is the TV free? I'm worn out and was thinking of renting a movie. Is that cool?"

Cooper hesitated before answering. "Go for it, Mac. Mitch and myself are grabbing a bite to eat. We might hang out a while so don't worry about it."

"Thanks, Coop. See you later."

McNeal and Maria soon arrived at the apartment after picking up a movie at the local video store. McNeal unlocked the door and began walking up the steps. He heard the sounds of an infomercial on the living room television set.

Maria looked worried. "I thought no one was watching TV?"

"You heard me call Coop. He must have left the TV on. What the heck was he watching?" McNeal led Maria into the living room where they planned on watching the movie from the couch. On the couch, however, lay a sleeping Seamus O'Toole, mouth agape, hand down his pants, loudly snoring.

"Ahh!" Maria screamed at the shock of finding a strange man sleeping on the sofa. "Who's that?"

"That, Maria, is Seamus O'Toole. He's our coach."

"Why is he sleeping on your couch?"

"I can't answer that question."

O'Toole sat up and yawned, raising his arms high above his head as he stretched. "Well, since I'm awake..." O'Toole again yawned. "I was waiting for you."

"Why? What's wrong?"

"No, Joseph, there's nothing the matter. I figured I'd check on Mitch and you. I see you must be ok since you're out gallivanting with this lass here." O'Toole frowned. "Women and training mix like peanut butter and mayonnaise, Joseph. No offense, lassie. I'm sure you're just delightful. But I digress. While I'm here, I think we should discuss the game plan."

218

McNeal gave O'Toole a puzzled look. "What game plan?"

"The game plan to get you qualified for the Olympic Trials."

Maria's eyes grew wide with excitement. She punched McNeal on his shoulder. "You never told me you were going to the Olympics!"

"Ouch, I'm not. Or probably not. Seamus this is Maria, Maria, Seamus."

Maria reached out her hand to shake O'Toole's but he merely nodded and continued talking. "Joseph, I think a lot of benefit would come with some altitude training. If you look back at the medalists of the last twenty plus years, almost all have done an altitude cycle. And right now is the perfect time. Right before we start getting fast.

"Seamus, you know I still have to qualify for the Trials. I mean I need to run at least 1:48.50 just to reach the "B" standard. It'll take 1:46 to guarantee entry."

"How about the 1500?"

"3:43 flat for the "B" standard, 3:38 for the "A"."

This gave O'Toole the fuel he needed. "So you are thinking about the Olympics, Joseph? I mean someone who knows the exact mark needed to get in the meet, must be thinking about it. Don't you agree, what was your name again? Mary?"

A confused Maria didn't know how to answer. "It's Maria. Sure, I agree."

McNeal shot Maria a stare that begged "Please don't encourage him." Just then the door downstairs opened.

"Great, I come here to watch a movie and we get a great big family reunion. I can't believe they didn't warn me."

"Mr. Cooper and Mr. Maloney, your presence is needed in the gathering room," shouted O'Toole as they entered the apartment.

Maloney's forehead wrinkled. "The what?"

Cooper helped Mitch hop up the steps. "He means the living room."

McNeal glared at Cooper who merely shrugged his shoulders and mouthed the word "Sorry."

O'Toole turned his attention to Cooper and Maloney. "Gentlemen, I have two things for you."

McNeal whispered to Maria. "The last time he said two things, he kept me on the phone for twenty minutes with a list at least ten items long."

O'Toole paid no attention to McNeal's comment. He had a captive audience in Cooper and Maloney, and he knew if he sold them, McNeal would have no choice. "As I was telling Joseph, the Olympic Trials are a little less than five months away. I think now would be a perfect time for a period of altitude training. Research has proven beyond a shadow of a doubt that it's almost mandatory for a runner to spend time in the mountains if he wants to run with the Kenyans."

"Seamus, if you didn't notice, my leg's freakin' broken. I don't think I need altitude training to learn how to use these stinkin' crutches."

"Sorry, Maloney, but I was referring to McNeal. I believe he should relocate for about two months before we really start hitting the track hard."

Cooper, while supportive of McNeal, had grown weary of Seamus and his incessant fawning over Joe. Himself and O'Donnell had run some pretty quick races themselves. "Seamus, and no offense to you, Mac, but didn't we arrange for you to coach the four of us? Joe, me, OD and Mitch. It seems as if all you care about now is Joey Mac and his new found Olympic dream. You know the rest of us would like some attention. It's not like we're a bunch of scrubs. Hey, maybe we ain't going to Beijing, or even to Oregon for the Trials, but a deal's a deal."

"Ryan, you are right, I did agree to work with the four of you. And I do want all of you to spend some time in the mountains. In fact, it'd be good to keep you guys working together. It seems to be working quite well. I know some people in Arizona who could help you guys settle in."

"Seamus, and I don't mean to interrupt here, Coop, but we all have jobs. We can't just pick up at the drop of a dime and go run our tails off for two months. I mean I wish I could, but I've got a team to coach, me and Coop both have the Café to take care of, and OD has a job. It's just not that easy."

"Point taken, Joseph, but this is a once in a lifetime opportunity. None of you guys are getting any younger. You owe it to yourselves to see this through."

"Seamus, I'm with you. I want to see this through, I truly do, but I got to do it my way. I've still got student loans to pay off, credit cards, real life stuff to take care off. I can't just get up and go. I wish I could, believe me I do. Seamus, I want to take this as far as I can, but I can't just leave my life. I'm sorry."

O'Toole paced the apartment floor. "Fine, have it your way but tell me this, how far do you want to go? That's the question. Nobody knows. You say stuff like 'see how far' and 'take a shot at it'. Well, damn it, what the bloody hell do you want to do? Cause whatever it is, you can't do it until you admit to yourself. So, tell me, Joseph, what do you want? Why are you putting in more miles than ever? Why such dedication to doing everything the right way? Why, Joseph?"

"I told you, to see what I can do. So there won't be any doubts, any regrets. And I don't think I need to go into the mountains to do that."

"Be specific damnit. No one runs with Bernard Lagat, and goes through what you've gone through without a concrete goal."

"He's right, Joe," agreed Maloney. "You tell your kids all the time. You've got to conceive it, then believe it before you can achieve it. What do you want to achieve?"

McNeal began to think. Deep down inside, he dreamt of going to the Olympics. He had dreamt it since he was a little boy. The dream originally took the form of anchoring the 4x100 meter relay, or of playing point guard for the Dream Team. As those dreams proved too improbable even for dreams, the dream evolved to wanting to be an Olympic half miler. After he became convinced he'd never get there in track, McNeal began thinking of other, less popular sports he had a shot at, sports like table-tennis, bobsledding, skeleton, and team handball. McNeal would see them on ESPN2 on a lackluster Saturday afternoon and become temporarily captivated. After watching the winter Olympics, McNeal researched bobsledding and saw that while he possessed the speed they were looking for in a potential athlete, he was too small. The governing body for skeleton, on the other hand, looked for athletes with characteristics similar to McNeal's. They even invited him to a month long camp at the USOC Lake Placid Training Facility. McNeal eventually came to the conclusion that since he didn't like the cold, didn't want to break any bones, and would probably be terrified out of his mind while flying face first down an ice covered tunnel at speeds in excess of 100 MPH, skeleton might not be for him.

Eventually, his Olympic dream died, like that of so many other aspiring athletes. But now, here he stood, running better than ever. He knew he had a long way to go, but if Seamus O'Toole, who had qualified for the Games himself, believed it might be possible, then why not.

"Fine, you're right. Deep down in my core, I still dream about going to the Olympics. I don't know how realistic it is, and I've been too embarrassed to tell anyone, but yeah, I'd like to make a run at it. Take a shot and see what happens."

Maria reached over and gave the red-faced McNeal a one-armed hug.

"That's what I've been waiting for you to say. Seamus O'Toole believes you've got the ingredients to be in the mix. That's all you can ask for, to be in the mix. Once you're there anything can happen. But, Joseph, you have to want this more than you've ever wanted anything else. You need to eat, sleep and breathe this. That's your only shot, to let it take over." O'Toole stood up, nodded at everyone in the room, descended the stairs, and left the apartment.

"Joe, I think I should go now. It seems like you've got a lot to think about. I'll call you tomorrow. OK?"

"What about the movie? I thought we were going to watch a movie tonight?"

"Joe, don't worry about a movie. I'm going to head out. We'll watch a movie later on this week."

"Maria, you don't need to leave."

"No really, it's ok. You should probably get some rest anyway after your backyard brawl last night."

"Fine, let me at least walk you to your car."

"A gentleman and an athlete, I see."

"Don't forget a scholar."

"Don't push it."

McNeal walked Maria down the steps and out front to her 2005 blue Volkswagen. "Gimme a call, ok."

"I'll think about it, Joey Mac." Maria reached in close to McNeal and softly kissed him on the lips. Goosebumps ran down his back as she pulled away. He couldn't remember goosebumps like that since high school. "Good night, Joe."

"Good night, Maria."

McNeal returned to the apartment to find Maloney and Cooper both already asleep. He sat down on the couch and turned on the television. After ten minutes of flipping through the channels to no avail, McNeal stood up and went to bed. McNeal drifted off to sleep, his mind again wandering in and out of various dreams, from O'Toole's Olympic talk, to Maloney's cracked shinbone to Maria's kiss good night, to his uncertain future at Bishop O'Connell and again to the little boy in the stands unable to get on the court.

chapter 22

THE FOLLOWING SUNDAY was a typically busy weekend morning at the Café. The weekend crowd differed from the Monday through Friday customers. Weekday customers were mainly commuters heading to work with a few telecommuters taking advantage of the Café's free Wifi access. There was also a lunchtime rush of sandwich orders and Joey Mac specials. Weekends were different; busy, but only until the late morning. Fathers woke up early to grab a dozen donuts to take home to the kids. When the Café opened, it kept the same hours seven days a week, open at 6:30 in the morning, close at 2:30 in the afternoon. While a bustling weekday lunch rush aided the bottom line, Cooper and McNeal soon realized afternoon hours on the weekend weren't so profitable. Eventually, they began closing early on the weekends. A major benefit of the reduced weekend hours was extra time to hit the trails for a long run.

After closing the Café at twelve, Cooper and McNeal met O'Donnell at Valley Green for a leisurely hour run. "The Green," was a runner's paradise, with a rolling five-mile crushed stone path and countless miles of challenging dirt trails. The Wissahickon Creek ran the length of the park, flowing over rocks and around bends. Ducks and geese swam playfully in the water, hoping to coerce a bread crumb or two from a passerby. All within the city limits of Philadelphia, a true urban oasis.

Cooper and O'Donnell were each entered in the Winter Warrior 5k the following weekend. It would be their first race since December at the Armory. They were anxious to see where they stood, to see if their bodies were responding as well to the increased workload of the past six months as McNeal's. Today, however, would just be a romp through the woods.

They began the run at about seven minutes per mile pace, and only picked up the pace slightly on the way back. They chatted about last weekend's events. Each man felt sorrow over Maloney's injury. The whole night seemed surreal to McNeal, as if straight from a movie. Mitch liked to say he owed McNeal his life, but it was McNeal who now felt indebted.

The conversation drifted to McNeal's battle with Lagat and Mottram.

"Wasn't really much of a battle," joked McNeal.

"Well, for twelve hundred meters, you had all of Madison Square Garden wondering who the hell you were," said O'Donnell.

"Joe, you really think you got a shot at Beijing?" asked Cooper.

"I don't know. I mean, I hope so, and O'Toole thinks I do, but I'm still a world away from that level. Who knows, maybe one of you guys will do something sick in that 5k next week and he can start drooling over you."

The hour run seemed to fly by and before they knew it, they were descending the steep trail that led to the parking lot where they began. Back in the lot, they stretched and grabbed a couple of bottles of water from the back of O'Donnell's car.

"They might be a little warm since they've been in my trunk instead of the refrigerator."

"Now OD, I know global warming is a very real threat. Heck, I've even watched that Al Gore movie. But it's February. I bet your trunk isn't any warmer than my fridge," joked Cooper.

"It's the sun. The sun heats them up, not the air."

Over on the other side of the parking lot, two forty something women and a man of the same age prepared to walk a pair of Rottweilers. Cooper had a well-known fear of dogs, especially those of the "man-eating variety" as he called pit bulls, Rottweilers and any dog larger than a toy poodle. O'Donnell figured this was a fine time to needle Cooper about that fear. "Yo, Coop, why don't you go do a strider?"

Cooper, oblivious to the pair of canines, nearly set off in their direction until loud barking caught his attention. "Real funny, man. That's real funny til I come back without a leg. I'm sure you'll laugh your face off when that happens."

McNeal laughed. "Aight, Len, we'll try to get together later in the week. You wanna go to the gym with us?"

"No way, Mac. I ain't trying to play hamster. I'll catch up with you guys later."

❧ ❧

February turned out to be a bitterly cold month. It seemed as if the temperature never rose above thirty degrees. Most nights, by the time McNeal returned home from practice at Bishop O'Connell, it was pitch black, and the temperature had dipped well below freezing. Cooper and McNeal spent an increasing amount of time training at the indoor track at the Family Fitness Center. One of the downsides was the time investment. The gym stood about twenty minutes away; a drive that easily increased to half an hour with the slightest hint of traffic, or snow on the ground. Add in locker room time, and it was nearly a three hour round trip from home to the gym. Ten o'clock increasingly became dinner time.

"This ain't no way to live," said Cooper after a particularly long day. "Look at this place. It's a mess."

"Coop, do you feel like cleaning? It's ten o'clock and we ain't even ate dinner yet. By the time Domino's delivers, you're talking 10:30."

While McNeal had made a conscious effort to better his diet, sometimes the convenience of ordering out outweighed the health benefits of cooking.

"I know, I know, that's what I'm saying. I don't know what the alternative is, man but I'm exhausted. I felt it out there last weekend at the Winter Warrior 5k."

"Coop, you ran 14:39 and it was thirty-eight degrees outside. That's freakin' ridiculous. You and OD were animals." O'Donnell had finished second with a time of 14:43.

"Thanks, but I could still feel the strain of this exhausting routine. I know I battled through it, but it was still there, man. I'm worried it's going to catch up with us. You know the quickest way to mess up a season is to get sick, or worse injured. By the way, where's your cousin Mitch at?"

"He's spending the night at his girl's crib. She took him to PT earlier and he decided to crash there."

"Seems like he's always there."

"I know. I think being around us depresses him."

"What? Now I know I was just commenting on what a mess this place was and how exhausted I've been, but depressing?"

"It's not us, it's the running. It's having something that meant so much to him taken away but still having it right in front of his face, day after day. It's got to be hard."

Cooper nodded his head in agreement. Unable to wait for the pizza, he made himself a heaping bowl of Honey Nut Cheerios and went to bed, leaving McNeal alone to wait for the delivery. McNeal used the time to call Maria, to see how her day went.

"Pretty good, Joe," she answered. "How was your run today?"

Her sweet voice never failed to brighten McNeal's mood. "Pretty rough, but ok. Did you get to work out?"

"Yeah, me and my roommate ran at like four o'clock. It wasn't too bad in the sun."

"Amazing, here I am trying to go to the Olympic Trials and I'm too much of a wuss to run outside, and you and your roommate are putting me to shame by braving the elements. That's pretty hardcore."

"Haha, me hardcore? That's funny, Joe."

The pizza finally arrived, and McNeal said goodnight to Maria. It was after ten-thirty, and the last thing he felt like doing was eating pizza. McNeal shook his head, stuffed the unopened box into the refrigerator, opting instead for an apple and a granola bar and went to bed.

At 6:00 AM the next day, the process began again. A morning run, eight hours at the Café, two hours of coaching, an hour ride back to the apartment, and then off to the gym for the nightly run. This was followed by yet another late night dinner at ten o'clock. Rather than order a pizza, however, McNeal, boiled a pot of water, tossed in some spaghetti and microwaved a pair of frozen turkey meatballs.

February ended with McNeal and the Bishop O'Connell girls' team traveling to Penn State to compete in the indoor state championships. In order to qualify, athletes needed to obtain a standard during the regular season. The Wildcats' focus was the 4x800 meter relay, an event they took much pride in over the years. While several of the members of the relay qualified in individual events, the girls collectively decided to run the 4x800 meter relay fresh, and then try to come back in the 4x400. In past years, Wildcat squads had placed in the top three at States, but were unable to capture the top spot. This year they entered the meet with a state leading time of 9:29, but knew they would need to run much faster if they hoped to earn the gold.

McNeal and the girls shared a mini-bus with Myers and the members of his 4x800 meter relay. Three of the girls on the 4x800 were doubling back in the mile relay. McNeal brought an alternate in case someone struggled to recover in such a short amount of time. The schedule allowed only an hour of recovery.

Both coaches knew the route to State College well, and assumed Lou, their bus driver, was also familiar with it. After all, Lou had transported the team the previous year. Myers used the time to nap while McNeal immersed himself in the day's sports section. An hour into the trip, however, McNeal's phone buzzed, and he looked down to see a text message from one of the seniors. McNeal did not particularly care for texting and was about to ask what the problem was when he looked down to read the message. "I think we're lost. Look outside."

McNeal glanced out the window to see a "Welcome to Maryland" sign. "Yo, Myers, I don't think we're supposed to cross into Maryland on the way to Penn State, are we?"

"Not any route I've ever taken."

McNeal stood up and walked to the front of the bus to see what Lou was doing. "Lou, um, we're in Maryland. I don't think that's right."

Lou was a retired truck driver who drove school buses part-time now. This was not the first slip up that occurred with Lou at the wheel, but McNeal had trouble getting upset at the affable driver due to the fact that he was just too friendly.

"I'm sorry, Joe, I think I must have gone the wrong direction on the highway."

Lou wore an embarrassed look on his face; if it was possible for an African-American to blush, Lou would have been blushing. McNeal sighed, patted Lou on the shoulder and returned to his seat, shrugging his shoulders at Myers' questioning of "What the heck is going on?"

Several hours later, the team arrived at the Super Eight motel a bit later than McNeal would have preferred, but none the worse for wear. As per team tradition, and in fact the tradition of many a high school track team, they went out for pasta at the Olive Garden. The guys and girls sat together, joking and having fun as they waited for their orders. McNeal and Myers dined at a table ten feet away from their teams. "Pat, I've got something to tell you."

"What's up, Joe?"

"This is my last meet. I'm stepping down after tomorrow."

Myers' jaw dropped. He tried to gather the words, but the shock of McNeal's announcement stole the sounds. After several seconds of awkward silence, Myers finally spoke. "Have you told the girls yet?"

"Not yet. I was going to tell them tonight, but I thought that might put unnecessary pressure on them. They don't need any 'Win one for the Gipper' motivation. I'll probably tell them when we get back to school and eat dinner with the rest of the team."

It was a Bishop O'Connell tradition that upon returning from states the entire indoor track team, whether they qualified or not, had a celebratory team dinner at the school.

"That makes sense. What about Flouers? Did you tell him?"

"Yeah, I called Butch last week to inform him of the news."

"What'd he have to say?"

"Pat, you know as well as I do that Butch Flouers don't give two cents about track. He couldn't care less. His only concern was who'll take over the team. He didn't want to have to go through a long drawn out process of interviewing various candidates."

That was precisely what concerned Myers. "Joe, it's one thing to take the girls for a meet, but I'm not sure...."

McNeal cut off Myers before he could finish. "Don't worry about it, Pat. I wouldn't drop that on you at the last minute."

"Then who?"

"Remember Chris Zimmerman?"

"Yeah, he graduated the year before I started helping out. School record holder in the hurdles?"

"Yeah, well, he's in grad school at Temple and available to take over for the short term. He's moving down to Florida this summer, so it's just on an interim basis. But I hoped you and Frank Williams could show him the ropes."

"Of course. So you're really going to take a shot at the Olympics, huh?"

"I'm gonna give it a try. This has probably been the hardest decision of my life, Pat. Those girls, well, you know, how it is."

"Yeah, man. They'll understand. It's obvious what a passion you have for coaching, and how much you give to the team. They'll know that if you're leaving, it wasn't a decision you came upon lightly, that there's a good reason for it."

McNeal felt a little better about his decision after the talk with Myers. It was something he had been contemplating since Millrose.

The recent string of late night workouts followed by ten o'clock dinners helped clarify things. McNeal looked at the outdoor schedule, saw it packed with potential conflicts and knew he had to step away, at least for the short term.

The meal concluded just after eight o'clock and the team returned to the hotel. McNeal reminded everyone of the ten o'clock curfew and of the rule regarding members of the opposite sex being in their rooms. He gave them his standard "We're not here for a one night vacation" speech.

At ten o'clock, everyone was accounted for and McNeal and Myers returned to their room. They turned on ESPN Sports Center to watch as the night winded down.

"Yo, Mac," called out Myers from his pull-out bed.

"What's up, Pat?"

"Thanks for helping me get started in coaching. I'm going to miss having you around."

McNeal smiled. "I'm gonna miss being there, man."

❧❦

McNeal barely slept a wink that night. He woke every hour, checking the alarm clock that rested on the nightstand. Finally at 6:03, McNeal decided to just get up out of bed and go run.

"Dude, what the hell are you doing?" mumbled Myers as he saw McNeal leaving.

"Can't sleep. Going out for a run. I'll be back in a little bit."

Myers shook his head, half in amazement, half in bewilderment and went back to sleep. An hour later, McNeal returned to the room. "Wake up, Pat. Let's go eat breakfast downstairs before the bus leaves."

"Joe, I have no idea how you are so damn chipper at 7:00 in the morning."

"Man, today's states. I couldn't sleep all night. Never can the night before a big race. This is the best part of coaching."

"You think so?" Myers sat up, pulled on a pair of sweats and slipped on his shoes.

McNeal paused for a second to mull it over as they walked down the hall. "Well, it's one of them. There's nothing like the feeling before a big meet where you get to see your team go head to head with the best there is. That's what get the juices flowing."

"Without a doubt. But is it the best thing?" asked Myers as they exited the elevator and sat down in the lounge where the continental breakfast was served.

"It's tough to pick one best thing. I mean I love coaching. The best thing might simply be seeing the kids develop as athletes. Seeing them improve each year and take an ownership over their own running. That's great to see. And the relationships you develop; having alumni return to see you and check on the program. That stuff's priceless."

"And you really think you're ready to give it all up?"

"I know I'm not, Pat. But I also know I can't keep running at eight o'clock and eating dinner at ten. Not if I want to be serious. I know it sounds cold, but coaching is always going to be there; maybe not this particular class and team, but coaching. I plan on doing this the rest of my life. This is probably my only shot to try and make the Olympics."

"When you look at it that way, I guess you don't have much of a choice."

"Yeah. This has been killing me for weeks. Like I told you last night, this has been the toughest decision I ever had to make."

The two finished their breakfasts of choice, McNeal oatmeal and an English muffin with a thick covering of peanut butter, Myers a bowl of Corn Flakes and a chocolate donut, and returned to their room to pack up for the meet. At eight o'clock the two coaches and all of the athletes congregated down in the lobby. McNeal did a quick head count before instructing everyone to board the bus which Lou had waiting outside the main lobby.

Before long they were inside the Athletic Center waiting for the 4x800 meter relays. At 1:30, an hour prior to their scheduled start, both O'Connell teams went out for their respective warm-ups.

"So Pat, how do you think the guys are gonna fare?"

"I'm nervous, but I think we'll do all right. Obviously North Penn is tough every year but who knows. You think the girls can take home the gold?"

"Can they? Yes. Will they? I hope so, but there's probably five teams capable of winning, so we'll just have to see what happens."

"Spoken like a true coach."

"Haha. I guess that was a little bit of coach speak."

The girls returned from their warm-up jog and began stretching. McNeal took this opportunity to gather the girls together for one final pep talk.

"Alright, ladies. Remember, we've done all the workouts necessary to make this possible. Trust your fitness and take a chance out there. Sullivan, you're leading off, make sure you get out and stay out of a box and you'll be golden. We don't need any miracles to win, all you have to do is run the way you have all season. OK, girls go get 'em."

The foursome grabbed their spikes and baton and headed off to the clerk of course.

"Oh, one last thing," McNeal yelled as they walked away. "Have fun. Don't forget that this is supposed to be fun."

The girls giggled a nervous laugh as they entered the clerking area.

McNeal was leading off the freshman Brittany Sullivan because she didn't know any better than to hand off the stick in the lead. Sullivan was fearless on the track and possessed experience beyond her years due to several summers of running age-group track. Running the second leg was junior Brittany Ansley, followed by senior sisters Mary and Colleen Sherman. Although in the same grade, the sisters were not twins. Mary had fallen ill as young child and missed a full year of school. From fifth grade on, the two sisters were in the same grade. Teachers tried to keep them separate through grade school. Colleen was the better student and they thought it might be difficult on the older sister to be outperformed. Once Mary discovered running, however, she found something to shine in, even if Colleen was her

equal. Mary's grades improved as she became more and more dedicated to the sport. Both sisters were now headed to Gonzaga University
in Washington where they planned on living together and continuing
their running careers.

The lead-off runners now lined up on the track. Since the Wildcats were seeded first, Sullivan stood on the far inside. McNeal worried
that she risked being boxed in if she did not react aggressively to the
gun, but his fears were quickly vanquished as she shot immediately to
the lead once the starter's pistol rang out. Sullivan hit the first 200 in
thirty-one and McNeal hoped she didn't expend too much energy too
soon. She passed the quarter-mile in sixty-four, holding a two-meter
lead on the field.

"Smooth and fast," shouted McNeal from his perch on the backstretch.

The chase pack closed ground on the third lap and heading
into her last lap, Sullivan led a tightly packed field of five runners.
Sullivan's form tightened up in her final fifty meters, the strain of the
race evident on her face. The lead-off runner from Cumberland Valley
passed her. She managed to hang on to second place, running a split
of 2:16.3, an indoor best. Ansley took the baton and immediately ran
up on the shoulder of the CV runner. It was now a pack of four teams,
O'Connell, Cumberland Valley, Northern Berks and their old rival
Springtown Academy, the defending state champions. It remained a
tightly gathered pack throughout the second leg until Ansley broke
free with 150 meters to go, unleashing a powerful kick to give the
Wildcats a twenty-meter lead. McNeal and Myers stood on the sideline, screaming wildly as she tore down the home stretch. Ansley's
split was 2:19, a three-second PR. Mary Sherman grabbed the stick
from Ansley and steadily expanded the lead, covering the distance in
2:18. The Wildcats now held a sizable advantage over the field and had
a shot at breaking 9:10. Colleen Sherman breezed through her opening
400 in sixty-nine seconds and the runner from Springtown Academy
closed to within five meters of the lead. Their anchor had earlier won
the open 800 in a time of 2:11. McNeal hoped the strain of the earlier

race and her fast initial quarter would take some of the kick out of her legs. By the bell lap, she had moved up on Colleen Sherman and taken the lead on the outside.

"React! React!" screamed McNeal.

React was exactly what Sherman did as she tore down the backstretch, pulling away from the fatigued anchor of Springtown Academy. With each stride she drew further away from her opponent and closer to a state title. Sherman crossed the line in first, her split of 2:17 put them at 9:10.53, the third fastest time nationally all year. McNeal pumped his fist in excitement as he watched the girls celebrate on the infield. With the mile relay less than an hour away, the girls jogged down in the infield as they awaited the awards ceremony, taking time to cheer on their male counterparts. The Wildcat guys completed the Bishop O'Connell double as they took down the five-time defending champion North Penn squad, running a school record time of 7:52.46.

The girls' expectations in the mile relay weren't as high as they had been in the 4x8 so anything they accomplished would be gravy. Running with tired legs, but boosted by their victory, Ansley, Sullivan, Colleen Sherman and senior sprinter Kelly Barnaby sped around the track in 3:59.85, the first time in school history a girls' mile relay had broken four minutes. Their time placed them third in the state, adding extra icing to an already sweet cake.

The girls and guys celebrated their achievements throughout the four-hour ride home, recanting stories of the season, joking and passing around assorted bags of junk food. With a bittersweet smile on his face, McNeal watched from the front of the bus, not wanting this last ride to end. He truly would miss this.

The bus returned to the school just after nine o'clock. The entire team, various alumni, and parents awaited in the cafeteria. The school cafeteria was adorned with decorations and a banner welcoming back the state champion relay runners. The kids exited the bus first and as McNeal gathered his stuff to step off the bus, Myers stopped him. "I know how hard this is gonna be for you. Thanks for everything. I've learned a lot from you and thoroughly enjoyed every minute of it. Make us proud, Joe."

The two embraced before leaving the bus. McNeal took a deep breath and walked down the steps and into the cafeteria where his team awaited him. Athletes, parents and alumni mingled throughout the cafeteria, laughing and joking as they munched on food supplied by the team parents. McNeal used this time to gather his thoughts. Speeches normally flowed easily for McNeal. He enjoyed the opportunity to entertain and inform a crowd, be it at school wide banquet, or a pre-practice meeting. Today was different. The lump in his throat the size of a golf ball made swallowing difficult and his palms felt clammy, like a nervous middle-schooler during his first slow dance with a pretty girl. After a few minutes, McNeal called everyone to take their seats so he could give his end of season speech.

McNeal began the speech with a recap of the ups and downs of the season. This was followed by the handing out of various awards, ranging from Most Outstanding Performer, to Newcomer of the Year, as well as some lighter ones, like the Wildcat Roar for the runner who consistently showed the most enthusiasm in cheering for her teammates. McNeal then began a review of his time at Bishop O'Connell. "When I took the job here back in 2000, I had no idea what I was getting into. All I knew was that I wanted to coach, I wanted to help young runners reach their goals the way some of my coaches helped me. I've talked about believing in yourself and your teammates, about working hard, and dreaming big. I think that we've done pretty good following that philosophy. We've won league titles, set school records, earned All-Americans, and today won a state title to match the boys."

The crowd all cheered at the mention of winning the state titles. McNeal took a deep breath. He could feel himself beginning to lose composure. Myers patted him on the back and McNeal continued. "The best part about this job—if you can call it a job, because I have loved every minute of it—has been seeing young kids grow up, seeing them develop not just as athletes, but as people."

The crowd buzzed as people realized something was amiss. Parents and athletes alike turned in their seats, hoping to find an answer on the faces of those around them, but instead saw mouths agape as everyone tried to grasp what they were about to hear.

"Today, I need to follow my own advice. As most of you know, I have been training pretty seriously for close to a year now. I have surprised even myself by how fast I've progressed. I didn't expect to be standing here giving this speech when I decided to train hard again. Heck, I might not have gotten back into it if I knew it'd lead to this. But I did and it has. Anyway, it's become increasingly difficult to run after working a full day, and then coaching. I find myself too tired, and often eating dinner at close to ten o'clock. In order to chase my dream of qualifying for the Olympics this summer, I can no longer coach here at Bishop O'Connell High School."

A river of tears streamed down the side of McNeal's face. He could no longer hold them in. He paused and wiped his cheeks with a tissue, but it was in vain as the wiped away tears were soon replaced by a new batch.

"I want all of you to know, however, that just because I won't be here coaching you everyday, it doesn't mean I'm going to disappear, or leave you ladies out to dry. Wildcat alumnus Chris Zimmerman will be the interim coach for the spring with boys' coach Pat Myers helping when needed. And don't hesitate for a minute to call me, email me, whatever, if you need something. Thanks for everything. Go Wildcats!"

McNeal stepped away from the podium and hugged Myers. He gazed into the cafeteria and saw the stunned and tear-filled eyes of not only his girls' team but of many members of the boys' team also. McNeal began the long, slow process of circulating through the cafeteria, hugging each girl, telling them everything was going to be just fine without him there, and thanking them for their kind wishes. The whole process took over an hour before the cafeteria finally emptied. McNeal surveyed the place where they had gathered day after day for over eight years. It had been quite a remarkable run ever since.

"You ready to leave here one last time?" asked Myers.

"I don't think so, but I doubt maintenance will let me sleep on the high jump mat."

At that the two men, who had first shared Bishop O'Connell as a coach-athlete relationship, left the school not just as colleagues, but as friends.

"Alright, Joe, good luck. I'm sure we'll talk."

"Good luck to you too, Pat. Keep those girls in line."

Myers laughed as he climbed into his car. He pumped his fist at McNeal as he drove away. McNeal slowly opened his door and sat down, staring out his window. The tears he had worked so hard to keep at a trickle now flowed freely. McNeal took a few minutes to compose himself, put his key in the ignition and turned on his car to begin the long, lonely drive home.

God, I hope I'm doing the right thing, he thought as he left the Bishop O'Connell parking lot one final time.

chapter 23

McNEAL STRUGGLED TO sleep for the next week, doubts about his recent decision plaguing his thoughts.

"Joe, I didn't get to see much of your coaching, but I know how much those kids meant to you. Sometimes though, life's about making tough choices. You've always been about giving, giving, giving. Now, this one time, you have to do what's best for you. Those kids'll be alright, you left them in good hands," Maria told McNeal.

McNeal knew Maria was right. He had grown so accustomed to the coaching routine that he didn't know what to do with his new found free time. Running during the day opened up the night for McNeal to spend more time with Maria, and actually cook more often. Contrary to the popular saying, the month of March arrived and it seemed as if spring instantly appeared. McNeal enjoyed the opportunity to train in mild weather for the first time since fall. Although he missed the day to day interactions of coaching, he believed he made the right decision. Summer was just around the corner. He still needed a qualifying time in either the 800 or 1500 for the Olympic Trials, which doubled as the USA Track and Field National Championships. They would be held in Eugene, Oregon at historic Hayward Field between June 27th and July 6th. McNeal hoped to qualify in the 800, but if the 1500 proved to be his ticket there, then so be it. O'Toole's training methods left him stronger than ever, and he felt comfortable in either event. The 800 was his first love, and much like a first girlfriend, held a special place in Joey Mac's heart. When remembering past 800s, McNeal was apt to fondly reminisce, recalling the victories and the battles waged with himself and his opponents. Not often thought of were the mistimed kicks, races where McNeal went too hard too soon, resulting in both of his legs tying up before the finish line, and him staggering the last twenty to thirty yards. Similar in thinking of an ex-girlfriend: the good times are warmly remembered while the healing power of time tends to gloss over the reasons she became an ex-girlfriend in the first place. While up to this point in the season, the mile had been McNeal's primary event, he was not quite ready to label the half a former fling. McNeal remained hopeful that as he added more faster running to the mix, his half mile times would improve.

McNeal awoke the morning of March 17th to discover that the early signs of spring were merely a tease. Snowflakes the size of quarters rapidly fell from the sky. McNeal turned on the radio to check the forecast. The weatherman predicted snow throughout the remainder of the day and total accumulation could top two feet. McNeal sighed. "Just when it seemed like we'd be done with the gym and that damn indoor track, Jack Frost slaps us across the face," he said to Cooper as he drove them to the Grilled Donut Café.

"So much for global warming. I can't remember the last time winter kicked our ass this bad."

Business undoubtedly would be slow today; it always was the day of a snowstorm. McNeal wondered if it was even worth the effort of opening up.

"Probably not from a financial standpoint," answered Cooper. "But from a goodwill and credibility standpoint, it can really help add customer loyalty. You know the Dunkin Donuts across the street is open. If we're closed, we risk losing customers forever."

McNeal reluctantly agreed and continued navigating his car through the storm. It would just be the two of them working today as their staff had called out. With the expected slow day, neither McNeal nor Cooper worried about the prospect of running the shop themselves. The snow continued to fall in droves, and by noon, they decided to shut their doors. Hopefully, they acquired some goodwill with the hardy customers who made a stop on their way to work, but they figured that by now, anyone brave, desperate, or just plain crazy, enough to be out in the midst of a blizzard had already made their stop. McNeal again took the challenge of steering his Aires through the nearly deserted streets of Philadelphia. After an hour of slow and sloppy driving, McNeal parked his car in front of the apartment.

"So what do we do for running?" asked Cooper.

"I guess we head over to the Family Fitness Center and hop up on the elevated oval. Unless you have a better idea, like running through the snow covered streets."

"The gym it is, then. The gym it is. When do you want the suffering to commence?"

"The sooner the better. What do you say we head out around two, get some mileage and lifting in and be back by dinner time."

"Sounds like a plan."

An hour later, the two runners once again braved the elements. Upon arriving at their destination, however, they found that the gym had closed at noon.

McNeal threw up his hands in frustration. "What the heck? You mean on the day we most need an indoor place to work out is the day they decide to shut down? I can't believe it."

Cooper shrugged his shoulders and headed back to the car. "Steps and core?"

"Whatever."

McNeal drove home and called Maria before embarking on the thirty-minute step routine that they designed during a previous cold spell. It called for alternating sets of ten flights hitting every step and ten flights skipping a step. "Hey, Maria. Enjoying your snow day?"

"You know it. How 'bout you?"

"Well, we closed the Café early."

"Wait, you even bothered to open? Why?"

"Something about acquiring goodwill with the customers and not losing them to Dunkin' Donuts."

"Hmmm. How many customers showed up?"

"Uh, five I think."

"Oh, ok then. I guess risking life and limb for five insane bagel buyers is worth it."

McNeal chuckled. "Yeah, the gym was closed too. I was kind of pissed. You figure the day you need the track they'd be smart enough so stay open. Now we got to do a step workout. "

"Joe, now you know that I'm all in favor of you and your fanatical running. But you do realize the gym employs real live people. People might not feel safe driving in a blizzard so you and Coop can chase each other around the track. It's not like the Family Fitness Center is on the list of necessities to stay open, like a supermarket or a hospital."

McNeal reluctantly agreed with Maria. Maybe closing the gym due to a blizzard wasn't all that ridiculous. "Well, anyway, I've gotta go workout. I'll call you later."

"See ya, Joe. Have fun running up and down your steps. I'm sure the neighbors will love it."

Upon finishing their indoor workout, McNeal logged onto Cooper's computer to check the weather. "The one good thing about a late season blizzard, is that it gets warm the next day, and the snow melts as quickly as it came," McNeal told Cooper as he checked weather.com to see if his theory held weight.

"Does that mean it's going to be seventy-five degrees tomorrow and we can break out the flip-flops and bathing suits?"

"Well, I thought you wore flip-flops all year? Something about it being your trademark."

"Yeah, they are."

"So then the fact that it's going to be a balmy twenty-nine degrees tomorrow shouldn't really disappoint you."

"What happened to your warm weather meltdown theory?"

"Well, I guess it was more of a hypothesis. More research is needed to make it a theory."

Moments after logging off of Cooper's computer, McNeal heard a long banging at the front door. "Uh, Coop, you expecting company?"

"No. You?"

"If I was, I wouldn't have asked if the loud banging downstairs belonged to your expected guest, now would I?"

Before Cooper could reply, the voice of Seamus O'Toole rang out. "Can somebody get the hell down here and let me in before I bloody freeze to death?"

McNeal and Cooper looked at each other in amazement. O'Toole did not own a car; he occasionally rented one when necessary. SEPTA, not the most reliable mode of transportation in the best of circumstances, did not exactly function on all cylinders during the worst storm of the season.

"He's your boy, Joe. You go let him in. Besides, he's liable to whack me with a snowball if I open the door. You know he hates me."

McNeal walked down the steps, yelling up at Cooper as he did so. "He does not."

"Does so."

McNeal opened the door to see Seamus O'Toole standing, snow covered from head to toe. O'Toole wore a yellow ski parka with a black ski mask and black leather gloves. He walked by McNeal as soon as the door opened, and shook off at the bottom of the steps.

"Seamus, what are you doing here? And how did you get here?"

"I need to talk to you so I walked here."

Seamus O'Toole lived several neighborhoods away from McNeal, a distance of at least five miles.

"Why didn't you just call me? Whatever you need to talk to me about surely could be discussed over the phone? I mean face-to-face conversation, that's only necessary for real serious stuff like breaking up with someone. You're not breaking up with me, now are you? Most normal conversations can be held over the phone. I mean, heck, there are some people who only communicate via e-mail and text messages nowadays."

"What the hell are you blabbering about? Damn it, I figured some fresh air would do me good. Seamus O'Toole don't let a little dandruff falling from the angels' heads tell me what to do."

Cooper joined O'Toole and McNeal in the kitchen. "Seamus, you want something to eat or drink?"

"Umm, you know what, old Seamus would love a nice cup of hot coffee. Black with whiskey if you guys have any."

"I thought you didn't drink, Coach."

"I don't drink that piss you call beer. Whiskey, now that'll put some hair on your chest. Besides, last time I checked, good old Seamus O'Toole wasn't in training."

Standing 5'5 and weighing nearly two hundred pounds presently, Seamus O'Toole was a far cry from the running machine he once was.

"No, Seamus, we don't have any whiskey, sorry."

"Then just a coffee. Black. Hot."

"How about we move this discussion about whatever it is that needs to be discussed into the living room?" asked McNeal.

McNeal and Cooper sat down on their green, fuzzy couch. O'Toole grabbed a plastic chair leaning on the wall and pulled it up a couple of feet away. He sipped his coffee. "You guys run yet today?"

McNeal nodded. "Yeah, we just got done doing steps, core and stuff."

"Stuff? What kind of stuff?"

"You know, like jumping-jacks, push-ups, drills and all. It was a good workout."

"Now correct old Seamus if he's wrong, the hearing's not as fine as it once was, but I thought that earlier you said you ran today."

Cooper replied this time. "Yeah. We ran up and down the steps a gazillion times."

"A gazillion flights of steps? Is that so, Joseph?"

O'Toole and McNeal's mother were the only two people on earth who called McNeal 'Joseph.' "Well, my boy 'Hot Sauce' might be slightly exaggerating the exact number of times we went up and down, but I know we ran them for thirty minutes. Then did thirty minutes of other exercises."

"Hmmm. Do you think Alan Webb was inside running steps today? You know it snowed in Virginia today too. Were you aware of that?"

"Um, no I didn't know it snowed in Virginia."

"Yeah, the Weather Channel told me. Anyway, Seamus O'Toole can guarantee your oversized calves Alan Webb did not run up and down a dinky little flight of stairs today. Hey, you, 'Hot Sausage'?"

"It's 'Hot Sauce'."

"Whatever. How many sub fourteen minute 5K guys do you think ran steps for a half an hour today?"

"I don't know."

"Well, I do. Zero. And as long as you keep doing that crap, it's going to remain zero."

"Seamus, there's a freakin' blizzard outside. We did the best we could do," said McNeal.

"The best you could do? Is that it? You know what the great General MacArthur once said? 'We will either find a way or we will make a way.' Where do you think this country would be if he settled for that pansy 'best we could' crap you're trying to sell me?"

McNeal opened his mouth but thought better of it. O'Toole stood up, nodded his head and left.

"Should we have offered him a ride home?" asked Cooper.

"He'll be alright. He walked here, didn't he?"

"Yeah, I guess so. I'm kind of glad he yelled at me and not just you."

"You agree with him?"

"No. I mean, I don't think so. Maybe? It just felt good to get yelled at."

"It felt good to get yelled at? Really? To think, I've thought O'Toole was the crazy one all this time."

To Cooper, O'Toole's tongue-lashing represented a sign that he cared about his progress and not just Joe's pursuit of Olympic glory. It improved Cooper's opinion of O'Toole. Although considering Cooper's and O'Toole's rocky relationship, an improvement wasn't saying much.

The storm ended around ten, but not before dumping over two feet of snow on the entire Philadelphia area. McNeal and Cooper decided, good will be damned, the Grilled Donut Café would not open on Tuesday.

McNeal stepped outside Tuesday morning to survey the damage left by the storm. Snowplows had done their best to clear the main streets, leaving huge piles of snow in their wake. McNeal had parked his car several blocks away in an Acme parking lot to avoid getting blocked in. Their small side street was plowed early in the storm and salted, but as the conditions worsened, more of Penndot's resources were dispersed to major arteries of the region. McNeal returned inside to find Cooper sitting at the dining table, eating a bowl of cereal. Cooper looked up from his bowl. "What's the plan for today?"

"For what?"

"Running wise. We gonna brave the elements today?"

"Wow, Coop. O'Toole's visit yesterday really hit home with you, didn't it?"

"Well, he's wacked two sides of the moon, but he's probably right. I mean one day of steps won't kill us, but we should probably try to get in a legitimate run today, you know?"

"Alright. Where we gonna do this? How about the Acme parking lot. We could do some pick-ups around the lot."

"Yeah, that'll work. I'll call Len and see if he wants to run. How's Mitch been by the way?"

"He's actually healing faster than predicted. It turns out it was just a hairline fracture on the shin and the knee was only a moderate sprain, not an actual full tear. He's been rehabbing, going to the pool and working out on the bike pretty religiously."

"Any idea on when he'll be back?"

"As far as I know, there's no time table yet."

At one o'clock, McNeal, Cooper and O'Donnell were carefully trotting down the street towards the Acme parking lot. Large, twelve-foot high mounds of snow surrounded the perimeter of the lot. The inner square of the lot, approximately a quarter mile, had been plowed and presented a relatively clear area to work out on.

"So what do you guys say? Ten times a minute hard, minute off?" asked McNeal.

"Sure, go ahead and pick something a couple of mid-distance guys would like."

"Yo, Sauce, we're looping a parking lot here, I don't think a ten mile tempo run is really fitting considering the circumstances."

O'Donnell nodded his head in agreement. "Yeah, Coop, I know how much you love flying around that little track of yours at the gym for hours at a time, but I'm not really feeling anything substantially longer than pick-ups. And for your information, I'm not exactly a 400 meter guy any more. Last I checked, you and I have been running the same races."

"O'Donnell, O'Donnell, O'Donnell. Once a sprinter, always a sprinter. You can't change your stripes."

"Spoken just as I would expect a bitter life-time long distance runner to speak."

The lot slowly filled with cars making the run an exercise in agility as well as a challenge to their fitness. The thermometer touched forty degrees causing enough melting to allow those fighting a case of cabin fever to venture out of their homes. With the forecast calling for temperatures to drop below freezing over night, many people headed to the Acme to stock up on food and other household essentials before the roads refroze. Without fail, as drivers left their cars and carefully walked to the supermarket, they would gaze at the fleet-footed trifecta with an open mouthed stare.

While the workout itself was nothing spectacular, McNeal and the guys felt pleased with themselves for braving the elements and showing true commitment to the cause.

"Nice run, guys. Thanks for getting my ass out the door," said a breathless O'Donnell.

"Yeah, man. That's what I needed," said McNeal

"I must admit it, that was a pretty good workout," said Cooper. "It felt good to get out and run."

"Even if it was a middle distance workout?" joked McNeal.

"These chicken legs got some juice in them, don't you doubt it."

"Man, that's exactly what Mac and I've been saying for years, You ain't slow."

"I never said I was slow. I just said I can't keep up when you guys start hammering two hundreds in twenty-five seconds."

They ran the mile back to McNeal and Cooper's apartment, carefully watching each step. Once at the apartment, Cooper opened up some music on his computer and the three completed four sets of push-ups and chair dips, as well as a fifteen minute core workout.

"So I guess tomorrow we open the Café back up, Coop?"

"I would say that's a good idea. I think by the afternoon it should be in the mid 40's."

O'Donnell stood up to leave. "This weather is wacked, man. By Friday they say it's going to be pushing sixty-five degrees. That ain't normal; a blizzard on Monday and Bermuda shorts on Friday. Al Gore was right, global warming is a nasty son of a bitch. You never know what you gonna get. You could go to bed and it be a nice clear, fifty degree night, and wake up in the midst of a blizzard, or even worse a fiery mess of ashes raining from the sky."

A bewildered Cooper began to ask "Who wears Bermuda shorts anymore?" but McNeal stopped him.

"He's on a roll, man; just let him flow."

"Alight, fellows, I got to get out of here before the roads start icing up again. Good job today."

By the end of the week the weather had broken, allowing normal training to resume. Business at the Grilled Donut Café returned to prestorm levels and when the long range forecast called for temperatures topping seventy degrees, spring fever had officially arrived.

chapter 24

MITCH MALONEY COMPLETED his last set of push-ups and walked over to the exercise bike he recently purchased from a yard sale for twenty dollars. He kept the exercise bike at his girlfriend Renee's house. Maloney was in his sixth week of rehab and had made remarkable improvement. After four weeks at Temple University SportsMedicine, his doctor cleared him to start jogging. Maloney progressed to running twenty minutes supplemented with work on the exercise bike. Maloney's routine consisted of performing a core workout, followed by a twenty minute jog, four sets of push-ups, or an upper body lifting work-out, depending on the day, and concluded with sets of thirty seconds all out on the bike. O'Toole devised the program to help rehab Mitch's knee while simultaneously maintaining his fitness and leg speed.

Maloney knocked out ten repeats of thirty seconds fast with a one-minute recovery, pedaling with a fervor rarely seen on an exercise bike. He tackled each thirty-second segment as if Lance Armstrong attacking another climb during one of his epic seven Tour de France victories. By the time he finished the tenth and final repeat, his sweat-soaked grey t-shirt clung to his chest, perspiration dripped from his forehead, and his legs wobbled. In spite of this, or possibly because of this, Mitch Maloney felt great. Maloney hoped this maniac approach to rehab would allow him to compete at the Penn Relays, a mere three weeks away, on the 24th-26th of April. O'Toole had entered the guys in the Olympic Development Distance Medley Relay, under the name Misfit Track Club. According to O'Toole "A more fitting name has never been given."

Maloney, if healthy, was slated to run the four hundred leg of the relay. A DMR traditionally consists of a 1200 leg, 400 leg, 800 leg, and 1600 leg. The planned order was O'Donnell leading off in the 1200, Maloney in the 400, McNeal in the 800, and Cooper anchoring with the 1600 leg. Penn would be McNeal's debut in the 800. For Mitch Maloney, competing at Penn would cap a remarkable comeback. It was early February when Maloney suffered a cracked shin bone and meniscus damage to his knee. Luckily, the shin injury was merely a hairline fracture and the strained meniscus was repaired with arthroscopic surgery, a minimally invasive medical procedure. He called McNeal to inform him of his progress.

"Hello? Who's this? Hey, Coop, do you recognize this number? I mean it looks familiar, but I just can't place it."

"Real funny, real funny. You guys know I've been busting my ass trying to get back."

"Just messing with you, Mitch. What's up?"

"I've got a doctor's appointment tomorrow. If all goes well, I should be able to really up the intensity of my training. I thought that you clowns might actually care that good old Mitch was on the comeback trail. I hope to be ready for Penn so I can run the DMR with you guys. You didn't find a replacement for me yet, did you?"

"Mitch, I told you, the spot is yours if you're able to go. So the rehab's going well?"

"Yeah, I think so. I'll know more tomorrow. Anyway, I was wondering if you could gimme a ride down to Temple for my appointment."

"Oh, yeah, sure. I'll just tell Coop I need to come into the Café late. What time you need me to pick you up?"

"Eight o'clock ok?"

"Yeah, that's fine. It'll let me run before I come get you. See you then."

McNeal awoke the next day, Thursday March 27th and ran four miles with a few pick-ups before driving to pick Maloney up at his girl-friend's house. Maloney practically skipped down the steps to the car.

"How's it going, Mitch?"

Maloney sat down in the passenger seat with a large smile on his face. "Good. Thanks a lot. God, I really hope this goes well."

If all did go well, Maloney would have three weeks to prepare for Penn. Not exactly ideal, but he could do a crash course of anaerobic work to get ready to run a solid quarter mile, and then start training with more of a long-term purpose. For now, Maloney simply wanted to get back on the track and really run; to just be one of the guys again. Mitch never competed in college, so this was his first opportunity to be on a team since high school. His injury helped him realize just how much he missed it.

McNeal drove the thirty minutes to Temple University with Maloney nervously switching radio stations the whole way. "Geesh, Mitch, pick a station. Personally, I like sports talk in the morning. You nervous?"

"You think? I feel like I'm about to take a final back in high school. I hated that feeling. Not knowing is killing me."

McNeal dropped Maloney in front of the office and parked the car in the in-patient lot out back. If Maloney wasn't ready to go, Mc-Neal had no idea who would replace him on the relay. McNeal walked into the waiting room, grabbed a copy of National Geographic from an end table and sat down. His right leg shook as he took turns pe-rusing the pages of the two-year old magazine and glancing at the television where the latest adventures of Jerry Springer played. Today's episode focused on mothers dating their daughters boyfriends. *Do these people really exist?* he wondered. While not a fan of tabloid talk shows, McNeal couldn't help but to pay attention. It was like watching a train wreck. Ten minutes passed and he looked down at his watch. His stomach felt nervous, as if he was the one seeing the doctor. He began reading an article about the communicating abilities of non-human mammals. Finally, after learning all the ways dolphins "speak" to each other, the door to the waiting room opened. Out walked a beaming Mitch Maloney.

"I'm good to go, baby!" Maloney grabbed McNeal in a bear hug. "Penn Relays here I come!"

"Welcome back, Mitch."

chapter 25

THE OLYMPIC DEVELOPMENT Distance Medley Relay was slated for Saturday April 26th at 1:00. Saturday was the prime time day for Penn; the day all of track's biggest stars came out. Highlighting the day was the USA vs. the World series featuring all-star teams from various nations competing in the 4x100, 4x400 and Sprint Medley Relays. These, as well as the high school Championship of America Races, were the featured events of the carnival. Most years they evolved into a head-to-head battle between Team USA and the tiny track-crazed island of Jamaica. The DMR followed the 4x1 so the crowd should be in a frenzy by then. Simply sitting in the stands had given McNeal goosebumps in the past; he had no idea what'd he do actually standing on the track in the midst of the hysteria.

With parking at Franklin Field next to impossible, McNeal and the gang took the 9:25 train to 30th Street Station and walked from there. McNeal had made the trip on Thursday to watch the girls from Bishop O'Connell compete in the Championship of America 4x800 meter relay. In an exciting race, the Wildcats placed fifth, the second American team, behind national record setters Eleanor Roosevelt and three Jamaican powerhouses. *I guess they're doing ok without me.*

The train pulled into the station at 9:57. The streets outside Franklin Field were mobbed. Vendors lined the sidewalks, selling everything from knock off Penn Relay merchandise to Oakley sunglasses—some even real—to an assortment of delicious Caribbean foods and island themed souvenirs. For one weekend a year, West Philadelphia transformed into Jamaica North.

"I can't wait to come out here and pick up a chicken patty," said O'Donnell. "As soon as our race is over, I'm out here. Heck, I might not even wait that long. I might hand Mitch the stick and jog right out the gate."

Cooper glanced over at O'Donnell. "Thanks for the support, Len."

"Hey, no problem, Coop."

Seamus O'Toole met the foursome outside the aged red brick coated stadium in front of the tennis courts. "So, gentlemen, and I use the term loosely, are we ready to run today? How those chicken legs of yours feeling, Mr. Hot Sauce Cooper?"

"Never felt better, Coach. Never felt better."

"That's good. You all need to be at the top of your bloody games today. These other teams are big time athletic clubs and want nothing more than to mop the track with your carcasses. I hope you fellows understand."

"Don't worry, Coach, we'll be alright," McNeal assured O'Toole.

"Good. Well, here are your passes. Seamus O'Toole has some gambling to do with my Jamaican brethren. I'll be in the northwest corner of the stadium if you need me. Good luck. Be smart and run tough."

"Is that it? That's all the coaching we get today?" asked Maloney.

"What the hell do you want old Seamus to do for you, Mr. Maloney? Hold your hand like a little girl? Should I remind you how to run the bloody quarter mile? Did your injury cause amnesia? Run as hard as you can til your legs burn and you don't think you can go anymore, then run some more, ok? Collapse and puke at the finish. Like I said, if you need Seamus O'Toole, you know where to find him."

O'Toole walked off towards the northwest section of the stadium. His balding red hair and Irish accent led one to easily forget that Seamus was a quarter Jamaican. His grandfather Colin Kelly traveled to Jamaica on vacation and fell in love with a beautiful Jamaican woman, Veronica Smith. Colin Kelly stayed there for five years, until their eventual divorce. O'Toole's mother spent the first twenty years of her life on the island before moving to the states to attend college on a track scholarship. It was while attending the University of Villanova that she met Seamus' father, Patrick O'Toole, an Irish miler for the team. The two married after school and moved back to Ireland shortly after Seamus' birth. O'Toole followed in his parents' footsteps and moved to the States to attend college where he developed into one of the world's top half-milers.

"That man is an absolute piece of work. If we all weren't running better than ever, I swear I'd fire him," said O'Donnell.

"Well, for one, we are. And for another, in case you forgot, we don't pay Seamus. He coaches us for free, unless you count all the meals we buy him at meets. But basically, he volunteers," McNeal reminded OD.

"I'd still fire him. I just wouldn't have to worry about notifying payroll or anything," retorted O'Donnell as they entered the gates of the stadium.

They walked into the stands, saw barely an available seat, and decided they'd be better off sitting out back behind Franklin Field. The scent of funnel cake, french fries and deep-fried Oreos emanated from the many kiosks in the area. Numerous sponsors set up tents back there, adding to the carnival like atmosphere of the meet. Among the many tents were Nike, the Army, AT&T, and Dunkin' Donuts, the primary sponsor of the meet. "I just don't get it. I wait my whole life to run at Penn, and the year I do, my bib number has Dunkin' Donuts on it," said O'Donnell.

Cooper pinned his number onto his green and white jersey. "America runs on Dunkin', man, you've seen the commercials."

"Yeah, but runners don't run on Dunkin'. Can you imagine going out there in the DMR after housing a vanilla cream donut?"

"I think I could break four after eating a cream donut."

McNeal and Maloney walked off to the restroom while Cooper and O'Donnell debated whether or not Cooper could run a sub-four minute mile after eating a cream donut. "Joe, what's Coop's PR without a donut? It ain't sub-four, is it?"

"Nah, Mitch, not even close. Like 4:15 or something."

The restroom was located at the bottom of a long concrete ramp inside the stadium. Once inside, the walls were one large metal urinal. Water dripped down from the top and the aluminum stretched around the entire bathroom.

"That's unlike any bathroom I've ever seen before."

"You never saw that before?"

"Nah, back in high school we always used the port a potties."

"Just another one of the charms of good ol' Franklin Field. So you ready to rock, Mitch? Your knee good to go?"

"Oh yeah, it's good. I just wish I had some more workouts in me, but I'm healthy as can be. Nervous as all get out, but other than that, I'm alright."

"Don't even sweat it, man. You'll be fine. Get out that first two relaxed but fast, work the third hundred and let the crowd carry you down the home stretch. Lift your legs, pump your arms and you'll be fine. What'd you run here your senior year? Forty-nine?"

"Yeah. Hopefully, I can match that. You ready for the eight leg? This'll be your first half, right?"

"Yes it is. We'll see if I'm ready. Last week I did a ladder where I went 4:35 for the mile, 2:03 for the half and fifty-four for the quarter. I finished up with a few two's in twenty-six so I think I'll be ok."

Inside the stadium, heat after heat of high school boys 4x400s circled the track. Loud roars would erupt from the seats every time a Jamaican team stepped onto the track. Soon enough, the time to warm-up arrived and the four runners ran ten minutes through the streets of West Philadelphia. During the warm-up they encountered members of several other clubs in their race, including New York Athletic, Greater Boston Track Club, Shore AC, and Nike Farm Team. All promised to pose a serious threat to McNeal and the guys, with Nike Farm Team being particularly loaded. The blocks closest to Franklin Field were flooded with hundreds, if not thousands of people. This made finding a rhythm difficult, but within a few blocks the crowds eased and they found a decent enough rhythm to shake out the legs. After the warm-up run, each man went through their individual routine of stretching and drills.

At 12:30 they entered the paddock to check in for the event. The best word to describe the paddock area at Penn Relays is chaos. Slightly controlled chaos, but chaos nevertheless. Runners from high school to the professional level gather and wait for a gentleman in a red hat seated on a chair high above them to call their event number. After an event number is called, the runners are herded like cattle to the next paddock area where they await the calling of their assigned letter. With literally thousands of athletes competing over the span of three days, there was not a second to waste. If a team missed their check-in, the outcome was potentially disastrous. The Penn Relays, like life itself, waited for no one.

"Event number 104, Men's Olympic Development Distance Medley Relay," yelled the man in the ten-foot chair. "Move up, move up. Let's go gentleman."

During the course of the meet, several different men serve as paddock chief. McNeal recognized the current chief from his days of running CYO in grade school. It was Ernie Forrest, former president of the CYO track association.

"Joey McNeal! How are you?"

"Good, Mr. Forrest. Yourself?" McNeal tried to be polite but was quite busy putting his spikes on and lubing up his legs with Icy Hot.

"So you've got a team entered in the DMR, eh?"

"Yes, sir."

"Team F, Misfits Track Club? Misfits Track Club where are you at?" Another gentleman in a red hat was yelling for McNeal and his team to check in.

"Good luck, Joseph," said Forrest as McNeal hopped on his one spikeless foot to the next waiting area.

O'Donnell walked with the other lead off runners along the brick wall that surrounded the outside of the track. In a matter of seconds, the starter would call them to the starting line. Above the wall sat thousands of screaming fans. The USA Red had just defeated the Jamaican men in the 4x100, running a blistering time of 38.79 and the crowd roar shook the old stadium. Maloney, McNeal and Cooper lined up along the wall, waiting their turn on the track. McNeal took a second to look around the stadium and take it all in. Over fifty thousand track nuts packed the over one hundred year old stadium, yelling and shaking it to its core. The awesomeness of the moment temporarily overcame McNeal.

Cooper patted McNeal on the back. "Yo, Mac! You there?"

"Yeah, man. Look around guys. Suck it all in and enjoy the moment. Track doesn't get any better than this. Now let's get the job done."

O'Donnell stood on the far outside of the track, practically against the brick wall that separated the track from the stands. Shore Athletic Club's lead off runner stood to his left. The field consisted of eight teams, Zap Fitness, Team XO, the Indiana Invaders and the four teams the Misfits passed while warming-up. The eight runners stepped up to the line. O'Donnell took a deep breath, trying to slow down his heart rate. His heart felt as if it was beating a million times a minute. BANG! The gun sounded and the eight runners took off. The 1200 leg posed many difficulties to most runners; it was too long to run balls to the wall like an 800, but a full quarter-mile less than the more strategic mile. O'Donnell found himself in the back of the pack at the 200 meter mark. The runners from Farm Team and Zap Fitness set the early pace. O'Donnell hit the quarter-mile mark at fifty-eight seconds, still trailing the pack.

"Move up, OD," McNeal shouted from his spot on the wall.

The runner from Shore AC began falling off the pace and O'Donnell moved past him on the backstretch. The half mile split read 1:58 and O'Donnell sat in sixth place after passing the lead-off leg from NYAC. Zap Fitness, Team XO and Nike Farm Team had distanced themselves from the field, all passing the half mile mark at 1:54. O'Donnell now felt the burning as his legs began to fill with lactic acid. The crowd cheered loudly as the announcer referred to the Misfits as the "Philadelphia Misfits." O'Donnell closed the gap on the runners in fourth and fifth place throughout the next two hundred meters. With 150 meters to go, O'Donnell unleashed a lethal kick, his arms pumping and his legs lifting as he powerfully sprinted down the homestretch. O'Donnell galloped past the Greater Boston Track Club and The Indiana Invaders, handing the stick off to Mitch Maloney in fourth place. His time was 2:57, and the Misfits were three seconds off the lead. Immediately upon passing Maloney the baton, O'Donnell stumbled to the turf and collapsed.

Maloney took the stick and aggressively sprinted after the lead pack of three. The gap shrunk with each step Mitch took. He passed the half-way mark in 22.5 and closed to within a step of the lead. The crowd on the far turn urged him on and Maloney obliged, moving into the lead at the 300 meter mark. Watching his cousin's fearless run, McNeal moved past the other runners into lane one as Maloney took over the lead. McNeal could not believe his eyes. Mitch Maloney, on three weeks of training, was actually going to give him the lead.

The thought of getting the stick in the lead raised the hairs on the back of McNeal's neck. At the 350 mark, however, the blistering early pace caught up to Maloney, and he began to pay the piper. The runners from Farm Team and Zap Fitness passed Mitch as his legs tied up. Maloney leaned back as he tried to fight his way through the fatigue, eventually handing off to McNeal in third place. Maloney, in his first race since the injury, had split 48.7, eclipsing his previous personal record of 49.2 set back in high school.

McNeal received the baton ten yards off the lead and a stride ahead of fourth place. He aggressively ran his first 200 meters, carefully stalking the lead duo. McNeal's eyes focused in on the shoulder blades of the runner from Farm Team, each step pulling him closer to his prey. McNeal continued bridging the gap for the next half lap and the crowd roared as McNeal pulled even with the leaders just before the 400 meter mark. The old familiar pain of the eight set in now and McNeal had to focus to maintain pace. On the turn, he seized the lead and the cheers grew louder. O'Donnell, back on his feet, stood on the infield encouraging McNeal as he smoothly raced down the backstretch. The runners from Farm Team and Zap Fitness remained in tight pursuit of McNeal, edging closer to him as they entered the final turn. McNeal refused to wilt, however. He used the adrenaline from the crowd and the race itself to summon a final unmatchable gear and handed off the stick to Cooper with a slight lead; his time of 1:49.8 his fastest ever.

Ryan Cooper's whole career he had considered himself a long distance runner. Today, however, Cooper was banging heads with some of the country's top milers. Cooper's only shot at bringing home the gold would be to run the kick out of the runners chasing him. Cooper covered the first 400 meters in sixty-one seconds, maintaining the five yard lead. By the half mile mark, the lead was down to three meters. He changed tactics, relaxing the pace to gear up for one final charge from four hundred meters out. The runners from Zap Fitness and Farm Team maintained their positions on Cooper's shoulder. The pace slowed remarkably on the third lap and they passed the 1200 meter mark at 3:10, covering the previous lap in close to sixty-eight seconds. Cooper needed to move so he lowered his head and took off as the official rang the bell signaling the final lap. O'Toole screamed for him to "Move your chicken legs, Cooper! You need to bloody go NOW!" Move his chicken legs is exactly what he did. He appeared to catch the other two runners by surprise as they struggled to react and Cooper reopened the lead. With 300 meters to go, however, all three runners were running flat out full speed, Cooper with a slight lead, Farm Team and Zap Fitness just behind. With half a track to go, Cooper maintained the lead. Halfway through the final turn, however, the anchor from Nike Farm Team blasted into the lead, opening up a gap almost instantly. Cooper tried desperately to go with him, but was already at top speed and could not accelerate. As he entered the final stretch, the Zap Fitness runner pulled even with him. Cooper fought against the burning in his muscles and the pounding in his head as he gamely battled the Zap Fitness runner. He strained more and more with each step. Just when it appeared Cooper would cross the line in third place, the Zap Fitness runner began to fade, apparently the victim of a mistimed move and Cooper crossed the line in second place, covering the final lap in fifty-eight seconds to run a 4:09 mile, a PR of six seconds. McNeal, Maloney and O'Donnell ran onto the track where O'Donnell wrapped his arms around the exhausted Cooper.

"Way to go, man. Way to go," whispered O'Donnell.

"I can't feel my legs."

"Don't worry about it Hot Sauce, you're not supposed to. That's what it feels like to run a sub 4:10 mile," said McNeal.

"Then I don't even want to know what sub four feels like. That was the longest four minutes of my life."

The four runners walked off the track, their own place in Penn Relay lore secure. A pleased Seamus O'Toole met the relay runners out back. "Now you critters know that Seamus O'Toole isn't much of a fan of second place finishes. That being said, I think today was a pretty good race." Such words passed as high praise coming from the curmudgeonly O'Toole. "Hope really might be springing eternal this year."

"Thanks, Seamus. I think I speak for all of us when I say that without your guidance, we probably wouldn't be here," said McNeal.

"Well, don't thank old Seamus too much, cause we aren't halfway to nowhere just yet. There's still a lot of work to be done, a lot of dynamite that needs to be set off before we go around getting all sentimental."

Maria, who watched the race from the stands with O'Donnell and Maloney's girlfriends, arrived just in time to hear O'Toole talk about blowing up dynamite. She ran over to a still exhausted McNeal to offer her congratulations. "That was an awesome race, Joe. All you guys did great. You were right, Joe, there really isn't anything like this. I've been to NBA Finals games and this ranks right up there for excitement, with all the flag waving and chanting. It's just wild."

"Eh, leave it to a dame to compare Penn Relays to a stinking basketball game," muttered O'Toole.

"Thanks, Maria. We'll be right back. We need to go cooldown."

"Ok, Joe. See you soon."

The four runners jogged a dead man's trot around the block before stopping. "Who wants a chicken patty?" asked O'Donnell.

Cooper shook his head from side to side. "You're a sick SOB. I can't feel my insides and you want me to eat some spicy-as-hell chicken patty?"

"I thought they called you Hot Sauce for a reason?"

McNeal and Maloney laughed as they both knew Cooper would be unable to turn down O'Donnell's challenge. "I'll take two."

"Coop, you don't need to be eating two chicken patties less than an hour after running 4:09," said McNeal, attempting to be a voice of reason.

"You saying I can't eat two chicken patties?"

"I'm saying you shouldn't."

"Man, you've seen me eat two cheese steaks after a night out like it was nothing, haven't you?"

"I've also seen you eat one and use the other as a missile, launching it out the car as I drove down the boulevard."

"Hey, that was a dark moment in my life. I'd appreciate it if you don't bring it up. The point is, you don't think I can eat two. I don't see you calling out OD."

"Fine, I don't think you can eat two."

McNeal shook his head as Cooper and OD each ordered two chicken patties. Cooper bit into the chicken patty, a yellow flour tortilla filled with spicy ground chicken. "Oh my gosh, that's hot. It's like chicken wings mushed up and wrapped inside a taco. Only hotter and a lot less tasty."

"It's pure deliciousness is what it is."

"I'm going to go inside and watch some races. I'll see you guys inside," said McNeal as he and Maloney walked off to watch the conclusion of the meet with their respective girlfriends.

chapter 26

PENN RELAYS MARKED the first time in his career that Joey McNeal broke 1:50. It validated his belief that maybe, just maybe, he could qualify for the Olympics. McNeal knew there was a world of difference between splitting 1:49 at Penn and running the 1:45 necessary to have a shot at reaching Beijing. But it was no further away than 1:49 seemed back in September.

Back in September, McNeal merely wanted to test his limits one more time, to write one last chapter in the book known as his running career. Since then, McNeal had dedicated himself fully to wringing every last drop out of his potential. Everything from his eating habits to how many hours a night he slept had improved. Neither were perfect, but each was a serious improvement. He lifted twice a week, did daily core sessions and stretched regularly. Now he stood on the cusp of greatness, of having a shot at donning the red, white and blue jersey of Team USA. Like all elite athletes, he had sacrificed much to get this close; he missed family functions, sacrificed his social life, constantly felt some sort of pain, and suffered the loss of his job and girlfriend in the same day. He even quit coaching, something he never envisioned doing. While happy with the path he chose, McNeal often thought about Bishop O'Connell. There were even moments when McNeal missed teaching at Second Chances. Since these moments mostly came at six o'clock in the morning in the midst of a morning run, McNeal more precisely pined for the days of arriving at work by nine o'clock. He hoped these sacrifices would not prove to be in vain. While making the Olympic team was the ultimate prize, McNeal still needed to reach the preliminary goal of running a qualifying time for the Olympic Trials. He needed a 1:48 to get the provisional standard and a 1:47 and change to automatically qualify. If the meet officials felt an event needed more competitors, they would dip into the pool of provisional qualifiers. For the 800, the magic number stood at thirty-two. McNeal needed to be among the thirty-two fastest half milers in the nation.

For Cooper and O'Donnell, the next big fish to fry was the Broad Street Run. McNeal decided to sit out this year's Broad Street Run and focus completely on the track. O'Toole didn't think it wise to race ten miles during your competitive phase of 800 meter training. Instead, McNeal would race the following Tuesday at the Tuppeny Twilight meet held at Villanova University. While McNeal agreed with Seamus O'Toole, part of him wished he could be out there competing with his teammates and friends. It was a small part, however, and all in all, McNeal would not miss the ten mile jaunt down Broad Street all that much.

Broad Street was held the first Sunday morning of May every year. This year that fell eight days after Penn Relays. As of the Monday prior to the race, Cooper and O'Donnell had not yet sent in their entries. McNeal, Maria, Cooper and O'Donnell sat in the apartment living room, watching the Phillies. "Coop, we don't have enough guys for a team entry this year, do we?" asked O'Donnell.

"No, we need at least three guys to score," said Cooper as he filled out his entry form.

Maria had been running regularly since she began dating McNeal and was planning on running Broad Street. Something about Broad Street attracted new runners. Maybe it was the allure of running from one end of the city to the other. Or the fact that there would be over 15,000 fellow runners out there so now matter how fast or slow one ran, there would be a crowd to run with. It could have been Broad

Street's reputation as a relatively "easy and fast" ten miler since it was straight and flat, even ever so slightly downhill in some parts. McNeal disagreed with this notion wholeheartedly, feeling that no ten mile race should be classified as "easy and fast." To him it was like a quick and painless death. At the end of the day, you're still dead. Whatever the appeal, the race drew a wide variety of experienced and novice runners. "Why don't you guys enter the co-ed division?"

O'Donnell looked at McNeal quizzically. "Do I look like I'm gonna wear a skirt?"

"No, man. Not that you don't have nice, sexy legs. Especially if you shaved those bad boys. But seriously. Maria's running it. You need one girl and two guys to score in co-ed right, Coop?"

Cooper tried to hide the fact that he was not at all in favor of teaming up with McNeal's rookie runner of a girlfriend. "Um, yeah, I think so."

"And I doubt it's all that competitive. You guys could probably win."

"I bet Lancaster Ave Runners puts together a pretty decent squad. I mean they got like a dozen guys who can run in the fifty to fifty-two minute range."

"Joe, I don't want to slow those guys down. There's now way I can race with them."

"Race with them?" McNeal chuckled. "No, you won't have to. They just add the three of your times and the lowest score wins. Like golf. Everyone runs their own race, same as if you were entered as an individual. Really, there's nothing to lose."

"Pride," Cooper mumbled. "Ain't gonna be any damn Kenyans running in the co-ed division. I better not get a stinking pink bib number or something."

O'Donnell walked over to McNeal. "You know the way I feel about bib numbers, Mac. I'm all in for running co-ed. Heck, it's the only chance I got to win something here. But bib numbers are like my wallpaper, if I got to hang a pink bib...I mean I'm already advertising Dunkin' Donuts. That's all I'm saying."

"Don't worry about it. I've never seen anyone with a pink bib at Broad. I'm sure you'll have the same bib as anyone else."

Cooper, much to his chagrin, filled out his entry blank and checked the box marked co-ed next to the team section. "Leave your entries here and I'll mail them together in the morning," he told O'Donnell and Maria.

෴

McNeal and Cooper each woke early the next morning to get a thirty-minute run in prior to work. Both deep into their specific training, running done together had greatly decreased. Cooper would often help McNeal out at the track by getting splits after he completed his own scheduled run, sometimes hopping in for a repeat or two to work on his leg speed. "So, Coop, ready for Broad?"

"Ask me again in a week."

"In a week? Broad Street'll be over in a week."

"Exactly. Then I'll know if I was ready. Seriously, though, I've never been in better shape. I've been averaging over seventy miles a week now since February. I don't think I ever touched that before, let alone put together three consecutive months. Yeah, if I'm not ready now, I never will be."

"What's the best you ever ran? Fifty-one something?"

"Yeah, three years ago. Last year I ran fifty-two and change. The year I went fifty-one, I was only running, like maybe forty miles a week. I think that's the year you ran fifty-three."

"Yeah, I remember now. We were in pretty decent shape that year. I think we did a whole lot of fartlek and tempo to make up for the lack of big time mileage. Where'd that place you?"

"Twenty-first. Got out kicked by some forty-year old beast for top twenty. I'm still pissed about that."

McNeal laughed. "Haha, I remember that. That's the year I had the death pains." After the race, Cooper and O'Donnell had stood at the road cheering on runners whom they knew while McNeal lie prone on the sidewalk in agony. "I never felt so bad in my life. I honestly thought I was dying. So what kind of time do you think you can run now?"

"I don't want to sound crazy or anything, but I think I can go sub-fifty. I mean if I ran 4:09 at Penn, how slow is 4:50 pace going to feel?"

"Probably pretty slow," McNeal said as they arrived at the apartment. "You can get first shower while I do some quick lifting."

McNeal sweated through a couple sets of lunges and step-ups while Cooper prepared for work. Leg lifting was something new to McNeal. At first, he struggled with it. He always felt sore the next day, especially in his hip flexors. He soon realized he needed to treat a lifting session the same way as a hard track workout, complete with a full warm-up and cool down. Now his legs felt stronger than ever, and with his new found strength, hopefully came some additional pop in his legs. Only time would tell.

Business at the Grilled Donut Café had taken a hit now that a Starbucks opened within a block of the Café. Statistics claimed the existence of a Starbucks nearby actually helped independent cafés but McNeal remained skeptical. McNeal and Cooper worried that if things didn't improve they would need to let go of one of their workers. Times were challenging for businesses and consumers alike and the Grilled Donut Café was no different. With gas prices through the roof, the cost of ingredients also skyrocketed. In order to keep some sort of sustainable profit margin, they had to increase prices. Cooper and McNeal worried that too much of a price increase could result in the loss of customers. Too little of a price increase, and it didn't matter how many customers came to the store if the profit margin was too small. Such was the challenge of running a small business.

All week long, the Café offered the Broad Street Run special. It featured a dish of pasta, served with grilled chicken and a slice of garlic bread. Runners of all sorts, but especially recreational ones, religiously carbo-loaded before a big event. The Café offered a chance at an early start. In addition to providing a head start on the carbo-loading process, at $8.99, the lunch special was quite the deal. With an assortment of running related memorabilia decorating the Café, it was impossible for customers not to know McNeal and Cooper took running pretty seriously. Many of the regulars discussed the upcoming big race with Cooper, asking him for pointers while wishing him luck. For Cooper, there was no race bigger than Broad. The Penn Relays were great, but Broad Street was his race. It was his annual personal Olympic final. Even in down years, Cooper had managed the motivation to run Broad. This year was his eighth consecutive year running Broad. Unlike the previous seven years, this time Ryan Cooper would be running with the leaders. And that scared Ryan Cooper more than anything.

꙳

McNeal awoke early the morning of Broad Street. The plan entailed him taking Cooper, O'Donnell and Maria to the starting line near Broad and Olney, and then driving south to wait at the finish line. McNeal drove to the gas station for a quick fill up and returned. He found Maria and Len waiting outside and let them in. "Good morning Maria, good morning, Len. Ready for today?"

Maria looked especially nervous. A successful basketball player in high school and college despite her short stature, today would be her first dip into the pool of competitive running. "I'm ready as I'm going to be. Are we leaving soon?"

"As soon as Hot Sauce is ready. I'll go check and see what the hold up is."

McNeal bounded up the steps two at a time. Skipping steps was one of many little things that told McNeal when he was nearing peak shape. He had some extra bounce in his gait; he grew increasingly fidgety between workouts and races and obsessed over things like checking his weight and heart rate each morning and making sure he stayed hydrated by checking his pee to see if it was clear. He banged loudly on Cooper's door. "Yo, Sauce! Len and Maria are downstairs? You ready?"

"Almost, Mac. I can't find my other flat."

McNeal walked into Cooper's room to find it totally torn apart, as if a cyclone swept through overnight. A mountain of clothes, towels and linens lay spread throughout the floor, nary a spot of the dark green carpet remained visible.

"Do that thing you do with my keys, Joe."

In the past, when Cooper's keys were missing, McNeal had shouted "Coop's keys!!" and they had an eerie habit of turning up just after being summoned. McNeal opened Cooper's closet door. "Coop's flats!"

"Already checked there. Ain't no way they're in there."

Just then Len O'Donnell exited the bathroom, one red racing flat in hand. "You looking for this?"

"What the? Yeah! Where'd you find that?"

"In the sink. I don't know what kind of weird race day rituals you got, but having your shoes sleep in the sink or brush their laces, that's bizarre, man. Whatever, dude, you go out and beat the Kenyans, and I'll let you wash my flats in your sink, too."

"Dude, I must've dropped it. I had them in my hands to put in my bag when I came in here. My phone rang and I guess I got distracted."

"Sure Sauce, whatever. Let's hit the road. Joe, you mind driving my car? No offense to your lovely vintage 1988 Dodge Aries, but, I, uh, would feel a little more comfortable in my slightly less used Matrix."

"So I filled my gas tank for nothing, you're saying? Sure, unlike running, the less that bad boy is on the road the better."

The race was scheduled for an 8:30 start. Broad and Olney was about a twenty-minute ride from the apartment. McNeal's clock read 6:42, and as long as he got them there by 7:10, they should have plenty of time to prepare. Extra time was needed at a race the scale of Broad Street. Over fourteen thousand runners would cram onto the road, many of them warming up on the cinder track of Central High School. McNeal, normally not an aggressive driver, took his job as chauffeur seriously and weaved in and out of traffic, trying to save every minute he could.

Maria, sitting shotgun next to McNeal, had never seen McNeal drive in such a manner and the pale look on her face said that she wasn't enjoying it. "Joe, can you please slow down? If you get arrested, we're not going to make the race at all. Plus, I think I'm getting car sick."

"I won't get arrested."

"If we crash, we won't make it anywhere," said Cooper from the backseat.

"Hey, I'm just trying to be helpful here. I still remember the time we were almost late two years ago. Remember, it was me, you, Cliff Johnson and Alan King. By the time we got warmed up, it was 8:15. Then we had to carry that body bag Allentown Running Company provided to the equipment bus, each of us lifting it high over our heads as we pushed and shoved our way through the crowd. Then, after we finally dropped it off, we had to sprint to the starting line so we didn't start the race back with the nine-minute milers. Remember running over people's lawns and hurdling yellow tape? I'm just trying to help you guys avoid that mess."

"Thanks for the effort, but we're only a minute away now, Jeff Gordon. I think you can slow the pace a bit."

McNeal slowed down and within a minute dropped the three runners off outside the Central High gates. "Good luck," he said as they exited. He quickly kissed Maria and whispered some last minute wisdom before she departed. "Just relax and have fun. The first mile's going to feel easy. You'll have plenty of time to make up for running it too slow, but if you run it too fast, you'll have nine miles to pay the price."

She nodded and was on her way with O'Donnell and Cooper. McNeal drove off to meet Seamus O'Toole down by the Navy Yard. McNeal knew that Maria must be having huge butterflies right now. He had barely slept the entire week prior to the first time he ran Broad Street. He vividly recalled waking up in a cold sweat throughout the week. The thought of racing ten miles for an eight hundred meter runner was terrifying. For a girl who grew up a basketball player and was now, not only running, but competing on a team with two pretty solid runners, it must be even worse, he thought. McNeal pulled onto the Schuylkill Expressway as he thought that maybe he shouldn't have encouraged them to run in the co-ed division. He fidgeted with the radio for a few minutes and soon was departing the highway and pulling into the nearest Wawa to grab a Chai tea and banana. McNeal then drove to the Wachovia Center parking lot and walked several blocks to meet Seamus O'Toole.

O'Toole stood amongst a group of runners from his charity training program. In addition to Cooper and O'Donnell, a full platoon of his runners, wearing the distinctive orange colors of the Strides for Hope organization, were running Broad. The Strides for Hope members not competing had set up an orange hospitality tent, underneath which a full supply of bagels, orange slices, bananas, water and Gatorade lay. O'Toole immediately paused his conversation upon seeing McNeal approach. "Joseph McNeal! Come here, lad. Seamus wants to introduce you to some of my friends."

McNeal found it odd to hear Seamus O'Toole call anyone his friend. The O'Toole McNeal and the guys knew was gruff and surly. McNeal doubted this attitude endeared him to a bunch of recreational charity runners. This version of Seamus O'Toole was different, however, shaking hands and laughing with everyone around. Several of O'Toole's 'friends' came up to McNeal to wish him luck, catching him off guard. It wasn't everyday that well wishers approached McNeal just to say "Good luck."

Back at Broad and Olney, Cooper, O'Donnell and Maria had just finished warming-up and now needed to weave through the masses to get a starting position near the front. Maria settled in near the sign calling for eight-minute milers, while Cooper and O'Donnell made their way to the front line. Despite Joey Mac's assertions to the contrary, the three were sporting pink and blue bib numbers. Runners competing as an individual or as a member of a single sex team wore either blue or pink, respectively. As Cooper correctly predicted, none of the Kenyans wore mixed color bibs. "That damn McNeal," grumbled O'Donnell as he took his position on the front line. "Another bib number ruined."

Mayor Michael Nutter, in race tradition, spoke a few words to the throng of ten thousand plus runners that stretched back several city blocks. Unlike the previous mayor, the Philadelphia crowd did not greet Mayor Nutter with a chorus of boos. In his first year as city mayor, his honeymoon period was still in effect.

After the mayor finished his customary greeting and well wishing, the siren serving as a starter's pistol sounded and Cooper, O'Donnell, Maria and thousands of companions began the journey south down Broad Street.

O'Toole's plan for Cooper and O'Donnell entailed immediately seizing the lead, an unusual tactic in a ten mile race. The common school of thought for a ten mile race was to hang back early, conserving energy so enough remained in the tank for the final few miles. O'Toole, not one for conventional wisdom, thought he found information telling him otherwise. In recent years, all won by runners of Kenyan descent, the leaders went out relaxed, hitting the first couple of miles in just about five flat pace before turning it up a notch. O'Toole felt, their Penn Relay performances withstanding, Cooper and O'Donnell were enough under the radar that the Kenyans were likely to let them go, figuring they could catch them later in the race. If O'Toole calculated correctly, Cooper would bank enough time early on to hold off the hard charging Kenyan challengers. O'Donnell did not feel that he possessed the required strength to win a race as long and with such a talented field as Broad Street. Thus, he readily agreed to serve Cooper's interests in the race, much the way members of Lance Armstrong's teams had ridden with the goal of Armstrong winning the Tour De France. O'Donnell helping with the pace would enable Cooper to not totally be on an island. O'Donnell figured he could hang on long enough to run a time comparable if he went out more conservatively, albeit in a much more painful fashion.

By two miles Cooper and O'Donnell had built a thirty-second lead, reaching the mark in 9:20. The chase pack hit the two-mile mark at 9:50. O'Toole had set up members of his Strides for Hope team throughout the course, each with a cell phone, with the task of calling out the gap on the chase pack to Cooper and O'Donnell, as well as calling O'Toole with mile updates.

"Haha! I knew they'd let them go. Perfect, that's simply perfect!"

McNeal trusted in Seamus' coaching but worried ten miles might be too long for Cooper and O'Donnell to simply run away from a world class field. He did not dare express his uncertainty to Seamus. "Seamus, do you think one of your spies could tell me how Maria is doing? She's wearing number...?"

"Seamus don't care what your dame's number is. There is something like twenty thousand bloody runners out there, approximately half female. Do you honestly think my spies, as you call them, could pick out your sweet little princess out of that madness? To think that all this time, I thought of you as the intelligent one of the group."

"I just thought maybe...I mean it couldn't hurt anything."

"Joseph, it's bad enough that you—without consulting old Seamus—signed her up as part of our 'team'. Now you want my people to find the proverbial paperclip in a forest?"

"Needle. The correct saying is 'needle in a haystack.'"

"Have you ever tried to find a paperclip in a forest?"

"What?"

"Well? Have you?"

"No, of course not. That's ridiculous."

"Exactly."

By now Cooper and O'Donnell had reached the three-mile mark in 14:00. The chase group had picked up the pace and was no longer getting gapped, but remained thirty seconds back. Maria steadily clipped off seven-minute miles, enjoying the sights and sounds of the course. Throngs of spectators lined the course shouting words of encouragement to the passing runners.

Out on the course, Cooper and O'Donnell grabbed their first waters at the aid station just prior to the four-mile mark. O'Toole's meticulous plan even called for when and where to grab their waters. They were to get them at the end of the station, and each station, run by a local organization or track team, had been contacted by Seamus and told exactly what he wanted them to do. Members of a local church manned this station, and one of them ran along side the two runners, handing each of them their water so they would not need to break stride. O'Toole left nothing to chance.

Cooper felt strong and confident at the half way mark. A group of four Kenyans had broken away from the pack and narrowed the gap to twenty-five seconds. O'Donnell did not feel as good as Cooper and wondered how much longer he could keep the pace. "I'm starting to hurt, Hot Sauce," he mumbled between breaths.

"Stay smooth, OD. Smooth and strong."

O'Toole split his time talking on the phone, giving orders to tell the two leaders, and walking around the increasingly more crowded tent. Here Seamus O'Toole acted like the mayor, shaking hands, laughing easily, kissing babies on the forehead. It was a side of the old coach McNeal rarely, if ever, saw. McNeal found himself in the uncomfortable position of taking questions on the Olympics, coupled with inquires of whether he thought Cooper and O'Donnell could hang on. "Um, it'd be a great opportunity and honor just to compete and have a shot at going to Beijing to represent the US," he answered, sounding a bit rehearsed. "Ryan and Len are in great shape and I'm sure they'll give it all they've got," McNeal responded in another tried and true cliché.

Geesh, I must sound like a robot, McNeal thought after answering the same set of questions for what felt like the thousandth time, but in reality was probably closer to the tenth. McNeal wondered what it must be like to be a pro athlete in one of the four major sports dealing with those type of questions on a daily basis. "I guess that goes with the million dollar a year contract."

The Kenyan foursome had narrowed the gap even more by the six mile mark. The lead had shrunk to nineteen seconds. The Kenyans were now clipping off sub 4:40 miles while Cooper and O'Donnell's splits ballooned closer to 4:50. The Kenyans chopped eleven seconds off the lead in the last two miles. At this rate, Cooper and O'Donnell would be caught somewhere in the final mile.

Two of the four Kenyans, Simon Kiptop and Peter Kagwe broke away from their countrymen at the six-mile mark. Their pace quickly dropped to 4:30 and by mile seven Cooper and O'Donnell's lead was down to just six seconds. One of O'Toole's workers relayed this to them along with O'Toole's words.

"Two Kenyans have closed to within six seconds. Seamus says to move your bloody arses!"

Cooper's heart jumped upon hearing the news. He had fully expected to get caught, and then he figured he would need to muster one last move. He had hoped it wouldn't be until the final mile. With thirteen seconds chopped off in the last mile, it appeared likely to happen much sooner.

O'Donnell was running on fumes at this point. He took a deep breath and turned to Cooper. "I got tops one more good mile in me, man. Get on my back and let me carry you through to the eight."

Cooper obliged and fell in half a step behind OD. O'Donnell's legs fought the urge to slow down, turning over and over. They covered the next mile in 4:39 with O'Donnell struggling to maintain a breathing rhythm. His loud, pained gasps for air signaled that he was running on borrowed time. Cooper needed to make a decision. Does he ride the game O'Donnell any further, or does he make a move now before getting caught? Kiptop and Kagwe lurked in the background, a mere four seconds back. O'Donnell's surge may have halted the bleeding, but the wound remained open.

McNeal paced back and forth at the tent, anxiously agonizing over his decision to not run Broad. Deep inside, he knew it was the right move, but in the heat of the moment, he yearned for the competition. He half thought of running onto the course and finishing the race with Cooper, before quickly realizing that doing so would be grounds for Cooper's disqualification. Hopping out on the road to finish with a mid-packer; that was ok. Trying to help your buddy cross the line first, not so much.

"You got to go, man," whispered a fully spent O'Donnell to Cooper. "Do what you gotta do."

Cooper nodded, muttered "Thanks, Len," and passed the weary runner.

With a mile and a half left, it was a three-man race. Kiptop and Kagwe sat directly on Cooper's shoulders, one on each side. Having hunted him down, they waited to see who would move first.

The threesome hit the nine-mile mark at 43:31. McNeal and O'Toole stood just past there, urging Cooper on. "You got this, Coop. No regrets, leave it all on the course," yelled McNeal.

"Listen, Ryan Cooper. Seamus needs you to move those chicken legs of yours and he needs you to move them now, damn it."

Cooper, exhausted and focused on the seemingly simple process of putting one foot in front of the other as fast as he possibly could, cracked a slight smile at hearing O'Toole again call him "chicken legs."

With a half-mile to go, it became apparent that a ten-mile race, a race completed in slightly under fifty minutes, would boil down to one final mad dash for the tape. Cooper flashed back to Penn, acutely aware of his near miss in a race also decided by a finishing kick. He could only hope the similarities ended there.

Two hundred meters from the tape, all three runners strode side by side, each man fighting for all he was worth. First Kipgot pulled ahead, then Kagwe, with Cooper falling a stride back. Just when it appeared Cooper could muster nothing else and was destined for the third slot, he summoned one last gear, surging past each man in the final stride and breaking the tape first, in a time of 47:59. With all three men under forty-eight minutes, it would go down as the closest finish in Broad Street Run history.

Len O'Donnell hung on to cross the line sixth in a time of 49:03, behind two more Kenyans and the top guy from Lancaster Avenue.

McNeal and O'Toole rushed from the tent to see whether or not Cooper had won. The roar of the crowd signified that he most likely had.

"Haha! Those chicken legs did it! Those chicken legs did it!"

Cooper smiled, tried to get up, but instead collapsed back into the fold up chair he was resting on. O'Donnell lay prone on the ground next to Cooper. If not for the slight rising of his chest with each breath, OD could be mistaken for dead.

"Is he alright?" asked McNeal as he shook Cooper's hand.

O'Donnell flashed the thumbs up sign. "Just more tired than any man in the world's ever been."

"Alright, guys, I'm going to run up the course to check on Maria. You guys did great. Made us misfits look real good out there."

McNeal found her just past nine miles, still on pace to run under seventy minutes. He could not believe the clock when he saw it, amazed at her ability to run so fast with no experience. "Hey, Maria, you look great," he said, running along side her for a couple of steps.

"Thanks. What are you doing?"

"Huh? Oh, I was going to run with you to the finish."

"You don't have to do that. I made it this far, I can make it the last mile."

McNeal stopped, taken aback slightly by her refusal of his company.

"Thanks, anyway. It was a sweet gesture."

Maria ran off and McNeal stopped to walk back to the finish line, proud of his girlfriend. She would finish in a time of 69:47 and Team Misfits easily won the co-ed division, outdistancing their closest competition by half an hour.

After the awards ceremony, McNeal again congratulated Cooper, O'Donnell and Maria on their fine efforts. "You even looked good with those pink and blue bib numbers," he joked as they walked to the car and prepared for the long process of leaving the Wachovia Center parking lot. Their departure was complicated by the incoming crowd for the afternoon Phillies game, prolonging the ride by nearly an hour. The long ride home, however, could not dampen the spirits of the happy, tired bunch in the car. It had been quite the day.

chapter 27

WITH THE HEART of the outdoor season upon him, McNeal's track workouts heated up with the weather. He had planned to run the Tuppeny Twilight Invite, held at Villanova University and always a high quality event, but a slight head cold canceled those plans. O'Toole did not want to risk McNeal getting sicker, or worse yet, straining a muscle because the cold left him weakened. Despite McNeal's assurance that he was fine, O'Toole insisted on holding him out of the race. Instead, the following week he entered an All-Comers meet at Plymouth Whitemarsh High School. The only problem was no one came. He led wire to wire, finishing in 1:50.76, not a terrible race, but nowhere near the necessary qualifying time of 1:48.5. If McNeal was serious about qualifying for the Olympic Games, he first needed to qualify for the Trials.

Today's workout posed quite the challenge. While it only called for four repeats of a quarter mile, it was the manner of which they needed to be run. O'Toole split the four into sets of two. The first in each set were to be run in fifty seconds with a minute rest in between. Upon completion of the first set, McNeal would get a recovery period of ten or so minutes, depending on how he felt. Maloney planned on running the first 400 in each set with McNeal. This would be especially helpful during the second set when McNeal's legs would most likely feel like jelly, and running a flat out 400 would be torture of the worst possible kind.

McNeal and Maloney warmed up a mile then went through a vigorous routine of drills and stretching. For McNeal, this type of warm-up worked best. The old standard process of jog, stretch, do a few drills and striders that he followed for years no longer got the job done. Instead, McNeal jogged one lap nice and easy, followed by a brief stretching routine. He then ran a mile, each lap progressively faster than the previous. This was followed by doing a drill, for example knee lifts, or butt kickers, followed by ten to thirty seconds of stretching, touching on each major muscle group. After thirty minutes, McNeal laced up his spikes, rubbed in some Icy Hot and ran six hard striders. "You ready, Mitch?"

"Joe, I've been waiting for you for ten minutes. Of course, I'm ready."

"Some of us actually warm-up."

"Some of us ain't so ancient that it takes a year to oil up our old joints."

"Alright, alright, let's do this."

"It's about time we got this started," yelled Seamus O'Toole as he approached the track. "Here I was hurrying to get here, and you blokes are just getting started."

O'Toole had given McNeal explicit instructions as to how to run the first quarter. He wanted even splits, twenty-five and twenty-five. Going out in twenty-three and holding on for a twenty-seven provided little benefit for the challenges one faced in racing a half mile.

McNeal and Maloney followed the plan perfectly, covering the opening 200 in twenty-five seconds flat, and maintaining that speed to hit the 400 in 50.2. O'Toole clapped his hands in approval. "That's it my boy, that's how we do it."

Maloney bent over, hands on knees, mouth agape, sucking in air with each breath. "Good luck running another one of them in a minute, Joe."

"You sure you don't want in?"

"You must be crazy." McNeal nodded and used the remaining time to jog, trying to shake his legs out.

After fifty seconds, McNeal approached the line, inhaled deeply and began to run. McNeal's heart pounded furiously as he ran down the backstretch. The short break prevented a return to a relaxed rhythm. He breathed loud, labored breaths and his legs burned with every step. McNeal hit the 200 meter mark in thirty seconds and negative thoughts flooded his psyche. *What good is a thirty-second third 200 going to do me in a big race?*

McNeal briefly contemplated stepping off the track but thought better of it. He reminded himself to control his thoughts. It was advice he had given his athletes hundreds of times and now found himself repeating the mantra inside his head.

Maloney stood along the track, yelling at McNeal to drive hard down the final straight. McNeal switched gears as he came off the turn, pumping his arms furiously, hoping his legs would follow suit. Ten meters from the line, the clock crossed the sixty second barrier and by the time McNeal finished, it read 61.7. While McNeal did not expect to duplicate the fifty-second quarter-mile he opened with, he certainly hoped for better than a 61.7. O'Toole silently shook his head from his spot outside the track. McNeal let loose a guttural sounding cry. "ARRRRGGGHHH!"

He put his head in his hands and wobbled off the track, heart still pounding and his legs barely able to support his weight. Maloney jogged over to meet him. "Yo, Joe, you ok?"

"I don't know, man. That sucked."

"What happened?"

"My legs weren't there and I lost focus. Ran like a mental midget."

Maloney nodded his head. "Your legs ain't supposed to be there after running fifty seconds for a quarter. You know that. The whole point of this workout is for you to adapt to that feeling so come race day, your legs don't go into shock. Get yourself together and let's nail this second set."

McNeal sighed and slumped up against a wall outside the track. It was the one spot out of the blistering sun. While the calendar still read May, the thermometer topped ninety degrees for the second consecutive day. The heat radiated off the track. He appreciated the pep talk from Maloney, but knew that when it was time to run the final four hundred, he'd be out there on an island. McNeal sipped from his water bottle and tried to refocus for the second set.

O'Toole wobbled over to McNeal. "Joseph, this is where it happens. This is where the rocks turn to diamonds. Ten minutes are up, time to go."

Ten minutes may seem like an eternity when in the midst of a grueling, hilly hour long run. It can seem even longer when visiting in-laws and certain family members, but ten minutes flies by when talking to a pretty girl and between sets of 400s. McNeal and Maloney again toed the line, standing side by side.

"Alright, let's rock," said McNeal as the two runners took off.

Maloney led through the first 200, hitting it in 26.3 with McNeal on his shoulder. With 100 meters to go, McNeal pulled even with Maloney and they began sprinting side by side down the track, each man pumping his arms, lifting his legs and breathing loudly. They crossed the line in 52.2, covering the second half faster than the first. McNeal walked to his bag and grabbed his water bottle, sucking down a gulp of sun warmed water.

"Well done, fellows. But the next one's the real test, Joseph. Show me what you're made of."

"Alright, Mac, you know what you got to do." McNeal approached the line one last time, exhausted from his previous three efforts and the merciless toll the heat took on him.

"This is where Beijing happens, this is where it happens," said Maloney. "Go get it!"

Once again McNeal took off around the opening turn, determined not to fall victim to his own thoughts. *Focus, Mac. Focus. Smooth and fast*, he reminded himself as he sprinted down the backstretch, reaching the halfway point in 27.5 seconds. He felt the lactic acid burning in his legs and his head pounded as he ran the turn. With 150 meters to go, McNeal's legs felt like anvils. Mitch Maloney, who had jogged down the opposite side of the track, hopped in the repeat. "Come on, Mac, you got this."

Maloney ran two strides ahead of McNeal, looking over his shoulder and calling out words of encouragement. "I'm that third spot. Get me and you're an Olympian, get me and you're in."

McNeal zeroed in on Maloney and attempted to wheel him in as they ran the last hundred meters of the day. His feet burned from the friction powerfully sprinting on a red hot track produced. His arms felt heavy as he tried to pump them and they struggled to cooperate. But each step brought him closer to Maloney, no longer shouting back words of encouragement, but fighting to hold off McNeal. Just before crossing the line, McNeal edged ahead of Maloney, his legs buckling as he tumbled across the finish in fifty-five seconds flat. He fell to the track fully spent, but satisfied with his last effort. He knew he shouldn't lie down after a workout, but it felt too good to get up. "Thanks for helping me out, Mitch. I couldn't have done that with out you, man."

"Don't even worry about it. I told you before I owe you my life. Consider this a small token of my appreciation."

O'Toole walked onto the track. "How about we cut the sentimental crap and cool down? Could we do that? Nice second set, but if you fall asleep in Eugene like you did on that first set, you can kiss Beijing good-bye. Hell, you won't even toe the line in Oregon if you pull that crap again."

McNeal knew O'Toole spoke the truth. He didn't think he'd let that happen again, that moment of weakness, but the thing about running is, you never know how you're going to respond to the fire until you're in the midst of the heat. Yes, the more a runner subjected himself to the suffering, the more adept he became at running through it. But the voices of doubt can never be fully extinguished. Just temporarily quieted.

McNeal pulled off his spikes and checked his feet for blisters. Nothing too serious, just a few friction spots on the soles. They'd hurt like heck on the cooldown, but shouldn't pose any long term problems. He slipped on his training shoes and struggled through a mile cool down, shuffling along the track in barely under ten minutes.

Later that evening, McNeal sat on his couch, watching an early season Phillies game when O'Donnell and Cooper returned from a run. It had been a week since Broad and both men were still feeling the effects of it. Cooper took a seat next to McNeal. "Yo, Mac, how'd that workout go?"

"Eh, it went ok. The second four could have been better, though."

"Phils winning?" asked O'Donnell.

"Scoreless game. The ageless wonder Jamie Moyer is throwing a gem, but so far no run support."

"OD and myself were talking about going out tonight. Maybe go down to Second Street Pub?"

"So, Len, you're allowed out tonight? The warden unlocked your chains?"

"Very funny, Mac. Very funny. Yes I am allowed out tonight."

"It sounds fun but I think I need to sit this one out guys. That workout wiped me out, and I got to get up early tomorrow to get in the pool. I was planning on hitting the pool in the AM and then running at Pennypack later on."

Many a night the past few years, McNeal had served as the designated driver. Nearly without fail, he enjoyed himself immensely on the rare occasions the guys got together for a night on the town. But things were different now. With a race in a week, he needed to monitor his rest and recovery. O'Toole figured he had at most three realistic opportunities to qualify for the Olympic Trials before the deadline. He wanted to be sure he did everything he could to give himself the best possible shot. A missed hour of sleep here and there adds up and before long, legs get sore, colds get caught and performances suffer.

Burning the candle at both ends is a risky proposition and more often than not, a losing one.

"Ah come on, Joe. You can sleep in and go to the pool a little later in the day. When's the last time OD went out?"

"I'll tell you right now the last day I was allowed to go out. Friday, February 2nd."

McNeal's eyes grew wide. "You remember the exact day, Len?"

"Yeah, 'cause it was Groundhog's Day. But unlike the Bill Murray movie, it didn't repeat itself for me."

"Wow. I don't know if I'm impressed or worried. And I do realize the significance of the situation, guys. Trust me, I do. But right now I'm on the verge of red-lining. Between working eight hours a day, spending time with Maria, and then busting my hump running, lifting and all that jazz, I can barely drag myself out of bed each morning. If anyone realizes this, it's got to be you two."

O'Donnell and Cooper looked at each other and bowed their heads in shame. They knew McNeal was right and felt bad about pressuring him to go out. "Alright, Mac. You got us. How about this? We head over to Chickie and Pete's and watch the rest of the game there and have some food. We'll be back at a decent hour and everybody's happy," suggested Cooper.

McNeal mulled over this suggestion for a second. He had put off cooking dinner and a roast pork sandwich sounded mighty delicious. He figured he'd wash it down with a few waters and be ok. With all of Philadelphia now smoke free indoors, cigarette smoke was no longer an issue. McNeal decided to go, but he wanted to make them wait a little before letting them know.

"I don't know. I mean Maria had her heart set on seeing the new movie 'Young @ Heart' down at the Ritz."

"Dude, ain't that the movie with the old folks singing?" asked O'Donnell.

"Yeah, man, it got rave reviews at the Sundance Film Festival. It's one of those rare beauties that make you laugh and cry, often at the same time."

Cooper shook his head in shock. It was one thing for Joey Mac to not go out to a bar and spend an all-nighter on the town. That he understood. But to go see a bunch of elderly men and women singing songs instead of grabbing a bite to eat and watching the game. That was downright disgraceful. "Mac, if what you're saying is true, I think you need to move out. I mean, and I thought I liked Maria, but this is unforgivable. Frankly, I'm flabbergasted and I don't easily flabbergast."

McNeal looked from left to right at his two friends and burst into laughter. "Nah, man, I'm just kidding. Maria's visiting her sister tonight. Let's go to Chickie's."

After Cooper and O'Donnell washed up, the three headed to OD's car. They stopped along the way to pick up Maloney at his girl-friend's. He hopped into the backseat with Cooper. "Thanks for rescuing me, guys."

Cooper shook Maloney's hand. "Rescue? That's not a real good way of thinking about hanging out with your girlfriend, Mitch. It's not like we just flew in on a helicopter and saved you from Al Queda."

"Ah, you guys know I love the old broad, but it's nice to get out every now and then."

"Amen to that," agreed O'Donnell.

The foursome walked into the popular eating and drinking es-tablishment on Roosevelt Boulevard. A long line of people stood at the front of the store, waiting for their tables.

"How 'bout we just go straight to the back deck?" suggested Cooper.

"Sounds like a plan," said Maloney "I can't imagine why anyone would rather wait then just head out back."

"Plastic," said Cooper. The other three turned their heads to look at him. "They could be allergic to plastic."

"Yeah, that's rampant these days. Maybe it's too noisy and crowded out there for some," said McNeal. "Frankly, I don't give a hoot, I just want some grub."

McNeal led the way as the four friends fought through the crowds to reach the back deck. Upon arriving, he was surprised to see numerous family and friends waiting for him. He turned to look at Maloney, Cooper and O'Donnell. They just shrugged their shoulders.

"Surprise!"

McNeal's thirtieth birthday was tomorrow. Apparently plans for a surprise party had been in the works for sometime. Maria walked up to McNeal, hugged him and kissed him on the cheek. "Happy Birthday!"

"Was this your doing?"

"With some help from your parents. And of course those guys." She pointed to Cooper, Maloney and O'Donnell. "Thirty's a big deal. I wanted to do something special for you."

McNeal gazed around the deck. Cousins, aunts, uncles and friends gathered throughout. He saw his parents and sisters in the corner, grabbed a hold of Maria's hand and walked over to them. "Hey, fam! Thanks a lot." McNeal hugged his parents and two sisters. "This is really cool. I don't think I've had a birthday party since I was sixteen."

"One more than I ever got," said his sister Teresa.

"Happy Birthday, Joe," said Mr. McNeal. "How's the running going?"

"Pretty good. The next big race is May 31st in New Jersey. Hopefully, I'll get the qualifier there."

Mr. McNeal nodded his head. "I'm sure you will."

McNeal's mother brought over a gift bag for McNeal.

"Aw, you didn't have to do that."

"We wanted to Joe. Look inside."

McNeal reached into the large red and yellow bag with the words "Happy Birthday!" and pulled out a framed picture. In it stood McNeal after his first collegiate cross country race, mud from the course caked over his legs, with his parents and two sisters. Engraved on the frame was "Gold medal winning son and brother."

McNeal's youngest sister Kimmy squeezed McNeal. "No matter what happens, big bro, you're already a gold medalist to us."

McNeal's eyes welled up as he looked at the gift. "Aw, thanks. This is awesome. You guys are the best."

McNeal hugged his parents and sister Teresa. "I better go talk to some of these people who came to see me."

He spent the next hour walking around the deck talking to friends and family members, introducing Maria and answering questions about his running. While he had had been carefully logging everything he ate recently, McNeal gladly chowed down on a roast pork sandwich and Chickie's trademark crab fries. He knew it was not the best fuel, but tonight was a special occasion.

"Alright, Joe, come here. It's time for the cake," called McNeal's mother. It was 9:45 and in fifteen minutes the deck opened to the public and all guests under twenty-one had to leave.

"Happy Birthday to you! Happy Birthday to you..."

McNeal knew what he would wish for. This could be his one and only shot at Olympic glory. Four years from now he'd be thirty-four years old, ancient for a half miler. Most half-milers reached their peak well before their thirtieth birthday. McNeal was trying to buck that trend.

"Make your wish!"

McNeal closed his eyes, imagined hearing the sounds of the Stars and Stripes playing as they raised the American flag at the Olympic Games and blew out the candles on the cake, extinguishing each one. After cake was distributed, most of the guests left, including McNeal's family. McNeal and his parents and sisters shared one last embrace.

"I'm proud of you, big bro," said Teresa.

"Thanks, sis. I'll talk to you guys later."

Maloney, Cooper, O'Donnell and Maria remained with McNeal to hang out a little longer. Across the bar, a couple of women sipped cocktails while periodically stealing looks at McNeal's table. A tall, tan, brunette in particular seemed to be interested in one of the runners. She glanced over her shoulder, quickly turned her head back and giggled, similar to a grade school girl at recess.

"Yo, Coop, I think the woman on the other side of the bar is checking the Sauce Man out," said McNeal.

"How do you know she's not checking out one of you guys?"

"Well, for one, we all have girl friends. So she has to be checking you out, Coop," explained Maloney.

"Mitch, that makes no sense. Number one, she doesn't know you three have girlfriends. And furthermore, everybody knows having a girlfriend automatically makes you at least ten percent more attractive. I mean, look at Joey Mac. Mac, who gave you that shirt?"

"This one?"

"No, the one in the back of your closet. Of course, that one."

"Maria gave it to me today for my birthday. I showed it to you earlier. Remember?"

"Of course, I do. That's why I picked you."

"Look, Coop, no excuses," said McNeal. "Here's what I want you to do. Listen close 'cause it's real important that you do exactly as I say. Ok?"

"I'm not guaranteeing that I'll do anything. I'm pretty positive actually that I won't do anything you say, but I'll listen anyway. Go ahead and hit me with it."

McNeal smiled in amusement. "Listen, Coop. You know I would never lead you astray. So just relax, and follow my instructions. Now you're going to walk over there and say "I noticed you noticing me, and I just wanted to put you on notice, that I noticed you too."

Maloney nodded his head in agreement.

"What? Ain't that a line from an episode of the Fresh Prince?"

"Mac, I'm all in favor of Cooper picking up this broad, and I'm a big fan of Will Smith. But that was the worst thing I ever heard. I think I just lost ten points off my IQ."

"Look, it ain't like Mac told you to go over there and do the Carlton dance. At least Will got girls on the show."

Maria resisted the urge to laugh. "I think it's a great idea."

"To be honest, I think I'd be better off doing the Carlton dance than saying all that mumbo jumbo you told me to say, Mac."

Philip J Reilly

"Fine, fine, fine. Just go over there and do something. She's still looking over here, but you delay, some clown is going to swoop in on her, and then you'll be complaining the rest of the night about why hot girls talk to clowns."

"I will not."

"I've got to agree with McNeal here, Hot Sauce. If you don't go make a move and some donkey does, you'll be livid. That's all I'm saying," said O'Donnell.

Before Cooper could respond, the brunette in question approached the table. "Excuse me. Aren't you the guy from the Grilled Donut Café?"

"Um, yeah. I'm one of the owners," Cooper answered.

She turned her attention to McNeal. "You work there too, don't you?"

"Yes, I do."

"Ok, guys. Just checking. I guess I'll see you around. By the way, I like the place." She turned around and walked away from the table.

"If she looks back before a three count, Coop, it means you're in. One, two..." Before McNeal could say three, their visitor turned her head to look back.

"That's her," said Cooper.

"That's who?" asked O'Donnell.

"The girl from the Café I'd been talking about," Cooper responded. Cooper had told the fellows about a particular customer he thought was attractive.

"Haha!" yelled McNeal. "You didn't say she was South American. I knew it, Coop, I always knew it about you."

O'Donnell and Maloney looked at each other, each slightly confused, and shrugged their shoulders.

"What exactly did you know? And how can you tell she's South American?"

"Didn't you hear her accent? I'm telling you, she's South American, probably Brazilian. And you can't beat Brazilian. Brazilian waxes,

292

bikinis. Heck, Pele was Brazilian and he's like Babe Ruth or Michael Jordan, but for soccer. They're like the best of everything. I think Maxim magazine recently named them the most beautiful women in the world. You Brazilian-macking son of a gun."

Maria shot McNeal a look. "I'm not Brazilian."

McNeal tried to cover his tracks. "You're the exception, baby."

The table exploded into a riot of laughter after McNeal's comments. The rest of the night, however, passed uneventfully as the object of Cooper's affections went unseen.

On Monday, she returned to the Grilled Donut Café. The hint of an accent McNeal was so certain of, however, was nowhere to be found. In fact, after closer investigation, it turned out that she was a South Philly Italian girl named Isabelle Capellini. By the third straight day that she stopped in to buy a green tea, McNeal had seen enough. He went into the back to get Cooper. "Coop, this is the third day in a row she stopped in. That's no coincidence. Our green tea isn't even all that good. I mean it ain't bad, but it's nothing special. I put a tea bag in a cup, boil some water, pour it overtop, add some agave nectar and a splash of lemon and presto, green tea. Maybe it is pretty good, but that's besides the point. You've got to the end of the week to seal the deal with her, or else."

"Or else what? And what do you mean by seal the deal?"

"I don't know what the or else is, but you need to either get a phone number or schedule a date. You've been thinking about this girl non-stop since a month before Broad Street. So I'm giving you a deadline. Seal it, or move on with your life."

"Whatever, Mac. How do you even know she'll say yes?"

"First of all, because I'm Joey Mac. Second, because she comes in here every day."

"So does Old Man Magee. Does that mean he wants to date me?"

"Old Man Magee is a seventy-five-year-old retired gym teacher. What else does he have to do other than come here and talk sports? This is different. Friday, Hot Sauce. Friday."

By Friday, Cooper was a nervous wreck. At two o'clock there was no sighting of Isabelle and they were set to close the shop. Just before locking up, however, she walked through the door.

"I'm sorry. Were you guys about to close up?"

"Soon, but it's ok," answered McNeal, as he straightened up the dining area. "I'll be right there."

"No need to, Mac. I'll help Miss Capellini."

McNeal returned to cleaning, careful not to get in Cooper's way. He did notice, however, that Isabelle Capellini appeared to hang on every word out of Cooper's mouth, responding to most of them with a giggle or a touch. Ten minutes later, the two of them were still talking. He looked over at Cooper, caught eyes, and pointed to his watch, mouthing the words "Got to go to the track."

Cooper took the hint, walked Isabelle to the door and bid her farewell.

"Well?"

"Well what?"

"You darn well know well what. Did you get the number?"

"Not exactly. But she's going to come by tomorrow and we're going to go out for a coffee after we close."

"Coop, we run a café. And you're taking her for coffee? So, you're either going to A) Take her here for an after hours coffee or B) Go to one of our competitors?"

"Well, it's the first thing that came to mind. The important thing is, she said yes."

"True, she did. Well done, Hot Sauce. Well done."

chapter 28

THROUGHOUT AMERICA, MEMORIAL Day weekend officially kicked off the summer season. But Joey McNeal's mind was not on picnics and barbeques, but on a more important task. Today was the New Jersey USATF Championships. It promised to be a high quality meet and posed a terrific opportunity for McNeal qualify. Maloney also entered the meet, but in the 400. The two of them, Maria and Holly, Mitch's girlfriend, drove up together. Maria had offered to drive to Monmouth College so the two could relax and focus on their races. Cooper and O'Donnell, who each decided to shut down from racing after Broad Street, were driving up later with Seamus O'Toole. Both men planned to resume serious training the following week, following a month of recharging the batteries.

"Thanks for driving, Maria."

"Of course, Joe. I just want to see the two of you run well."

Maria's support represented a refreshing change for McNeal. With his former girlfriend Kelly, McNeal often felt as if he had to choose one or the other, running or Kelly. Maria provided no such challenges. In fact, on the rare occasion McNeal lacked the motivation to get out the door, Maria was not afraid to kick his butt into gear. "Listen, Joe. I don't want to be sitting around one day and have to listen to you lament about how close you came to making the Olympics. Now put down the Play-station controller and go run," she once told him.

They arrived at the track two hours before the 12:10 scheduled start time of the 800. Maloney's race was slated for a 2:20 start. McNeal had entertained thoughts of doubling in the quarter just to see what kind of time he could run, but Seamus O'Toole had quickly squashed that idea. "What in the name of Peter Snell do you want to do that for? Damn it, man, focus on the task at hand. Qualifying for Eugene, alright."

McNeal found a quiet spot underneath the stands and out of the sun. He sat in a red fold-up chair, sipping on a bottle of water, listening to his MP3 player, visualizing the perfect race. Before he knew it, the clock read 11:20 and it was time to warm-up. "Alright, gang, I got to go get ready. See you all soon."

"You coming back here before checking in?" asked Maria.

"No, I'm going to take my stuff with me and go right to the check in area."

"Good luck then, Joe." She gave him a kiss on the cheek for good measure.

Maloney grabbed McNeal in a bear hug. "Good thing O'Toole ain't here. Get the job done, Joe."

McNeal chuckled and fist bumped Mitch. Next he ran to the bathroom, a normal pre-race ritual for McNeal and countless other runners. *Ah, I feel about ten pounds lighter,* thought McNeal after exiting. He stopped by the registration table to check the entries in his event. Six athletes were entered with times of 1:50 or better. A lack of competition would not suffice as an excuse to qualify today.

McNeal listened to the sounds of P. Diddy, or whatever Sean Combs called himself these days, as he ran his mile warm-up. "Come With Me," a remake of the classic Jimmy Page song Cashmere, resonated in McNeal's headphones. It had recently become one of his favorite pre-race tunes. He had noticed that a lot of the music on his play list had begun to over stimulate him before workouts, so he cut back and found a few songs able to psyche him up, but not rev him up so much that his heart felt like it was ready to explode. Twenty minutes before the start, a flash of lightning shot across the sky. A loud rumble of thunder followed and within seconds, a torrential downpour of rain began. McNeal and the other entrants huddled together under the officials' tent, awaiting word on what would be done as spectators scrambled for cover. The forecast had called for possible thunderstorms in the evening, but nothing this soon. A man's voice came over the PA system, announcing the plan. "We are going to delay the meet. According to USATF rules, we cannot resume competition until thirty minutes after the final flash of lightening. Everyone please leave the stands in an orderly fashion and proceed to the gymnasium. Thank you for your cooperation."

McNeal looked up at the dark, ominous clouds, hoping they were not a sign of things to come. With a limited number of opportunities to qualify, he needed to race.

An official told the runners to evacuate the tent. It was not considered safe with the threat of lightening present. McNeal gathered his things and ran to the gym area where he saw Maria, Mitch, and Holly. "Any O'Toole sightings?"

"Coop called my cell five minutes ago. They got caught in traffic but were pulling into the parking lot when he called."

The storm lasted ten minutes and not long after the last drop had fallen, the sun returned. The announcer returned to the PA system. "We will restart the meet in twenty minutes. The first event on the track will be the remaining semifinal heats of the women's 100. That will be followed by the men's 800 at 12:45. The remaining events will proceed in order from there."

"Time to go again." He jogged out of the gym where he bumped into O'Toole, Cooper and O'Donnell.

"Joseph! Come here. How you feel today?"

"I'm fine. Hate having my warm-up interrupted, but what can you do, you know."

"Don't pay it no thought. Step out on that track and run the race we've been training for, alright? You do that, and rubber will burn."

O'Toole raised his nose to the sky and breathed in deeply. "Ah, I love the smell of burning rubber on a warm spring day. Now get out of my sight."

McNeal exchanged fist bumps with Cooper and O'Donnell and again went on his way. Ten minutes prior to start time, he removed his headphones, and changed his socks and shoes. McNeal liked to race in a fresh pair of thin socks. He put on his racing singlet, massaged a large glob of Icy Hot into his legs and ran four fast striders down the backstretch. He felt some slight soreness in his left hamstring, but nothing to prevent him from competing. At this point in his training, it was a rare day when some muscle wasn't aching.

The starter called for all 800 meter runners to report to receive their hip numbers. McNeal was assigned number four, placing him in the middle of the ten-man field. The start would be a straight start from the line, no stagger of any sort.

"Gentlemen, let's keep this clean. No elbows, make sure you have a stride before cutting in. They'll be two commands. On set, step up to the line, but not on it. Then the gun. Any questions?"

There never were any questions at a meet like this, but the starter asked just in case. McNeal was sometimes tempted to ask something along the lines of "So we're not using blocks today?" but never mustered up the courage to do so.

"Runners SET!" BANG!

McNeal broke for the pole, catching an elbow in the chest from the runner to his left as he did so. He stumbled, nearly falling to the track, but recovered his balance just in time. McNeal found himself at the back of the pack after the first hundred meters, sitting in tenth place. He knew the last couple of runners in the fast heat were seeded in 1:52 and he couldn't stay in the back for long and harbor any hope of qualifying. McNeal veered into lane two and moved up in the pack. By the 200 meter mark, he sat in sixth place, hitting the split in twenty-six seconds and change. With no room in lane one, McNeal remained in the outside on the turn and fought his way up to fourth place. His legs felt strong, but his breathing labored, probably from the elbow and the ensuing hard charge down the backstretch. At the quarter-mile, McNeal remained in fourth, passing the halfway point in 53.5.

"Let's go, Joseph. Today's the day, today's the day."

The pace remained the same for the third 200 meters and McNeal knew he would be close. At the 600 meter mark, he sat in third place a couple of meters off the lead, and the clock read 1:20. He would need a strong finish to hit the time, but he still had a shot.

With 150 meters remaining in the race, McNeal began his kick. His arms pumped and his legs powerfully churned around the turn and down the track. With fifty meters to go, McNeal ran shoulder to shoulder with the leader and tried to accelerate one final time. Just as he did, however, his legs began to give out. The intensity of the effort to get back in the race had taken its toll and McNeal now struggled to remain on his feet, let alone pass the leader. His eyes squinted and his vision blurred. The pain felt like nothing he had ever experienced in all of his days of racing and he doubted he would even reach the finish line. Each step felt as if in slow motion and his hamstring and butt muscles seized up. Desperate, he focused solely on his form, but his arms flailed out to the side, catching the runner who had bumped him at the start, and further knocking him off balance. Somehow, McNeal remained on his feet and crossed the line before tumbling to the hard, unforgiving track, scraping the skin off his hands and knees in the process. The clock read 1:48.87 unofficially, just short of the provisional standard. He lay there for a moment, in too much pain to move. In addition to his cuts, bumps and muscle soreness, McNeal felt as if his internal organs were waging war to free themselves from his body. Cooper and Maloney stepped onto the track to help him up. Cooper reached down and grabbed McNeal's hand. "Great race, Mac. How you feeling?"

"Like a got run over by a Mac truck. Did I get it? Did I qualify for the Trials?"

"I don't know, the official time isn't posted yet."

McNeal, bloody from his fall, knelt on the infield, staring up at the scoreboard. Ten minutes passed before the scoreboard flashed the results making it official. McNeal had not qualified for Eugene. The psychological pain was far greater than any physical soreness. It would be a long silent ride home for McNeal; a ride that didn't begin for another two hours as McNeal had to play the role of good soldier and watch Maloney run the quarter in a time of 48.21.

McNeal took Maria to a movie that night, partially as a way to treat her, but just as much to distract himself from the near miss of earlier in the day.

"So, Joe, what do you want to see?"

Maria yearned to help McNeal cope with the disappointment of not yet qualifying for the trials. What had once seemed like an eternity and plenty of races to get the required time, now boiled down to one final moment. McNeal would be racing in Icahn Stadium in New York City in two weeks on June 12th. It represented his final shot Eugene.

"Hmmm, I don't know. What's out?"

Maria checked the Daily News and saw the typical assortment. There was the chick flick, the gross-out comedy, the action adventure, the superhero movie. "Looks like the usual suspects. Do you want to see the new Adam Sandler movie, about a Zohan or something like that?"

Maria typically did not enjoy Adam Sandler, but she knew what a big fan of his comedy Joey Mac was.

"You sure? You don't even like Adam Sandler. Didn't you want to go see those singing senior citizens?"

"Yeah, but that's only playing downtown. We can save a lot of time just going to Neshaminy to see Zohan. It'll be funny."

McNeal knew that Maria, unlike Kelly, was not particularly fond of Adam Sandler's brand of humor. This made McNeal quite grateful of her offer to see 'Don't Mess with the Zohan.' "Ok, let's see that. Heaven knows I could use a little laughter."

Maria could hear the disappointment ringing in his voice. "Joe, you ran a hell of a race today, you really did. What'd you miss qualifying by? A couple tenths of a second? You'll get it next time, I know you will."

"Thanks, Maria. I sure hope so. I'm running out of time though."

"How many shots have you had? I mean, realistically today was the first race you actually could have run it. You missed the Villanova meet and then your other race, I don't think anyone was within five seconds of you."

McNeal appreciated Maria's confidence in his ability, but he had doubts. He felt capable of running at least the provisional standard of 1:48.5 but wasn't quite as confident he could run the automatic mark of 1:46.5. An athlete with the provisional standard had the pleasure of waiting to see if he ranked among the top thirty-two athletes who declared for the event. If an athlete reached the automatic time, he was granted a spot in the field, no matter how many athletes reached it. Normally, several athletes with the provisional, or "B" standard, got into the meet. They just had to sweat it out.

"I know, I know. I trust Seamus but I just wish we had a few more races built into the schedule to give me some wiggle room."

"Seamus must be very confident you can hit it when you need to. Now, let's forget about it for a while and go watch Adam Sandler make an ass of himself."

McNeal laughed, stepped out of the car and walked with Maria to buy tickets. The movie, already in theaters for three weeks, did not approach sell out numbers for tickets sold. In fact, once Maria and Joey Mac entered the theater with their Snow Caps, popcorn and two bottles of water, they had their choice of seats. Maria gestured to a row of seats midway up the steps and they took their seats. By the start of the film, a few other couples and a small group of teenagers joined them in the theater. Two hours later, McNeal and Maria emerged from the movie, each with widely differing views on 'The Zohan.'

"One of the best movies of the year," said McNeal, just slightly tongue in cheek.

"You have got to be joking, right? That was awful! I can't remember seeing anything worse."

"I think you just don't understand Adam Sandler's humor."

"What's to understand? It's not like it's some highbrow intellectual humor. A twelve-year-old would get it."

"Best movie of the spring and summer. Hands down."

"Better than Iron Man?"

McNeal opened his car door, sat down and started the car. "Oh, of course."

Maria joined him in the vehicle and buckled her seat belt. "I think you are ridiculous."

McNeal looked at Maria and smiled as he drove away. She just shook her head and laughed. The movie, whether brilliant or terrible, served its purpose of brightening McNeal's mood. Until he fell asleep later that night and dreamt the day's race several times, each time waking up in a disappointed sweat after again just missing the standard. After the fourth occurrence, McNeal got out of bed, put on a pair of shorts and his running shoes and stepped into the darkness and ran.

chapter 29

SUNDAY, JUNE 8TH would be McNeal's last long run prior to his final attempt at qualifying for the Trials. O'Donnell and Cooper were joining him. O'Donnell hoped to run a few fast races at some local track meets during the summer, while Cooper stood at a cross roads. He had put in so much time and work into his past year of training and it all paid off with his Broad Street victory. Unlike McNeal, however, he entertained no dreams of Olympic glory. His best event, the ten-miler, wasn't in the Olympics. He did not consider himself a marathoner, and even if he was, that ship had sailed in the fall with the Olympic Marathon Trials. Cooper's tentative plan was to hop in a few races this summer and hopefully log an ample amount of mileage to prepare him to run the Philadelphia Distance Run, a half marathon widely considered one of the top races of its distance in the country, if not the world.

The three of them drove to Kelly Drive, home of an 8.4 mile loop frequented by runners, bikers, and in-line skaters. It felt like just the other day he and Mitch Maloney ran five miles at the Drive, complete with a dash up the Art Museum steps. It was here back in September that Maloney proclaimed himself to be "all in." Mitch had recently run a PR of 1:53 in the 800, not a bad time after missing nearly two months with injuries. Today, the three runners would actually venture inside the museum. Maria would be driving down with

OD's girlfriend, as well as Isabelle, whom Cooper had been spending increasingly more time with. Mitch passed on the invitation to join them, saying "I ain't ready to actually set foot in the Art Museum yet."

The runners ran at a relaxed pace at the onset of the run, taking the opportunity to discuss a motley of topics, ranging from McNeal's confidence about qualifying for the Trials in a week (high he claimed), the status of Cooper's relationship with Isabelle ("a work in progress") to Cooper and O'Donnell's post Broad Street training ("I finally feel like I'm recovered and ready to go" said O'Donnell.) The first four miles defined the term "conversational pace." As so often occurs when two or more runners of a competitive nature get together, the pace slowly began to quicken. Talking ceased somewhere in the middle of the sixth mile as the run changed from "conversational" to "hammering." After running a pair of miles under 5:30, McNeal had had enough, and decided to back off the pace for the last mile. "I'll be the guy," he said as he suddenly slowed. "No offense to you guys, but I'm not trying to leave my race at Kelly Drive. I've only got a few days until my last shot at this."

Cooper and O'Donnell agreed and both men backed off the throttle as well. "I was hoping somebody would say something 'cause I was dying," said Cooper.

The three runners finished their run and changed in the restroom at Plaisted Hall at the base of Boathouse Row, the Philadelphia landmark that serves as the start and finish of the loop. "Nothing like a little spray-on deodorant and a birdbath in the sink before going to a classy place like the Art Museum," joked O'Donnell as they walked the quarter mile to the museum. Entrance to the museum was free on Sunday mornings before eleven.

"To think I've lived here over twenty-five years, and this is my first time actually going inside this place," said Cooper.

"My second, and just like the first, on a free Sunday with a date," said McNeal.

They met their respective dates at the top of the steps as countless tourists flashed pictures of each other posing at the top of the steps in the classic Rocky Balboa pose. O'Donnell shook his head.

"We live in the cradle of liberty and our top tourist attraction is museum steps that a fictional boxer ran up. Not even the museum itself."

"When's the last time you stopped by to see the Liberty Bell, Len?" asked Maria.

"Ummm, I don't know. Probably on some school trip back in grade school."

They entered the museum and proceeded to the café where lunch was sold. An eight-plus mile run works up the appetite. Sandwiches, soups, and salads made up the majority of the available options. McNeal chose a soup and salad combo, despite the ribbing he knew he'd take from Cooper and O'Donnell, two runners who espoused the philosophy "If the furnace is hot enough, it'll burn anything," of eating.

Each couple eventually went their own way, touring the cavernous museum as they saw fit. McNeal, by no means an art aficionado, surprised himself with how much he enjoyed perusing the relics throughout the museum. He particularly enjoyed the medieval exhibit which featured artifacts from the era of King Arthur's Knights of the Round Table. Maria, on the other hand, immersed herself in the Impressionist exhibit. After an hour exploring the Impressionist Era, McNeal and Maria moved on to a more abstract section of the museum. While McNeal could appreciate the skill and attention to detail in much of the Impressionist work, he found himself thoroughly perplexed by paintings that appeared to be made of random splashes on a canvas. "I think I could do that."

"Joe, you can't even draw a stick man. How can you say you could create a valuable piece of art?"

"That's my point. It's just a random assortment of colors splashed on a canvas. My five-year-old cousin could do that."

"Well, he'd have a better shot than you."

McNeal shook his head and checked his watch. He had played the good soldier throughout the day, but was approaching his limit. Luckily, they were near the finish line.

Just before exiting, they arrived at an exhibit spotlighting the history of the Olympic Games, from its origins in Ancient Greece, to the modern incarnation that began in 1896 in Athens. McNeal's mood immediately brightened and his focus sharpened. Legends of track and field were prominently displayed throughout the exhibit. Paintings of Jesse Owens, Carl Lewis, Steve Prefontaine, and Jim Ryun lined the walls.

Maria pointed to the portrait of Prefontaine. "Who's the guy with the porn star 'stache?"

McNeal turned to Maria with a puzzled look. "Porn star 'stache? Uh, that's Steve Prefontaine."

"Oh. Well, what made him special?"

McNeal again quizzically stared at Maria. "Hmm. Well, I guess what people most loved about him was the passion he raced with. He raced like it was an art form and tried to give the fans a show. They made two movies about him. We should rent one."

"Yeah, that'd be cool. Do you think of racing as an art form?"

"Me? Haha, no, not my racing at least. I'm just trying to survive out there."

Maria playfully punched McNeal on the shoulder for his display of humility. McNeal moved to the next branch of the exhibit where bronze sculptures of chiseled figures running, jumping and throwing showed idealized versions of the human body in action. Soon the remaining members of their party joined McNeal and Maria in the Olympic display.

"Joe just transformed from absolutely dying to leave into a little kid in a candy shop. It's kind of cute," Maria told Cooper.

Cooper glanced at Maria, rolled his eyes and walked up behind McNeal, who currently was looking at a collection of medals that had been donated to the museum. Next to the medals was a collage of scenes from different opening ceremonies. McNeal paused there. "Just check out the looks on everyone's faces. It's indescribable. It's the moment of a lifetime. I know I don't need to say this, but I'd do anything for a moment like that."

"Joey Mac, you already have," Cooper told him. "You've totally dedicated yourself to the cause for the past year and now you're on the cusp of competing for an Olympic berth. After next week's race in New York, you'll be going to Eugene to take a shot at Beijing. That's all you can ask for, a shot."

"Yeah. A shot, that's all I want." McNeal slowly spoke the words as he walked away. In order to get that shot, however, McNeal needed to run significantly faster than he had ever run. He needed to transform the potential that Seamus O'Toole saw into the performance of a lifetime. Even then, it might not be enough.

chapter 30

McNeal left for New York mid-afternoon on Wednesday. While a trip to New York only lasted about two hours, McNeal wanted to be well rested for Thursday's race. Sitting in the gridlock of NYC traffic didn't fit McNeal's notion of ideal race preparation. Maria accompanied McNeal on the trip. She just wrapped up her year as school nurse at Second Chances. Mitch Maloney also traveled to the meet and would compete along side McNeal in the 800. He harbored no aspirations of qualifying for the Olympic Trials, he simply hoped to better his best time of 1:53. Cooper remained home to run the Café. He would travel up on Thursday with O'Donnell and O'Toole to watch McNeal and Maloney race.

Maria offered McNeal the use of her car, a 2003 Volkswagen Jetta, as long as he agreed to drive. The prospect of driving through the city of New York terrified her. McNeal, eager to drive a car with an air conditioner and a CD player, readily agreed. Save for a brief backup on the Jersey Turnpike, the ride proved to be uneventful. Traffic in the normally jammed Lincoln Tunnel even moved at a steady, if not swift, rate of thirty miles per hour.

At four o'clock, they arrived at the Hampton Inn in Queens, a mere three miles from Ichan Stadium, site of the race. The Hampton housed a contingent of Philadelphia Phillies fans who had traveled up

I-95 to see the Phillies battle the hated New York Mets. "I wonder if there's any tickets left?"

"Joe, do you really think it's a good idea to go to a game the night before a big race?"

"I doubt it would hurt anything. I don't plan on playing centerfield or anything," joked McNeal. "And I'm definitely not going to get behind the plate and catch. That would be suicidal, catching nine innings the day before a race. But just sitting out in the bleachers and watching the game will probably be relaxing, you know. It's not like I want to sit in a chair for five hours with my eyes closed chanting "I must run fast" over and over again."

Maria rolled her eyes before responding. "I'm just saying, you didn't come up here to go to a game. I mean we can watch it in the room or down in the lounge, but walking up the steps, being out in the crowd, if it was me, I'd prefer some peace and quiet."

Maloney nodded his agreement as the three boarded the elevator to their third floor room. "Joe, I hate to do this to you, but I got to agree with Maria."

McNeal thought about what Maria said and knew she was correct. While most likely no harm would come from going to the game, there was no need to tempt fate. He needed to be on top of his game tomorrow, a mere hundredth of a second could be the difference between competing in Oregon and staying home, Olympic dreams dashed. "You guys are right, I just got excited at the prospect of watching the Phils beat the Mets in New York."

They exited the elevator and walked down the long carpeted hallway to their room. McNeal slid the key into the door and walked inside where one lonely double bed sat. No second bed. No pullout couch, no couch at all. In addition to the double bed, two end tables with small, orange lamps, and a twenty-nine inch television inhabited the sparsely decorated room. The three travelers looked around the tiny room, then at each other.

"Um, Joe, what kind of room did you order?" Maria asked.

"I booked it online. There's supposed to be two queen beds and a fold-out couch."

Not only were the other beds not in the room, there was no space in the minute room for them.

"There must be some sort of mix-up. I'll call downstairs to see if we can get this resolved."

Mitch and Maria enthusiastically agreed with McNeal's decision to call the front desk. Neither appeared thrilled with the prospect of squeezing three across a bed made for one.

"What do you mean this is all that's available? The site said a standard room came with two queen-sized beds and a pull-out couch."

Maloney and Maria sat silently, trying to hear the response of the person on the other end of the line. The agitated look on McNeal's face told them all they needed to know.

"Listen, I don't want to get the difference in rooms refunded, I want a different room." McNeal paused as he listened again to her explanation. "No, thank you for all of your help. Oh, yes I will be sure to have a wonderful night. You do the same." McNeal hung up the phone. "Supposedly, the travel site only guarantees a room. It doesn't guarantee any type of room and the best rooms go to those customers who booked with the hotel themselves. They said we can't even get a cot because there's no space for it. Which there isn't." McNeal glanced around the room, hoping to see space that wasn't there.

Maria tried to make the best of the situation. "It's ok, Joe. You take the bed, we'll each take a side of the floor. Just make sure not to step on me in the morning."

"I can't make you guys sleep on the floor. Why don't you take the bed, Maria?"

"I'm not sharing a bed with you with your cousin here."

"That's not what I meant."

"Then there's no way I'm making you sleep on the floor the night before a big race. No discussion, it's final."

Mitch Maloney looked from Maria to his cousin and tried not to laugh. "So I don't get any say here on where I sleep?"

"Oh, I'm sorry, Mitch. It's just that, well, you know," Maria stammered.

"That my cousin Joe is trying to get to the Olympics and poor little Mitch isn't? So now we're being racist? Dr. King would be ashamed."

"Racist? Not only are we cousins, we're both white, Mitch. How can that be racist?"

"Not that kind of racist. Racist as in your race is more important than mine."

"Then what does Martin Luther King have to do with that?"

"Not a damn thing. I just thought it sounded good. I'm taking a pillow and sleeping in the bathtub, that's final. It's 2008. You two have been dating for nearly six months. Go ahead and share a bed. Now let's get some dinner."

They checked out the restaurant in the lobby, but decided the menu was overpriced for what it offered, a combination of typical pub food and seafood entrees. They walked down the street to a series of shops and restaurants and chose a small Italian shop. McNeal ordered the spaghetti with turkey meatballs, while Maria got the chicken parmesan platter and Maloney ordered lasagna. The cozy bistro satisfied their appetites and they returned to their undersized room where they watched the Phillies defeat the rival Mets before heading to bed..

"Goodnight, Maria, goodnight, Mitch. Thanks for giving me the bed," said McNeal as he turned off the TV and lights. "There's plenty of room if someone wants to share."

"No way, man," yelled Maloney from the bathroom. "You kick and fart in your sleep. I remember from having to share a bed with you way too many times on travel trips."

"No thanks. I really do hope that he's kidding though," said Maria.

"I don't know. I'm sleeping when I'm sleeping."

All three laughed, then silently went to sleep. Soon enough, McNeal would be stepping onto the track. For now, though, he just wanted to visualize the perfect race as he fell asleep. Tired from the long day, he struggled to keep focus for the entire race, and dozed off somewhere on the second lap. He'd have to wait for the real thing to see how it ended.

McNeal awoke early the next day; he rarely slept well the night before a big race, whether his own, or one his team was competing in. He looked around the cozy quarters and saw Maria and Mitch still asleep. Maria began to stir upon hearing McNeal get out of bed.

"Where you going?"

"I don't know. I was just going to go out for a walk. Get some fresh air, loosen up the legs and see if I can find some breakfast. Do you want anything?"

Maria sat up, rubbing the sleep out of her eyes. McNeal was impressed that even just waking up from a night of sleeping on a hard, hotel room floor, she still looked beautiful. "Um, I guess if you can, pick me up a coffee and a bagel, please?"

"Sure, no problem."

Maria smiled at McNeal. "You want me to go with you?"

"Nah, you can lay down and rest. Hop up in the bed. I'll be back in a few."

"Ok, see you later."

McNeal took the elevator down and stepped out into the warm New York air. The temperature was already eighty-one degrees and it was not quite eight o'clock in the morning. McNeal didn't mind racing in the heat, especially events less than a mile. Had he been running a 5k, his thoughts might have been different. With a start time after nine o'clock, the heat might not be a factor anyway.

McNeal walked down 31st Street towards Broadway. He saw a deli on the corner and walked inside. With signs in both Spanish and English, McNeal understood why New York was considered to be a cross section of the county, a true cultural melting pot. McNeal searched the aisles, picking up a quart of orange juice, a six-pack of bottled water, a bag of cinnamon raisin bagels, and a small jar of peanut butter. McNeal's mind wandered as he walked the several blocks back to the hotel. From thoughts like "Would there be someone to push him in the race?" and "Am I really ready for this?" to "How long of a flight is it to Eugene?" and "I bet Chinese food in Beijing is awesome."

McNeal spent the time after breakfast watching reruns of Sports Center, reading the newspaper and trying not to think that in a few short hours, he'd be running, up to this point, the biggest race of his life. If all went well, it would only hold the top spot until his next race.

McNeal drove Maria's Jetta to Ichan Stadium arriving at seven o'clock. O'Toole, Cooper and O'Donnell arrived at the stadium an hour later, just prior to Maloney and McNeal warming-up.

"Joseph, how are those pistons you call legs feeling?"

"Feeling good, Seamus. How you doin' today?"

"First of all, Seamus O'Toole doesn't have bad days. Second of all, good old Seamus isn't running any races tonight."

"Seamus, are you going to ask the 'Mitch Man' how I'm feeling?"

"Well, I guess Seamus has no choice, now Mr. Maloney, do I? How is the slower of the two McNeal cousins doing?"

"What? My last names Maloney and you—whatever, I'm good, I'm good," Maloney answered. "Crazy old man."

Cooper and O'Donnell exchanged hugs with McNeal and Maloney, wishing each man luck.

"So, cuz, is today the day?"

"We'll see, Mitch. I know I've put the work in, now we'll just have to see what happens. I don't really want to jinx myself by making some bold prediction."

The two returned from their ten-minute run, and each went about their own particular routine of stretching and drills. McNeal reached into his track bag and pulled out his headphones. Being superstitious, he skipped the Olympic theme song, figuring it would be bad karma. Now if he qualified for the Trials, he might play the theme song. Instead he listened to "Chariots of Fire" as he went through a vigorous series of drills. At five of nine, the final call for the 800 was made and McNeal and Maloney checked in with the clerk.

"Good luck, Mitch, good luck, Mac. Do what you've been training for, man. Today's the reward," said Cooper.

McNeal made a pit stop to get a good luck kiss from Maria, thinking that Seamus wasn't looking.

"Damn it, Joseph, get your blarney-kissing arse over there."

McNeal unsuccessfully tried not to laugh at O'Toole's remarks. O'Toole could always be counted on to say something memorable. He stepped onto the track and ran his last two striders down the homestretch. The starter called for all half-milers to step to the line. McNeal held the second position from the inside. Directly to his left stood Lucas Cortez, the runner who bumped McNeal at the start of his last race. Cortez ran 1:46.31 that day to win the race and qualify for Eugene. He was using this race as one final tune-up for the Trials. The starter took his place ten meters down the track and uttered the directions McNeal had heard hundreds of times in the past twenty years. The gun sounded and all eight men in the field exploded from the line, each hoping to establish good position. McNeal ran the first turn aggressively, knowing every tenth of a second was vital. He settled into second place, tucked behind Cortez where he remained through the first 3meters, run in forty seconds flat. By this time, two runners had pulled up along of McNeal and boxed him in. *"I've got to get out of here,"* thought McNeal as he ran down the homestretch of the opening lap. He heard O'Toole and the guys screaming those same instructions to him. Just before the quarter mile mark, McNeal attempted to break out of the box by squeezing through a small space between Cortez and a runner from Central Park Track Club. Like a football running back hitting a hole, McNeal quickly split the gap. Just when he thought he had successfully broken free, his left foot was clipped from behind. He stumbled, struggling to remain on his feet. After three strides, McNeal nearly regained his balance, until his flailing right arm caught a passing runner, sending him tumbling to the ground. Mitch Maloney hurdled McNeal as he lay on the ground, looking down at him as if to say "sorry" although he was not responsible for the fall. McNeal slammed his fists on the ground, his Olympic dreams now crushed.

"Get up, Joe, get up!" screamed Maria.

McNeal did just that, climbing back to his feet, and resumed running. *Suck it up and run for pride.*

McNeal ran as hard as he could that second lap, even passing a few runners who had fallen off of the pace. It was all in vain, however, as he crossed the line in 1:52 in a virtual dead heat with his cousin Mitch Maloney, well off the qualifying standard.

McNeal continued running after crossing the line, immediately exiting the track. He headed straight for the men's room where he stood facing a sink, staring straight into the cracked mirror, broken, just like his Olympic dream. Tears slowly ran down his face, leaving a trail of tears from his eyes to the corners of his mouth. McNeal grabbed a paper towel from above the sink and wiped them from his face. Mitch Maloney walked into the room to try and console his cousin, but couldn't find the words. "I'm...uh, I'm sorry, Joe." Maloney patted McNeal on the back and walked out the door.

McNeal inhaled deeply, closed his eyes and attempted to collect himself before leaving the confines of the restroom. When he felt satisfactorily composed, McNeal walked out the door and into the arms of the waiting Maria, who squeezed him tightly, whispering into his ears that it would be alright as the tears again began to flow.

Seamus O'Toole approached the couple, and for once, bit his tongue and waited for them to end their embrace. "Joseph! Come here. Now you listen to me. Lift your bloody head up off your chest, damn it. Your neck works, does it not? You have absolutely no reason to hang your head. Do you hear me?"

McNeal reluctantly nodded his head. One day he might look back fondly on the past year and recall the great progress himself and the guys made, the crazy workouts, racing Bernard Lagat and Craig Mottram at Millrose, and just missing out on a gold watch at the Penn Relays. At the present moment, all of that meant nothing to McNeal, however.

"Just to be one of those rare individuals who can think about the Olympics without making a mockery of the Games says something, Joseph. Qualifying time or not, the races you ran, the fitness you possess, that can't be taken away. I've got some phone calls to make, but I'll talk to you later."

O'Toole and McNeal shook hands. O'Toole planned on visiting family in New York so Cooper and O'Donnell would be returning home in Maria's car. Despite Maria offering to drive back to Philadelphia, McNeal insisted on driving. He hoped the act of driving would allow him to clear his head and not think about the race for a while.

This strategy worked for about twenty minutes. Once they left the city limits and began the monotonous drive down the Jersey Turnpike, McNeal's mind proceeded to wander and his thoughts drifted to what might have been if only he had remained on his feet. If he had simply fallen short of the qualifying time, he'd be upset, but at least he would know that he simply was not fast enough. Instead he fell, and would never know what would have happened if he had remained on his feet for the entire eight hundred meters. If: the biggest little word in the English language. If only he had run a few tenths faster in New Jersey. If there had been more competition at the meet at Plymouth Whitemarsh High School. If he hadn't gotten sick. If he had just one more race to run. If, if, if. The list was endless. Sadly, none of it mattered. Ifs never did. Ifs led to sleepless nights, caused old men regret, and added to the heartache and pain. But change something? No, ifs never did that.

chapter 31

THAT NIGHT MARIA offered to take McNeal to a movie. He declined. After falling short in New Jersey, McNeal knew he still had another shot. No such shot existed now. The guys encouraged McNeal to make a trip downtown with them but he was in no mood to play the role of designated driver. For the first time in his life, he understood the need for some people to drink away a tough day. He didn't indulge in the idea, but he understood. "I think I'm just gonna stay in and watch TV. You guys go ahead without me. You too, Maria, call some of your friends."

Despite McNeal's insistence, neither Maria nor his three brothers in training went out. Instead Cooper ordered a pair of pizzas and the five of them hung out at the apartment.

"Joe, I know that in the end it didn't work out for ya, but I'm proud of you," said Maria. "You did what most people are afraid to do. You took a chance at something special. You risked everything. And I know if you hadn't fallen you'd be going to Eugene."

"That's just it though. I did risk everything. And for what? A scraped up knee? I mean, I quit coaching, lost my job, my girlfriend—well that was actually good—and what do I have to show for it? A couple of scrapes on my knees, that's it.

"Really? Is that really all you got?" asked Cooper. "Cause if it is, then I guess the three of us don't have anything worth a damn either."

McNeal sat silently for a minute. "I ain't saying that, Coop. I'm saying that I—not you—hell you won Broad Street—I feel like it's all been for nothing. I almost wish I never would've started this stupid comeback, or mission, or whatever the hell I've been on."

"Well, Coop might have won Broad Street, but I didn't, Mac. In fact, I haven't won crap," said O'Donnell. "And I wouldn't trade in the past ten months of training for nothing. Joey Mac, we've touched the fire, pushed the limits, and gave everything we had to a noble cause. Regrets? I've got a few in this life, but these last ten, crazy months? No way, man. Neither should you."

McNeal sighed. He knew they were right. It didn't make him feel any better, but it was true. "I hear you Len, I really do. One day, I'll probably even agree. But right here, right now, I don't know. It's still too raw."

"Fair enough," O'Donnell answered.

"Hey, Joe," said Maloney.

"Yeah, Mitch?"

"This don't have to be the end of the line. I didn't think I'd race again this season after getting my leg cracked in a freakin' brawl, but I did, didn't I? Just 'cause you ain't going to the Olympics, don't mean it's gotta stop here. There's a helluva lot more races out there to run. Remember that. Just like you told me back in high school. There's always another race. No matter how good or how bad your last race was, there's always another one waiting to be run."

McNeal nodded. "We'll see if there is for me. I'm goin' to bed." He gave Maria a hug and a kiss goodnight. "I'm sorry I'm such a depressing bum."

"Shut your mouth! Don't call yourself a bum. I don't ever want to hear you say that again, ok?"

"Ok."

"I love you, Joe. Call me in the morning."

"I love you too, Maria. Good night."

McNeal woke up the next day and went to Pennypack Park. Cooper insisted he not work, and McNeal was in no mood to argue.

He laced up his running shoes and began to do what he always did when life dealt a bad hand. But how do you run away from a problem when running is the problem? After a half-mile in the park, McNeal stopped and began to walk. He didn't have the energy or the desire to run. He walked over to the creek's edge, sat on a rock and attempted to skip a few stones. Instead, they sank like his Olympic aspirations. After ten minutes of unsuccessfully skipping stones, he stood up, walked back to his car, drove home and went back to bed. This was one cut that wasn't going to heal easily.

McNeal returned to work Sunday morning, despite Cooper insisting he take off the whole weekend. He figured there was no sense in laying around another day feeling sorry for himself. Moping just wasn't part of his nature. There was no denying the fact that McNeal was distracted as he had burnt two sandwiches before noon. He was grilling a peanut butter, honey and blueberry sandwich on whole wheat bread when he heard a familiar voice. "Joseph! How are you doing?"

"Excuse me? I'm working, Seamus."

"I see that. Joseph, I need to speak with you right away."

McNeal's customer turned to look at Seamus O'Toole, annoyed that the preparation of his breakfast was being interrupted.

"Seamus, I'm working here. Give me a minute, ok."

"Hurry it up then, will you? This bloke is probably starving halfway to Belfast."

The customer, a thirty-something year old business man wearing a grey pinstriped suit with gelled back jet black hair again shot O'Toole a look of agitation. O'Toole paid the man no mind and took a seat at a table in the corner. McNeal soon joined him. "So, Seamus, how do you like the place?"

"It's surprisingly nice. I often thought of opening a café myself. I saw some that were quite impressive over in Ireland. But that's neither here nor there. I have much a more pressing matter to discuss with you. I contacted some people at USATF and they granted me permission to run a certified 800 meter dash tomorrow, as long as we provide FAT timing, of course."

"What? What do you mean? Like host your own race?"

"Exactly. This will give you one more shot to make it to Eugene, Joseph."

McNeal was temporarily speechless. He thought his Olympics hopes were dashed the moment he lost footing in New York and crashed to the track. Now O'Toole arrives and resurrects his shattered dreams.

"Well, who am I going to run against? I can't very well run that kind of time all by myself, you know."

"That does pose quite the dilemma, but I think I have the solution, Joseph, my boy. Mitch and the fellows will rabbit you. Take you out in fifty-two and hang on as long as they can, then get out the bloody way."

McNeal shook his head as he attempted to take it all in. "Ok, what do I got to lose? What time we doing this, and where?"

"Seven o'clock tomorrow at Upper Darby High School. It's the fastest track in the area and I know someone out there with a timing system. I've already made some phone calls to the local papers to try and drum up some interest. Figure a little bit of a crowd can only ratchet up the intensity. Where's Cooper at?"

"He's in the back, why?"

O'Toole didn't take the time to answer McNeal's question. He had already stood up and begun walking back to find Ryan Cooper, diligently working on food orders and balancing the budget. "Ryan? How are you and your little chicken legs doing?"

Cooper looked up from his desk, shocked to see Seamus O'Toole standing in front of him. "I'm good, Seamus. To what do I owe the honor of your presence? In my office, no less."

"Well, you need to let Joseph go home and rest, for one."

"Rest? Why? Is he sick?"

"No, not at all."

"Then why does he need to rest?"

"Seamus here has managed to get the proper paperwork to host a certified half mile race tomorrow and I need Joseph to go home, shake out those legs, and start preparing. I was also hoping you could provide your services as a rabbit tomorrow?"

"Wow, that's great, but, Seamus, you don't call me chicken legs 'cause of my blazing speed. I haven't done any speed work since Penn. Heck, I've barely worked out at all since I won Broad."

"Just give it all you've got for as long as you got then get out the bloody way. That's all I ask."

"Alright, Seamus, I'll do my best for Mac, but I'm not making any promises."

O'Toole shook Cooper's hand and left the back room. "McNeal! Get out of here. Hot Sausage has it all under control."

McNeal looked back towards Cooper, who nodded his head as if to say, "Go ahead."

"I'm going to go to the track to do a pre-meet and I'll pick you up at one ok?" McNeal told Cooper, not wanting to leave him without a ride.

"Don't worry about it. I'll just run home since I need to loosen up for tomorrow myself."

McNeal could not believe what just happened. All of a sudden, his hopes of being an Olympian were renewed. Now that he had another shot, the thought of failing again sickened him. He didn't think he could bear to fall short again. The dreadful idea of missing the standard again almost caused McNeal pause before accepting Seamus' proposal. Almost. *Then I'll just have to get the job done,* he told himself, trying to silence the doubts.

He called Maria to relay to her the good news. She shrieked with excitement upon hearing it, and McNeal calmed her down and reminded her that it was just a shot, not a guarantee by any stretch of the imagination. Maria quickly dismissed the possibility of McNeal falling short yet again. "Third times the charm, right?"

"But this is my fourth attempt, isn't it?"

"Yeah, but one of them you had no competition, and another one you fell down, so they both only count as half. So, like I said, third times the charm."

McNeal made no attempt to disprove her theory as to why he would qualify for the Trials, figuring he could use a bit of luck, even if the thinking behind it was a bit convoluted.

Joey McNeal barely slept a wink that night. The normal pre-race jitters seemed to multiply ten fold with this second chance. He woke up early in the morning and grabbed a newspaper to read and went to the Café, but as a customer, not to work. He ate a bowl of plain oatmeal, flavored with fresh bananas and a touch of cinnamon and sipped from a tall glass of water. He perused the sports page, checking for anything of interest. One item stood out: "Local runner takes one more shot" was the headline and underneath lay a story about McNeal and his quest to qualify for the Olympic Trials. McNeal could not believe his eyes. "Did you see this?" He waved the sports section in Cooper's direction.

"See what? You know I can't read."

"Well, I thought maybe you had Isabella read it for you when she made her daily visit. Anyway, O'Toole got them to publish an article about tonight's 'race'."

"Really? That little leprechaun is amazing."

McNeal finished his breakfast and returned to the apartment. Maria came over at lunch to hang out and help keep McNeal relaxed. At four o'clock, Maloney, Cooper and O'Donnell arrived and the five of them drove to Upper Darby High School. Traffic on I-476 was often brutal, but today the traffic flowed smoothly. McNeal hoped this was a sign of things to come. After spending some time sitting in the bleachers, joking around, McNeal and his pacemakers began warming up. For McNeal, it felt weird warming up for a race that nobody else would be finishing. By 6:30, half an hour before the start time, the stands began to fill and many of McNeal's former runners were on hand to cheer their old coach on. Music blared loudly from the sound system. Pat Myers stood in the press box, serving as the official MC of the event. O'Toole really had gone all out in arranging the event. By 7:00, there must have been well over two hundred people at what was basically a time trial. He saw freshman sensation Brittany Sullivan and senior middle-distance sisters Mary and Colleen Sherman. The three girls left the stands and bounced over to see their former coach.

"Hey, Coach! How you feeling?" asked Sullivan.

"Pretty good. I hear you're doing quite well. That was an awesome 4x8 you ladies ran down at Penn."

"Thanks," said Mary Sherman. "You know we wouldn't be where we are if it wasn't for you. Well, good luck, Coach Mac."

Her sister Colleen echoed her sentiments. "Good luck, Coach."

Sullivan, remembering a speech that McNeal once gave her, said "Good nerves, right coach? All positive thoughts."

McNeal laughed as he ran off to do his final pre-race preparations. He really did miss the team. Now was not the time to think about that, however. After a few minutes, O'Toole, the race's starter, called the runners to the line. "Alright, you all know why we're here." He reached into his red bag and pulled out a shiny black starter's pistol.

O'Donnell recognized it immediately as the gun O'Toole fired into the air that fateful night back in February. "Isn't that the..."

"Of course it is. You don't really think they'd allow Seamus O'Toole to carry a loaded gun, now do you? Enough of that, let's get to business."

Seconds later, O'Toole fired the gun and they were off. The agreement was that O'Donnell and Cooper would basically go all out for a quarter mile and pull McNeal through in fifty-two seconds. If by the 200 meter mark, they were too slow, Maloney would take control. But if they were on pace, he would wait until the quarter to take over, and then try to take McNeal through the 600 in 1:19 flat. He would then peel out to the side and let McNeal finish it himself.

O'Donnell and Cooper covered the first opening two in twenty-six seconds, each man driving for all he was worth, neither wanting to let their good friend Joey Mac down. Cooper and O'Donnell each held the pace through the quarter, with Maloney and McNeal close in tow. Myers called out all of the action over the sound system. "Mitch Maloney now moves into the lead and Joey McNeal sits right behind him, waiting to take his turn."

The stands were rocking with fans cheering McNeal on, trying to urge him further and faster with the sheer power of their voices. Maloney smoothly rounded the turn as the bell rang and he continued the assault on a qualifying time. Just as planned, the clock read 1:19 as the two men hit the 600 meter mark. Mitch Maloney stepped to the inside to let his cousin pass, shouting encouragement as he did so. "This is it, Joe, this is it!"

McNeal briefly wondered why Maloney had stopped running if he had the energy to scream at him, but quickly regained his concentration. He focused on the movement of his arms, pulling each down past his hips. He focused on snapping his legs through the stride cycle as he rounded the final turn and entered the homestretch, running all alone, just himself and the clock.

"Joey Mac, Joey Mac," chanted the crowd so loudly that the bleachers shook as they rhythmically stomped their feet. McNeal had never heard his name chanted before and it seemed to provide an extra push when he needed it most. He got up on his toes, powering down the track with each step as the crowd roared louder as he approached the finish. McNeal could feel his legs tiring and prayed for another thirty meters. His lungs seared and his head throbbed. Running for fitness may be good for the body, but this type of all-out effort wrecked utter havoc on the body and his begged for him to stop. It was now that the mind needed to take control and convince the body to cooperate. Each step closer to the line McNeal got, he grew tighter and more tired, but still he fought to stay smooth. A fast runner needed to be relaxed even when it felt as if all of his body was about to explode. Finally, McNeal collapsed across the line, looking for the clock set up on the infield to see what he had run. It read 1:47.89, unofficially. The men sitting behind the camera checked the tape for the official reading. It read 1:47.82 as McNeal's torso crossed the line. He had successfully run faster than the provisional standard. His time placed him thirty-third in the nation. The top thirty-two runners who declared for the event would be accepted into the meet. Since today was the last day for qualifying, it was unlikely that anyone would jump ahead of him. When O'Toole checked the list and saw that miler Alan Webb was one of the runners on it, he knew McNeal would be in. Webb, despite running the world's second fastest time in the 800 in 2007, would not jeopardize his primary event, the 1500, by competing in the 800.

"You did it, Joseph, you did it," O'Toole yelled as he waved the competitor's list at McNeal.

"Are you certain, Seamus? I don't want to get all excited and then find out some cat in Kalamazoo ran faster to knock me out."

"As certain as I am that the grass in Ireland is the greenest on God's green earth."

McNeal's face beamed with a mixture of excitement, relief and joy as he smiled ear to ear. He rushed over to Cooper, Maloney and O'Donnell to thank them for their help. "Thanks fellows, thanks so much. None of this would be possible without you. And I don't just mean the pacing—although I definitely could never have run that fast all alone—just everything, all of the day to day training together and support."

"Yo, man, none of this would be possible without you," said Cooper, pointing to himself, O'Donnell and Maloney.

"Yeah, Joey Mac, if it wasn't for you getting the crazy idea to get after it one night last summer in a bar, then none of us would have accomplished what we have this year. You're the one who's owed the thanks," agreed O'Donnell.

"These cats might not want any of your gratitude, cuz, but you can thank me. That 600 was the freakin' hardest thing I ever did. We even now."

The four runners shared a laugh and hugs and handshakes were given all around. McNeal then turned his attention to Maria.

"Thanks, Maria, you've been nothing but supportive these last six months." McNeal pulled her close for a hug.

O'Toole had seen enough. "Hey, now I don't mean to rain on your picnic, or anything like that, but I do believe there is still another goal to achieve. So let's not get too overly sentimental here and forget there's a race to be run."

McNeal let go of Maria and walked over to O'Toole, gesturing for the other guys to join him. Despite O'Toole's best efforts to convince them otherwise, the four runners embraced the old coach in a group hug, with Maloney rubbing the remaining reddish grey hair on O'Toole's head. McNeal then did a victory lap of sort, walking around the stadium, talking to his parents, ex-runners and parents of ex-runners, thanking them for coming and seeing how their seasons were going, even though he already knew most of the details. He had kept in close contact with Myers since turning over the program. Myers descended from the press box to congratulate McNeal. Eventually, McNeal changed into his training shoes and went for his cool down. The reality of what he just accomplished hit him full force as he circled the tartan oval; Joey McNeal was going to Eugene, Oregon to compete in the United States Olympic Trials.

chapter 32

COOPER SCREAMED UPSTAIRS to McNeal. "Let's go, man, you've got a plane to catch!"

The roles were reversed today; normally McNeal waited for Cooper, all the while impatiently pacing across the living room. Today it was Cooper's turn to hurry McNeal. Cooper had agreed to drive McNeal and Maria to the airport for their flight to Eugene. They were supposed to leave by 6:15 but the clock on the wall already read 6:20. McNeal suddenly came barreling out of his room, dragging a large blue bag, fresh off a fight with the dryer, nearly tumbling down the steps headfirst in the process. "Dude, that dryer sucks! I put in a load last night before I went to bed figuring it would dry overnight, and I woke up this morning and it was still wet. So I'm in there trying to pack, but still waiting for all of my socks and underwear to dry. Where's Maria?"

"She called and asked me if we could grab her on the way. She said she called your cell, but you didn't pick up."

"Crap, hold on, my phone's still in my room charging."

Cooper led the frazzled McNeal through a checklist of things he needed for the trip. "You're not taking a toothbrush or razor?"

"Nah, man, I never do on a trip."

"So what do you do, not brush your teeth?"

"No way, that's disgusting. I can't believe you'd ask me that. I get the complimentary toiletries from the front desk. With all the airport security guidelines, it's just easier. Alright, let's head out of here," said McNeal, suddenly telling Cooper it was time to go.

Cooper stopped at Maria's apartment on the way to I-95 and they were on their way. O'Toole was already in Eugene, meeting some old friends of his. It was O'Toole's first taste of big time track since his own running days. Traffic on the highway was light and McNeal and Maria arrived two hours before their 9:30 flight. Maria exited the car first, as Cooper stopped McNeal just before he stepped out. "I just wanted to say thanks, man."

McNeal looked at Cooper with a quizzical look on his face. "For letting you drive me to the airport? Anytime, man."

"This past year's been amazing, on and off the track. Without you, none of it would have ever been possible."

"Thanks, Coop, that means a lot. Without you and the guys, I wouldn't be making this trip. You guys have been there every step of the journey, pushing me to my limits."

The driver in the car behind Cooper honked his horn loudly. The two runners shook hands and McNeal hopped out of the car.

"Give 'em hell, Mac," Cooper yelled as McNeal shut the door behind him, giving Cooper a final wave.

"Alright, Maria, here we go." He grabbed his luggage and they began the lengthy walk to Terminal A to catch their US Air flight. McNeal loved flying. It gave him the feeling of doing something important, which in this instance he actually was. It also reminded him of childhood trips to Florida where his family would vacation and visit family. McNeal's family wasn't the richest in the neighborhood, but this never prevented them from taking a family vacation. McNeal's excitement level rose as his mind drifted, prompting him to walk faster.

Maria struggled to keep pace. "Joe, can you please slow down?"

"Oh, sorry. I was just...excited."

"Thinking about the race again?"

"Actually no," answered McNeal, feeling slightly embarrassed. "I was really just excited to fly. I always get psyched up when I fly. I'm not sure what it is, but it gets my juices going."

"Really? That's kind of cute, but can you and your juices please wait for me?"

McNeal slowed down and soon enough they were through the security checkpoint and waiting at the gate. McNeal had worried about his spikes clearing security so he removed the metal spikes and figured there would be ample opportunity to purchase replacements in Eugene. The city wasn't billed as Track Town, USA for nothing. The woman behind the counter made the call for all passengers in rows 1-17 to begin boarding and McNeal and Maria stood up. They would be sitting in row 9, seats A and B.

"Do you want the window?" McNeal asked.

"You don't mind?"

"Nah, not at all." McNeal raised their bags into the overhead storage compartment.

Moments later the engines began to roar and the jumbo jet accelerated down the runway, taking off just before the end of the asphalt straightaway.

McNeal exchanged high-fives with Maria, who could only smile at his child like enthusiasm. "Eugene, here we come."

☙❧

After a long flight, McNeal needed to loosen up his legs so he met Seamus O'Toole at the practice track available for competing athletes. "Joseph, I have a pair of spikes I'd like you to try. I met with an old friend of mine who works for Nike. These are top of the line half miler spikes. They're not due out until next year, but they have released a limited number to a few athletes."

"Seamus, I don't know if it's a good idea to try new spikes for the biggest race of my life."

"Precisely why I want you to try them now my boy. If what I think is true, you'll be more than pleased."

McNeal relented and tried on the new spike. They were white with red and blue coloring, appropriate for an Olympic year. The heel had a hole cut out, allowing a runner to run sockless and not worry about developing a blister. McNeal slid his feet into them, tied them tightly and stood up. "Wow, these are snug."

"Do a strider and let Seamus know what you think."

McNeal ran down the straightaway, accelerating with each step. O'Toole was correct, the shoes felt good. "Seamus, these are amazing. They feel like I'm wearing socks with spikes sticking out of them. I think I'll race in 'em. Thanks."

"I told you, my boy. No stone left unturned. They just might provide the extra tenth of a second needed to make it to Beijing."

≈∽

Ryan Cooper, Len O'Donnell and Mitch Maloney gathered around Cooper's laptop. Today marked the first round of the men's 800 and the only way to watch was via a live webcast. The three nervously chewed on their pizza as they awaited McNeal's heat. According to the start list, he would be competing in the third of four heats. They watched the first two heats, each won in a time of 1:46 and some change.

"What's the qualifying procedure again?" inquired Maloney.

"They take twenty four to the semis, so they only eliminate eight. The top four in each heat automatically advance, and then the next eight fastest times," answered O'Donnell.

"Alright, guys, quiet down, he's up now," said Cooper.

Back in Eugene, McNeal toed the line, awaiting the sound of the gun. Maria and Seamus O'Toole watched from the stands, each fidgeting anxiously. The starter raised his hand high in the air, holding the runners for several long seconds before firing his pistol.

McNeal immediately broke for the lead, hoping to secure a spot in the top four while safely avoiding traffic. The remaining members of the field sat back, content to let an unknown do the work. McNeal held the lead through the quarter-mile mile mark, hitting it in 50.8, causing O'Toole to shake his head in worry at the fast split.

"What's wrong? He's winning?" asked Maria.

"Not now, my dear, not now, no questions."

At the 500 meter mark, McNeal remained in the lead, but the eight-man field had closed the gap on him. He held the lead down the backstretch where, with 200 meters to go, the race broke into an all out sprint and McNeal was swallowed up by the pack, falling back into fourth place. McNeal held the coveted fourth and final guaranteed qualifier until fifty meters remained. He gamely struggled to keep form, but his legs betrayed him, tying up with each step. McNeal's head shot back and his shoulders raised as the strain of the fast early pace began to inflict a heavy toll. By the time he crossed the line, McNeal had fallen to seventh place and found himself in the unenviable position of waiting to see if his time of 1:48.07 would hold up. Going into the final heat, he sat seventh among runners who had not qualified automatically. His time needed to be faster than the sixth place finisher. He stood on the infield, hands on his knees and intently watched the fourth and final section. None of the runners in section four wanted to lead, and they came through the 400 in a pedestrian fifty-five seconds, setting up a fast and furious final lap. McNeal held his breath as a horde of runners rumbled down the homestretch six across, praying his time would hold up. McNeal seldom prayed about sports, believing God had bigger things to attend to, but this time he could not help himself. The final runner crossed the line, and McNeal looked up at the scoreboard, waiting for the official results.

1st Elliot- 1:47.23

2nd Gonzalez—1:47.34

3rd Smith—1:47.49

4th Thomson- 1:47.88

5th McNamara- 1:48.01

6th Cortez- 1:48.09

McNeal let out a huge sigh of relief and fell to the ground, knowing he had survived to run another day. That's what the first two rounds of the Trials were about: survival. And McNeal had done so, vanquishing his rival Hector Cortez in the process. He climbed back to his feet and walked over to the stands where he saw a beaming Maria standing next to a still nervous looking Seamus O'Toole, sweat dripping from his brow.

"Joseph, you are going to give me a premature heart attack, you know that? What on earth were you doing out there that first 200 ? You looked like a bloody madman, opening up a ten-meter gap so early in the race. Don't try anything stupid like that in the semis or you'll be burnt like day old ham and cabbage."

McNeal smiled and turned away to cool down.

"Congrats, Joe," called Maria. "Nice race."

"Thanks," yelled McNeal as he jogged away.

"Hmmmph. Don't encourage him."

Back in Philadelphia, Cooper, Maloney and O'Donnell exchanged hugs after they read the qualifiers for the semifinals.

"Alright, cuz. One round down, two to go."

∾∾

The next day, McNeal rose early to shake his legs out and prep them for that night's race. Early in the afternoon, McNeal and Maria stopped by the track to watch some of the other events. McNeal considered himself a fan, first and foremost, of the sport and could not resist the lore of watching some of the greatest athletes in the world battle it out for just three spots on the Olympic team. The best and worst thing about the US system was how no one was guaranteed a spot on the squad. World Champion in the 100 meter, Tyson Gay? Nope. Olympic gold medalist in the 400 meter, Jeremy Wariner? Not him either. American record-holder in the mile, Alan Webb? Not in the US. Not even Bernard Lagat, a two-time Olympic medalist, and a double World Champion in 2007. Fall down in the final, get sick at the wrong time, or just pick a bad day to have a bad day, and you could be watching the Olympics from afar. The American system of qualifying is brutal and plays no favorites. Top three, with an "A" standard, or go home. Like the Trials themselves, participation in the Olympics requires an athlete to obtain a certain standard. For a nation to be granted three berths in an event, each athlete must have met the

"A" standard within the past year. Unlike in past years, however, an athlete's window of opportunity to gain an "A" standard closed at the conclusion of his or her event at the Trials. This was a new wrinkle in the system; in past years a runner who placed in the top three, but fell short of the standard, could travel to Europe to chase a fast time and still reach the Olympics. That was not the case this year. In fact, there had already been one instance of a fourth place finisher who previously hit the standard earning a trip to Beijing ahead of a third place finisher who came up short. Currently, McNeal did not have the "A" standard. He figured to have even a remote shot at placing top three in the final he would need to surpass the "A" standard.

After sitting through a few events, McNeal decided that watching the meet was adding to his nerves. The temperature was also quite cool, and Maria had forgotten to wear a jacket, so she sat there, shivering, while insisting the whole time that she was fine. So, after watching a heat of the 100 meter dash, McNeal opted to head back to the hotel for a few hours. The hotel had an indoor pool which Maria swam in while McNeal sat on the ledge, content to dip his legs in the cool, refreshing water.

Maria's athletically-built body looked quite good in a bikini. McNeal knew he had out-kicked his coverage with her. In Maria, he had a girlfriend who understood his need to run, and in fact wanted to be a part of his competitive life. With her wet, curly brown hair, glued to her shoulders, and her lightly tanned skin shining from a combination of the pool water and the lighting, Maria looked better than McNeal could remember in their six months of dating. Sitting on the edge of the pool, McNeal reflected on the tumultuous past year, the hardships he had fought to overcome, and the day in day out toll the grind of high-level running took on a body and soul. It made him appreciate that much more the opportunity in front of him. Maria's soothing voice awakened McNeal from his thoughts. "Hey, daydreamer, don't you need to get ready?"

"Oh, yeah, you're right. I was just thinking a little."

"You looked pretty into it there. Thinking about the race?"

"Kind of. Just sort of replaying the past year in my head a little. Alright, I'm gonna go get ready. You coming?"

"Yeah, I'll be right there."

McNeal went up to his room, showered, and left with Maria for the track. The time schedule for the evening session called for the 800 semifinal to be run at 9:05, Pacific time, which for McNeal was the equivalent to racing just past midnight. Good thing he had been in Oregon a few days to adjust to the time difference. Back home, Cooper, O'Donnell and Maloney again gathered around the small screen of Cooper's laptop. NBC would be airing the final, but McNeal first needed to qualify.

McNeal's semifinal heat was loaded. On paper, it appeared to be the more difficult of the two sections. Qualifying for the final was simple, finish in the top four in your heat. Unlike the first round, there would be no period of limbo spent wondering whether or not you qualified. Today, barring a disqualification, McNeal would know as soon as he crossed the line if he was moving on to the final or heading back to Philadelphia.

O'Toole reminded McNeal about running a more tactically sound race in the semis. "Don't be the rabbit," O'Toole cautioned him. "Put yourself in striking position, and from 300 yards out, run like the wind, Joseph. Avoid the box like the plague."

At precisely 9:05, McNeal stepped up to the line, ready to carry out O'Toole's plan. Unlike the first round, in the semifinal each runner stayed in their lane for the first hundred meters, before breaking for the pole. The gun fired and McNeal and his competitors took off, running around the turn, each man hoping to establish position before they cut in at the one- hundred meter mark. McNeal found himself in sixth place at the break. Keith Johnson, the defending US champ, led the pack, with collegiate champion Tomas Gonzalez hot on his heels. Johnson took the field through the 400 in fifty-three seconds flat, a relaxed but honest pace. McNeal lay slightly off the pace, still sitting in sixth place, at 53.5. Barring a miracle, there would be no "A" standard today; that would have to wait until the final. He held the sixth spot until 300 meters remained in the race, and then, just as O'Toole had diagrammed, McNeal slid into the second lane and shifted gears. By the 600 meter mark, McNeal had moved into fourth, rapidly closing on the top three runners with each stride. At the top of the final stretch, the top four runners were Johnson, Gonzalez, Mc-Neal and Matt McNamara. Johnson held the lead and was running in lane one with Gonzalez virtually even in lane two. McNeal ran right behind with McNamara on his outside, in danger of being boxed in if any other runners were to make a late move. McNeal took a quick glance over his left shoulder and saw a runner charging hard, about five yards back.

I've got to go now, he thought, knowing he still had another gear. It would be a dreadful feeling to know he could have made the final, but missed out due to a tactical error. With eighty meters remaining in the race, McNeal made his move, splitting Johnson and Gonzalez and powering down the track, arms pumping vigorously in tune with the piston like movement of his legs. McNeal felt as if in slow motion the final fifty meters. Not because he was dying, in fact, he was pulling away from the field with every step he took as Johnson and Gonzalez appeared content to cruise across the line as McNamara battled a late charging Leed Grant for the fourth and final spot. Rather, it was as if McNeal was in the zone, that rare state athletes reach in the midst of peak performances. He felt the movement of every muscle, he tasted each breath of oxygen he inhaled, and felt as if he could hear the individual voice of each of the thousands of fans in the stadium. McNeal could even feel the dribble of spit running from his lips to his chin. Somehow, he deciphered Seamus O'Toole's voice, screaming for McNeal to "put the hammer down." It was a feeling he had read about great athletes like Michael Jordan or Muhammad Ali experiencing, but had never previously felt himself. His peripheral vision allowed him to see that he had pulled clear from the field but he continued charging hard for the line, driving his legs forward with each step. Finally, after what seemed like an eternity, but in reality was mere seconds, McNeal crossed the line, victorious in the first semifinal heat.

The euphoria from winning soon was joined by that all too familiar post-race pain. Pain never felt so good to Joey McNeal, however, as he realized he would be amongst the eight men competing in Monday night's 800 meter final. He had once again lived to run another day.

᭐᭐᭐᭐

McNeal awoke early Sunday morning, ran a few miles to loosen up his legs and went to the local church with Maria. He favored running his pre-meets early in the morning, believing the extra few hours of rest came in handy. After Mass, McNeal met O'Toole at a coffee shop to discuss the various scenarios in which the race could unfold, attempting to devise the best possible strategy for all circumstances. Out of the eight competitors in the final, McNeal would be the only runner without an "A" standard for Beijing. They decided McNeal's best bet would be to sit off the lead, somewhere around fourth or fifth place for the first 300 meters of the race. At that point, he would need to make a decision: Go now, and anyone who wants to go can try and stay? Or bide his time and wait for 300 or less to go? It was a question that could only be answered on the track in the moment.

"I think you should just take the lead from the start, strategies be damned," Maria chimed in.

O'Toole looked up from his coffee, served black, and grumbled. "I think some people don't know when their opinion isn't needed, much less wanted. Just how many championship races have you run in, lassie? Oh, I forgot, zero. Now, as I was saying, Joseph, you're just going to have to make that decision on your feet. If it feels honest, and you think you've got the wheels, you can wait. But if in the unlikely event it feels slow, then you're going to need to get plugging sooner, rather than later. You understand?"

"Yeah, I got it. I'll just have to roll with the punches and see what happens."

"Roll with the punches? Who do you think you are Rocky Balboa? Damn Philadelphians. You do realize he's a fictional character, don't you, Joseph?"

"Uh, yeah, but I didn't say anything about Rocky. I just said, ah, never mind." McNeal had learned it was usually easier to just nod at what Seamus O'Toole said than to argue over the details.

Joey McNeal's family flew out to Eugene for the final. Due to a previous commitment, they missed the opening two rounds. McNeal told them not to worry about it, that if he didn't make the final, it wouldn't be worth watching anyway. McNeal and Maria met them for dinner on Sunday at Track Towne Pizza, a local spot where various competitors could be found chowing down on a well-earned meal after a tough competition, or loading up the night before the big event. McNeal ordered a slice of grilled chicken, a small plate of angel haired pasta with marina sauce, and a side order of yams.

"So, Joe, how those legs of yours feeling?" asked McNeal's mother.

"A little sore but nothing too serious. I'll go back to the room and soak in Epsom salt, and see if I can convince my masseuse here to give them a little rub."

McNeal enjoyed the meal with is family. While the discussion mainly focused on the race, it still gave him a needed break from thinking about tomorrow's race. When the waiter asked if anyone wanted dessert, McNeal was the first to answer. "Not today, well, at least not for me. You guys can have some but I need to fight this sweet tooth at least for one night."

No one took up the waiter's offer of dessert. McNeal's sister Teresa said they'd return tomorrow to celebrate. McNeal hoped she was right.

On Monday evening, McNeal arrived at a Hayward Field that buzzed with energy. Hometown hero Galan Rupp had just qualified in the 10,000 meter and the crowd was fired up. Several local athletes had made the 800 final, again scheduled for 9:00, and hoped to use the home field advantage to propel them to Beijing. McNeal, a decided underdog, had developed a bit of a following himself. Earlier in the day, he had done his first pair of interviews, one for the local newspaper, *The Intelligencer*, and a second for the popular running website "Let's Run." His curly hair and good looks won him a cheering section of female fans who cheered loudly upon seeing McNeal enter the stadium, much to the chagrin of Maria. "Looks like I've got some competition."

"Haha, I wouldn't lose too much sleep over the, uh, competition."

McNeal had also been exposed to his first drug test. Upon arriving at the stadium, the officials from USADA gave him a cup to pee in, and followed with a request for a blood test. McNeal, not at all fond of needles, and absolutely hating the sight of his own blood, contemplated asking the official if it could wait until after the final, but did not want to be thought of as avoiding the test. O'Toole spoke up for him, however. "Sir? Do you think we could wait until after tonight's final? Whatever's in his system now will surely still be there in a few hours, will it not? This young man is going to need absolutely every drop of blood, sweat and tears in his body if he is going to have a shot at gaining a top three spot tonight. Could we spare the needle for now?"

The official paused a moment to think. Track's reputation had been ravaged recently by drug cheats and USATF had promised a clean meet to the public. On the other hand, there would be no harm in waiting until after the completion of the event. "Go on, Mr. McNeal. The urine test will suffice for now. Just be prepared for a blood test later on, ok?"

McNeal eagerly agreed, relieved to avoid a needle. O'Toole was right, he would need everything he had to make the team.

Just after eight o'clock, McNeal left the stands where he had been sitting with Maria, his family and Seamus O'Toole to go warm-up. The manner in which O'Toole and McNeal's father got along amazed McNeal. It was as if they had been best friends for years. As McNeal departed, well wishes rang out from his cheering section. McNeal headed for the fields behind Hayward Field to warm-up. He hoped to escape the madness currently engulfing the stadium. McNeal jogged, stretched lightly, then completed his usual assortment of drills and stretching. He felt ready, his legs feeling as if they possessed the pop necessary to break through onto the Olympic team. Just before 7:30, a loud roar was heard coming from the stadium and McNeal knew the men's 400 meter semis were currently being contested. He could only imagine the level of noise that would emanate from the stands during an actual final. Gigantic goose bumps covered McNeal's arms and legs at the thought. *Focus, Mac. Stay in the moment,* he reminded himself, and returned to his drills.

Soon enough, McNeal finished his routine, and returned to Hayward Field. As he reentered the stadium, McNeal inhaled deeply and took a look around. Ten thousand rabid track fans stood on their feet, wildly cheering the runners in the women's 800 meter final. It was an awe inspiring moment. O'Toole noticed that McNeal appeared to be caught up in the moment, and walked over to the railing to grab his attention. "Joseph!"

McNeal looked up to find O'Toole waving him over.

"Listen, Joseph. Remember what got you here. Now is not the time to grow awestruck. Enjoy the moment, but don't get caught up in it. Suck it all in, chances are this is going to be your one and only dance at the prom. Make the most of it."

O'Toole's words added to the buzzards currently flying circles in McNeal's stomach.

"So I want you to take a look around one last time and remember it. Got it?"

McNeal took one long look around the stadium and the screaming fans. Within minutes, they would all be cheering for him, or at least he liked to think of it that way.

"Now, forget about it. It's just got to be you and your seven competitors out there running the same distance you grew up loving. Today, Joseph, is the day you've dreamed about for the last twenty years. Thousands of runners wish they could be in your bloody spikes, but they're not."

The announcement for all men's 800 runners to check into the clerking area came over the sound system as O'Toole was speaking.

"Alright, Joseph, there's no need to get into strategy. We've done that already. Do what you know how to do, what you're capable of doing, and the results will follow. Go check in and give 'em bloody hell out there."

McNeal gave one last wave to Maria and his family and ran to the check in area. He thought back to the Millrose Games, and the difficulty he had checking in there, all because an official had mistaken the then twenty-nine year old McNeal for a high-schooler. At thirty, McNeal would be the second oldest entrant in the event, after three-time US Champion Marcus Tomlinson, who was McNeal's senior by six months. Experience wise, however, McNeal was a noob. The trials represented McNeal's first national championship appearance.

Back at McNeal's apartment, his friends stood around the television ready to scream their lungs out cheering for him. Each of their hearts raced with excitement as they watched their good friend make his bid to be an Olympian. At the check in area, McNeal gave the gentleman in the blue USATF blazer his name, who in turn, handed McNeal his hip number. McNeal looked down to see the number four, and hoped it was not a sign. Fourth was the worse place to be at the Trials, it meant being oh so close, but not quite close enough. He peeled the sticker off and carefully applied it to his left hip. McNeal wore black spandex, slightly above his knee, with a tight, white singlet and his new blue and white Nike spikes. He bent down to tie them one more time, carefully double knotting each shoe before stepping onto the track to run several striders before the race began. The starter called for all eight runners to head to the starting line and he took his place in lane four. To his inside in lane three was defending USATF champion Keith Johnson, and to his immediate outside was Tomlinson, one of the greatest mid-distance runners in US history. The starter raised his arm and the crowd quieted to a hush. McNeal took a deep breath, and crouched in his stance, waiting for the gun to fire. Once it did all eight competitors took off aggressively. At the break mark he sat in seventh place. Tomlinson and Johnson ran one-two up front, setting a furious pace and challenging the other members of the field to follow. McNeal ran stride for stride with Tomas Gonzalez down the backstretch, reaching the 200 meter mark in 25.5 seconds, nearly a second behind the lead. He remained in the seventh spot through the far turn, his eyes locked on the leaders, watching their every step. McNeal held a good position on the outside of lane one, with a clear path ahead. *Start moving up,* he told himself, as he neared the half way mark of the race.

"Fifty-one!"

McNeal sat in fifth place at the bell. O'Toole stood at the rail of the stands screaming for McNeal to make a move. "It's now or never, Joseph. Don't leave any hay in the barn, let it all loose."

McNeal already felt the burning in his legs as he raced around the turn. Normally that sensation waited until the 600 mark to set in, but the combined effect of the fast early pace and the previous two rounds had taken a toll on him. He knew he couldn't fall off the pace, however. *Fight it, fight it with all you got.*

With 300 meters to go, McNeal knew it was time to go. He dipped his head one time, began pumping his arms faster, and took off down the backstretch, passing one, two runners and moving up to the coveted third position as he reached the 600 meter mark. The lead trio now consisted of Tomlinson, Gonzales and McNeal, with Johnson a stride back in fourth. McNeal ran in lane two, causing him to run extra distance. It appeared not to matter as McNeal moved to the lead with 150 meters to go and unleashed his kick, exploding into an all out sprint. The crowd cheered wildly for the newcomer, and a deafening roar shook the stadium.

This is it, I'm actually going to do this, thought McNeal, as he turned for home in the lead.

McNeal drove his legs powerfully up, focusing on every minute detail of his form, not wanting to waste any motion, or lose even a tenth of a second. In the stands, O'Toole, his family, and Maria were hopping up and down, yelling as loudly as they could for him. But McNeal heard none of them. While in the semifinal, he felt as if in slow motion and his senses seemed to pick up, this time it was a completely different experience. He felt the sensation of every muscle in his body working in perfect sync with each other. All he could see was the finish, all he could hear was his breathing and the footsteps of the runners around him. It was as if the rest of the world had grown silent and dark. With fifty meters to go, hometown favorite McNamara passed McNeal, finishing with his patented strong kick. McNeal battled to go with him, fighting tooth and nail for every step, every inch as his body began the process of shutting down, not wanting to cooperate with his will to win. Gonzalez, the collegiate champion pulled up on his shoulder but McNeal gamely struggled to hold him off.

Get there, get there, he urged himself on, closer and closer to the line.

McNeal's legs were in a total state of shutdown now, his form beginning to break down, arms flailing to the side, but Gonzalez was equally spent. Johnson and Tomlinson had fallen to fourth and fifth, the aggressive pace proving to be their downfall. With twenty meters to go, it was no longer a matter of placing top three, the only question was if McNeal would reach the Olympic "A" standard of 1:46.0, and whether or not he would finish second or third.

McNamara crossed the line victorious with McNeal several yards back, outleaning Gonzalez for the silver. McNeal crossed the line and immediately looked for his time on the scoreboard, his legs wobbling. McNamara walked over to congratulate who he thought were his new Olympic teammates, grasping McNeal, helping to hold him up. The eyes of O'Toole, Maria and McNeal's family were glued to the scoreboard while Cooper and company stared at the television screen waiting to see what time was posted.

Eventually, several nail biting minutes later, the scoreboard lit up and the times were posted.

1st McNamara: 1:45.32 A
2nd McNeal: 1:46.01
3rd Gonzalez 1:46.12 A
4th Tomlinson 1:46.71 A

McNeal collapsed to the track in disappointment. He would not be an Olympian. He could not believe that he had come so far, to miss by so little. One hundredth of a second, less than the amount of time it took to blink, an amount so miniscule to most of the world, but to Joey McNeal, so big. Tomlinson, who by virtue of his time earlier in the year would be going to Beijing, walked over to McNeal and pulled him up off the track. "Great race, man. Just a helluva race. You ought to be wearing the red, white and blue instead of me."

McNeal appreciated the gesture, and the two athletes embraced. It was now apparent to everyone that McNeal would not be going to Beijing, and the other runners walked past him, patting him on the back, each saying something to console him. McNeal jogged off the track, down the tunnel and the fans at the entrance stood and cheered for him. McNeal paused, expecting to see familiar faces leading the applause, but it was merely people who respected the effort McNeal gave in chasing his dream. McNeal, a tear in his eye, raised his right arm and waved to the crowd, acknowledging their cheers as he entered the tunnel.

McNeal slowly walked down the tunnel, pass the interview area to the athlete's locker room, where he sunk down onto the metal bench that ran the length of the room. One day, possibly one day in the near future, McNeal would fondly reminisce on the day he was the second best half miler in the nation. That day was not today. His second place finish felt hollow, knowing two runners whom he beat would be traveling to Beijing to compete in the Olympics. McNeal put his hands over his face, and the emotion of the moment overcame him. Tears flooded his eyes, rushing down his face as he sat there in silence. A few runners walked by and patted him on the back, or shoulder as they passed, each saying something along the lines of "Good race."

O'Toole soon entered, informing McNeal that his presence was requested in the interview tent. McNeal was not in an interviewing mood, but he thought of all the times he watched an athlete face the media on television, and how much more respect he felt for those who stood there and faced the music after a tough loss, as opposed to those who quietly snuck out the back door, leaving their coaches and team-mates to answer the questions. McNeal stood up, composed himself, and trudged up the steps to the interview area, sitting amongst the men who would actually be going to Beijing.

The bright lights of the cameras focused squarely on McNeal and a slew of questions came his way.

"Joe, do you have any regrets about how the race went?"

"Well, I guess my only regret is not running faster."

"Looking back, would you have done anything differently in preparing for this race?"

"I don't think so. I would have liked to have run a few more races, but I was sick for about a week, and that set us back a bit. But I think my coach had me as well prepared as possible."

"Do you feel any bitterness at the rule change preventing you from chasing the "A" standard now, as opposed to past years?"

"Bitterness? No, not at all. I mean I'm disappointed as heck to not be going, but no, I don't feel any bitterness. What's to be bitter about?"

"What are your plans for the future? At your age, do you think you'll take a shot at London 2012?"

"Wow, I don't know about the future. I was so focused on today, that I haven't given it much thought, to be honest with you. At my age, huh? I don't really think I'm that old, but I can't say whether or not I'll take a shot at London."

"Joe, you were a total unknown prior to this year. You didn't even qualify for the Trials until the last possible day. What would you attribute your breakthrough to this year?"

"That's a good question." McNeal inhaled deeply as he thought how to properly answer the question. "I've run my whole life, but a few years back, I got injured and running became secondary to other things, like coaching. About a year ago, I started having some regrets about my career, and decided that I needed to vanquish any ghosts of my past, or I'd always wonder 'what if?' So, with the help of some of my friends and Coach Seamus over there, I decided to, so to say, chase the ghost. And a year of hard work later, here I am. Coop, Mitch, and OD, if you guys are watching thanks for the help. Maria and family, thanks for all of your support. And of course, none of this is possible without God."

The reporters appeared slightly stunned as McNeal thanked those who helped him, despite not qualifying. One last question was raised. "So, then Joe, do you think you've caught the ghost? Are you finally satisfied?"

"Um, I don't know, honestly. Once you're satisfied, then I think you lose that hunger to improve. Today's result withstanding, I'm happy with the year I've had to be sure. But have I finally caught the ghost? Not sure about that, he's one fast cookie."

At that the throng of reporters broke into laughter and the press conference ended. McNeal shook hands with the men who would represent the United States in Beijing and left the stage, where Maria and his family awaited. Surprisingly, the interview process left McNeal feeling slightly better, maybe verbalizing some of his thoughts and feelings helped him sort them out.

McNeal's youngest sister, Kimberly, ran over to McNeal and hugged him. "Good race, Joe. I'm proud of you."

McNeal gave her a hug and then proceeded to hug his parents and other sister, Teresa, each of whom told McNeal how well he had done and that they were, of course, proud of him. McNeal then turned his attention to Maria, his girlfriend who provided so much support over the last several months when McNeal had been so focused on running and nothing else.

"You ran awesome, Joe. I love you."

"Thanks, Maria. I love you too."

The whole crew walked off into the distance, but McNeal stopped short, just before exiting the stadium. He looked around Hayward Field, one final time, sucking it all in, trying to extend the moment just a bit longer. O'Toole approached McNeal, put his arm around his shoulders and spoke. "Joseph, thank you. You brought me back to this great sport of track and field, and for that, I will forever be grateful. For a long time, I had turned my back to track. You changed that. One day, one day soon, you will think of this day, of this season, and wonder if you must have kissed the blarney stone. You and the boys accomplished much, you ought to be proud. Take some time to let it marinate, then we can decide where to go from here. Alright, old Seamus is tired and needs to go get some sleep; you should go grab a bite to eat with your family and that dame of yours, who truth be told, isn't half bad, not sure what she wants to do with a skinny runner like you, but that's besides the point. I'll get in touch in a couple of days."

O'Toole shook McNeal's hand one last time and walked back to his hotel while McNeal heeded his advice and dined with his family and Maria. The next morning he would be flying back to Philadelphia, not as an Olympian, but he would be flying back with the silver medal in the United States Track and Field Championships, a remarkable feat in its own right.

chapter 33

McNeal reflected on the past two-plus years of his life as he walked through the fields. He could not believe that it had really been over two years since the night in the bar when he proclaimed to his flag football teammates that he was going to get back into running. No one could have predicted the wild ride he would travel from that point on. After the Olympic Trials, Puma had offered a one year contract to sponsor him. It entailed free shoes and training apparel, as well as a small stipend and health benefits. It also granted him usage of certain Puma paid services, like chiropractors, massage therapists, and a nutritionist. Obviously, it would also require him to run, something he wasn't sure he wanted to do after the Olympic Trials final. He felt as is he had done what he needed to do, he had finally proven to everyone, especially himself, that he was truly a gifted runner, not just a local all-comers wonder. McNeal had, in his words, "caught the ghost." He didn't know if he could handle another year of living the lifestyle necessary to run at a high level. A talk with Maria helped McNeal make up his mind.

"So, why don't you do it because you can?"

"Well, I know that I can. What do you mean?"

"Hate to break it to you, Joe, but one day you won't be able to. Take Brett Favre. You defended his right to come back because he still could play, and he knew his time there was fleeting. Well, Joe, you can still run. This last year, from what you've told me, has been about proving to yourself that you were good enough, about chasing that damn ghost. So, why don't you run now for the pure love of it? You've done what you needed to do, now do what you want to do."

Right then, McNeal knew Maria was right. He called Seamus O'Toole, now doubling as his agent, and told him to accept the contract. The only condition was that Puma outfit Cooper, Maloney and O'Donnell, each of whom had been instrumental in McNeal's rise to the top. The Puma rep agreed to give them each two pairs of trainers and spikes per year, as well as a few articles of clothing. A little extra publicity certainly wouldn't hurt the shoe company.

Over the course of the next year, McNeal built upon his success. His level of fitness grew with each passing day, allowing him to complete more challenging workouts. In Europe after the Olympic Trials, McNeal joined the exclusive sub-four club, running a 3:57 mile at a small meet in England. Two weeks later, he ran a personal best 1:45.31 in the 800 while winning a race in Stockholm, a time well under the Olympic "A" standard. McNeal felt especially proud of that performance, knowing that in past Olympiads, he would have been competing. The next summer, McNeal finally qualified for the national team after again placing second in the 800 at the USATF National Championships. This performance enabled McNeal to compete at the IAAF World Track and Field Championships in Berlin, Germany, the second biggest meet in track and field. McNeal again tasted the bitter taste of coming oh so close, but not quite close enough as he just missed a medal in the finals, running 1:44.08 to place fourth, less than a tenth away from the bronze medal.

McNeal ran that race with a nagging pain in the bottom of his foot, which turned out to be a stress fracture, prematurely ending his 2009 season with a few big European meets left on the schedule.

McNeal soon realized he had been walking for the better part of an hour. In sixty minutes, his Bishop O'Connell harriers, led by junior Brittany Sullivan and sophomore Kimberly McNeal, would be toeing the line in the PIAA state championships. He needed to give them their final instructions before they warmed-up. He jogged over to where they had set up earlier that morning, passing his cousin Mitch Maloney on the way.

"Mitch, I didn't know you'd be here."

"I wanted to see Kim run. I got here early so I could get in some hills though. Seamus thinks I got a shot to get invited to run in the Elite Mile at the New Balance Games in February so I need to be ready."

"Yeah, I heard. Carrying on the family name. Well, I got to get over to the girls before they think I got lost or something."

"What about you, Joe? How's that foot? You know it's getting pretty lonely out here training without you now that Cooper and O'Donnell have both moved on to marathons."

"It's holding up alright. We'll see what happens I guess, no promises, though. I've been busy enough working at the Café and coaching. I don't know how I ever did that and run."

"What you got to get permission from the old lady?" joked Maloney, referring to Maria, now McNeal's fiancé.

"Real funny. No, like I said, we'll see what happens."

McNeal left Maloney to finish his workout while he dealt with the task of calming down his team one last time. He gathered the girls into a circle before they headed out to warm-up. "Alright ladies, this is the moment we've been waiting for, the day that you girls have worked so hard to reach since July. All of the ingredients have been added, it's gone through the heat of the oven, now all you have to do is put the icing on the cake. That's what today is, icing on the cake of a terrific season. If each of you run the way you are capable of running, the way you have run this entire season, good things will happen, no great things will happen, and you will have yourselves the memory of a lifetime. If you don't, you'll always wonder, what might have been if I had run my best. You'll always be chasing that ghost. Today is the day we make history happen."

The Wildcats went on to secure the first state title in school history that afternoon and McNeal knew no matter where life's road may take him, it would not take him away from coaching again.

Made in the USA
Columbia, SC
26 November 2017